The Muse

A ROTHVALE LEGACY HISTORICAL PREQUEL

I

RAINE MILLER

RMR

Raine Miller Romance

Cover Design: *Jena Brignola* & *Michelle Preast*
Editing: *Making Manuscripts*
ISBN-13: 978-1942095040
ISBN-10: 194209504X

DEDICATION

To Dreams, and for making them real.

Are you sure
That we are awake? It seems to me
That yet we sleep, we dream

—**William Shakespeare** - *A Midsummer Night's Dream*

CONTENTS

AUTHOR'S NOTE

This is the first story I ever wrote. It has been tucked away in a box under my bed for more than six years. A few people have read it and probably forgotten the story by now because they last saw it so long ago. I wrote every word from the heart and crafted the whole basis of the world in which all of my later books were born into. Blackstone Affair was born out of ***The Muse***. Rothvale Legacy was as well. Every book, every story, every main character, connects in some way to what was begun right here on the pages following this message. I hope you enjoy where it all began. To beginnings. May they lead to something very wonderful for you.

xxoo R

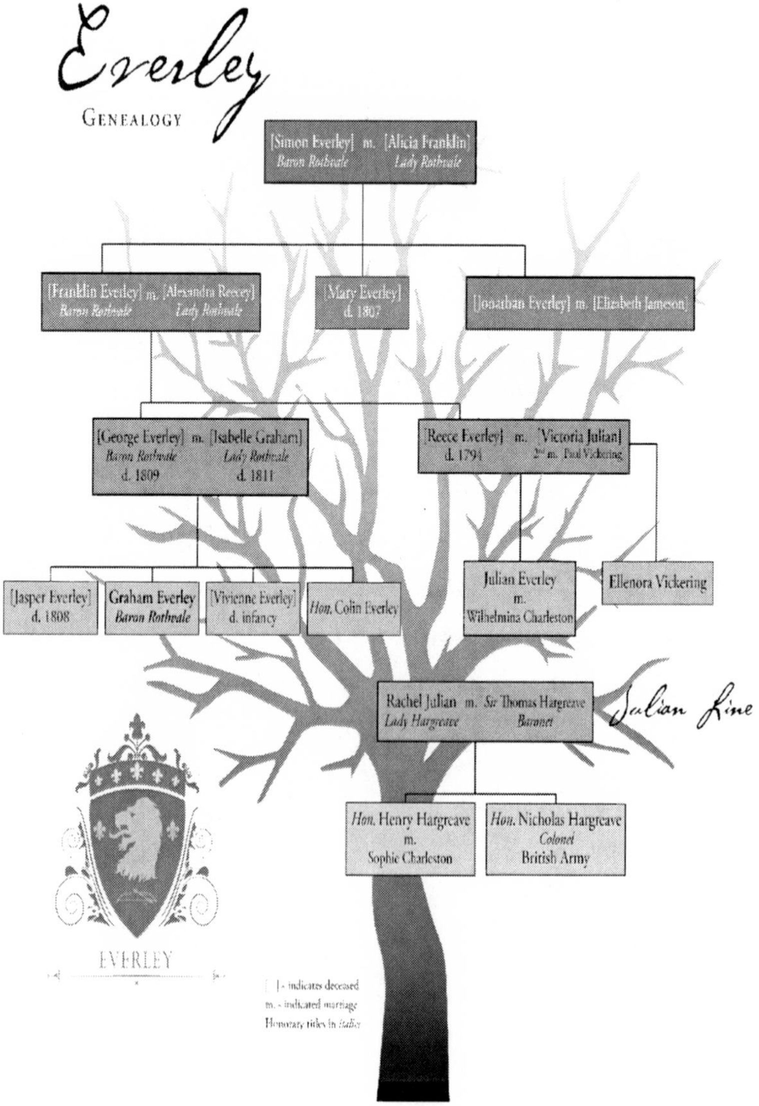

Everley
Genealogy
[Simon Everley] m. [Alicia Franklin]
Baron Rothvale Lady Rothvale
[Franklin Everley] m. [Alexandra Reecey]
Baron Rothvale Lady Rothvale
[Mary Everley]
d. 1807
[Jonathan Everley] m. [Elizabeth Jameson]
[George Everley] m. [Isabelle Graham]
Baron Rothvale Lady Rothvale
d. 1809 d. 1811
[Reece Everley] m. [Victoria Julian]
d. 1794 2nd m. Paul Vickering
[Jasper Everley]
d. 1808
Graham Everley
Baron Rothvale
[Vivienne Everley]
d. infancy
Hon. Colin Everley
Julian Everley
m.
Wilhelmina Charleston
Ellenora Vickering
Rachel Julian m. Sir Thomas Hargreave
Lady Hargreave Baronet
Julian Line
Hon. Henry Hargreave
m.
Sophie Charleston
Hon. Nicholas Hargreave
Colonel
British Army
EVERLEY
[ ] - indicates deceased
m. - indicated marriage
Honorary titles in italics

Byron-Cole & Wilton

Genealogy

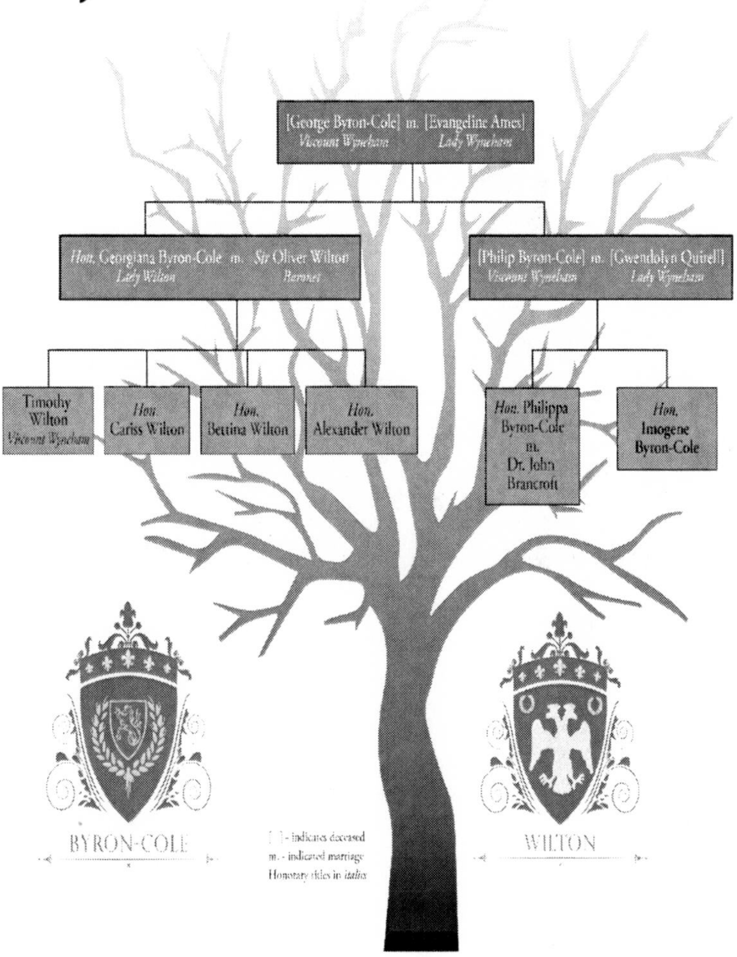
[George Byron-Cole] m. [Evangeline Ames]
Viscount Wyneham
Lady Wyneham
Hon. Georgiana Byron-Cole m. Sir Oliver Wilton
Lady Wilton
Baronet
[Philip Byron-Cole] m. [Gwendolyn Quirell]
Viscount Wyneham
Lady Wyneham
Timothy Wilton
Viscount Wyncham
Hon. Cariss Wilton
Hon. Bettina Wilton
Hon. Alexander Wilton
Hon. Philippa Byron-Cole m. Dr. John Brancroft
Hon. Imogene Byron-Cole
BYRON-COLE
WILTON
[ ] - indicates deceased
m. - indicated marriage
Honorary titles in italics

Prologue

sim·u·la·crum [sim-*yuh*-**ley**-kr*uh* m]
--noun
1. a slight, unreal or superficial likeness or semblance
2. an effigy, image or representation

London, 1895

"It is completed." Removing the cloth covering, Frederic stepped back to show his work.

His companion studied the painting for a long time before he spoke. "Beautiful. Simmering and seductive through the use of such vibrant orange. Sure to garner attention, don't you think, Frederic?"

"Perhaps. I hope it will." Sighing, he felt weary and tired, unwilling to waste the energy of thought on how his newest painting might be received.

"What will you call it?"

"I am calling it 'Flaming June.'"

"Who is she, asleep in the chair, in that flowing gown? Was she June?"

Frederic shook his head. "There was a different painting, before this one, another version—the original. I saw it one time and could never forget, so seared was the image into my memory."

He touched a finger to the canvas, remembering details of what she looked like, even though it had been a very long time since his own eyes had been granted the view in all her magnificent glory.

"When was this?"

"Oh, many years ago when I was first starting out. I met the great man himself at a house party in Warwickshire. He had to have done that painting more than eighty years ago by now."

"Who?"

"Mallerton. He painted her first. Conceived in the warmth of summer, he said. He told me he painted her during the month of June. Sometime in June."

Frederic felt wistful now, lost in the remembrance of that other painting. "She wore a yellow dress, jonquil yellow, and had a splendid shawl draped over her."

"Who was she?"

"Mallerton said she was…Imogene."

Chapter 1

Little Lamb who made thee?
Dost thou know who made thee?
Gave thee life and bid thee feed,
By the stream and o'er the mead…

William Blake ~ Songs of Innocence, 1789

Kent, 1812

Imogene looked up and saw all she needed to know. The November sun had just about conquered the clouds and that was good enough for her. The air was cold but it didn't matter because the opportunity to ride overruled. This was her time to be liberated and she welcomed it. Riding out was the only time she could really put everything aside. Moments like this took her back in time…to before.

Rambling up to the top of the meadow, she looked down upon the dry creek below. Her eyes caught the ball of white easily among the dark rocks, subconscious memory focusing in on what did not belong there. Urging Terra down into the crevasse, she found the white spot to be a lamb, just hours old. Without a thought, she dismounted and reached for the solitary creature. Warm baby wool stirred under her hand, melting her heart in an instant. She knew there would be no way she could leave it here to die. This was an off-season lamb, unusual for late fall, but not unheard of.

She scanned the landscape slowly until she saw what she suspected. The mother was dead, her body mostly obscured by vegetation a few yards distant. Imogene could see that there was blood on the ground too. It had seeped into the earth leaving a wide, dark spot. The poor thing had likely died giving birth, a harsh reality of daily life for human and animal alike.

Taking up the bleating baby, she secured it in front of her saddle while Terra snorted in annoyance. A large rock made do as a mounting block, and slowly they picked their way out of the rocky trench, back up to the firmer ground of the meadow. Orienting herself toward the Kenilbrooke farm entrance, she figured the best plan was to relinquish the lamb to Mr. Jacks and inform him about the dead ewe.

Terra was having none of it though. Tossing her head and stepping awkwardly, the beautiful bay was clearly having trouble bearing the weight. Imogene leapt down for the second time and tried to discover what ailed her. "Did you pick up a rock in that trench, my beauty?" Soothing her with soft words and stroking, she investigated the favoured hoof as best she could but found nothing. Unfortunately the lamb's bleating only became more incessant. "That is not helping a bit, is it, my darling?" Terra eyed her patiently as if she understood every word.

Gathering up the lamb from the saddle, Imogene held it against her until it quieted. Once Terra had calmed enough, she wrapped the reins around her hand and began to lead her slowly. "I suppose we'll just have to walk our way back."

Terra nickered in seeming agreement. The only thing Imogene could see to do was to lead Terra as gently as possible and seek help at Kenilbrooke Park. She would never risk injuring her horse just for her own comfort anyway, and a walk would not kill her. It might not be so pleasant with a lamb in her arms, though. And that November sun might be a bit warmer than she originally thought, but she would survive. This wasn't so hard she thought, as she picked her way over rocks and scrub, and very uneven heath—just vigorous exercise is all. The miles would pass quickly.

Keep telling yourself that, girl.

BROODING was what he did best, or so that was what his brother told him quite often. Coming to Kent for their cousin's wedding was the right thing to do. Didn't mean he wanted to be here, but then again, want and need were rarely in agreement. At least he'd never known them to be. So Kent it was for the moment. Graham Everley, 9th Lord Rothvale, Baron, master of Gavandon, Member of Parliament, unrealized portrait painter, and most of all, miserable bastard, stared out the window of his friend's house and thought about the past year. Returning to England brought back his numerous feelings of helplessness and regret. Ireland was different. Easier. Slower. He'd missed it from the day he had left.

"So, any plans for Town while you're here?" Hargreave asked behind him from the couch.

"Yes, actually," Graham answered, still looking out the window. "Next week I'll make my way down. What is it, two hours by horseba—" He lost his words. His voice just vanished as the pain struck him deep and struck him hard. It felt like an actual piercing into his flesh. The harsh thumping that accompanied that pain told him his heart had gotten in on the battle as well. All of it was in direct response to what his eyes were taking in. "Hargreave? There is the most extraordinary sight. Just right here." He motioned for his friend to come. "Who is—who is the young beauty carrying a new lamb and leading a lame mare down your path?"

Henry Hargreave joined him at the window and frowned as soon as he saw. "Miss Byron-Cole appears to be needing some assistance. I'll go down and find out what's happened." Graham followed right behind his friend. Rude manners or not, he was getting a better look at her.

"Miss Byron-Cole, good morning. I think you've had a bit of trouble, it looks like," Hargreave announced as he approached.

"Mr. Hargreave." She looked flustered. Hell, she looked like a goddess. Graham couldn't take his eyes off her. And that voice of hers. He'd only heard her speak Hargreave's name but it was enough to tantalize his senses. There was huskiness to the sound of her, a breath of sensuality, putting images into his head of naked skin and bodies entwined in beds. *Her* naked body in *his* bed, more specifically.

He watched Miss Byron-Cole explain to Hargreave and chose to ignore he was staring like an idiot. "I had thought to beg assistance from your manager. Yes sir, it has been an eventful morning. I came upon this lamb, newborn, and its dead mother in the dry creek of the upper meadow, and I could not abandon the baby. I meant to deliver it to the estate and quickly found upon our return that my horse was coming up lame. She appears to have an impediment, possibly a stone or some such, imbedded in the hoof of her right foreleg. I fear we have had a slow, ponderous walk instead of a ride."

Hargreave called for his estate manager and addressed her again. "Miss Byron-Cole, you must be exhausted from your trek carrying that lamb so far. Will you take some refreshment and sit down?"

"You are too kind, but no thank you," she declined, shaking her head. "I dread my intrusion, as you are receiving visitors, and have no wish to call you away from your guests." Her eyes followed to where he stood on the steps. Graham froze and took in the sight of her, compelled to look, unable to do anything but stare. "My aunt will be missing me by now, I fear. I am well past my time—they will be asking for me at home," she said solemnly.

"Of course, but rest assured it is no intrusion. I am quite sure you are providing a welcome diversion for my guests in any case." Hargreave turned slightly, directing his eyes to where Graham stood, still rooted to the steps and gawking like a half-wit. Hargreave cocked an amused brow at Graham before turning back to address the lovely Miss Byron-Cole once more.

The lucky goddamn sod.

"At any rate, we are neighbours, and you have bravely risked yourself in returning my property to the estate. I should be thanking you as I am now in your debt," Hargreave prattled on as the estate manager walked onto the scene. "Ah, here is Mr. Jacks. He will take the lamb and see to your horse…um…what do you call her?"

"Terra. Terra is her name, Mr. Hargreave. Mr. Jacks knows."

Graham thought Miss Byron-Cole looked like she wanted to bolt, and he was struck with the very irrational idea that he should demand she stay and take refreshment as Hargreave had suggested. He was not finished staring yet. And he wanted to hear her talking some more. But all of those 'wants' were forced to wait while a groom transferred her saddle from her lame mount onto a regal dark horse bearing a white splash across his front, a perfect rendering of a crashing, ocean wave.

"Terra, meaning *firma* earth? How appropriate. You see, the horse on which you will return, is called Triton, god of the sea. The earth and sea both represented as it were," Hargreave joked, pointing to both horses.

Graham wanted to roll his eyes, but waited for her response instead.

"So they are, earth and sea indeed." She did not laugh at the joke. "Triton is known to me. I daresay I can manage him. He is a swift lad, but gentle. Thank you, sir, for your kindness and for the loan of him. My uncle can send a groom for Terra on the morrow, returning Triton at the same time. Will that be acceptable?"

"Most assuredly, it is no trouble." Hargreave assisted her mount from the block while Graham had to keep his feet on the steps by force of will. He wanted to assist her up from the block. He wanted to put his hands on her waist and hold her—what in the bloody hell had infected his brain? "Will you and your family be attending the ball this evening?" Hargreave asked her. *Good bloody question.*

"Yes, sir, an event most anticipated at Wilton Court. I believe everyone is looking forward to it with great enthusiasm," she answered politely, but looked to the side of the gravel path like it was her best friend. She wanted to be gone.

"Are you to be counted among those who anticipate it?" *Thank you, Hargreave!* Graham hoped she would say yes. The ball tonight meant he could see her again. Talk to her. Dance with her. Touch her.

"Yes, of course." Her reply gave away nothing. Miss Byron-Cole was a reserved beauty. "Again, my thanks, Mr.

Hargreave, for your help today. Please do give my best to Mrs. Hargreave, Miss Mina, and to Mr. Everley. Good day, sir."

Hearing his name come from her lips felt good, even though he realized she wasn't referring to him when she'd said 'Mr. Everley.' Miss Byron-Cole had named his cousin, Julian Everley, prospective bridegroom and the very reason Graham was even back in England after more than a year and a half. If his cousin was not about to marry, then he never would've left Donadea on his own accord.

Smiling stiffly, she dipped her head in farewell. When she lifted her head, her eyes drifted over to his for just a moment and held. Feeling suddenly like a schoolboy, Graham couldn't keep back the grin. But as soon as she caught his smile, she abruptly turned away. *Damn.*

"Miss Byron-Cole, until tonight then." Hargreave bowed before joining Graham on the steps. Both watched her ride swiftly down the drive, Triton's hooves kicking up bits of gravel as she was carried away and out of sight. That black horse of Hargreave's was magnificent. In fact, the whole scene had been magnificent—horse and rider.

"You must tell me everything about her, Hargreave." Graham decided not to waste any time discovering whatever he might learn about Miss Byron-Cole.

His friend arched another brow at him but offered nothing. At their return to the drawing room, all heads turned to meet them, eager for the gossipy news.

"Well?" Sophie inquired.

"Miss Byron-Cole sends her best regards to all of you." Hargreave quickly explained to the group what had occurred as he took up his wife's hand and brought it to his lips for a kiss.

"She looked worn out, Henry. You should have brought her in for a rest and refreshment," Sophie admonished.

"Yes, my dear, and I did offer, but she seemed very concerned about being missed at Wilton Court, and anxious to be on her way. As I'm sure you saw, she literally bolted away from here. I would have worried for her safety on Triton if I didn't know her as such a talented rider."

Graham surprised himself by blurting, "I dare to say she behaved quite remarkably and in good sense of the situation and of the duty pressed upon her. She had the forethought not only to rescue the lamb, but also spared her horse permanent injury by knowing well enough not to ride. I think she must be more sensible than most ladies of twice her age."

They all turned to stare at him like he'd grown another head. "I believe we can all agree on that, Graham." Hargreave came to his rescue. "She will be in attendance tonight at the ball."

"But who is she?" He did it again. His mouth working completely independent of good manners or logic. "Er, she is quite—quite unusual." He knew he was being insistent, and looked a certifiable idiot, but he had to know.

Miss Wilhelmina Charleston, or Mina, as she was affectionately known, his cousin's fiancée, and the sister of Mrs. Hargreave, answered first. "That remarkable young lady is the Honorable Imogene Byron-Cole and no stranger to duty, sir, as you correctly observed. She has come to Shelburne to live with her family called Wilton. Lady Wilton being her aunt, and the sister to Miss Imogene's father, the late Lord Wyneham. Miss Imogene was raised on a country estate in Essex, where she was recently orphaned, and it would be safe to say, still suffering from the grief of her loss."

"Wyneham, I have heard of him. I think I even met him once. Was Lord Wyneham a politician? And what of her circumstances in losing her parents? I daresay I noticed the sadness about her, ever present during her exchange just now—"

Graham wished for a knife to cut out his tongue.

Mina and Sophie exchanged looks, their sisterly glance a sure sign they were noticing what a foolish arse he was making of himself.

"You are correct. Lord Wyneham was popular in the House of Lords, and served quite distinctively until his untimely death." Mina hesitated before offering more. "Miss Imogene has become close friends with our sister, Jocelyn, and has not shared but only a little even with her. And she's just barely out of official mourning."

Graham nodded respectfully, waiting for Mina to carry on. It bothered him that he was so eager to know everything about this Imogene Byron-Cole. What in the hell was wrong with him? He must be losing his mind. He'd been away from England for far too long.

Mina smiled gently and continued with her story. "As I understand it, Imogene has experienced her multiple losses in the space of only a year. The first, being separated from her beloved sister, and only sibling, due to the lady's marriage to a gentleman and her departure to, I believe, Gloucestershire. Next, her mother, Lady Wyneham, succumbed to a wasting illness after years of affliction just a few months after the wedding. And then there was the unfortunate death of Lord Wyneham just seven months past. He was killed in a shooting accident of uncertain circumstance, some putting it about it was done purposefully, owning to the grief of losing his wife. About six months ago, after the furor died down and arrangements settled, Lady Wilton returned from Essex with Imogene. Needless to say, she is struggling to adapt to the loss of everyone she loved and the lack of security in her life this past year."

Graham could not resist the question, thinking he hated the idea of her being sent off to a family who might not want her. "And you say she is welcomed by her relations?"

Mina nodded, but not before a knowing smile escaped first. "I believe her to be much loved though I imagine some of their devotion has got to be partial gratitude, as her great loss has enriched their family enormously. Since Lord Wyneham died without a male heir, his title, estate and peerage have passed to his nephew, her cousin, Timothy Wilton, who will take it all when he reaches his majority next year. Though for now, he is still at university, Cambridge."

"And what is her age?" Graham wanted to know more. "Has she come out?" He knew he was showing himself to be a pathetic fool but could not find it in him to be very concerned.

"I do not think she has yet attained her twentieth year from what Jocelyn has said. She did have a London season last winter, but limited due to her mother's illness."

"And she rides often?" he asked recklessly.

His cousin, Julian Everley, who up to this point had remained quiet during the conversation, finally spoke up. "Christ in heaven, Graham, this is a certain surprise. Yes, she rides often." Jules bore a confident smirk as he doled out a little more information. "We have encountered her several times whilst riding out. She appears very confident and experienced, but clearly prefers her solitude to the company of other riders."

Hargreave chimed in next. "Yes, she's a practiced rider as Jules says. Always very polite and modest, everything a young lady should be. Her uncle, Sir Oliver Wilton, approached me soon after her arrival to Shelburne. I was given to understand that riding is her one true comfort, and he indulges her wishes to be allowed the freedom to ride out solitary. Her horse was brought here from her home in Essex. Upon our first meeting, I was happy to grant her access to Kenilbrooke, as Sir Oliver felt should she ride within the boundaries of the estate where her safety could be better secured. My manager, Jacks, arranged everything and absolutely dotes on her like a daughter. He sees to it that she can enjoy her riding in peace under the protection Kenilbrooke offers her."

Graham responded decidedly. "I see. Well then, Hargreave, I shall require an introduction to Miss Byron-Cole at the ball this evening."

Hargreave pursed his lips in amusement, ready to start in on the mockery. "Really. I was under the impression you were only showing the merest passing interest."

Graham narrowed his eyes and thought all manner of retorts he would never speak in the presence of ladies. *How about a passing interest in my Hessians up your arse?* Hargreave knew it, too, and seemed to be enjoying himself immensely.

"Consider it done, my friend. But please remember she is a young lady of good standing, and not a person to be trifled with. She has many protectors." Hargreave spoke the last cautiously.

Feeling his hackles rise, he fixed his eyes upon Hargreave with the authority and assertion that came easily to man of his station, his words firm and precise. "You know me. I am a gentleman, am I not? I do not *trifle* with young ladies…*ever*." He must have looked a menace because Hargreave leaned back, putting a wide space between them.

"Never in doubt, Graham, I know that," Hargreave assured him.

Attempting to shake off the defensiveness, he made an

effort to soften his tone. "I think I will take my leave for now, locate my brother, and get settled. Until later, then? Mrs. Hargreave, Miss Mina, Jules, Henry." He bowed to them before quitting the room, knowing gossip would fly the minute he was gone. His cousin and friends would speculate on him. More ribbing and teasing would follow that. He could be sure to expect a thorough lampooning about his interest in the lovely Miss Imogene Byron-Cole before, during, and after the ball tonight. And there was nothing to be done about it now.

Imogene...an Irish name. Can she be real? I've been run through with a broadsword, it feels like. If I am dreaming...do I want to awaken?

His response to the sight of her had been visceral. He tried to get his head wrapped around the idea, his body reacting independently with no regard for the rational at all. As Graham walked to the stables, he had an epiphany realizing events had been put into motion through fate that reached far beyond his control. It was not what he had expected to find here, but he would no more be able to turn away from Imogene Byron-Cole than he could stop time. His head began to ache, his heart, however, was coming alive.

Once at the stables the familiar smells and sounds soothed him a little. Graham selected a spirited looking grey and ordered it saddled. While he waited, he spotted her horse alone in a stall. *Terra is her name, Mr. Hargreave.* He spoke to the horse by name, and stroked her neck before bending down to examine her right foreleg carefully. She didn't appear to be favouring it now, which was a good sign. Terra was a fine piece of horseflesh and it would be a shame for such an animal to be damaged…or for her rider to be hurt because of it.

The groom spoke, "That one is not of the estate sir, and she came up lame today."

"Yes, I saw the lady lead her in. Is she recovered?"

"Yes, sir. She had somethin' like a rock hurtin' her. Mr. Jacks had the horseman see her. She'll be good as new for her lady."

"Do you know of the lamb that the lady brought in this morning? What of it?"

"Here, sir. I'm feedin' it cow's milk with a bottle 'til the shepherd can be found. Takin' to it just fine."

Graham peered into the corner of the stall, and there it was covered with an old horse blanket. The lamb lifted its head to look at him, blinking big round soulful eyes. He thought about the lamb being held in her arms during the long walk back, pressed against her body, cradled in the warmth of her breasts. He was bloody jealous of that lamb.

The groom's voice broke through his ponderings. "Yer horse is ready for ya, sir."

Graham rode the grey hard across the fields, trying to clear his mind and think of peaceful things. But peace eluded him. The vision of her with her dark golden hair, and those poignant brown eyes was stuck firmly in his head—going nowhere.

I have exposed my attraction to her now. What if she doesn't like me? They'll all be watching me with her tonight. Christ Almighty.

Chapter 2

A dance is a measured pace, as a verse is a measured speech.

Francis Bacon ~The Advancement of Learning, 1605

Racing away from Kenilbrooke on Triton's steady back, feeling both embarrassed and horrified, she wished she could ride right off the face of the earth. Her intrusion upon Mr. Hargreave, and as he was receiving guests, too, was not an experience she cared to repeat. Imogene was on friendly terms with Mr. Jacks, and had expected to deal with him today, but how wrong she had been.

She thought about what had just occurred. Mr. Hargreave standing to talk to her with a visitor looking on had been agonizing. They must have thought her addled in the head, wandering across fields with helpless animals. She'd prayed for escape. Forced to remember her manners, she'd tried to show a sincere interest in the ball tonight, but quite frankly, didn't know if she was up for it. This ball was the first formal occasion since putting the black aside. Was she even ready for this? And who was the tall man standing upon the steps? His intense staring had made her feel she was wearing no more than her shift. That couldn't be proper, now could it? Imogene shook her head to try to clear it a little. Whoever he was, he must be here for the wedding of Mina and Mr. Everley. Maybe even someone with family connections. As much as she'd like to avoid the idea of an attraction, the stranger had been darkly handsome and mysterious.

After handing Triton over to a groom at the stables, she walked the path to her home. But it wasn't really her home, was it? She was a visitor here. Even though she knew they loved her, her life was not the same, and never would be again. The contrast between Wilton Court and her own home growing up was starkly dissimilar. Her four cousins were a definite distraction from the harsh reality of grief though, and that was something at least.

She remembered back to her sister's wedding. Just a year ago, they had celebrated Philippa's joy with not a hint of what was to come. Imogene supposed time would ease her melancholy, but for now it still wrapped around her like a cloak.

The usual disorder greeted her. "Alexander! Take that muddy dog outside at once. And, Bettina, look at you! You have as much mud on you as the dog." Aunt Wilton scolded them both.

"Sorry, Mamma." The twins deferred to their mother before hurrying away to do her bidding.

Imogene could not hold back her grin. "Bettina reminds me of…me at that age."

"Imogene. We were beginning to worry, dear. You are past your time," she admonished.

"Yes, Aunt, I am sorry. Terra came up lame and I found an orphaned lamb and brought it to Kenilbrooke. They've loaned me a horse to get back."

"Always an easy mark for the creatures." She put her hand up to Imogene's face. "But you are a sweet girl with a gentle heart who cannot help it, can you?"

"No, Aunt. I cannot help it." She shrugged helplessly.

"Be an angel and go up and help Cariss prepare for the ball tonight. I heard from Mrs. Charleston today that Mr. Everley's cousins have arrived at Kenilbrooke for the wedding. I daresay there will be new introductions this evening, my dear, so wear your finest and, Imogene, do try to enjoy yourself tonight." Aunt Wilton took Imogene's chin gently in her hand. "You are young and beautiful and worthy. You deserve to be happy, my darling. Your mamma and papa would have wanted it." At the mention of her parents, Imogene's countenance fell, and her aunt saw, but carried on. "Now, dear heart, please do not let the mention of them sadden you. They are together in heaven and at peace. I know their fondest wish is for their beloved child to find happiness and to be settled into a life of her own as your sister is. This is a time for amusement and diversion, for you to be carefree and to meet new people. You will catch the eye of some gentleman soon. I know it. How could you not? So, a happy face then? You will try?"

"Yes, Aunt, I will try." Imogene gave her aunt a gentle embrace.

Aunt Wilton kissed her forehead. "That's my brave girl. Off you go now to make yourself beautiful."

Hours later, Imogene had taken her aunt's advice to heart and was determined to make an effort to find some enjoyment in the evening. The gown she chose was blush, chiffon silk, short-sleeved and high-waisted, with an intricate, golden brocade-embellished belt. She left off the requisite long white gloves. Her adornment was her mother's pearl and diamond choker. The choker was very old and contained four horizontal ropes of pearls, with the middle being secured with a diamond and pearl encrusted oval. Wearing it made her feel close in spirit to her mother. Imogene arranged her dark blonde hair so most was gathered up, but a few long curls were allowed to hang down on one side.

Her cousin, Cariss, wore a similar concoction, but in pale blue. Cariss was Imogene's closest friend, save her own sister, but younger by two years. In the carriage en-route to Kenilbrooke she held Imogene's hand, chatting about the different dances, what the ladies might wear, wondering who their dance partners might be. Pulling up the drive, the glow cast from the blazing torches lit up the courtyard steps. Imogene was instantly taken back to her earlier encounter just today, right here upon this spot. She felt a peculiar sensation sweep over her—odd, with a strangeness of feeling—unaware it was an omen that things were about to change.

SIR Oliver and Lady Wilton were announced first, then Timothy, Cariss, and finally Imogene. "Miss Byron-Cole," the footman's voice boomed through the noisy room. She lifted her head, feeling many eyes fixed on her. Summoning every speck of courage she could muster, she held her chin high and stepped forward.

The mistress of the house, Sophie Hargreave, immediately approached, holding out both hands in welcome. "Dear Imogene, how utterly lovely you look tonight. May I say that Henry told us of your eventful morning and we were all struck by your steady nerve in dealing with the situation you found yourself to be in. My dear, how did you do it?"

"Thank you, Sophie, and may *I* say that the general

splendour of the room is very pleasing tonight. You are kind in your praise of me, but I was only doing what I should in the circumstance."

"Miss Byron-Cole, I think you underestimate your good sense and remarkably strong spirit." This was Mr. Hargreave's voice coming from her far left.

Imogene turned to answer him directly and looked straight into the arresting green eyes of the man who had stood upon the steps of Kenilbrooke just this forenoon, watching her. *It is him.* Imogene did not reply to Mr. Hargreave immediately. She couldn't with those green eyes staring at her. "I thank you—th-thank you for the compliment, Mr. Hargreave." Imogene finally found her voice.

Mr. Hargreave did the introductions. "Miss Byron-Cole, allow me to introduce my friend, Graham Everley, Lord Rothvale, Gavandon, and Warwickshire."

She curtsied. "Lord Rothvale." *Graham Everley. He must be related to Mr. Everley. A cousin perhaps? And he is a lord. His eyes are so…green.*

Lord Rothvale bowed. "Miss Byron-Cole, it is an honor." He kept staring. She was just as guilty, though. And she could not seem to stop herself from staring, either. He smiled just the faintest bit, his solemn expression softening. "Your horse is recovered, Miss Byron-Cole."

"THAT is very excellent news," she answered with a smile, "but how do you know about my horse, Lord Rothvale?"

There is definitely a God and I am somehow in his favour. You're smiling at me. He leaned forward to whisper, "I saw you lead her in this morning whilst carrying that lamb."

She blushed beautifully and lowered her eyes. "My lord, you misunderstand. I observed you this morning as well, standing on the steps. What I meant was how did you *know* she is recovered?" She then lifted her eyes directly, looking for an answer.

Miss Byron-Cole missed nothing, and she was no shrinking violet, which was even better. And that beautiful blush was delectable to the point he felt his mouth start to water, but when she looked up at him he felt his cock wake up. He was really going to have to concentrate tonight in her presence so as not to embarrass himself. "When I rode out later, I saw your horse in the stables. Terra, I believe you said? Well, your Terra is no longer lame, and the lamb you rescued is thriving apparently. You see? A happy ending all around, and all due to your efforts." He felt himself smile right back.

"I am very glad to hear of it, sir. And thank you for checking upon my Terra."

The words came from his mouth before he could even sort them out. "Miss Byron-Cole, may I claim the first set of the dancing?"

"You may." He didn't miss the slight flare of her eyes when she agreed.

"And the dinner set as well?" he proposed. "I daresay your conversation over dinner would be welcome." *I'll have to strive to converse coherently—that'll be difficult. I'd rather just look at you. And imagine you in my bed.*

"Yes," she whispered, sounding a little less sure. He didn't care about that part though. She'd agreed and that was all that mattered. Her natural acquiescence pleased him.

The spell was broken when Jules and Mina joined the group. Mina held out her hands to Miss Byron-Cole in welcome. "You look lovely, Imogene. I hope you are enjoying the evening after your eventful ride this morning."

"Thank you, Mina. You look beautiful as always. Indeed, I am finding the evening very pleasant." She smiled brilliantly at the engaged couple, and Graham was content to simply observe as she chatted with her friends. "Has Jocelyn come tonight? I do not see her."

"No, she claimed to feel unwell, but I think she really wanted to avoid the ball. We are quite at a loss of how to encourage our sister to put herself into society," Mina said.

"Crowds are difficult for Jocelyn. But a kinder friend could not be found. I am grateful for her and for her friendship." She fixed her countenance upon Mina and Jules. "If I may say, you and Mr. Everley make a striking couple tonight—your happiness together is evident."

Jules responded. "Thank you, Miss Byron-Cole, for your kind sentiments. I think you have quite expressed the meaning of it. We are very happy indeed." He kissed Mina's hand lovingly. "And I am glad that others can easily see it." Jules put his hand on Graham's shoulder. "I've noticed that you have been introduced to my wayward cousin."

"Wayward, is he? But even so, he holds the Everley title?" Imogene shot back.

"Correct. He is the *titled* Everley, but I have a bigger house and grow more turnips than he does," Jules joked.

"I am not wayward in the slightest! What is your purpose, Jules?" Graham rolled his eyes at his cousin's attempt at a joke. "More turnips? That is the most idiotic thing you have ever spoken I am sure."

"Ah, Graham, my purpose is to follow convention this evening and secure dancing partners for two of the sets. As you well know, I cannot dance more than three with Mina," he said slyly. "Miss Byron-Cole, what have you available?" Jules asked her smoothly. Maybe Jules had more sense than Graham originally thought, as he saw where his cousin was leading.

"Ah…well, Lord Rothvale has secured the first and dinner sets." Her brown eyes locked onto Graham's. "The second and fourth and final are open, Mr. Everley." Imogene replied to Jules, but continued looking into Graham's eyes while she said the words.

Graham interrupted, "The final set is taken as well." His eyes never left hers. He was determined to have his way with her.

Jules spoke to the whole group. "What say you to this, Miss Byron-Cole? Do me the honor of the second set, and Hargreave the fourth. Graham, you will partner Mina for the second and Mrs. Hargreave for the forth. Hargreave and I can partner with Elle for the other set we each need. Will this arrangement suit everybody?"

"Yes," Graham said firmly. Imogene did not say anything in agreement, but then she did not say no, either. It was enough for now. The mysterious beauty had deferred to him a second time and that was all that concerned him. *Yes, a natural.*

TAKING their places for the first set, Imogene felt oddly, different. Her hand burned where his skin touched hers. He gazed at her a great deal. She found it a relief to simply stay quiet and not have to speak as they moved through the steps down the line.

Mr. Graham Everley, Lord Rothvale, was tall and broad shouldered, brilliantly fit into his clothes. His noble features were very pleasing, and combined with those expressive green eyes of his, made him a handsome man. At least, Imogene thought so. His dark brown hair was straight, reaching just to the tops of his shoulders, worn in the old style: tied back in a queue, and wrapped in a ribbon. He was some years older than her, with an intellectual quality, so she imagined he was educated. His countenance was on the sombre side, somewhat domineering, but not taciturn or haughty. He possessed a gracious smile when he gave one up and there was a gentle quality about him, too. There was also a perceptible sadness about him, a weight, something burdensome. Imogene recognized it because she was no stranger to those feelings herself.

The second set of dancing with Mr. Julian Everley was certainly enlightening. He was a perfect gentleman as always, but she felt an undercurrent, sensing he was up to something. "Miss Byron-Cole, at the conclusion of the dance I would very much like to make your introduction to my sister, Ellenora. I think the two of you would enjoy one another's company. She rides as do you and would be grateful for the companionship here at Shelburne, for these few weeks away from home. Would you be willing to meet her?"

"Of course, Mr. Everley. It would be my pleasure to make your sister's acquaintance. It is always nice to meet another who appreciates the joys of riding." Imogene was touched by the warm demeanour of Ellenora Everley and they connected right away. Mr. Everley seemed pleased that his sister had some company of her general age. The girls were enjoying an easy conversation about horses, when Lord Rothvale joined them, coming to claim Imogene for the dinner set. He'd brought with him a younger man, most likely his brother, the resemblance so clearly evident, it was no surprise when Lord Rothvale introduced him. "Colin Everley, my younger brother. Miss Byron-Cole."

"Mr. Everley." Imogene curtsied. *He has the same green eyes as his brother.*

"How do you do, Miss Byron-Cole?" He bowed.

Imogene addressed all four cousins. "Has it been a very long while since you were all together?"

Mr. Julian Everley spoke for the whole group. "Indeed, this reunion is the first in over a year for us." He brightened when his Mina approached, his eyes visibly lighting up at the sight of his fiancée. "And as it is a happy reunion for our family, we also have the joy of adding *another* Everley to our number."

Imogene tilted her head in congratulations. "The support of one's family is a wonderful thing, is it not? I daresay I am a little envious of you all being together tonight. You are blessed to have each other." She looked to each of them with sincerity.

Lord Rothvale trained his insightful eyes on her again. "Quite right, Miss Byron-Cole, it is good and proper that we are reunited upon this happy occasion. It has been far too long since we have been in company. What of your siblings?"

"I have only one. My elder sister, Philippa. She is Mrs. Brancroft now and makes her home at Wellick in Gloucester. I have missed her very much since her marriage to Dr. Brancroft. He is a practicing physician at the new hospital there." Imogene heard the excitement in her own voice as she continued, "Arrangements have been made for me to go to them after the new year. I want to be with my sister as she prepares for the birth of her first child."

"Wellick, did you say?"

"Yes, my lord, do you know it?"

"Indeed, Miss Byron-Cole. Wellick is no more than ten

miles from Gavandon, my home. Gavandon lies along the south western edge of Warwickshire where it borders Gloucestershire, and the two are of an easy distance."

His voice was liquid as he looked at her and talked about his home. Imogene was finding herself a bit unnerved at how easy it was to be with this man—a man she had only laid eyes upon this morning and met formally this evening. When he looked at her she felt something different, an excitement that made her breathing come harder than it should. Like he was seeing more of her than anyone had ever seen before. And she was shocked to find he lived so very close to her sister's home. Surely she would see him again when she went north to stay. *I very much want to see you again.*

Seated next to each other at dinner, they were mostly quiet, but strangely it was not at all uncomfortable in the silence. He did break it finally, though. "The pearls you wear are quite distinctive and handsome. Are they a family heirloom?"

Imogene brought her hand to her throat. "They were given to me by my mamma, and also to her, by her mother. They are very precious to me and I feel…close…to her when I wear them. She was lost to us eight months past." Immediately she wondered what had loosed her tongue. Why was she telling him this? What was wrong with her?

"My deepest condolences." He bowed his head slightly. "Colin and I have also lost our mother, little over a year ago." They became quiet again for a moment. "At times, I daresay I feel rather cheated."

Imogene set down her spoon and turned to him. "I know of what you mean. You have expressed my feelings exactly. That is precisely how I feel about it but never have been able to put it as you have just done." She shook her head. "It is extraordinary, sir, I care not to speak of my loss, but strangely, it does feel liberating having this discussion with you." Imogene pondered his way with her. He was direct but not offensive. She liked how he didn't pry or hover, but was patient in conversation. In an effort to continue their dialogue, she asked, "Do you have particular interest in jewellery, Lord Rothvale?"

His eyes burned at her and she could swear he was thinking something other than what he replied. "It would be fair to say that I have an interest in fine art of all mediums. I appreciate the creative design aspect of it. But my particular interest is in paintings, specifically portraiture. I have always been fascinated by portraits, even as a child, pestering my parents to tell me of what they knew of some ancestors' portraits; wanting to know who the artist was as well as the sitter and the situation of the scene. One of my favourite places at home is the portrait gallery. I am continually working on the family history and find that portraits provide essential information. Have you ever sat for your portrait, Miss Byron-Cole?"

I was correct! He is a scholar. "Yes, actually I have. My papa commissioned a portrait of my sister and me together. We sat for it about four years ago now. Mr. John Opie was the artist; he completed it just before his death. It hangs at Drakenhurst Hall, my home in Essex.

GRAHAM found himself in a situation like nothing he'd ever experienced before. With every question and reply, he simply wanted more. So much more. The thoughts swimming around in his head were wild and totally unexpected, but that wasn't stopping him from moving a bit closer to her in his seat and drawing her further into intimate conversation. He would take any advantage he could. He sensed that if he didn't act quickly he would be making a mistake he could never recover from.

"A most excellent master of the craft. I should very much like to see it, your portrait. You know, John Opie painted my mother's portrait in the early days of her marriage. It is one of my favourites." *I so want a portrait of you, Imogene.* "A technical question for you, if you don't mind? Did Mr. Opie use an optical device, something like a wooden box that he looked into?"

"He did actually. He used it at the very beginning mostly and for our facial images I believe, for it was right up close to us."

"Was the room dark when he used it?"

"It was. And the device?"

"A camera obscura. It can project an image through a mirror and lens that is useful in replicating scenes and in drawing an image true to life. The artist must still possess his talent, mind you, but it can assist most excellently with scale and proportion." Graham smiled at her and tried to show calm when all he could really imagine was her in repose, covering minimal as he used the camera obscura to draw her. He felt himself stir at the thought and willed it down. Could this really be him? Was he getting stiff at the dinner table with a woman he'd just met?

Apparently so, you idiot!

IMOGENE thought the fourth set of the dancing just as

interesting as the one with Julian Everley earlier. Mr. Hargreave was such an amiable man and always very friendly, thus it surprised her when he asked directly, "Did you enjoy your conversation with Lord Rothvale at dinner?"

"Yes, sir. I found him to be very agreeable and we discussed portraits in particular. Do you know Lord Rothvale well, Mr. Hargreave?"

"Very well. We met up in our school days. Jules, Graham, and I all up together at Eton, and as thick as thieves since," he announced, grinning. "He's an expert on paintings and very cultured, fluent in French and Italian. I daresay he would have devoted all of his time solely to art pursuits if fate had not intervened and made him the heir to the barony and Gavandon."

"He was not born the heir?"

"No, he is a second son. His elder brother died some years ago now, and under…difficult circumstances. Graham has borne a great many burdens and troubles since, but you would not hear him tell of it. The loss of both of his parents, responsibilities for a younger brother, *and* Parliamentary obligations in the House of Lords…you can see his plate has been rather full. His brother Colin, is nearly five years his junior, and also here for our wedding, having just one more term at Cambridge, Trinity, before he completes his formal studies. A serious scholar, Colin is—mathematics and astronomy. He researches for Sir William Herschel, you know, the discoverer of the new planet, *Georgium Sidus*, cataloguing and mapping stars for him. The brothers are close, and more loyal friends could not be found. We do not share blood, but almost. Rothvale and Colin are Jules's cousins on their fathers' side. I am Jules's cousin on our mothers' side. We feel like family."

Imogene listened to every word Mr. Hargreave had to share during their set and she had to wonder why he was so forthcoming about Lord Rothvale and his family. She was greatly interested, but still, this whole evening was turning out very differently from what she had imagined. She got that feeling again, that flutter inside her stomach. There was that sense of change and she was on the edge.

As the dance with Mr. Hargreave ended, Lord Rothvale pulled up to return Mrs. Hargreave to her husband. He then faced Imogene solemnly. "Miss Byron-Cole, would you bestow me the honor of the final set of the evening?"

"I was wondering, my lord, if you had formally asked for the final set before. I was not completely sure."

He made a slight tightening of his jaw. "I did assume and I humbly offer apology for my presumption. But will you…give me the final set?"

Imogene regarded him and the look upon his face told her he would be crushed if she declined. She took pity on him immediately, for the thought of causing him distress bothered her. "Oh, why not. Yes, I believe I will," she said teasingly. "I am often accused of being too solemn, my lord, so if I must be jovial tonight I daresay others must join me in the expression."

"Well said, Miss Byron-Cole." He gifted her with a glowing smile and looked dashingly handsome doing it. Imogene got the feeling Lord Rothvale did not pass along smiles freely, so the fact he was giving them to her made her feel special. They stood together for a moment and Imogene repeated the behaviour she had indulged in quite a few times over the course of the evening, looking into his eyes and forgetting there was a party going on around them.

THE *Muse*

GRAHAM was a vivid dreamer. Not so much in the sense of a visionary, but he regularly experienced visualization of scenes that appealed to him and had vibrant dreams while sleeping. Tonight a new presence entered his subconscious just like he knew it would, tormenting him in all manner of ways.

He'd expected to be tormented, too, so his dreams were no surprise. Some of his visions were honorable, some downright unmentionable, but always there, forceful, arousing, and compelling. He could not get her out of his head, and did not want to. One idea stood out above all others though. *Mine…*

Imogene Byron-Cole was meant for him.

He was lost. So lost, already.

And all he could think about—dream of—all he could see…was her.

Chapter 3

How sweet is harmless solitude!
What can its joys control?
Tumults and noise may not intrude,
To interrupt the soul.

Marie Mollineau ~ 'Solitude,' 1670

Imogene went straight to Terra in the stall just like he'd expected. Graham watched everything from the doorway as he leaned against it.

Terra stamped her hooves and nickered, excited to see her mistress who draped her arms around the beast's neck and rested her cheek there. Imogene's eyes were closed as she indulged in the simple joy of reuniting. God she looked fine today, fitted into a blue riding dress that contrasted her colouring perfectly. He wanted to touch her.

What if she held on to me like that? Graham was reluctant to break the spell of the moment. He watched instead, a voyeur, held in his place by the scene before him. Finally he spoke up, "It is hard to tell who has missed the other more."

Imogene jumped, releasing Terra and stepping away. "Oh, Lord Rothvale—you are h-here," she stammered.

"I am." He grinned at how she'd worded it. "That

sounds as if you were anticipating me?" He asked the question and loved the flush that crept up her beautiful neck.

"No." She swallowed hard and looked back at Terra, not at all effective in covering up her lie. "Yes well, Terra and I are very close. We have been together for five years and she is the dearest, best friend a girl could ever have. I should be lost without her."

"Indeed, she is lucky to have such a loving, benevolent mistress. Will you ride today? It is very cold." The idea of her off alone did not set well. At all.

"Yes, I shall. I've prepared for it and dressed warmly. I'm afraid I'm not content to sit inside all day."

"And you ride alone? What if you should encounter trouble or have an accident?" He tried to keep his voice even but feared that was impossible. *I'd never allow it if you were mine.*

"That is a sentiment I hear often, my lord. My reply to it is this: I am a fairly capable rider, and Terra is reliable. My uncle, Sir Oliver, has restricted my riding to the Kenilbrooke estate when I am solitary, with Mr. Hargreave's kind approval and knowledge. I must always notify Mr. Jacks, the manager when I set out, so he can mark the time as I am allowed two hours." Her eyes swept down. "You see? I have many gallant protectors watching over me and we have worked out an arrangement that suits everybody."

"It does not suit me." He wanted to tell her to come into the house instead and that she would definitely not be riding alone today, but how in the hell could he do that? He had no claim over her. Not yet at least.

"I beg your pardon?" She widened her eyes at him.

"Miss Byron-Cole, I don't doubt your level of competence, it is clearly evident you *can* ride, but you cannot say you have control over all the unexpected dangers that exist." Graham knew he sounded hard but he did not want her to go alone and that was all there was to it.

"No sir, I cannot control every danger in the world," she admitted, her face flushing. "Something I know to be true. Sadly, that has been made very clear to me in my life," she trailed off, like she regretted saying the last part.

As it has also been made clear to me.

"So you would willingly expose yourself to danger, Miss Byron-Cole? How could you do it? And even to the ones who care for you?"

"Sir, I would not consciously wish to give pain to any of those who care for me. You do not know me, or you would not suggest such a thing. It is simply—it is necessary for me to do this," she said, her voice growing softer as she continued to look down, "for it is all that remains of my life…from before."

He'd struck a nerve and she took him to task for it. This girl had some spirit in her. And he would so love to be the beneficiary of that spirit. Images of beds and bodies entwined flashed through his head again. He really was losing his mind he was sure. He walked up to her and took a finger to her chin. He added some gentle pressure. "Look at me."

She opened her beautiful eyes as she lifted her face upon his command. Graham swallowed hard as she complied. Everything about her got to him - her acquiescence, her beauty, her voice, even her scent. The shape of her face was distinctive - high cheekbones and a wide mouth with beautiful lips he wanted to taste. Her eyes were brown but there was nothing dull about them. They sparkled with flecks of gold and green and amber. It was the same with her hair, not really brown, but shimmering with light throughout. He wanted his hands in her hair, pulling her against him to accept his touch and body inside hers. Oh yes. He'd had plenty of those thoughts already. He wanted Imogene in his bed, underneath him, taking him in as he made love to her.

Her eyes grew wet as he tipped her chin up to look at him. He dropped his finger.

To refrain from touching her took all of his strength. He could see her distress at being reminded of painful remembrances, and knowing a little of them already from his family, he wanted to comfort and soothe her.

Graham couldn't help looking longingly before speaking, his eyes sweeping over her from head to toe. She was dressed in riding clothes. The tight jacket fitted over willowy curves that looked too damn delectable for her to be off all on her own. "But I want to know you…*very* much."

She took in a sharp breath that made her breasts rise up underneath the jacket.

"If I could go with you today I would." He *should* be with her, but he knew that wouldn't be happening today. "Damn propriety!" The frustration of being unable to act, forced him to say goodbye so he could leave her to her riding. It would be best for him to take his sorry lump of flesh away from her before he did something really stupid anyway. Like try to kiss her. God, he wanted to. "I regret causing you distress just now. Please forgive me? I do hope you have a safe and pleasant ride."

Imogene's eyes flared at him. Frozen, she stared for a minute and then nodded an acknowledgement of his apology. He wished she'd say something more, but she stayed quiet. A blast of autumn air blew into the stables at that moment, lifting her hair and making it dance. The chill in the air made her shiver. He saw it happen as clear as day and wondered if it was really the chill, or had it been what he'd said to her.

"Miss Byron-Cole, until next time." He bowed, turned on

his heel and left her in the stables. *God help me to walk away. Just get me off without some grave breech of manners. If something happens to her I don't know what—*

Graham talked in his head all the way back to the house, whipping stray stalks with his riding crop mercilessly as he went. He made it back in time to see her ride out from the window, hair streaming behind her in the cold wind. It was the longest two hours he could remember spending. He reread the same passage in his book over and over until he grew disgusted and flung it down.

Graham welcomed the relief that washed over him when he saw her ride back in. He observed her signal to Mr. Jacks that she had safely returned. The pang in his chest drilled through his body as she galloped down the drive, away from Kenilbrooke, away from where he was.

Graham was well aware of the constraints of society. Imogene was aware, too. They understood the rules. He could not go with her alone. Someone was needed who could serve as chaperone. If it weren't for those rules she would be in his arms already and his lips would know what it felt like to be against hers. A plan began to form of a possible solution to this hindrance. Graham went in search of his sweet cousin Elle.

A week later and Graham could not remember a more pleasant time at church. The lovely view of Imogene's profile as she sat with her family was his sole focus and he relished it gratefully. The rector's droning message, uninspiring and condescending in tone, was put aside as he allowed himself to study her intently without too conspicuous of notice by others, or so he thought.

In the churchyard, Graham watched his cousin, Elle, approach to invite Imogene and her family to the games that had been organized at Kenilbrooke for the recreation of the young people. Imogene appeared to accept the invitation gracefully, and chatted easily with her new friend. Jules and Hargreave were watching everything transpire, too, and apparently with great amusement. Graham felt clearly on edge, not completely sure if he should approach Elle and Imogene, but it was obvious he wouldn't be able to stay away for long. His self-control evaporated when it came to her. *Keep talking, Elle,* he begged silently. Finally, he started toward them, hat in hand.

Behind him, Hargreave and Jules were in full amusement. "He is moving in," Hargreave whispered loud enough for him to hear.

"Yes, yes, go to her, my boy," Jules mocked.

"Ease your beating heart, lad," Hargreave sang. They laughed together and took sport at his expense.

Graham turned back and glared over his shoulder. "Would you two shut up!"

"Good day to you, Miss Byron-Cole, a pleasure to see you again so soon." Jules probably thought his imitation was amusing, but Graham wanted to land him on his arse.

"Oh, Miss Byron-Cole, would you do me the honor of partnering me at croquet?" Hargreave imitated next. They collapsed into laughter then, and were so noisy that people around them were beginning to laugh as well, without even knowing of the joke.

Imogene definitely heard them and turned to look at them quizzically.

Elle looked over as well, disbelievingly.

Graham glanced back again at the idiots and thought

fondly of disembowelment.

"Miss Everley, why are your brother and Mr. Hargreave laughing like schoolboys in the churchyard?" he heard Imogene ask.

Elle replied, shaking her head, "I am sure I do not know, Miss Byron-Cole, their behaviour is very odd."

Graham went next as he pulled up into their conversation. "I know why. They are absolute, insensible idiots." He bowed. "Miss Byron-Cole, I look forward to seeing you this afternoon at Kenilbrooke."

"Lord Rothvale." That was all she said. His name. It was enough for him though. Her acknowledgement and her eyes on him were enough. The husky sound of her voice at complete odds with her physical form, and utterly sensual in a way that made his mind turn wicked in an instant, and highly blasphemous for where he stood with her—in a churchyard.

"Until later then, ladies." He tipped his hat, strode away from the girls and back toward those who took their amusement at his expense.

"What in the *bloody hell* are you two doing?" he said a little too loudly, palms up. The reverend, who was speaking to Mrs. Charleston, gasped and turned to deliver him a shocked, open-mouthed glare. Jules and Hargreave burst into new fits of laughter at this final humiliation. Graham winced, put his hand to his head and ground his teeth. "Many pardons, Reverend, Madam, that was regrettable, please accept my apologies." He pointed his hand out and continued forward toward his source of harassment.

"Peace, Cousin." Jules clapped Graham on the back affectionately as he drew up.

"Do you always behave this disgracefully in proper company and on the occasion of church? It is a miracle you both have secured the society of respectable people and brides as well. Do not ever do that again." Graham stabbed a pointed finger at them. "You will regret it, I promise you. I'll give you a basting you'll not forget!"

"You've got your bristles all set up, Cousin." Jules paused but then bent in laughter again. "Cursing in the churchyard, right in the parson's ear—that was in high-ropes, Graham!" Jules and Hargreave were still lost in idiotic laughter as the three walked away.

"I cannot wait until you are married; there might be some relief then, from you cutting up my peace."

Hargreave replied, "Well you shan't have long to wait then. So you'll be staying on, after Jules' wedding? Please consider Kenilbrooke open to your needs, Graham."

"No, you moronic dolt. She's going to her sister at Wellick after the new year. And I just happen to have the acquaintance of a certain Dr. John Brancroft of Gloucester Hospital. I do not need your help, either of you. You have done your parts, and I thank you. Now you may leave me be. By God, I mean it or I shall have to thrash you both and you will not look winsome for your wives!"

WHEN her carriage drove up he was there waiting. No other person was going to touch her as she got out but him—of that he was certain. He looked at his hand when he reached for the door handle and envisioned it was her bare skin he was touching. Graham had always been told he had big hands. Imogene's hands were elegant and perfect. He gripped firmly when she placed her hand in his and felt the jolt down low of arousal. The merest touch and he felt stirred. He really needed to get some control over his reactions. His imagination, and his cock, had minds of their own apparently, especially when it came to Imogene, and they were in public for Christ's sake!

Imogene offered the introductions for her family. "Lord Rothvale, I do not believe you have made the acquaintance of my cousins, Timothy Wilton, and his sister, Miss Cariss Wilton."

"It is a pleasure, Miss Wilton. Mr. Wilton, I hear you take your studies at Cambridge. Today I shall introduce you to my brother, Colin Everley. He's at Trinity finishing now, but it can never hurt to have further acquaintances away from home."

Timothy Wilton thanked him and led his young sister into the party.

Now that he had her all to himself, he smiled down at the beautiful Imogene and offered his arm. When she took his arm and returned the smile he felt a burst of happiness shoot through him. "You seem to be in happier spirits than you were this morning at church, my lord."

He nodded in agreement, and kept his expression bland on purpose. "What think you of croquet, Miss Byron-Cole? Are you any good at it?"

"I am tolerable at it, but I am told I can be devilishly competitive at sport."

"Excellent. Do me a kindness, please. Should you encounter my cousin or Hargreave's ball in the course of the game, at any time, be merciless and send them into oblivion."

She seemed to find his comments hilarious. So much so that she laughed out loud. "We have a pact, my lord. On my honor I *will* definitely do it."

"I have made you laugh. I love the sound of your laugh.

It was worth it, this morning's debacle, to hear you laughing just now."

"A good laugh is always worth it," she said, as he led her toward the games.

Graham enjoyed the game very much, the least of it being revenge upon his cousin and friend. The greatest pleasure for him was being able to watch her at liberty, mallet in hand, striking the ball with a skillful flourish, laughing and floating over the grass, dark golden hair, shifting in the wind, her smiles at amusing conversations. To him she was ethereally beautiful and he loved to look at beauty. True to her word, she sacrificed any shot in which there was the opportunity to send Hargreave or Jules.

"Well done, Cousin," Jules whispered in his ear. "I am impressed you have gained her loyalty so quickly. Looks as if I have helped you after all, doesn't it?" Graham put out his hand in greeting and Jules took it. Graham gripped painfully hard and was satisfied to see his cousin wince through the handshake. Jules complimented, "She is lovely, perfect for you. So she's the one that will make you happy, eh? So fast…but I can already see a change in you."

"Thank you for the kind sentiment. I have never known such unshakable feelings. Like it was meant to be or—well yes, I dare to hope that she will be mine. How did you get through this experience with Mina?"

Jules shook his head. "It was utterly dreadful. I wish I could say it was not. But you'll manoeuver through just fine. You have the advantage of coming together amiably from the first. She likes you. How did you manage that so easily?"

"By smiling and asking her to dance," Graham replied dryly.

"Ouch. I guess you have heard the stories of how it was

with Mina and me at the first. I was such a stupid arse and she fairly hated me. You are much wiser than I was. My advice? Be completely honest with her and declare yourself, soon. I suspect Miss Byron-Cole would appreciate some candor in her life about now. Don't wait too long. If you don't offer for her, someone else will. She's just out of her mourning and well dowered. Everyone's giving respectable deference to you now, mostly due to your rank, but that won't last forever."

Graham nodded his understanding, but felt his heart ditch at the thought of another courting her. *She is mine.*

Both men watched Elle approach Imogene to invite her for riding the next day, hearing her say, "My cousins Colin and Graham will be accompanying me. We will call for you at Wilton Court tomorrow at ten o'clock." They saw Imogene acknowledge the information and agree to go along.

Graham turned to Jules. "Your sister is the kindest, sweetest person I know and I owe her everything in this. I'll not forget what she has done here for me, Jules."

Jules smiled wistfully and nodded. "I know. She is, and I know you'll not forget."

It became too emotional then for the cousins to continue conversing. Too many memories of painful hurts, and children without parents, so they grew quiet.

Both of them understood.

"LORD Rothvale is in love with you." Her friend whispered into Imogene's ear from behind.

"Jocelyn! You just about frightened me to death. And how on earth can you say such a thing? He barely knows me." Imogene was shocked at her friend's candor, but could not deny the feelings of excitement that came with Jocelyn's words. It had been so long since she had embraced the emotion she hardly recognized it.

"I realize that, Imogene, but short time or no, that man is in love with you. He asked me about you."

"He asked about me? When was that? You were not at the ball, Jocelyn. By the way, why in the world not?"

Jocelyn ignored her last question. "Mamma and Papa invited them to dinner at our house. Jules, his sister Ellenora, and their cousins."

"Of course they did. Julian Everley will be your brother soon when he marries Mina." Imogene tried to divert the conversation. "What do you think of Ellenora?"

"I like her, but I was speaking of Lord Rothvale. Don't you want to know?"

Imogene felt her face flush. She couldn't speak, so she just nodded and waited for Jocelyn to tell it.

"When we sat to dinner, he put himself by me. Somehow he already knew that we are close friends. He told me of meeting you that day, how you brought back the lamb. Imogene, he is entranced when he speaks of you. He wanted to know what you like to read."

"What did you say?" she whispered.

"Poetry. Lord Byron. *Le Morte d'Arthur.* He liked that, I think." Jocelyn looked at her boldly. "He wanted to know your favourite colour as well?"

"And?"

"I told him it was…green. He liked that, too."

His eyes are green. "You should not have told him, Jocelyn. It's not right. I don't want people speculating."

"Too late for that, I think." Jocelyn took up Imogene's hands. "His eyes never leave you. If you turn and look now, you will find he is staring at your back as we speak. I think the better question for you is what do you think of him?"

He's looking at me right now? Imogene lifted her head, her stubbornness rising up. "I like him. He is a gentleman toward me. He has done nothing to cause me to see him as anything other than that." She dropped her eyes. "He will be in my riding party tomorrow. Would you like to join us, Jocelyn?"

"No thank you, dear. You must use your opportunity with him tomorrow to help him get to know you better. Don't let this chance slip away, encourage him."

Imogene pondered Jocelyn's words. Could he really be in love with her? How could he after just a few meetings? Could she love him? She had to admit, just thinking about him made her suddenly warm inside. She liked how that felt.

"YOU were magnificent today." Graham viewed her earnestly, trying to soak in as much of her presence as he could. He found that the urge to be with her every minute was surprisingly strong. Right now he could almost feel tinges of panic at the thought of her leaving.

"I had a wonderful time. It felt good to laugh and I truly enjoyed the games. Our conspiracy against Mr. Everley and Mr. Hargreave went quite well, I daresay. They were at the bottom of the heap in scores." Imogene's triumphant grin easily gave away her competitiveness.

"All thanks to you. You are possessed of a wicked competitive streak. It's true. 'Mark and learn from Miss Byron-Cole!' should be the cry of the day."

She laughed again. "Miss Imogene, please. Miss Byron-Cole has too many names in it. I look forward to riding tomorrow, Lord Rothvale," she told him easily, her eyes flashing.

He bowed, thrilled at her request that he address her by her Christian name. "Miss Imogene, as do I…very much."

You have no idea how much, beautiful Imogene.

Chapter 4

Love comforteth like sunshine after rain.

William Shakespeare ~Venus and Adonis, 1593

Dark clouds exuding the threat of rain were in full force by the time Imogene's riding party called at Wilton Court. Introductions were made all around for those who were in need of one and Lord Rothvale, looking handsome and somber as ever, gave assurance that should the weather turn, he would see her safely home. When assisting her in mounting Terra, the feel of his big hands around her waist burned right through her clothes. "All set?" he asked.

She nodded sharply at him, totally unable to form any words.

"Where to, Miss Imogene? You're the only one of us who has the advantage. Lead us on?"

"Very well, follow me." She guided Terra out.

Imogene took them to a high meadow dotted with trees, well beyond the boundaries of Kenilbrooke. There was an old rock wall, crumbling enough in places that it could be breeched on horseback. Beyond the wall upon the hill, were the ruins of a castle. Formidable centuries past, but now returning back to the earth in its waning days. The roof had been removed long ago, and with that one act, the castle's doom had been sealed. The walls immediately began to separate, tumbling down once there was nothing to keep the enormous weight of the stones forced together at the top. The ruin was still beautiful, even in winter and in its dying gasps. Outside the wall, sheep dotted the hillside, grazing and reminding her of the occasion she first saw him. The sheep had colonized the area and fixed themselves in and around the ancient toppled stones. His brother, Colin, and Ellenora Everley paired up and headed off, picking their way through the rubble.

Their pace slowed and Lord Rothvale pulled up next to her. "Where did you find it?"

Imogene knew that he was referring to the lamb she had rescued on the day he arrived, for the grazing sheep had reminded her of the same thing. "Way down there in the creek bed," she pointed below them to a meandering creek flowing with water. "It was dry then, nothing but rocks."

"So adventuresome. You were quite comfortable scrambling down into that rocky pit?"

"It wasn't comfortable, but had to be done. I could not have left the poor thing to die."

"You are rather fearless I think."

"More like a girl raised in the typical country way. It was nothing I would not have done were I at my home, at Drakenhurst."

"You consider yourself a typical country girl? I assure you, that you are not. I have never met anyone like you in my life."

I feel the same way about you. "Perhaps you've not spent enough time in the country, Lord Rothvale."

"I don't think that's it." He cocked a brow at her and shook his head. "What of your home, Drakenhurst? How did you occupy your days there?" What surprised Imogene the most was how he behaved as if he really wanted to know about her life. Most men would simply greet a lady as society dictated, showing little interest in her person or thoughts. Yet, he looked deeply into her eyes when he asked questions as if her answers were important information he desired to know.

"Drakenhurst is in Essex, a working estate, not far out of London at Waltham Forest. My father kept an excellent stable and enjoyed the hunting when his obligations to Parliament allowed him time to pursue it. From a young age, I realized being out of doors is much preferable to being in. I rode very frequently, and indulged in a bit of target practice as well. I find the required skill and precision of archery a challenge and like the quietness of it. The stillness and concentration necessary, before the arrow is released toward the target is…is satisfying to me, and feels like an accomplishment. I miss it. Since I have come to Shelburne, I've not had opportunity to take it up again." Her voice trailed off and she felt the sudden need to stop talking.

"You are an accomplished sportswoman. You see? I was right. You are not the typical country girl as you modestly claim. You sound like Artemis, goddess of archery and the hunt. What a portrait that would make, Miss Imogene. Just imagine it."

"My lord, I assure you, I am not the paragon of accomplishment you praise me to be. I had occasion to spend plenty of time indoors as well with the more ordinary and traditional occupations expected of a young lady. I write and keep a journal. I also read a great deal." *Which you know already.* "My mamma was ill for a long time, my sister and I attended to her continually. She dearly loved for us to read to her, and later, she had need of me to write her letters." Imogene looked at him challengingly, not wanting pity, for she was protective of her grief still, and not yet ready to share.

He nodded and wisely let it go. Lord Rothvale had good instincts, which was a fortunate for him, because she did not want to speak about her mother. Not today.

They rode along together in companionable quiet. Again she was impressed by his easiness. He didn't push. It was more like leading her where she wanted to go. She could speak freely and there wasn't a pressing need to fill the surprisingly comfortable silences with unnecessary conversation.

"My turn," she said. "I have answered several of your questions, so it's only fair you give up some answers, my lord. Agreed?"

"Ask away, Miss Imogene. I am yours to command," he answered lightly, seemingly glad the somber spirit of their conversation had passed.

"Why did your cousin, Mr. Everley, refer to you as wayward, at the ball? He called you his wayward cousin and I want to know why."

He gave her a lifted eyebrow first and then spoke. "A fair question I suppose. It is nothing sinister, I guarantee. I am 'wayward' in the sense of being away from home for a long time. I've been in Ireland for the past year putting business affairs to order. Remember, how I told you of the death of my mother last fall? Well, the Irish estate, Donadea, passed to my family upon her death. I had to attend to business there."

"And Ireland is very agreeable to you?"

"Yes, very much so. In fact, I stayed much longer than

was originally intended. When Julian wrote to me of his upcoming marriage to Miss Mina, I felt the time had come for me to return to England, and to my responsibilities here. My family is important to me, and I wished to offer support to Jules, of course," he finished quietly.

He is loyal to his family. "Do you miss Ireland?"

"It is bewitching to be sure. The old world still exists in Ireland and right along with it, the old world creatures…fairies, and brownies, and elves." He looked at her stone-faced for a minute before he winked, his green eyes teasing her.

"Even brownies, my lord? They are the naughty ones I've heard." She teased him right back.

"Indeed. I've never met a brownie I could trust. They are all wicked little demons."

"I think somebody else is wicked, telling imaginative tales about the residents of the Emerald Isle."

He threw his head back and laughed at her, the sound of his laughter hitting her right in the heart. "But truly, there is a magical beauty that pulls you in, captivates you. I know I will return someday." He looked directly into her eyes and Imogene could have sworn he was referring to her in his words. "Though I am happy to be here in England—it was time for me to leave Ireland, and right now I would not wish to be anywhere else."

Despite the chill of the day, she suddenly felt hot. "Your name, it is not commonly bestowed, is it? Was Graham your mother's surname, given you in respect?"

"Yes. You are exactly right. It is somewhat of a family tradition. I thank God my mother was not named Bumweald or Whitelegg, or something equally horrifying."

She could not hold back the comment. Lord Rothvale was easy to tease. "I don't know about that, I think Whitelegg

Everley has a good ring to it, don't you?" She kept her face serious even though she wanted to fall on the grass and howl. He saved her by laughing first and letting her join in.

"You have a lovely name," he said. "Imogene is an Irish name. Did you know? It means 'last daughter.' And your surname is shared with England's most celebrated poet."

Imogene didn't feel like talking about her name, rather she watched him intently, looking at his hair. She blurted, "You wear your hair in the old way. Is it because you have been in Ireland?" She immediately regretted her question. "Forgive me. That was rude of me to ask."

He shrugged. "I don't mind telling you. It just seemed easier at the time. Ireland is very different from England, simpler, less complicated. I have thought of cutting it now that I am back."

STUDYING her reaction to his words, he observed a quick furrow at her brow before she whispered the word, 'regrettable' so lightly, he barely heard. *She fancies the long hair.*

"But maybe I'll just leave it long." She smiled at him again.

Graham believed in fate. He believed in his frequent and vivid dreams, feeling it was fate that had brought him here to this place, with the purpose of finding her.

He was ready.

Ready to go home and claim his inheritance in the true sense of all it entailed.

Ready even, to take a wife.

The notion of a wife, now that he had met Imogene, was so strong that it was the only way in which he could see her. He needed to be sure though. Sure of her feelings. He could not share any of this with her yet, but held faith in it. His dreams were strong, and Imogene was an ever-present force.

Sleep was something he looked forward to each night, for in his sleep he might find her in a dream. He could go to her. He could touch her.

The laughing sounds of Elle and Colin broke through his musings as they pulled up, riding hard. Graham looked at them questioningly. "The sky, my brother," Colin directed scornfully pointing up. "It's going to pour!"

Christ! Graham looked up to ominous, rolling, storm clouds. Right then, the sky opened up and unleashed with a vengeance. The sound of it like a giant thundering beast coming at them gave the instinct to bolt. "We are caught and there's nothing for it! Prepare to get wet!" Graham shouted as the four of them headed back at a hard run.

Imogene looked like she was having the time of her life—so free and unconventional. Galloping in the rain, getting soaked, feeling the water run down his face, was the least of it. Having those things happen with her, stirred him. It felt wildly intimate. As their horses pounded over the turf, she looked over and met his eyes. Grinning widely, she yelled, "I love this."

He laughed out loud in response to her declaration, taking in the vision of her. So beautiful—even in the pouring rain—racing over the fields, soaked to the skin, clearly loving every minute of it. *And I love this…with you.*

As they approached the grounds of Kenilbrooke, Colin and Elle shouted their goodbyes and headed away toward the stables. Graham and Imogene continued on together toward Wilton Court at a gallop. It was not much farther to go, and too soon they arrived, riding straight into the barn to get out of the rain. Graham leapt down from Triton and was waiting to help her dismount, his hands latching on to her waist, pulling her down toward him. He wasn't going to miss this chance to touch her and have her body up against his. Not possible, and propriety could be damned.

Imogene closed her eyes when his hands grabbed hold, and opened them again when her feet touched the ground. She breathed heavily from the exertion of the ride, and a great smile broke out on her face. "That was the best ride I have had in ages. I'll never forget this day."

Me either. Graham was mesmerized again. Even soaked, she was exquisite. "Are you cold?" he managed to ask.

"Not in the slightest."

"Your clothes are soaked." *And in all the right places…* He tried not to stare at her damp bodice showing every delicious curve of her most perfect, lovely, and noticeably chilled breasts. What he wouldn't give to have his mouth on that part of her right now. He did try valiantly, but was not completely successful. *Saints help me!*

Imogene shook her head slightly. "It does not matter, this experience was worth it," she gulped, her breath still coming out strong and steady.

Graham could not stop what he did next. Reaching out to touch her face, he pushed a wet tendril of hair away from her eyebrow. Nothing could have prevented him. His fingers kept moving, with a will of their own, tracing down the side of her face, along her cheek, under her jaw line and finally ending at her chin. Imogene closed her eyes again at his touch.

"You amaze me, so unique, not like any other," he breathed, thrilling at her response to his touching. She felt something, he was sure.

"I thank you for that, my lord. It is meaningful to me that you think so."

"Would you like to go again? When the weather permits?"

"Oh, yes I would," she answered, nodding.

"I go to London today." He watched her carefully.

"You are leaving?" She frowned before she could school her response—he hoped that was the reason, at least. And that she didn't want him to leave.

"Just for a day or two. I have pressing business and must go." He'd caught her frown and was glad for it. "I'll be back before you know it, and when I am, I want to see you. To call upon you, formally." She did not react right away, but her eyes held. "Do you understand what I am proposing?" She nodded, her focus never leaving his eyes. "And do you wish it, Miss Imogene?" She nodded again. "Tell me, please. I need to hear you say it." His true demeanour was being revealed. The real him. The dominant part of him. He could not help it, and if she was to be truly his then she would have to accept him in this way.

"I wish for you to call upon me, Lord Rothvale." Her brown eyes glittered at him and he wanted to record this moment. How she looked at him right now, the beauty of her, how very fine she was.

"Well, then…." He nodded back, never breaking eye contact with her, taking up her hand and bringing it to his lips. He kissed it on the side, where he pulled her skin into his mouth a little. There was just the tiniest brush of his tongue and he held it much too long for propriety's sake. He was dying to touch her but he also wanted to see how she would react to him. Imogene allowed him to have his way for a moment then she drew in her breath sharply. The sound pushed Graham out of his trance, and he released her hand quickly. "I'm sorry," he whispered, but that was a lie. He wasn't a bit sorry he'd gotten to taste her skin.

Shaking her head the slightest little bit, she said, "Do not be," and then backed up slowly. "Good day, sir, and Godspeed on your journey." She stood before him, her expression unreadable.

He bowed first, and then watched as she turned and fled the stable. *What the bloody hell? You're supposed to court her, not devour her.*

But sweet Christ, she'd tasted good.

Graham knew he was in for a tortured dream sequence that night. To be relentlessly tormented by the blonde beauty he had yet to claim was indeed a sweet kind of torture. Soon, he would claim her. Soon, but not yet. He allowed himself indulgence in the thought.

The three-hour ride to London, in patchy rain, gave him plenty of time to reflect upon her reactions at what he'd done in the stables. He went over and over it again in his mind, knowing he had taken a liberty to be sure, but felt certain she had been affected, in a good way. Her little gasp had been one of passion, not fear. She was passionate. From her delight in riding freely in the rain, to her reaction to his kiss, he knew she was passionate. And he would be the one to discover the depths of it. He hoped he hadn't scared her off him. He would know soon enough, wouldn't he?

THE yelling, the arguments, the crying. The child was crying, and so was her mother, somewhere. The monster laughed at him again, at everyone. His mother, dressed in riding clothes, wept at his feet. His father lay cold in the coffin. He felt so alone, helpless, weak. "Don't ever turn your back on them, my son," his mother implored. "She is of your blood! If for no other reason, do it for me!"

He faced the monster. "Why do you torment me? Am I never to have any peace?"

The monster laughed at his pleas.

"Don't bring shame on the family, son!" his father shouted at him from the coffin. "Do your duty, nothing more. No more need be done. Let it go."

"I hate you!" he screamed at the monster.

The monster cackled with glee...

Graham crashed awake from his nightmare, bolting up in his bed. His eyes travelled down his body and got a gander at the cockstand he was sporting as he panted against the headboard. Not exactly the type of dreams he'd hoped for tonight.

He brought the image of Imogene into his mind—her beautiful face and body—and focused on them. He did this until his racing heart calmed and his head stopped spinning. His hand moved down to between his legs and found his rigid cock. It wouldn't take long and by God, he needed the release. He couldn't go out and take care of himself at a bordello, and he wouldn't want to anyway. Didn't think he would be capable. The days of bordellos and whores were over. He just wanted one woman now. His hand stroked a little faster. He imagined Imogene's mouth, with her beautiful lips kissing down his body, lower and lower. He sheathed his cock a little tighter in his palm until the tip wept. He saw her flicking out her lovely tongue to taste the droplet—and that was all it took. His bollocks tightened as the climax mastered him, and he spilled over his hand, the musky scent of spunk filling his head along with the images of her that he'd put there. The release was something, but it wasn't nearly enough. He wanted the real thing with her. He wanted to come buried deep between her sweet thighs, pleasuring her right along with him. He wanted it all with Imogene.

As he got up to wash his hands, he took a good look into the mirror above the washbasin. He saw the straight dark hair and the big body he'd been born with, the green eyes, and the decent teeth he could thank his mother for, and wished he could change the past. He wished it with all his heart, but again, that question of 'want' and 'reality' resurfaced to remind him life rarely gave up what you really desired. He prayed Imogene would be the exception.

When Graham got back into his bed, it took some time for him to find sleep again. But when he finally succumbed, it was of her that he dreamed.

Chapter 5

We do earnestly repent,
And are heartily sorry for these our misdoings;
The remembrance of them is grievous unto us;
The burden of them is intolerable.

***The Book of Common Prayer* ~ *Holy Communion*, 1662**

The hours Imogene spent reflecting on his kiss in the barn were extensive. Less concerning to her was the lack of propriety than her physical reaction to Lord Rothvale. Graham. His name was Graham. She wanted to be able to call him by his given name but wouldn't dare to do it until he asked it of her. When he touched his lips to her hand it was like nothing she had ever experienced. She found herself forgetting everything about the requirements of proper decorum. He simply took control of her body. While the feelings were exciting and wonderful, she still found them confusing. Even through it all, something deep inside told her he was not a dishonorable man or trying to prey upon her. How she knew it, she couldn't say, but she knew it all the same.

As he came into view, her heart beat faster. They were to

ride again. This time, her cousins, Timothy and Cariss, were included. Would he treat her differently now, she wondered. Especially after he'd made her repeat to him that she wished for him to call upon her formally. She had a very good understanding what that meant.

But Lord Rothvale appeared to be his same steady self when he came into view, riding upon Triton. Calm, intense, kind, steady—he seemed all of those things. She braced herself for his hands when he hoisted her up onto Terra's back. *Yes.* His firm touch, still divine, affected her just as much as the other times.

He leaned toward her neck and whispered, "Are you well, Miss Imogene?"

"I *am*, Lord Rothvale. And you?"

Very deliberately, he said, "I am *now*." She couldn't help the beam she gave him back, and she couldn't wait to talk to him again, but the riding would have to come first.

The party of six ended up at the same location as last time. Today they breeched the broken wall and entered the castle ruins. It was a magical place. One could not help but think on the inhabitants of centuries past and wonder of the people who had come and gone from this spot. After a time, they decided to dismount, exploring the stones on foot. He offered his arm and she took it, feeling his strength as he tucked her arm into his. They walked together away from the others and she was glad for the chance to be alone.

"There is something I wish to tell you. Will you hear me?" he asked.

Imogene's stomach did a little flip. "Yes, of course."

"I have not been completely honest with you. I have kept something—information—from you."

"Why would you do that?" She felt suddenly sick. Was

he going to tell her he was a cad, a rogue, that he had a wife, something terrible that would shatter her trust in him?

He held her arm close in to his side, firmly like he would be reluctant to let her go. "I did not wish to burden you or to push you too far, or overwhelm you."

"But you have never made me feel like that. In fact, upon reflection, you are very comfortable to be with. Your manner is easy, and I feel safe when I am with you."

He looked down at her, his expression softening in relief. "You have no idea how happy that makes me feel. I always want you to feel safe when you're with me." He squeezed her hand a little. "I know your sister's husband. We are well acquainted."

Imogene was confused. Was this the dark secret? "John? You know my brother-in-law, Dr. Brancroft? So why did you not say so before?"

He sighed. "There's so much more to it and most of it is a painfully, sad business. I wished to avoid it, to spare you any connection to the ugliness of it, or for it to spark sad remembrances of your own."

"I appreciate your honesty and consideration, my lord, but I wish to hear your story. Please tell me. I want to know."

He nodded solemnly. "In my family I was not born the heir. I am a second son."

"I know that already. Mr. Hargreave told me, the night of the ball." She could tell that her knowledge surprised him.

"He did? What did he tell you?"

"Only that. He said you had become the heir after the sad loss of your older brother, giving no details, just indicating that you had borne some burdens. He said it in the way of a friend, truly, and was almost—he seemed protective of you, concerned. That is all, there is nothing more," she told him honestly.

"Hargreave and I must 'chat' later I am afraid," he said tersely. "My brother, Jasper, was the great family tragedy. He destroyed himself and my parents along with him. Weak and selfish, he was unwilling to accept his duty. The simple explanation is that he dissipated himself to death, falling in and keeping company with dishonorable people who used him. He was an opium addict, drank too much, gambled away tremendous sums of money, holding no respect for himself or for his family. Shame is what he brought to us. That is the gist of it; you do not need to hear every disgusting detail." She looked at him calmly and stayed quiet, waiting for him to finish. "Near the end of it, Jasper grew very ill and was brought home to Gavandon. Dr. Brancroft became known to us then. He attended my brother, but the damage was too severe to bring Jasper back, most of it being the damage to his mind. The body cannot heal if the mind is unwilling."

"Was John able to do anything for your brother?"

"Not really. Brancroft is a good doctor and a fine man. He tried his best, but nothing more could be done for Jasper and he was lost despite Brancroft's best efforts. A shade of gloom fell over my family. The shame crushed my good father. Bad blood. Within a year his own body gave out in apoplexy. My father's passing was sudden, but he lingered long enough to discharge the duty on to me, to take up the responsibility for everything, and for my mother and Colin, of course. Dr. Brancroft also attended my father. He made him as comfortable as possible in those dark times, and he was very kind to my mother who suffered terribly in her grief. John Brancroft is an honorable man. I do not know your sister of course, as these events happened some years ago, before he had met her, but if she is anything like you, I suspect he is blessed to have found her." A smile was attempted, but sadness reined in his eyes.

Imogene looked into them compassionately. "What a tragic waste. I am so sorry."

"I agree. One gigantic waste, and—" He stopped and shook his head.

"What? Please tell me." Imogene waited. "Surely you realize that his actions do not stain you."

"But they do." He looked grim. "Jasper ruined everything. I hold anger and resentment against my brother. I do not forgive him for what he has done to my parents, to me, or to Colin. My brother was a selfish bastard—" Graham gave her an apologetic look. "He took and took and did nothing but take some more. I feel wrath for him, but that is my weight to bear."

"Did you resent the duty thrust upon you?"

"I suppose, but I was really just desperate at first to find my way and to be worthy. I had not been raised for it you see, and was ill prepared when it happened, believing I would live the life of a painter. But it was not to be and the years have resolved it now. I will carry on the responsibility to my family and continue to do it to the best of my ability, for as long as I am able." His green eyes had a cold look to them now.

"But I believe you *are* an honorable man. His actions don't mark you. You shouldn't fear the telling of your situation would alter my opinion of you. It is the same as before."

"Truly?"

She nodded. "Truly."

"Miss Imogene, I've been plagued with a bad conscience and I—I thank you for hearing all of this…repulsiveness. I am so sorry to have it touch you, I really am, but I could see no other way around it."

Imogene drew up, making him stop in their walking. "Well, I can only offer my support and the willingness to hear anything you wish to tell me. I assure you, nothing you have said today revises that status. I am your friend."

GRAHAM let go of her arm and took both her hands in his. He turned them palm up and stared at them. He caressed them for a moment before lifting his eyes to her beautiful brown ones, and relished her words. She would accept him, bad blood, and family skeletons and all. He knew in this moment that nothing would get in his way of having her. Not his shameful secret, and not the legacy his brother had left for him.

"Thank you," he whispered. "I hope it's more than a friend though. Tell me it is more than friendship." Imogene's breathing picked up. He saw the colour on her neck and her breasts moving underneath her clothes. "Tell me it is," he repeated the command.

She was so lovely. The flush of her skin in the clean cold air, strands of golden hair lifting in the breeze, her burgundy riding dress, the horses tethered and grazing nearby, ancient ruins crumbling behind, all coalesced into one gorgeous scene; a scene worthy of capturing. He tried to get it crammed into his head, willing the details to stick so he could remember how beautiful she looked when she told him she did not care about the ugliness of his past or the bad blood of his family. "It is more," she whispered and he wanted to kiss her lips right then and there but knew he couldn't. He drew her palm up to his mouth and kissed that instead, wanting her to know she was already precious to him.

Observing propriety is a hellish existence when I want you so badly.

They continued on with their walk. As they went along, Graham felt relieved but he sensed Imogene was troubled. She grew stiff and quiet.

He felt, and then saw the transition in her, dread filling him. Pulling her to an abrupt stop, he demanded, "What is wrong? You look like you have seen a ghost." Moving his hand up to her shoulders, he held her firmly, lowering his head to meet hers, his mind racing. "Do you regret your words of feeling toward me? Whatever it is I need you to tell me," he finished gently.

With anguish in her eyes, Imogene shook her head and said, "I have secrets to tell as well, bad ones, worse than yours. I have done something very wrong and no one knows."

He did not like this feeling at all—Imogene terribly upset and distraught. Seeing her in so much pain actually hurt him. Calmly, he led her to a ledge of rock that afforded a place for them to sit, providing some privacy and blocking the cool wind. Once they were seated, he gathered her hands in his and dipped his head so he could meet her eyes. "I can see you are distressed. It pains *me* to see you thus. Let me help. I am here for you. I will listen if you wish to speak. And if you don't wish to tell me then I will just be here." He reached up and stroked over a tendril of hair that had escaped her pins. He couldn't imagine she had done anything that was *very* bad. How was it even possible? Seeing her tears killed him but he forced himself not to press. She needed to tell whatever it was on her own terms.

After what seemed like an age, she looked down at her hands still held in one of his and began to talk. "Do you wonder how John Brancroft became known to my family?"

"Was it because of your mother?"

"Yes. She had been ill for years. Her lungs. Despite it, she was the best mother to us. She loved us so much, and tried so very hard to get better. Such a strong will she had, brave and never complaining, determined not to leave us alone without a mother."

Imogene struggled to tell her story. Her voice faltered and he knew it was hard for her. He just held her hand and continued to trace over the piece of hair framing her face.

"John had left the north and had come to Royal Sothington Hospital for a course of study and research, taking on patients with Mamma's particular illness as part of his investigation into the disease. He prescribed modern treatments for my mother, believing they might help. My parents were immediately taken with him and the relationship between them grew. He became more than a doctor, he became a friend. John and my sister, Philippa, were instantly attracted to one another—it was swift and mutual between them. They fell in love, eventually marrying. John's research study ended and the time had come to return to Gloucestershire. That time was just over a year ago from this day. John and Philippa's wedding was the last occasion my whole family was together in joy. That day was the beginning of losing them…one by one."

Graham felt the chill of the day seep inside him when she spoke of her pain but he couldn't do anything but listen. He wanted to know everything about Imogene, even the painful parts of her life.

"It's so clear in my mind. I felt miserable when Philippa left, but she was so happy with John and I was in turn happy for her. Later I realized my parents were relieved that she was settled and contentedly married to a gentleman they respected and knew could provide for her. He is a very wealthy man you know, and did not have to be a doctor for the living. He helped to found the hospital at Wellick. John is good in his heart and wants to help people and that is why he is a doctor. Papa said he would not be surprised if John received a knighthood in his lifetime."

Graham nodded. "I know. He is all that you say."

"My parents knew Philippa would be protected and safe—one less daughter for them to worry about." Graham squeezed her hands, but still she kept her head down, pushing on with her story. "My mother was doing well with the treatments John prescribed, or so it seemed. She wanted to spend a lot of time with me. Upon reflection, I believe she knew she was coming to the end and wanted to use the time left in the best way, by being together. She insisted on a large party for my birthday. It was the last party for her. Mamma was firm I go to the dances and partake in the Season for my coming-out. Her disease struck hard soon after and she was unable to rally. There is nothing sinister in her passing and I accept it. She fought valiantly, but her disease was stronger and it took her. It hurts and I miss her, but know she loved me as a mother should. I am grateful she no longer suffers on earth and is at peace."

Imogene finally looked up at Graham. Her expression just about did him in. To have someone to confide in felt freeing even if it was painful. At least he felt that way. He rubbed his thumbs back and forth over her wrists and stayed quiet. If he could touch her like this then he could be her strength.

Imogene forged on. "I tell you this only to make you understand the situation that had come to pass before the betrayal that changed everything." She paused before taking a deep breath. "Have you heard of the gossip surrounding the death of my father, Lord Wyneham? That he took his own life and attempted to make it look like a hunting accident?"

Graham did not flinch from her question even though he loathed to hurt her. He closed his eyes for a second but nodded his head in the affirmative.

"Well, it is true. All of it. He did take his life." The words came pouring out of her now and the tears began to surface as she threw it out in the open. "When the constables came and questioned me, I lied, saying it must have been an accident, for my father could never have done such a thing. I lied to them when they asked if he had indicated what he meant to do. Even when his sister, my Aunt Wilton, came for me, I did not tell. She does not even know that he meant to do it. In truth I have broken the law. It is a crime…a sin, what I have done. I was terribly frightened and all alone and I was so, so ashamed."

When the words left her lips, Graham's grip on her tensed and he felt his jaw tighten. "Why were you ashamed, *chérie*? His actions do not stain you." He used the same words she had said to him.

"Oh, but they do. I was ashamed because my father did not love me enough to stay with me…." Her voice broke and tears came, but she kept going. "On that day, he gave me duties to attend to so I could not join in the hunting party. I was much put out and he knew it. He tried to comfort me, telling me he was proud of me for being a dutiful daughter and for my care of Mamma during her illness. He kissed me and said I was so strong, and he knew I would be all right. He said, 'Find your happiness, Imogene.' His words sounded odd at the time, but later I understood he was saying goodbye to me."

Imogene paused for a moment like she was gathering

strength to keep speaking. His heart was breaking for the pain she had endured. "Once the initial shock wore away, it was replaced by anger, betrayal, shame, and humiliation. After losing my sister and my mother, my father killed himself because he was too weak to live without her. He left me all alone knowing everyone else was already gone to me. His child. I was not important enough for him and that is the truth!" She broke, her face bearing a grimace of pain so harsh before shaking into sobs. "How could he do that to me?" Pulling her hands away from his, she covered her face and wept.

Graham was stunned for just a second before protectiveness leapt forward. He wanted to avenge her. How dare Lord Wyneham treat his daughter with so little care? Reacting instantly, he pulled her into his arms. Closing his eyes, he forced himself to stay calm and strong for her. One hand moved up to touch her hair, but mostly he just held her, letting her cry against him. Finally he spoke softly, "I don't know how he could have done that to you. He must have been in incredible pain to consider it. I'm sure he loved you very much."

Many moments later, Imogene seemed to realize just where she was and stiffened. She was in his arms, being held by him, comforted and cherished where she belonged. He didn't want to let her go, but he did anyway. Her face flushed as she pulled away. "I am so sorry to have imposed upon—"

He stopped her words with two fingers to her lips. "*Never* be sorry for telling me. You have been through so much and I grieve for the pain you have suffered in your losses, but you must listen to me now. What happened was terrible and you've borne a heavy burden. It was iniquitous for truth, and I hate that such a thing was laid upon you. You've done nothing wrong or bad. Brave is what you are—brave to bear the truth as you have done. I believe it was right to keep that secret, though. Don't ever tell anyone else, Imogene. It's better if you don't. Do you understand?"

She nodded at him, her face streaked and red.

"Imogene, please know this of me—I am greatly honored you trusted me to tell of this painful, terrible thing that has happened to you. I am glad it was *me* you told. I hope you can understand and believe when I say, 'You honor me.'" He bored into her eyes with his own, reaching down deep, willing her to know he meant every word.

Graham felt something open up in his heart. It was like a door opened and the wind rushed in. Was it love? Gratitude? Relief? Whatever it was, he wanted it, and he wanted more and more of it. He wanted Imogene to be with him…always.

Leaning against his hand, she closed her eyes for a moment before responding, "I am grateful it was you as well. I feel less burdened now. Thank you for hearing me. You are a good friend, Lord Rothvale."

He caressed her cheek with his thumb. "More than a friend, remember? And after this day of painful confessions, do you think you could leave off with the titles? I wish to be just 'Graham' to you. Would that be all right, *chérie*?"

"Yes…Graham." The slight hesitation before she said his name was endearing. He loved the sound of it coming off her sweet lips.

"Thank you, *chérie*." He stood up then, holding out his hand to her. "I think we need to get out of this cold. What say you to going back to the house for tea? We might play cards afterward, perhaps Whist or *Vingt-et-un*? Would you like that?"

Imogene looked up at him for a moment and then stood,

taking his hand, a slow smile stretching until it became a grin really. "Well, all right, but you should know that I will try to win. I will probably win." She finished authoritatively with more nods.

"Ah yes, competition motivates you. That *is* a good thing though. It will make everything so much more amusing. You know, I think I have stumbled upon it. The knack with you is to find out what it is that you want. For once you know that, you'll fight like the devil to win it. Won't you?"

"Yes, Graham, I *will* fight for what I want." Her words made him soar.

"THE wedding is tomorrow, and I must leave the day after," Graham said.

"To London?"

"Initially yes, but then I must be on to Gavandon. It is time to return to my home. I've been away for so long."

Imogene could not meet his eyes. The reality of his words hurt. They hurt badly. He had been invited to dinner tonight and they were together in the garden. *Leaving? Not here any longer?* Surely he would seek her out again when she went north to Philippa and John. He would be only a few miles from her. She felt things could not be finished between them. From the day they had met, he had never wavered in his courtesy to her, asking permission to pay her court, even. They had occasion to meet nearly every day since their introduction. He had called on her at home and had dined with her family. She had been invited to Kenilbrooke on several occasions. They had ridden and walked together and enjoyed each other's company in society and at church. What was the purpose if he was just going to leave? She kept her face down to maintain her composure.

"Will you not look at me?"

She did, reluctantly. "You will be missed when you are gone, Graham."

"I can't tell you how good it feels to know that, Imogene." A hand moved up to touch her hair. "I don't want to leave you either, but you'll be at Wellick soon and I can come to you there."

"I will be there in six weeks' time." She made a brave attempt at a smile. "I will look forward to you calling upon me then."

Bringing both of her hands up, he kissed them back and forth. "Six weeks feels like an age of time to me. What do you think, *chérie*?"

"An age of time, for truth," she answered with a breathy laugh. "At least now I know you will miss me."

He pulled her close, wrapping her into his arms. "Imogene, what if we did not have to wait so long? What if we could be togeth—"

"Imogene! Time to go into the house now." Her uncle, Sir Oliver, interrupted them and guiltily they jumped apart. "Lord Rothvale and I must talk together," her uncle said firmly.

Blushing deeply, Imogene curtsied. She looked up at Graham to find him beaming, giving her the kind of smile that was rare for him.

"Goodnight, Miss Imogene." He bowed, his smiling green eyes glowing in the moonlight.

Chapter 6

I loved not yet, yet I loved to love…I sought what I might love, loving to love.

St. Augustine ~Confessions, AD 397-8

Julian Everley and Mina Charleston were blessed with a remarkably mild day for their wedding. When the bridal couple knelt together, and the words spoken, Imogene had cause to reflect upon the meaning of those words. The bride and groom looked wonderful, but the man standing up for the groom was the only one Imogene could see. She went to the wedding feast and dancing at Kenilbrooke Hall with a heavy heart under her smile, for she knew this was the last day. Graham would be leaving Shelburne in the morning.

Exuberant guests feeling the effects of wedding punch made for a lively celebration at Kenilbrooke Hall despite her gloominess. Graham danced with her as much as convention allowed but as soon as their set ended, he took her hand firmly and asked, "Imogene, I need to speak with you, alone. Will you come with me?" Her heart did a flip, her legs turned to jelly, but her head nodded, yes.

Outside, on the balcony, he took both of her hands into his and looked at her dead on. "I must tell you something, but I think you might know already. I think everybody knows." He shook his head a little. "Regardless, I will speak from my true heart to you now. My *chérie*, Imogene, you have captured my heart in these short few weeks. I knew it the first time I saw you, and then, when we met that night at the ball. The more I am with you, and the more I know you, the more I know you are the one for me. I have no wish to be parted from you, but if I have the promise of you, I know I can bear the separation."

Imogene leaned back upon the wall for support and closed her eyes for a moment, wanting to let his words fall over her, to feel every letter of them. She opened her eyes and focused on his beautiful green ones.

"I have a question I wish to ask, but before I do, you must understand that I do not want your answer…yet. Tomorrow, I am obliged to leave, as you know. I will come to you at Wilton Court before I depart, to bid you farewell and would have your answer then. It is important to me that you take some time to reflect upon what I ask of you tonight, before you respond. Can you do this for me, *chérie*?"

"I can." She nodded, her heart nearly pounding out of her chest.

"Imogene, I want to marry you. I offer myself to you with great affection and respect, and vow that my desire in this is with no other requirement than to allow me to care for you and to make a life together." He brought her hands up to his heart and pressed them over it. "Will you be my wife, Imogene, my Lady Rothvale?"

Starting to speak, she stopped herself, biting her bottom lip to keep from answering. "I will give you the answer tomorrow, as you have asked."

He moved her hands from over his heart up to his lips and kissed the palm of each one. "Do you understand why I am asking you to reflect upon my proposal before you give me your answer?"

"I think so, but tell me anyway."

He let out his breath. "I asked your uncle last night for his consent and he has given it, but I did make sure he understood that it is for you to decide, unequivocally. Frankly, I am grateful he found us together in the garden last night, but you are a young woman, not yet of age, alone, and without parental guidance in this most important decision. I am a good bit older than you, and could in a way, be seen as a guardian of sorts. I would never wish, could not bear for you to feel—to feel that you have been passed along from your parents, to your aunt and uncle, and then finally on to me. Everyone has good intentions. They feel pleased to know you could be settled, and their guilt and sorrow for your loss are erased. People are happy to see a pretty girl marry a rich man. It makes them feel better about their own miserable lives. But none of these are reasons for you to accept me. I want you to accept me because you know it is what *you* want, not because you have been influenced, or coaxed, or persuaded by the well-intentioned. I want you to marry me because you know you want *me*. And when you know, I will know it too."

Imogene moved one of her hands out of his grasp and brought it up to the side of his face. He closed his eyes for a moment and it felt to her as if he trembled under her touch. "And you're sure you want me?"

"I am sure. That first day, when I saw you carrying in that lamb, and later at the ball when we talked, I knew without a shadow of a doubt you were the one for me. Right away I knew you were the woman of my dreams, the one I hoped to find one day. I want no other but you. I love you, Imogene, and I want you to belong to me."

"You do?" Imogene nodded into his eyes. She was not able to speak or respond beyond that simple effort. *He loves me.*

"I do," he said solemnly, offering his arm, "shall we go back to the party then, *chérie*?" She let him lead her back inside to the eager expressions, the clapping, and the cheering of exuberant wedding guests. Graham turned to her and whispered, "See? Even now everyone assumes you have accepted me. Please ignore them. Let's pretend we're alone, and they are not here. Keep smiling and putting your eyes on me, *chérie.* It's just us, you and me. Better yet, it's just us, staring into a crowd of people that look like sheep."

She laughed silently at his words, and held onto his eyes. She would remember his eyes in this moment. His eyes told her everything she needed to know.

THE following day, Imogene prepared herself carefully to give Graham his answer. For him, she chose a cream brocade dress decorated with brown embroidery, topped with a brown crochet Spencer jacket. The jacket had a V-shaped neckline and was short-sleeved coming to just above her elbows. The bottom of the waist ruffle and the edge of the sleeve were both finished with cream crochet. Over that, she put on a long, cream, linen coat for warmth. She left her hair down in long curls, pulling it all to one side, and secured with a ribbon. A brown cameo on cream velvet was placed around her neck. She applied her soft honeysuckle scent, checked her package for him, and also the letter. Imogene was ready.

Cariss knocked at the door before bouncing into the room. "You look beautiful, Imogene, and I am so happy for you." Imogene embraced her sweet cousin tightly. "It is not such a great surprise that Lord Rothvale wants to marry you, though it is a relief to finally be able to speak of it with you." Cariss squeezed her hands.

"Was it so obvious to everyone, truly?"

"Oh, Imogene, you cannot say you don't already know it. Everyone with two eyes could see it and know it. For God's sake, the sky and the grass and the trees knew it. Did you never wonder why everyone left the two of you alone? They were loath to approach you when you were together, so lost you were in each other. We did not dare. And being proposed to at a wedding? It was quite magical seeing the two of you, like a fairy tale really, and nobody wished to break the spell. And now, the fairy tale will have a happy ending for you and Lord Rothvale, just as you both so richly deserve."

Imogene hugged her cousin, felt the emotion and tried to control it for she did not want a tear-stained face at the moment.

"Cari, you are so dear to me. I wish for you to attend me at my wedding. Will you?"

"It would be an honor." Cariss kissed her cheek.

Aunt Wilton interrupted them. "He is here, Imogene, and you must come down now."

Imogene looked at Cariss, took a deep breath, gathered her things, and went down with her aunt. "Here she is," Aunt Wilton announced, leading Imogene over to Graham, who stood next to her uncle in the drawing room.

He watched her approach, his eyes devouring her. He bowed. "Good morning, Imogene."

She curtsied. "Good morning, Graham." For the first

time in public they both used only their given Christian names in the familiar address.

Smiling at her, she knew he'd caught the gesture. "Will you walk in the garden with me?"

She nodded her answer mostly because she was busy looking at him. He was so handsome in his clothes, not dandified, but masculine—long dark brown coat, brown waistcoat, green shirt and tall boots. His hair was tied with a dark green ribbon today. How in the world would she bear it when he left this afternoon?

Clasping her hand, he led her out of the house, into the garden and to a bench with no sides or back. She sat with her legs off one edge; he sat with his over the other edge. Setting down her things, she turned to him. He took both of her hands into his. "You are so beautiful I can hardly speak for looking at you."

"I feel the same way about you, and I am glad you think so. I wanted to be beautiful for you today."

"BUT you always are." Graham forced the question out of mouth. "Do you have an answer for me to what I asked of you yesterday?"

Imogene looked down at their hands where he was holding them entwined. He gentled his grip immediately, knowing he must have been holding her too tight without realizing. He couldn't help it though. He was desperate. Now he just wanted her answer so he could find some blessed relief. He tilted her chin up gently with one finger so he could see those beautifully expressive eyes of hers. If he could see into her eyes he would know—

"Graham, I want you to know that I *did* spend some time reflecting upon your words last night. You said you did not wish for me to ever feel coerced to accept you, but only desired me if I knew that *you* were what I wanted."

"Yes." He nodded. This waiting was torture. He really just wanted to kiss her and take her away somewhere very private and not come away until he had discovered every secret about her.

"Well, I do know what I want."

Her eyes burned back at him. "Tell me." He waited and soaked up the vision of her.

"I want you, Graham. The title, the manor, the great estate, all mean far less to me. I have had all of those things, and I will never be poor. I know my father settled well on me, and I will never need to find a rich husband…just one that loves me."

He brought her hand to his lips and kissed it. And then because he could not stop himself from doing it, he brought his lips to her lips with just the lightest touch. He felt a shiver run through her and wanted to do more, but now was not the time. He pulled back and waited for her to continue.

"And since I trust you, and believe in your character, I know I have found that man." She took a deep breath. "So, I will say the words to you in this way, as I am guessing they will mean more to you like this. Firstly, Graham, I love you as well. I love your honesty, your easy manner, your sincerity, your strength, your kindness—the man that you are. Secondly, in answer to your proposal, I accept your hand in marriage. I do wish to be your wife, to love and honor you, and to live my life with you."

Graham leaned forward until their foreheads met and just rested against her for a moment. Imogene's words had touched him deeply, but also cleared away his many doubts.

"If I am quiet it is because I am unable to speak for being in awe of you. You have made me the happiest man, Imogene." He reached into his breast pocket and pulled out a carved gold ring. "You'll have another ring when I can get it from Gavandon." Slipping it on her finger, he kissed her hand and held it up to his beating heart. "Can you feel my heart beating? It's more like pounding really."

She nodded. "I can feel it, your heart…my heart."

"It *is* yours," he said.

"I have something for you, a gift, an improper gift, but I do not care. I must give it before you go away." She handed him a small package.

"An improper gift, from you? How intriguing." He accepted and opened the small packet. Inside a dozen ribbons of various sizes and colours were lined together, mostly dark, all cut to the same one foot length. He touched one of her long curls. "I know what this is. In your sweet way you are telling me not to cut my hair. You need not worry. I know you fancy my hair and I would not have cut it short. I might have to trim it though. I don't think I'd like it down my back. Will that be all right, *chérie,* if I just keep it trimmed to the length it is now?" He could not hold back the grin that was dying to get out. He loved teasing her and seeing the blush she would give him when she answered his question. Knowing and predicting her responses to him was an intense feeling. He still had so much to learn about her.

"Yes, of course," Imogene said. She blushed right on cue and looked down, as if the prospect of him arranging himself personally for her was making her shy.

Her blush also gave him a brutally stiff cock.

Imagining Imogene blushing in his bed, and all of the

things they would do together once she was his wife—

"Graham?" Her soft inquiry dragged him from his wicked thoughts and back into the present.

"Thank you for the ribbons. I will wear them, and think of you." Hell, if that weren't the truth. He'd wear her ribbon ties and think of both of them together wearing nothing *but* the ribbons.

"I have a letter for you as well, Graham. My very first letter to you. I'll give it to you now, but you mustn't open it until you get to London." She put the letter into his hands. "Put it in your pocket and I will know if you cheat," she warned.

He placed her letter in his waistcoat pocket where he could feel it against his chest. He wrapped up the ribbons and put them into a pocket of his coat. Rising from the bench, he offered his hand. "Walk with me?"

She let him lead her out of the garden and onto the grounds, her hand securely in his. He needed the touching, and he suspected Imogene did, too, because they were both dreading the parting that would come soon enough.

He made for a large tree that could afford some privacy from the outside world, and figured it would have to do. The moment they were under the canopy Graham pulled her into his arms, and breathed in the scent of her. The lavender she used on her hair and the honeysuckle for her skin. "You smell so good." He rested his chin on the top of her head.

"So do you."

"To hold you like this is heavenly, Imogene. I wish I didn't have to let you go. You've made me so happy, but it makes it no easier to leave you now. I'll have to take this memory with me so I can bear being parted."

"You will come for Christmas?"

"Yes, *chérie*, I will come to you at Christmas."

Graham looked down at her lips and knew what he wanted to do. He dipped his head and joined their lips. It was soft and slow, gentle and sweet. He did not want to push—get all worked up, for it would serve no purpose. By his best guess, it would be at the very least, four weeks before they could marry. He would just have to wait for her and console himself that he could bear it because he had the promise of her. Christmas was only ten days away and now they were engaged, it would be acceptable for him to write her letters and give her gifts. He consoled himself with that.

Graham lifted his head and could see tears starting in her eyes. "Did that make you cry?"

"No. Yes—I am so happy, and so sad that you must go. Oh, Graham, I am a mess of emotions. You must think I am foolish."

He fished out a handkerchief and gave it to her. He held her against his chest and spoke into her hair, "I think nothing of the sort other than to be a little jealous of you."

"Why?" she sniffed.

"Because you are a lady and you are allowed to express your emotions. I, on the other hand, must hold them all in. I daresay I should like a good cry right about now, as well," he teased.

"Last night, I had a vivid dream and it was—it was out of the ordinary."

His heart stuttered but he kept his voice calm. "Tell me about your dream."

"I was alone looking in on a scene, a party or celebration of sorts. There were four people, two couples, one of them being my parents. The other couple, I did not know, but the gentleman looked like an older version of you. They were toasting something, and they were making merry. All four of them, looked right at me and raised their glasses. My mamma spoke, she was the only one of them to do so, and she said, 'Imogene, we are so happy for you both.'" Imogene stopped then and pressed her hands to her face. It took a moment before she continued. "I bolted up in bed when I woke from that dream, and I felt touched by the netherworld, truly I did. It was not frightening, but it was genuine. Am I losing my mind? What did that dream mean?"

He put his hands on her shoulders firmly. "You are not losing your mind. It means just what it should mean. We were destined to find each other, through fate, or the help of our parents in heaven. We are meant to be together. I really, really believe that. It sounds like a lovely dream to me, and I am glad you shared with me just now. Remember your dream and hold onto it."

"I will then."

Graham understood her completely as he held her under the tree and trailed his fingers over her hair. For him, dreams such as the one she described happened all the time. It had been that way for his whole life, the vivid dreaming.

"We must go back, they will be expecting us for luncheon," she said sorrowfully.

"In a minute we will go. I'm not ready to give you up yet. I must kiss you for a while and erase away all traces of your tears."

She lifted her cheek off his chest and looked up at him, offering her lips so sweetly it was difficult to keep himself in check. But he managed—just barely. Graham held onto his woman and kissed her properly for the first time. He relished the taste of her lips and the scent of her skin so close, the melting softness of her body against his as she allowed him to lead her along.

And he kissed her, and kissed her, over and over again.

THEY returned to Wilton Court at a sedate pace, both wishing to avoid the inevitable. Graham looked down at her and wanted to pull her back under the tree. Her lips were so fine and soft. Right now they were puffy from all the liberties he'd taken while kissing her, but he loved the look of her being claimed by him. As they walked back, he wondered how in the hell would he survive the next few weeks. It would be bloody difficult for sure.

"Our engagement will be announced in the papers tomorrow. I'll put it in immediately when I get into Town," he told her.

"So the whole world will know?"

"Yes, indeed. I want the whole world to know you are promised to me."

"Will you write to me?"

"Yes, I will write to you." He tugged on her hand so they might stop walking for a moment. Touching his fingers to her lips, he caressed the soft pink skin. "Where would you like to marry? Here in Shelburne or Town? You don't have to answer now. Think on it and we will arrange everything when I come at Christmas. If you should choose London, my townhouse, Brentwood, will be at your disposal for as long as you and your family might like to stay in Town. Of course, I will not be there with you for I will be up north at Gavandon, but there is staff to take care of you if you do decide to stay. As soon as you choose where you'd like to marry, I can apply for the licence."

"A special licence? They cost a fortune."

"I can well afford it, and you are more than worth the price." He touched the tip of her nose. "I cannot wait too long for you, Imogene. Now that I have won you, I have no wish to be patient." He bent to kiss her again. "I want you to be my wife as soon as possible."

"And I do as well."

The soft reply she gave along with her welcoming lips when he bent to kiss her again utterly thrilled him. For all her innocence, Imogene showed passion, and he could not wait to explore the depths of where it would lead them together.

SIR Oliver invited Graham into his study to discuss her settlement as soon as they returned from their walk. Imogene went to her aunt who embraced her and asked, "Now we have a wedding to plan?"

"Yes, Aunt Wilton. Graham must be invited to Christmas. You must extend the invitation before he leaves today for Town."

Aunt Wilton touched Imogene's face. "We are so happy for you, my dear. You are become grown up before my eyes. Of course he shall be invited for Christmas and his brother, too."

At luncheon they shared several longing looks, both of them thinking about being separated. It was so strange an idea really. Just a month ago she didn't care about much at all in her life, but everything had changed the moment she'd met Graham. Now she was in love and engaged to be married to a man who said he loved her. So quickly her priorities had changed.

When it was time, Graham bid his farewell to everyone, and accepted Lady Wilton's invitation for Christmas when she asked him.

Nine days I must be without him.

Imogene watched him with her family, taking his leave, so politely reserved. He wasn't reserved with her though. She thought about them kissing under the tree and felt her face heat up. Graham, along with his thorough kisses would be greatly missed.

They were left alone to say their farewells in private.

Imogene stood before him in the drawing room, attempting a brave front. Graham pulled her close and held her firmly. "I am trying to memorize your shape, to take in your scent, to remember how you feel against me, for it will have to do for a good while," he whispered.

Imogene felt tears rising to the surface and remembered his handkerchief. She pulled it out and blurted, "I do not want to give this back to you."

Graham pressed his lips to the cloth and kissed it, then pushed it back into her hand and said, "Keep it."

"You should have one of mine so you have something from me. I'll run up and choose one—a plain one."

Graham grasped her hand as she turned to go. "Not a plain one, please."

She smiled at him, understanding that he wanted something decorative. Imogene chose a handkerchief of white linen with an elegant crochet lace ruffle all around. She had embroidered her initials in lavender thread into one corner: I. A. B. C. to represent her full name: Imogene Amelia Byron-Cole.

When she pushed the cloth into his hand, Graham unfolded it reverently. Seeing her initials, his head snapped up immediately. "Your initials." He put his other hand to her cheek. "So perfect. A perfect token I shall cherish and keep close to me every minute." He thought it read like a prophecy, too. *Falling in love with Imogene had been as easy as…A-B-C.*

Graham kissed her sweetly, lingering over her lips and then lastly on the forehead. Gentle kisses that would have to hold her until they could be together again. Her chest stung as he pulled away.

Graham cleared his throat and said the words she did not care to hear. "Farewell, Imogene, do not come outside please, it will be too hard to leave if you do."

"Goodbye, Graham, until Christmas Eve then." She could not resist one more question to hold him there for just a moment longer. "Do you ride Triton?"

"I do. He is fast and can convey me quickly." His eyes down, he spoke, "Imogene, you remind me of something. I wish to ask a favour. I think you will not like it, but I ask it of you selfishly, for me." He looked up and hit her with that solemn, green stare.

"I know what you wish. You do not want me to ride solitary."

"It would be easing my heart to know you are not alone when you ride. So, if you can agree to do it while I am away, I would be very relieved."

"For you, Graham, I promise to do as you ask. I'll drag Cari along with me I suppose."

"Thank you, my darling. Now I can leave you a little easier. I love you so much, *chérie.*" He kissed her again, caressed her face once more, and then he was gone.

Imogene stayed in the drawing room, frozen where she stood. She heard the sound of Triton's retreating hoof beats until they faded and there was nothing but empty silence.

GRAHAM rode hard to London, managing it in less than two hours. He entered his house and went straight to the study where he wrote out an announcement of their engagement, sending the missive off immediately.

Sitting at his desk, he removed her letter from his waistcoat, touched it lovingly for a moment and then broke the seal. Inside was a curl of her hair and he laughed out loud as he set it aside. *I needed this. Imogene, how did you know?* He opened her letter.

My Dearest Graham,

You have just asked me to marry you tonight and I wish to share my deepest feelings with you. I trust you as I have never trusted another person. You are honest and good. You are kind and gentle. You are wise and steadfast. I know you will love me and that alone will make me happy. I vow to spend my days in the pursuit of loving you in hopes of making you as happy as I will be. For the first time, in many months, tonight I go to sleep without a great sadness pushing against my heart. The pain of it is nearly gone. Your love heals it and it is fading away. Here is my kiss to seal my words to you. I am reminded of the Walsingham *ballad by Sir Walter Raleigh. This small part that I have written out expresses my true heart, and is meant to assure you of my constancy in loving you.*

But true love is a durable fire,
In the mind ever burning,
Never sick, never old, never dead,
From itself never turning.

Return to me Godspeed,
I.B.C.

Graham read her letter over many times and wondered at the miracle of her. She had used some coloured salve and made the mark of her lips upon the letter.

She is an angel, a princess, a goddess. And she is mine.

He touched the print of her lips with the tip of his finger…her beautiful lips.

Chapter 7

At Christmas I no more desire a rose
Than wish a snow on May's new-fangled mirth;
But like of each thing that in season grows.

William Shakespeare ~Love's Labour's Lost, 1595

Imogene lifted the door knocker and waited. Ellenora Everley was first on her list of calls before she left Shelburne. Now the wedding was over, there was nothing to hold the extended guests at Kenilbrooke. A servant showed her to the parlor and Ellenora's rapid footsteps preceded her arrival into the room just a few moments later. When she saw Imogene she embraced her immediately. "I am so happy for you and Graham. We are to be cousins," she said excitedly.

"Oh, Ellenora, I am happy. So happy. It hardly feels real as of yet."

"Elle. Please, you must call me Elle. All my family does, and you, *Cousin*, are as good as family now."

"I had to come and see you before you departed. Are you away soon?"

"Yes, today, but tell me, when is your wedding to be and where?"

"Soon, a few weeks. There is no point to a long

engagement and as you know, I must get north soon, for my sister. The final arrangements will be decided by Christmas, and I think we will probably marry in Town in the later part of January."

Elle looked wistful. "He loves you. God, he loves you, Imogene. When he came to me for assistance as a chaperone, my heart melted because I so wanted this outcome for him." She squeezed Imogene's hands. "To have helped, even a little, to bring the two of you together is a great honor."

"I suspected as much and wanted to, ah…thank you for your efforts." She felt herself flush. "I think perhaps your brother Jules was part of it as well?"

"We saw how smitten he was and wanted to help Graham in any way we could. Jules cares deeply for Graham. That first night at the ball, he worked so hard in his plotting to bring the two of you together and keep all others away. Well, we all care about him—Graham, Jules, Colin and Henry, they are all so good. They are the very best of men. Graham will want nothing but to make you happy, Imogene, and I believe you will do the same for him. He deserves someone like you." Elle sighed dreamily.

"Will you come to visit us at Gavandon when all is settled?" Imogene asked.

"Of course I will. You could not keep me away."

"Elle, where do you go now? With your brother and Mina on their honeymoon, where will you stay?"

"Today, I depart for Worcester to stay with my aunt and uncle, Sir Thomas and Lady Hargreave—my mother's sister. Sadly, I will probably not be able to come to your wedding. The roads in winter do not support the best of conditions for travel." She frowned. "I will miss it."

Both looked up at the arrival of Colin who swept into the

room bearing a great, delighted grin. "I thought I heard the two of you talking in here. Ah, and here is the beauty that has captured my brother's heart. Congratulations!" He gallantly bowed and kissed her hand. "I look forward to having a sister. You shall make the most magnificent Lady Rothvale, rivalling my dear mother, of course." His green eyes flickered as he smiled at her, the same colour and hue as Graham's. "My brother could not have chosen better. Welcome to the family, Imogene."

Imogene was touched by his kind gesture. Colin was such a gentleman, just like his brother. "You are both so kind in embracing me, and in putting me at ease. I feel as if I am getting more out of this than is Graham, however. I am gaining not only a husband but his wonderful family as well. I think it's safe to say I have made a good choice."

18th December, 1811

GRAHAM walked his property at Gavandon. He took in the winter fields, the trees, the dead grasses. Everything was in hibernation, asleep. Its entirety waiting for the warm breath of spring to gently stir the cycle of rebirth. Imogene was like that for him. Before her, his life was static, unchanging in its bleakness. He moved through the daily requirements, but was waiting for something yet to come. He had been asleep. Now he was awake. Her arrival into his world now brought purpose. He had a reason for walking the earth. Life had bestowed great responsibility, and great privilege upon him. He intended to accept both in full measure.

Making his way up the path to the stone house, he

thought of her, the way she looked that first time. The pain came again. He had such longing for her.

After being admitted by a servant, Graham announced himself, calling out as he walked toward a large, open room at the rear of the house. Many windows facing east provided beautiful light that warmed the room.

"You're back. Such a long time since setting my eyes upon you." His friend stuck out his hand and Graham shook it warmly.

"I am."

"You look different. That long hair suits you in a brooding, lordly way," he drawled. "Oh, and my sincerest congratulations as well. She appears very lovely."

"Well, you look exactly the same, my friend, and it is good to see you after so long a time, and I thank you." Graham gave a nod of appreciation for the salutations. "You have been in receipt of my letters, and the items have made it safely?"

"Yes, of course." He walked over to one wall and lifted the cloth covering.

Graham approached it reverently, breathing in long and hard at first sight of the image. "It is spectacular." He eyed his friend with determination. "I have a new priority for you though, and you'll be kept very busy. I will even have to help you."

"Let's hear it."

Graham tapped his forehead. "I have it here. It's all here, every detail, and we don't have much time."

His friend swept out his arm in a slight bow. "Shall we get to it then?"

THERE were so many things requiring his attention, but Gavandon Manor was not one of them. Fortunately Mrs. Griffin had charge of the house. It had not suffered from his absence even slightly. She ran her domain with efficiency and fairness, demanding hard work and loyalty in those under her, but organizing everything as if it was no effort at all. Graham could not have done without her. Mrs. Griffin had been with the family for twenty-five years. She had been the one to tell him he had a baby brother on the day Colin was born.

He awaited her in his study. She had been brought to tears upon hearing his news. Both of them likely thinking the same thoughts so there was no need to speak them aloud.

Your mother and father would be so happy for you.

Her soft knock touched the door, and at his call, she entered his study. "Lord Rothvale, how may I serve you this day?"

"Mrs. Griffin, I have need of your sensible mind in a matter that I fear has been left for far too long. It concerns the lady's chamber," he trailed off. "I need," he took a deep breath, "I need your help in readying that chamber for my bride. I know it cannot be left as it is but I am at a loss as to what should be done. What are your thoughts?"

"My lord, I am happy to be of help. May I suggest we go there and discuss? I believe that would be the best course."

Entering his mother's rooms with Mrs. Griffin, Graham felt like he was trespassing into forbidden territory. It could not be said it was grief actually for he believed he had conquered that emotion quite thoroughly in the past year. Rather, it was being in her private space. As her son, he had not come here except on very rare occasions, and then it had been to her adjoining sitting room, never into her bedroom. It was only at the very end of her life, during her lingering, after the accident—

He pushed those images of his mother down and away. They were too painful and did not honor her goodness and beauty. Graham felt out of place here and that worried him. These would be Imogene's rooms. She would dress here. She would bathe in this room. He would come to her here, to this bed. *Yes, you've spent plenty of time thinking about that part.* Feeling a headache coming, he moved to sit down on the settee. Graham looked around his mother's room slowly, taking it all in, seeing her things laid out, then looked to Mrs. Griffin helplessly, his hands palm up.

"How do I do this, Mrs. Griffin?"

Ever the efficient, she took pity on him. "My Lord, lord, do not worry yourself about this, it will sort itself out easily. These rooms will not evoke the same feelings for Miss Byron-Cole as they do for you right now. She is a lady, raised and bred, the daughter of a peer. She has been prepared for claiming a place such as this. If I might suggest, sir, it would be important for her to make these rooms her own by choosing the furnishings, fabrics and ornaments such as they please her. What if they were cleared of everything personal and stripped down? It would be a clean slate. Tell her you wish for her to make it up in the manner she prefers. I believe she would be honored by your confidence. Once the rooms are done up, you will find your countenance greatly changed in regards to this space. It will no longer belong to *Lady Rothvale*, your mamma—it will belong to *Lady Rothvale*, your wife."

Graham leapt up and embraced her hands. "You are the wisest woman! Thank you for your kindness. I knew you would know the best course of action," he whispered. "I'll leave everything in your capable hands then." He welcomed the relief he felt as he quitted the chambers.

THE *Muse*

24th December, 1811

IMOGENE stuck fast to the window seat. Graham was coming today but she knew not what time he might show. It was Christmas Eve and the family was making merry in full force. Colin had already arrived earlier in the day, riding in from Trinity College where he studied. Graham was coming from much farther away, from Gavandon. Imogene worried for him. Would the roads be safe? What of the weather? Was he warm enough?

"He is a lucky man, my brother. I daresay he is, but I am sure he well knows it."

Imogene looked to the voice. "Colin." She smiled at him. "I am so pleased you are here. Would you like to sit?"

"With you, Sister? But of course I would, if for no other reason than to cheer you. You look as if you need it."

"Am I that pathetic?" Imogene was thoughtful for a moment, but then her countenance changed to one of boldness. "I don't care. I miss him and wish him here with me," she charged a little too loudly. The room grew quiet and heads turned in her direction. Imogene hung her head in embarrassment and groaned, "Oh God. I am that pathetic."

Colin laughed and patted her hand. "It is charming really, to see you so worried and concerned for him. But you should know he would not like it."

Imogene looked at Colin in amazement. "He would not like that I worry for him?"

"God, no! If he knew you sat here waiting for him instead of joining in the party and having your enjoyment, he would be quite aggravated. And I should be punished for not seeing you happy and amused."

"Why ever for? That is the most ridiculous thing I have ever heard, Colin."

"Because it is *his* job to worry, no one else's. My brother takes his worrying very seriously, my dear, and has since I can remember. He can worry about everyone and everything, but no one can do so for him. I fear he grows worse with age." He smirked. "And now that you will top his priority list of things to worry over, I dread he'll be most fearsome in carrying it all out. He would gladly rip into me for not watching over you better. So, will you save me from the gruesome fate of my brother's wrath? Come and join in the games and he will be none the wiser. Graham will never know you sat here pining for him," Colin teased. "I certainly won't tell him. I must save my skin with any methods at my disposal, to ensure my own safety. So you see, it is a bit selfish on my part, dear Imogene."

"I do see, and I acquiesce but only because I have no wish to endanger you, Colin." Imogene stood and took his arm. "As for Graham being the only person allowed to do any worrying…well, we shall see about that. I daresay I can hold my own against him and I am not afraid. I can be wicked stubborn," she challenged.

Colin looked at her adoringly. "Having you in the family is going to be such fun. Are you sure you do not have another sister hidden away somewhere?"

Imogene was cheered as Colin led her to a game of cards. She became so engrossed; it was a joyful surprise when she later heard the maid announce, "Lord Rothvale."

Imogene's eyes locked on as she stood abruptly from the card table. Her heart pounded and her breath grew short. She felt lightheaded as she moved forward, wanting to launch herself into his arms, but that would not be proper, would it?

Not in front of all of her family at least. *Breathe. He's here now.*

Graham stood frozen as she came to him. He did not move, just stared at her in that solemn way of his.

"Graham." His name came from her lips in the softest whisper.

"Imogene." He took up her hand and kissed it lovingly, drawing her closer to him. She could smell his scent and she filled her head with it as his eyes raked over her.

The very loud and stern bellowing of Sir Oliver blasted through the room. "Nay! That simply will not do. I will see that custom is observed properly in my home. I demand it no less!"

Shocked, Imogene turned to stare at her uncle who had obviously lost his mind. Sir Oliver got up from his seat, tried to hold back a smile, then a chuckle, until he was unable, bending over at the waist and laughing with great thunderous guffaws. "Look up. It is Christmas after all. Now do it up proper and honor the tradition, son." He addressed Graham and pointed. They both looked up to see the kissing ball of mistletoe hanging in the doorway above their heads.

Graham gave a little growl as he reached for her; only Imogene could hear it. He tipped her back, supported her weight and planted a decadent, bawdy kiss on her lips in front of everybody, grinning from ear to ear when he lifted her back up to standing, the clapping and cheers of the family filling the room. Imogene brought her hand to her mouth in an embarrassed smile. All of the earlier tension she had borne had completely left her now.

"Merry Christmas, *chérie*," he purred in her ear.

"It may be merry now you have come back to me." Imogene sighed contentedly as she took him by the hand and led him forward to greet the others and join in the games.

AS they walked to the Christmas Eve service at Shelburne Church, Graham clutched her hand tucked around his arm like he would never let go. "So have you sorted it all out? Our wedding details? How long must I wait for you?" He sounded a little dramatic, firing questions at her one after the other.

Imogene squeezed his arm. "Yes, it is sorted and not long."

"How long though?" he groused.

"A month."

"An ocean of time, a month. Even a week would seem so to me when waiting for you," he said softly. "What is the date you have chosen?"

"The twenty-sixth of January. 'Tis a Tuesday."

"Where do you want it?"

"Ah…yes. I am not sure really and wanted to ask your opinion. Have you in mind a London church that would be suitable for us, Graham?"

"Actually, I do. Have you heard of St. Martin-in-the-Fields? I am a patron there and I think I could get an accommodation for us. Would it suit, do you think?"

"Yes. The shining white church; the one that welcomes the poor. I love the idea of it. I would have us marry there. " She nodded at him, deciding on the spot.

"Then you shall have your wish, *chérie.*" He looked at her adoringly. "How I shall get through a month apart from you, I have no idea."

LATE into the evening, after a delightful Christmas Eve

supper, Colin and Graham made ready to depart for Kenilbrooke Hall where they were staying with the Hargreaves. Imogene's whole family had been very warm in welcoming the brothers, and it was obvious they appreciated this happy, family Christmas. It was probably a pleasant change from the last time the holiday was upon them, their mother having so recently passed.

Imogene walked Graham outside and put her hands on his chest. He clasped his hands behind her back and held her loosely. "This has been the most lovely day." She choked out the words with emotion because she wasn't the only one feeling the pull of family memories and loss.

"It has, *chérie*. I'll be back in the morning though—you'll not be rid of me so easily as this." He leaned down to kiss her goodnight, his lips firm and seeking just as she remembered. "Sleep well, and I'll meet up with you in my dreams tonight."

"You will?"

"Oh yes. I most certainly will dream of you tonight as I always do." The look on his face was both bold and mysterious. She wondered what he dreamed about her. The thought of such an intimate image of Graham in his bed and dreaming of her made her stomach flutter.

His face hovering right over hers, he whispered, "If you could see into my dreams, my innocent beauty, I am afraid you would be soundly shocked at my wicked thoughts. It is a good thing they are private."

Imogene had absolutely no answer to that comment so she just smiled at him and said goodnight. She would have to ponder on that tonight in her bed.

CHRISTMAS Day, 1811, Imogene wrote at the top of the paper as she started a letter to Philippa and John, giving details of their wedding and to approximate when she might finally arrive at Gavandon. Graham was across the room from her writing his own letter to Jules. She watched him for a moment, the big muscles of his arms underneath the jacket flexing from his hand moving the pen. He wore glasses that made him look even more scholarly. She could just imagine him in professor's robes giving a lecture on portraiture with the somber expression of his. He looked up and winked at her. "Almost done."

This morning they had exchanged Christmas gifts. Imogene loved her presents and looked over at them sitting on the writing desk where she worked. Graham had given her his mother's emerald ring that she would wear next to the gold one he had presented before. He'd also ordered five, sumptuous, leather-bound writing journals, one for each of the next five years. Upon the front of the first, gold embossed script with her name and the year.

Journal of Lady Imogene Rothvale

1812

He had also given her a very special surprise of a gift, monogrammed stationary bearing the Rothvale crest and a lovely letter hallmark for pressing into sealing wax. These were not new items and contained the letters of their initials blended together: G R I.

Graham explained they shared the same exact initials with his parents, George and Isabelle, and that he couldn't think of a better omen of blessing upon them. And what an economical wife she was, he had joked. Pointing out she would save him a great deal of coin as none of the monogrammed items of the house would need altering.

Imogene had given Graham a framed miniature silhouette of herself she had ordered done in the village. The maker was fairly skilled and even she thought it a decent rendering of her profile. Graham clearly loved it. He put it in his breast coat pocket, patting where it rested next to his heart. "The very best gift of the day," he whispered to her quietly so no one else would hear.

He stood up and offered his hand when their letters were complete. "Walk with me."

"I would like that very much." She followed him to the coat room and they were off and away quickly. Graham led her to the same tree as before, where it was private. Imogene assumed they wouldn't be allowed a very long time, but they would take whatever they could, silently thanking her aunt and uncle for being more relaxed about the strict rules of propriety than most.

The second they were under and out of sight, he pulled her up against his body. Her head reached right to the top of his chest at his throat. She breathed in his scent. He smelled like clean linen and leather soap and something else she couldn't identify. Whatever it was, it was the scent she associated with him, heavenly and male. She could have stayed in his arms for hours and hours, but they didn't have a lot of time.

He cupped her face in his hands, tilting her toward his lips. "I need this, Imogene." And then he descended. Imogene was lost to everything he did. She remembered being grateful he was holding on to her because she didn't know if she had the power to remain standing on her own. Graham's lips were alive today. They did not stay still. Moving and caressing and seeking, he pulled her bottom lip into his mouth just a little. The gentle scrape of his teeth on her made her moan. He devoured her lips. It was done gently and lovingly, but he devoured her all the same.

Imogene could not have curbed him even if she had desired to. He was in total control of the situation and she a mere pawn in whatever boundaries might be breached today. His hands left her face and moved to her waist. They didn't stay there long before opening her coat and pushing inside. Making his way to her waist again, his fingers massaged her back while his kisses continued to melt her in that decadent, slow, teeth-grazing way of his. His hands moved up on her, sliding right up her sides, slowly, simultaneously. His fingers explored the sides of her breasts where they swelled out on the sides of her tight-fitting bodice. She arched into his touch and pressed closer. "Graham?"

"You taste so fine. I want to take you away where we can be alone together. I want to make love to y—" He brought his lips to her neck and then her throat, still gentle but more bold than before. His hands kept exploring the sides of her breasts. She felt hot and wanton. She wanted him to keep kissing her and keep touching her. She wanted more even though Graham was the one in charge and she had no idea what she should do.

He had made his way back up to her mouth again. "Yes. I want—" she breathed against his lips.

And then he stopped. He went no farther with his hands. He didn't try to cover her breasts even though she wanted to feel his hands on them. He just kept stroking light touches over the sides, making her want to press her body into his.

Graham continued caressing even after he pulled back from their kiss and stared into her eyes.

"Why did you pull away?" she mumbled, barely coherent.

"For your own good, *chérie*, and mine. You are so

beautiful right now, standing before me, with your eyes so earnest upon me, and the feel of you under my hands. I could do things right now that I should not do with you. Not yet. You deserve the best of everything, my *chérie*. I could not live with myself if I ever dishonored you." He brushed her cheek with the back of his hand.

"I love you."

"As I love you, *chérie*, and I will treasure loving you for the rest of my days… *Je chérirai notre amour pour le restant de mi vie.*"

GRAHAM pressed a slim volume into her hands as she walked him out to say goodnight. "One last gift, *chérie*. I marked a poem inside. Read it, and I hope you think of us as we were today under the tree." She accepted the book and nodded. He mouthed, "love you," before walking away into the night.

Imogene was intrigued by the mystery and went straightaway to her room to read. She opened to the page he had marked and found a poem entitled:

The Kiss: A Dialogue.

Among thy fancies, tell me this
What is the thing we call a kiss?
I shall resolve ye what it is:

It is a creature born and bred
Between the lips, all cherry-red,
By love and warm desires fed—
And makes more soft the bridal bed.

It is an active flame that flies
First to the babies of the eyes,
And charms them there with lullabies—
And still the bride, too, when she cries.

Then to the chin, the cheek, the ear,
It frisks and flies, now here, now there:
'Tis now far off, and then 'tis near—
And here, and there, and every where.

Has it a speaking virtue? Yes.
How speaks it, say? Do you but this,
Part your join'd lips, then speaks your kiss;
And this Love's sweetest language is.

Has it a body? Ay, and wings,
With thousand rare encolourings;
And as it flies, it gently sings—
Love honey yields, but never stings.

Robert Herrick, 1648

Imogene's heart stuttered as she read it through the first time. She read it many times over, the words becoming more beautiful at each reading, and knowing she was blessed to have such a man as him.

A man who did not fear showing her how much he would love her.

Chapter 8

And now I see with eye serene
The very pulse of the machine;
A being breathing thoughtful breath;
A traveler betwixt life and death.

William Wordsworth ~ 'She was a phantom of delight', 1807

28th December, 1811

"Angleo's will do for now, Stanton," Graham told his driver.

"As you wish, my lord."

Graham had to get out of his house tonight. And there were a lot of reasons why it was a good idea. The foremost being his beloved was upstairs in a guest bedroom right now. He looked out the window at his London home as Stanton pulled the carriage onto the street and pondered the realities staring him in the face. Showing Imogene, her cousin, Cariss, and Lady Wilton around Brentwood today, he'd realized his time here in London would have to be limited.

They would start their married life here in this house. They would begin here. The first time they made love would be here, under his roof, in his suite. He shook his head a little at the vision, thinking he needed to clear his mind before he did something he sorely regretted. Imogene was an innocent to be sure but there was passion in her—passion yet to be awakened, but it was definitely there. She responded to him so sweetly and with such trust that he knew it was a good thing they would be separated for the most part, doubting he could bring her chaste to their wedding day. He knew unless he censured them, she wouldn't be able to do it. She was too giving and generous and would struggle to deny him. Imogene had an uninhibited nature in general; it was part of her womanly attraction. He did not think he could remain under the same roof with her and stay under regulation for thinking about her. Tomorrow he would leave. It would be dreadful to be parted from her again, but it had to be. So tonight, after everyone had retired to bed, he'd slipped out. He needed the distraction to clear his mind enough so he could sleep there even this one night.

Graham entered Angelo's Fencing Academy on Bond Street and found exactly what he was looking for. "Well, well, well, look what just walked in. The wayward native son returned to Mother England," the man with the sardonic voice drawled.

Graham grinned. "Gravelle." He extended his hand in greeting.

Clive Gravelle took the hand, returning an enthusiastic welcome to his old friend. "I've seen your brother here and there; he's kept me apprised of you. Long time away, my friend," he said, shaking his head slowly from side to side. "What brings you in here tonight?"

"Thought I might clear my head with an assault if possible," Graham remarked easily, stretching his neck from one side to the other.

"I'd be happy to give you a go," Gravelle offered. "Foils or sabers?" he asked with a one-sided grin.

"Foils. It's been quite a while since I held a sword, Gravelle."

"Good for me then. I've heard some talk about you, you know."

"And what have you heard?" Graham asked, giving away nothing.

"Well for one, that you were back in country, and then that you wasted no time getting yourself leg-shackled. Furthermore, the lady in question is the late Lord Wyneham's daughter, the young one. I hear she's green, but lovely. It's said she didn't have much of a come-out last season due to mother's illness. It is true then?"

Graham nodded once. "Sounds as if you have the pertinent facts in order."

Gravelle whistled through his teeth. "How the mighty fall. Congratulations, my friend. I hope you shall be very happy in your wedded state. God! I cannot believe it."

"Believe it, Gravelle, and I have every intention of doing so." He tilted his head in acknowledgement of the congratulations.

"You know I heard there was some sniffing about up in Essex after Wyneham died. Word was, she was young, orphaned and well-dowered, but family swooped in and secreted her away before any who would try to take advantage, descended. How did you find her? Sad business about Lord Wyneham by the way; he was held in high regard."

Graham eyed Gravelle patiently before answering, "She was living in Kent with her aunt and uncle. We met when I was there for Julian's wedding. Hargreave also has married since I've been away. Their brides are in fact, sisters."

"Blasted hellfire! Is there anyone left unfettered?" he asked disgustedly.

"Just you, Gravelle." Graham winked. "Should you decide to jump into the pond, you'll be in excellent company."

"No thanks, Rothvale. I am perfectly fine as I am, but I daresay I should like to meet *your* diamond. You know, to see if she is as lovely as is said."

Graham pointed and levelled a lethal stare. "You do not come near her, Gravelle," he said evenly. "Have nothing to do with her, I mean it!"

"Oh, my God. She is here in Town? You have brought her to Town."

Graham flinched inwardly at Gravelle's words but appeared unaffected by them. Still giving away nothing, he replied, "This conversation has gone on for far too long. Are we having a go with the foils or not?"

"Yes, yes, just rufflin' your feathers. 'Twill make for a better assault that way. It's always a good idea to shake up your opponent, eh?"

"Let's get to it then."

Graham worked very hard at the assault. He had been away from his sport since he'd left for Ireland. Parrying against his friend, he realized how much he'd missed it. He would definitely make time for it again, now he was home.

A new face watched their assault and he congratulated Graham on his skills when it was over. Gravelle knew him and did the introductions. "Lord James Trenton, Hewbrooke Abbey, Essex. Trenton's father is the Marquess of Langley."

"How do you do?" Graham offered his hand. "Essex? My bride-to-be hails from Essex. We are to marry in a month. Imogene Byron-Cole of Drakenhurst?"

"Congratulations, Lord Rothvale. I know the family. We are of a neighbourly acquaintance. Very lovely, the Miss Byron-Coles." He nodded. "Most sad about Lord Wyneham though. My father served with him, mentioning his passing with much regret to me."

Graham nodded back. "Just Rothvale, please. How do you know Gravelle, here?"

"University. Oxford. Our friendship held out longer than Gravelle's studies did though." Trenton grinned.

"Ah. I attended Cambridge, or I would have remembered you. What brings you to Town, Trenton?"

"Just passing through on my way—"

Gravelle cut him off. "He's on his way to the Bishop of Winchester to take clerical orders," he said without admiration. "Just ghastly, Trenton! How can you do it?"

Trenton rolled his eyes. "I am pragmatic and have the luck of being a third son in birth order. I imagine I can muddle my way through. It cannot be so difficult, and I have to do something with my days. Unlike you, Gravelle, I would not have the taste for a career at dissipation with the same giddy enthusiasm that you possess. And let's not forget, also unlike you, I can read *and* write!"

"I am hardly a dissipate, Trenton! But how will you know what to say at those events, funerals, weddings, christenings?"

"It's all written out in the books, Gravelle, you simpleton. Oh, did I mention that I *can* read?"

Gravelle had the grace to look embarrassed. "But you will have to do it with sincerity."

"I have every intention of being most sincere, my irreverent friend. I may not subscribe to the habits of endless preaching and moralizing, but that aside, I should do an adequate job I think. It's about living a good life. Do you doubt my faith?" he asked with a grin.

"No, just your sanity." Gravelle was unconvinced.

The conversation caught Graham's attention though.

"What kind of sermons do you think you shall give, Trenton?"

"Very short ones."

Graham's eyes lit in a smile. "And you fence?"

Trenton nodded, "Indeed, I do at that."

Graham fished a card out of his pocket and gave it to him. "Write to me when you are finished with your orders. We may be able to work together. I could have a proposition for you—a good one." *He is exactly what I need for Gavandon parish.*

On his way home that evening, Graham made a mental note to speak to Colin and impress upon him the importance to get down to Town as often as possible for the purpose of checking on the ladies. He knew his friend Gravelle was trustworthy, but wouldn't take chances on others who might hear of Imogene. London was full of opportunists. Being here reminded him of why he stayed away most of the time. If not for the culture and art, and his duty to Parliament, he would probably never come.

For now he would have to put his faith in Lady Wilton. He had no choice. For all that he had observed, Lady Wilton seemed to act in Imogene's best interests, with discretion and sensibility, so putting his trust into her capable hands to keep Imogene safe and happy during the next weeks was an easy decision.

Graham prepared for sleep and got into his bed. Alone. He felt as if he'd never gone to Angelo's tonight and exhausted himself with fencing. His mind was plagued with a new worry. How would he be able to leave her again? Tomorrow morning he would have to do just that, leave Imogene in London on her own. Just pondering the thought of it was painful.

7th January, 1812

IMOGENE simply wanted to go home, but Aunt Wilton and Cariss were speaking to the modiste and didn't seem to be in any hurry to leave. She didn't wish to be rude and push them to rush so she drifted over to the glove case and looked in.

The gloves made her think of hands.

Hands made her think of Graham.

More specifically, Graham's hands touching her when he kissed her. She recalled some of the things he'd told her of his desires he'd shared the last time they'd been alone together. It was exciting to imagine the forbidden and the unknown with him. He'd said he would love her for hours, and make pleasures unlike anything she'd ever known—

"Which do you think more elegant, the white or the buff?"

The question startled her. She'd been so lost in her thoughts she'd not noticed anyone else approach. A gentleman, looking to purchase some ladies gloves it looked like, had just asked her opinion. He looked very polite and proper with his hands clasped behind his back, a pleasant smile on his handsome face.

"Well, that would depend on the lady's purpose in wearing them, of course, but I think I would select the buff. A bit more forgiving than white."

"Ahhh, yes, practicality is always something to consider. 'Tis a gift for my dear little sister and I do want her to be able to get good use from them." He bowed elegantly. "I am sorry, that was rather rude of me to just impose on you without an introduction. My name is Ralph Odeman, and I assure you I don't usually ask strangers for help in choosing gifts."

Imogene laughed. "Please don't think another thought about it, Mr. Odeman. I'm not in the least put out, and delighted to have helped." Knowing that she was waving propriety to the wind, she offered her name to him. "Imogene Byron-Cole, how do you do?"

"It is an honor, Miss Byron-Cole, or is it missus? My apologies if I am in error."

"The title of 'miss' will apply to me for another three weeks only."

"Ah, my congratulations to you upon your impending marriage—"

"Imogene, are you ready, darling?" Aunt Wilton called, indicating it was time to go.

"Thank you, Mr. Odeman, and I hope your sister enjoys her gift," Imogene offered before following Aunt Wilton and Cariss out of the shop.

As their carriage paused to pull onto the road, Imogene glanced out the window at the street traffic. She was surprised to see Mr. Odeman standing there staring right into her carriage window. Their eyes met across the distance before she felt compelled to turn away. The expression he wore made a shiver roll through her spine, and she suddenly wished she'd never told him her name.

"Who was that man speaking to you in the shop?" Aunt Wilton asked.

"A Mr. Odeman who was buying gloves for his sister, and asked me would I choose buff or white for myself."

"Do you know him, Imogene?" Cariss asked.

"Not at all."

19th January, 1812

IMOGENE was not happy. Truthfully, she was beginning to feel rather low, especially today of all days. And there had been nothing from Graham in nearly a week. No letters telling her how much he missed her. The hours of dress fittings and endless selections she'd endured this morning boded well for the smashing headache she felt coming on. Cariss and Aunt Wilton had already preceded her in another carriage more than an hour ago. As Imogene headed up the steps of Brentwood Manor to lift the knocker, she saw a flash of movement at the drapes. *That's odd.*

The front door opened but Mr. Finlay, the butler, was not there to receive her. She stepped carefully into the empty foyer and looked around the whole room.

And then she smelled him. The wonderful, unique scent recognizable only as his, met her nose. Instantly revived, she whispered, "Graham?"

Seconds later, she was rewarded with the most wonderful feeling she had experienced in days and days. Strong arms wrapped around her from behind and pulled her close. "Yes, *chérie*?"

"You *are* here!" She turned and faced him, her heart about to pound out of her chest. "I've had no letter in days and no knowledge of you coming to London."

His green eyes danced. "It was meant as a surprise, *chérie.* Are you happy to see me?"

"I have missed you, so much, it has been awfully hard to bear." He didn't unclasp her hand as he led her into the parlor, shutting the door behind them. It wasn't until Imogene was back in his arms that she felt free to indulge in a sigh of relief.

"I know exactly what you mean, *chérie*, it has indeed been dreadful." He looked hungry as he swept over her with his eyes. "I have thought of doing this, every minute, of every day since we have been apart." Then he descended, his lips claiming hers. Words were unnecessary for the next few minutes. Graham was intent upon one thing, and that seemed to be showing her just how much he'd missed her. Which appeared to be a great deal. "Open your mouth for me," he said on a moan.

Compressed up against his chest so tight she could feel the heat of him through his clothes, she opened her mouth to his seeking lips. He pushed his tongue inside and she got her first taste of him. She met his tongue with her own and touched him back—so soft but yet so bold—the sensation of him in her mouth made her weak and thrilled at the same time. Graham pressed her into the back of the settee they were on and plundered her mouth for a good long while. His hands did more travelling up the sides of her breasts and maybe even touched in more places than he'd done before. It was impossible to make him stop. Imogene did not want him to stop anyway. She wanted him to kiss her with his tongue and touch her with his hands. When he held her like this her mind lost all coherent thought and reasoning. Whatever Graham was offering, Imogene wanted. And that was the essence of how it had been for her from the very first. She did not question her response to him, it just…was.

Eventually he pulled away and she opened her heavy eyelids to look at him.

"Just before I reached for you, I think you were scenting me, am I right?"

"Yes. It was the most amazing awareness. I was feeling low and missing you dreadfully. When I came up the steps I saw a movement at the window and thought that was unusual. Then, I stepped into the empty foyer and caught the trace of your scent. I *knew* it was you, but was afraid to hope that you had come."

"I was weak from missing you as well, but nothing could have kept me from you on your birthday. Happy birthday, *chérie*," he whispered, triumph evident in his voice. "Lady Wilton is a very helpful conspirator. I shall have to be sure to thank her."

"You did remember." She cupped her hand under his chin. "I have been duped. Very successfully, but *very* happily. I would accept any excuse to have you here with me." Her eyes felt the beginnings of tears. "You are the best birthday present…the very best of all."

"No tears, *chérie*. Tonight is for celebration of my beloved's attainment of her twentieth year. I wish to squire you about town upon my arm, show you off a bit before we are married—make all the young bucks jealous," he teased her. "We are all due for the theatre tonight, and a late supper. Colin and Timothy have come down from Cambridge and will join us, and your aunt and Cariss of course. You see everything has all been very well planned."

"I must learn from your excellent example, but you never know when I may get back at you." She pushed away a strand of his hair that had slipped from the binding and tucked it behind his ear.

"I'll gratefully take any retribution from you. If you only knew how difficult it is to remain a gentleman with you like this in my arms."

"Is it so hard?"

"It is monumentally hard." He gave her a wide-eyed stare that told her he was saying more with that comment than just the words. "I have a gift for you, *chérie.* You would honor me if you wear it tonight." He produced a large jeweller's box, and placed it in her lap.

How romantic he is.

"Oh!" She looked down at the most magnificent emerald ensemble she had ever seen. It was simply stunning: emeralds and large pearls set in white gold, a choker, earrings and a wrist cuff all matching. "Graham, I do not have words to express how beautiful these are." Shaking her head slightly in wonder, she asked, "Did they belong to your mother?"

"They did." He swallowed hard. "She would have been happy for me, in finding you. No words are necessary. Just wear them, and seeing them on you will be enough for me." He kissed her neck, both of her ears and finally, lifted her wrist, kissing it as well—all of the places the jewels would touch her skin.

Imogene closed her eyes and tried to seal this moment in time into her mind, so she could remember it for her whole life. The tears came nonetheless.

Graham kissed the tears away. "I already told you there were to be no tears on this happy occasion," he said lovingly. "I'll be here for tonight only, and then will stay with an old friend. I'll be here in London though, and will come to see you each day, until next Tuesday." He smiled widely. "The very best day—the day that you shall marry me."

"My tears can only be a symbol of joy now, for you have taken all of my sadness away."

"Yes, well, that has all been part of the plan." His words teased, but she hoped that she was taking away some of his sadness too, just as he was doing for her.

THE twilight air sparkled when they both appeared for her special evening. Imogene was silenced by the sight of Graham in formal dress. He bowed to her in compliment. "You are a vision tonight, Imogene. The emeralds do justice to you. Thank you for wearing them."

"You are very welcome. May I say that *you* are the epitome of fashion in gentleman's dress this evening?"

"Thank you, *chérie*." Once in the carriage, he sat beside her rather than across from her as was custom. He took her hand and held it, looking so solemn she wondered about the mysteries of him. Graham was not a chatterer. He was a watcher.

"How did you manage to get everyone into the other carriage and us alone?" she asked.

He caressed every inch of her with his eyes. "I told the drivers and hoped Lady Wilton would allow it." He shrugged. "Being a lord should be good for something."

She squeezed his hand. "Well I am glad my aunt is so generous for I love to be alone together."

"I could never tire of gazing at you, Imogene. I look so I can seal the image into my mind and remember how you are at that moment. Later when we are apart, the image I have of you, will get me through the time I must be away from you."

"But now you will be in Town, really?"

"I will." He brought her hand up and kissed it. "I could not be away from you for a moment longer. I had to come. And tonight we celebrate your birthday." He proffered a soft package. "Here's a gift I chose. The colours remind me of you. I hope you like it. Happy birthday, *chérie*."

Out spilled the most elegant Indian shawl: the heavy silk a soft yellow gold with splendid designs in burgundy, blue, and green, shot through with gold thread, the fringed edges floating with each movement. "Graham, this is a work of art. It's so gorgeous, and I shall adore wearing it. Thank you. I love that you are knowledgeable of art and design. You have quite the artistic eye." She tilted up to give him a gentle kiss.

His eyes got that dark look again and he held her face up close against his. "Yes, I do have quite the eye for beauty. I look forward to the day when I might see you in that shawl and nothing—"

He let her go and changed position in the seat, looking a bit strained. "Are you all right, Graham?"

"I am fine. That the shawl pleases you makes me glad, for in all things that is my purpose." He bent to kiss her awaiting lips.

THE hour was very late. Surely no one would be awake. It would just take a moment to slip down the hallway and get her journal. Imogene remembered where she had left it. The library was the last place she'd written in it and she would have retrieved it this afternoon, but Graham's surprise visit had changed her plans. She often wrote at night, reflecting on the events of the day, and writing it down was comforting. Graham had treated them to a delightful evening as well a very special birthday celebration and she wanted to put it in her journal.

Imogene wrapped the new shawl around her nightdress, took up the candle carefully and walked swiftly down the hallway. As soon as she entered the library, she knew she wasn't alone. A light glowed from between some shelves. Quickly crossing to the desk where her journal lay, she picked it up and turned to leave without lingering. She jumped a foot when she found herself facing a pair of very familiar green eyes.

"Such a hurry, *chérie.* Whatever for? And you look so fetching in that shawl. It pleases me that you wear it." Graham carefully removed the candle from her hand, setting it down on a nearby table.

"You startled me, Graham. I came to retrieve my journal thinking everyone would be asleep at this—"

He silenced her with a very determined kiss, the sound of her journal dropping to the floor echoed off the walls. He filled his hands with her hair and pulled her close against him, his lips devouring, his body pressed hard into hers. "By all that is holy I can't help what I am doing. I want you so badly—looking like a goddess coming in here," he mumbled.

Imogene could hear warnings going off in her brain but was helpless to do anything about them. As he compressed against her, she could feel him hard at the hips through her thin gown. *I cannot make him stop. Don't want to stop—*

Graham had her pinned up against the library wall, raining kisses over her face and neck. She moved against him. Their breathing filled the silence of the library. His hands moved too, touching and feeling determinedly. Tracing down her neck, his nose dipped lower, below the loose neckline of the nightdress, toward her breasts. Searching hands shifted up from underneath, lifting them toward his lips.

"So soft. I need—I want to taste." His lips pushed the fabric of her gown open farther and trailed over the bared flesh of her breast.

A low moan escaped from her and the sound seemed to snap Graham out of the flare of desire that gripped him. He pulled back, his hands coming to rest on the wall upon either side of her face. Something compelled him to look up the wall and straight into the portrait of some stern-looking Everley ancestor, no doubt. She had seen those dour portraits every day she'd come into this room since she'd been staying in this house. She panted against the wall as he stared at her in the candlelight. The space between them felt cold now that his body had pulled away, and every place he'd touched with his mouth was still tingling. Imogene never would have asked him to stop.

Graham looked longingly at her for a moment before bending to pick up her journal and placing it in her hands.

Then he determinedly straightened her shawl, layering it over the front of her.

"My dearest, Imogene, *chérie,* beloved, you've caught me by surprise. I fear I have quite lost my manners, and sincerely apologize for my imposition upon you just now. Please forgive me?"

Imogene tried to control her breathing. "Of course, Graham. It was…reckless of me to come in here like this."

"Probably, yes, but you have made such a beautiful visual memory that I might take with me for the next few days, and for that, I thank you." He placed the candle into her other hand. "Until tomorrow then, my darling." Opening the door, he kissed her forehead, sighed heavily and led her out into the hallway. "Off to bed you go." He watched her walk away. "Imogene?" She turned back to look. "Lock your door when you get to your room please."

"All right." She nodded.

"Sleep well, *chérie.*"

"WHAT a beautiful shawl, Imogene," Aunt Wilton remarked at breakfast the next morning.

"Graham brought it for my birthday. He has quite the talent for choosing beautiful things, and I am fairly taken with it." Imogene stroked the elegant fringe.

"Lord Rothvale is very generous to be sure and honorable and everything a gentleman of his standing should be, but I daresay he is more taken with you than either of you realize, my dear Imogene," Aunt Wilton responded with a knowing smile.

Imogene blushed, lowering her eyes. Aunt Wilton put her hand atop Imogene's and squeezed it. "My dear, there are some things I feel it my duty to share with you—to prepare you for marital life with your husband. Your mamma is not here and she would not wish to send you away to be a wife, uninformed and ignorant of what will come to pass." Imogene nodded, listening. "Lord Rothvale loves you very much, Imogene. It is evident to the world and I am sure he will be gentle and kind in claiming his nuptial rights."

"His rights…yes I know, but I don't really know what that means."

"Well, you will have to submit to him, willingly, in the marriage bed. It is your duty. And with your figure, and the way he looks at you, you should expect him to be…ah…very keen on claiming them. But as I have said already, he will be good to you. I know it. He adores you so, and will lead you in the ways of what he desires." Aunt Wilton squeezed Imogene's hand again. "You should not dread it, darling. It is not unpleasant if accomplished in the correct attitude. With the possible exception of the very first time you come together. That first time, when you are no longer a maiden, it will hurt just at the beginning only, and even then not badly if he has prepared you, which he will. If you go to him willingly I am sure you will find him very careful and loving."

"But what exactly will he do?" Imogene was insistent. "Please tell me."

Aunt Wilton paused before answering, "He will join his body to yours, intimately, and stir it, spilling his seed in you. He will seize great pleasure from your joining and will want you in this way…often. It is typical of new husbands with their brides. If God is willing, the start of his child will take eventually. You will have a sign of this occurring, if your courses stop and do not come; that is the best indication that you are with child. There are other signs too and I will be happy to speak of them later, but I daresay you will know it when the time comes and you will have Philippa to go to, and Dr. Brancroft, of course. That is the way of it, my dear. We are all born to do our duty and yours will be to honor your husband, acquiesce to his wishes, and bear him the heir to Gavandon. Remember, Imogene, he has extensive properties, and a title to secure."

Imogene appreciated her aunt's direct approach. What is the point of skirting around issues, speak them and be done. Honesty was always the best course. As she pondered her aunt's words, understanding began to dawn. The look in Graham's eyes was sometimes puzzling. She had not truly recognized what she saw in them before. Especially now, it was becoming clearer: the encounter in the library last night, the powerful feelings when he touched her, her unwillingness to stop him, his request that she lock her door upon return to her room. She began to understand. Now she imagined, and correctly so, that he was thinking of all the things he wanted to do with her, but could not act upon them. Not yet, but soon he would. He would do all of those things he was thinking about. Imogene felt an involuntary shiver take hold and sweep through her as she thought about the things he might do, and it was not at all unpleasant.

GRAHAM sat opposite Imogene in the coach today. Looking, longing, loving her with his eyes only. After last night's passionate lapse in the library, maintaining a modicum of decorum seemed like the wise course. When he'd called upon her late this morning, explaining there was another gift, and they would go in the carriage, she had been full of questions. *Where are we going? We will go alone together?* Assuring Imogene that all was approved with Lady Wilton, Graham could only give thanks for the woman. He really needed to show his appreciation for her understanding in allowing him some liberties that other guardians would have never considered granting.

He lazily studied Imogene as she looked out the window at the passing scenery. She focused on her surroundings for a bit and then turned away from the window to address him. "I know where we are going," she said firmly.

"And does it please you then?" He needed assurance. "If not, just say the word and we'll go right back."

"No. It's a lovely gesture and I should—I should like to be there, again. And you'll be with me, Graham." Smiling bravely, she nodded her head.

"I just thought you might like to visit, and you know, get some of your things that you might like to have, with you, when you start—when *we* start our life," he trailed off, feeling much less sure. "I'm sorry, I'm not saying this right at all. What I meant was I did not want to take you away from everything, from your home, without you getting a chance to—a chance to say goodbye." He exhaled. "This was a mistake, wasn't it? Damn, I've made such a mess of things. I am so sorry, *chérie.*"

"Graham." She reached out to him. "Darling, it is fine and good that I go. You are quite right in this. I need to go back to my home. I want to, and I am so grateful you will be with me." She closed her eyes, still nodding.

Graham immediately moved from his seat to hers, drawing her into his arms. She rested her cheek on his chest and let him comfort her. He held her like that for the remainder of the journey and worried if he had done the right thing in bringing her.

The housekeeper, Mrs. Ellis, was waiting for them when the carriage pulled in the drive. Imogene flew into her arms. The elderly Mrs. Ellis took Imogene's face into her hands. "You are grown up so lovely, Miss Imogene. I know your mamma and papa are feeling very joyous for your happiness. Lady Wilton has written and told us of your love match, you see?" She turned to him and bestowed a sincere smile. "Lord Rothvale, bless you for loving our Imogene and caring for her so kindly. Our hearts here at Drakenhurst can now be eased to know she will be in such good hands."

Graham bowed graciously. "The honor is all mine, I assure you, Mrs. Ellis. I bless the day that fate allowed me to find her." Mrs. Ellis veritably glowed at his words.

"My dear, I took the liberty of putting together the things I thought you would surely wish to have, but please have a look around and make sure you get everything you wish for. We'll have a late luncheon served for you when you are ready."

Imogene excitedly showed Graham everything. The house, the stables, her favourite haunts as a child. The portrait gallery was his favourite though. Mrs. Ellis had packed thoroughly and there was really nothing Imogene wished to have in addition to what she had already gathered for her, apart from her bows and wrist gauntlets. Graham liked that she would have her bows for he intended to set up targets for her at Gavandon so she could take up the sport again. He'd teased her that the bows would be needed for the Artemis portrait he intended to have done of her.

Imagining the portraits to be created of Imogene was his absolute obsession. He tried not to blather about it too much to her, but he certainly thought about it constantly. Imogene was beautiful of course, but there was something about her that would evoke deep emotion in a portrait. Graham knew this to be irrevocably true. Just seeing her pick up her bow and sight it for a moment, got his creativity flowing with ideas for backdrop and pose. Watching her made him happy. It was such a simple thing, and yet it was…everything.

After a great deal of exploring and gathering of items, and the late luncheon, there was really only one thing left to be done. Mrs. Ellis pressed a thick wool blanket into Graham's hands. "The ground is damp," she told him. Graham nodded in understanding, realizing what it was for, and walked Imogene there.

He put the blanket on the ground in front of the crypt where her parents rested, and asked, "Is this all right, my darling?"

Imogene dropped down on the blanket as if being pressed from above with an immense weight. She looked so haunted he had to look away for a moment. Graham stood back then and gave her the privacy she needed. This was something he understood, very well.

Many, many long minutes and a river of tears later,

Graham saw when Imogene put her hand out to him. He came to her on the blanket, and held her as she said her final goodbye. And then it was done. On the ride back she allowed him to hold her again in the carriage. She was quiet for most of the trip and he left her to her thoughts, but toward the end she looked up at him and said, "I made my peace."

"I am glad, *chérie.* I only wanted to give you the chance to come home—"

She silenced him with two fingers to his lips. "It was good you brought me here today…to do this." She returned to her position of resting against his chest and settled back into quiet.

Holding his arms around her soft weight, he thought about his own demons. He'd be facing much the same when he brought her home to Gavandon in a few weeks. Would Imogene still love him if she knew? Would she rest so trustingly in his arms as she was right at this moment, if the truth about his secret were known? Speculation on the outcome was easy to figure. Imogene would turn away from him. She would not love him or want him anymore. And that fear drove him to secure her. Whatever it took, whatever must be leveraged, Imogene would be his. No other option was tolerable. The idea of losing her love, for any reason, quite simply…terrified him. She must never know.

"MISS Byron-Cole, I finally have the honor of meeting you. My friend has kept you quite secreted away in his plans for you. He was quite right to do it, your beauty and charm reasons enough for him to keep you all for himself."

"Gravelle, are you trying to charm my fiancée on the

night before she weds me? What kind of a friend are you anyway?" Graham glared at his friend even though it was apparent he was joking.

Imogene was having a wonderful time on the eve of her wedding. The Hargreaves, her dear friend, Jocelyn, her uncle and cousins, as well as Colin, had all arrived for the nuptials in the morning. Family and friends were in full support this evening at Brentwood along with some new faces. A Mr. Clive Gravelle was one of them. Very amusing, with as easy a manner as Graham had, but without the somberness.

"Thank you, Mr. Gravelle. I hope in the future, when we know one another better, you can feel free to share some of the memories you have of Graham. He's told me that you've known each other since childhood, with your parents being close friends and neighbours in Warwickshire. I should love to know some little thing of what he was like as a boy."

"By all means. I must have a veritable trunk-full of stories about his boyhood exploits. For all his outward seriousness there lies a mischievous bent to our Rothvale here." Gravelle replied with a nod and a rakish twinkle to his eyes.

"How wonderful, Mr. Gravelle. I look forward to a very long and reminiscent conversation with you then." She looked over at Graham.

Graham rolled his eyes. "Gravelle, you are such a loyal friend. It's so heartwarming to have one's true friends in support. Have I thanked you for putting me up in Town this past week?" He directed a menacing glare at his friend but all knew it was in jest and that he was truly grateful to have such a good friend with him on this day.

Mr. Gravelle then focused his attentions on her cousin, Cariss. "Miss Wilton, have you enjoyed your stay in Town?"

"Yes. Thank you, Mr. Gravelle. It has been a very busy

time with preparing for the wedding and the diversions of London. I fear it shall be quite a drear winter, now all of the doings will be at an end. I will miss Imogene dreadfully when she is gone."

"Perhaps you will be soon for a visit to Gavandon, Miss Wilton?" Gravelle suggested with a charming smile. Imogene was not unaware of Mr. Gravelle's very watchful interest in her cousin and wondered what Cari thought of him. She would have to ask her later.

Imogene replied, "In response to your suggestion, I hope Cari may be able to join us in the spring at Gavandon. We are working to arrange it. Are you at home in Warwickshire, Mr. Gravelle?"

"Yes. Kelldale Park is but three miles from Gavandon. I split the year between there and Town. I daresay we will all cross paths again soon when we are north."

Graham spoke up, "True that, Gravelle. We must make it so."

Imogene loved seeing Graham with his friends and losing some of his reserve. He was smiling more now and that pleased her too. She hoped his apparent happiness was because of her.

She wanted to be the reason.

Chapter 9

And soft adorings from their loves receive
Upon the honeyed middle of the night.

John Keats ~ 'The Eve of St .Agnes', 1820

St. Martin-in-the-Fields's shining whiteness was a beacon today—accepting and confirming the vows of the couple inside, hearing their promise to love, honor, cherish, protect and obey. Graham was in awe of the experience. When he knelt beside Imogene and the priest put their hands together, covered them with his own, and spoke the words, Graham knew them…truly.

As Imogene signed her maiden name for the last time on the marriage document, he finally allowed himself to indulge in a sliver of relief. She now belonged to him lawfully and spiritually. Until death chose to part them in this earthly life.

They stood on the steps and took their moment together while the trilling bells of St. Martin's went ringing out into the city of London.

THE man watched from across the street, knowing he must not be seen. He hung in the shadow, but still had a clear view of them. The bride was lovely, and what do you know? Very familiar in her looks. *God!* He thought this might work out even better than he had imagined, cheered that the satisfaction of getting what he deserved was going to be made all the sweeter for the sport in it. He licked his lips as he slithered down into the bowels of the old metropolis. Thinking the same thought over and over, as he made his way, "I have you over a barrel. One way or another, you're going to give me what I want."

A wedding breakfast at Brentwood followed the ceremony at St. Martin's, although it was well past noon before it got underway.

Graham admired his wife in her elegant wedding clothes. The dress was done in ivory satin with bold, vertical stripes in blue-grey, a faux waistcoat bodice and a long jacket with a slight train. Her hair was up with some of it left to tumble down her back, and she wore the magnificent pearl choker from her mother she'd worn to the ball the night they'd met. Utterly mouthwatering.

It took some time to say their goodbyes to their many guests. He sensed Imogene growing a bit emotional saying farewell to her family, especially Cariss, but they parted with promises of a visit in spring. She gave a special farewell to her friend Jocelyn Charleston, both agreeing to write and hoping to see each other again when Jocelyn might come to her sister

Mina at Everfell.

Gravelle was the last to leave, and it was late in the afternoon when all had departed.

"They have all gone. I think Colin is still about, but I imagine he'll make himself scarce." *He'd bloody better be scarce.* "We'll not see him again before he leaves. We are finally alone, *Mrs.* Everley." He pulled her into his arms and linked his hands at her back, letting the full flush of her against his body wash over him.

"I love for you to call me Mrs. Everley. I know we can only say it when we are alone together, but I do love the sound of it."

"What? You don't wish to be called Lady Rothvale? You've earned it. You are a baroness now. I'll have to call you Lady Rothvale sometimes. In any case, you must accustom yourself to it for that is what everyone else will call you. There's nothing for it. Sorry, *chérie*." He grinned down at her.

"I know, and it is an honor, but I love 'missus' when you say it to me," she said, while smoothing over the lapel of his new blue-grey jacket made to match the colour of the stripes in her dress to perfection.

"Well, I'll be sure to say it to you all of the time then." He glanced down at her, her eyes focusing intently on his jacket lapel until it lost her consideration, replaced by his pocket handkerchief for some fidgeting attentions. "I think Mr. Gravelle was quite taken with Cariss. He stared at her ever so much." She finally lifted her eyes up to meet his.

Graham would say his new bride was a bit nervous if he had to guess, but he supposed it was natural for her to feel that way. So, he forced a calm response and just held her loosely, content to just have her alone with him. "Well, your cousin Cariss is lovely despite being so young, and he could not do better than her, but *she* might do better than him," he said with a smirk. "No, I jest. For all of Gravelle's triviality, he is solid loyal—a good man. Knows horses better than anyone and a *very* successful man of business—a sharp fencer too. They could be well matched I suppose," Graham said thoughtfully as he pondered the possibility of the two together.

"Can we stay like this forever? It has been so very difficult to look at you all day and not be able to touch you."

Her comment got his attention as well as his cock's.

"Really? I cannot imagine whatever you mean, *chérie*."

She frowned at his teasing, her luscious bottom lip jutting out a little.

"All right, you've caught me in an enormous lie, Mrs. Everley. I thought I would die if they did not all leave this house."

Her frown transformed into a beautiful smile, and he couldn't wait anymore to have a little taste of his bride.

He kissed her first, softly and slowly, a finger under her chin, holding her to his lips before moving back to assess her from head to toe. "You are always beautiful to me, but today you are beyond description, and this dress—quite remarkable in colour and design, very modern. I know there will be mention of you and your dress in the columns tomorrow. I shall clip it out and save it for a keepsake. You choose the loveliest clothes. I have always thought so. Such a vision today when your uncle walked you into the church."

"*You* were my vision today, Graham. You were…ah…very handsome, as you always are." She blushed up at him. "I was nervous at first but as soon as I could see your eyes upon me, I felt a calmness wrap 'round me and I knew everything would be well."

He brought her back into his arms and held her, saying

nothing, preferring to simply indulge in his favourite activity of looking at her and close enough to touch. In truth, he was trying to bend his mind around the fact she was now his wife.

Graham made a decision about how their evening would progress.

"I must write some letters of correspondence. Would you like to join me in the study? Maybe you could write in your journal for a time? Mark the occasion?"

"All right. I'll just go and get my journal, and meet you in your study."

He watched her go, unable to tell from her reply what her thoughts were on his suggestion. *Christ! It's only four o'clock in the afternoon. I cannot just carry her upstairs and bed her right now. No. I am not doing that. I want everything to be perfect.*

Graham stood when she returned to his study, leading her to a writing table he had situated just across from his desk. "If you sit here, I may be able to look at you whenever I wish and I will be very, very content."

"It is your intention to work on your correspondence or to look at me?"

"Both. But since it is the first time I have tried it, I am not sure of how successful I will be," he said, leaning down to kiss her on the temple.

He helped her get settled first, then went to his own desk and sat down to write. Graham had very strong self-control. It was a reflex, honed by his life experiences. When he made a decision, he almost always carried it through, avoiding distraction by focusing unwavering concentration on the task at hand. But today was different. He could look at her and control himself, but the mental images of the coming night, beginning to bombard his thoughts, were more difficult to suppress.

He wondered if Imogene had similar thoughts as him. Probably not, he decided. Sitting across from him, she appeared very unfocused, and Graham had to work doubly hard to keep from laughing at her distractibility. She was so utterly charming; he could watch her unendingly and never grow tired.

Fidgeting and sighing, she rolled her neck over the top of her shoulder, the effect pushing her breasts upward in her bodice.

This last move of hers was so tempting he actually felt his mouth start to water. *Christ Almighty, this utter torture. How am I going to make it through dinner?*

Imogene stood up abruptly.

Graham leapt up out of his chair, looking inquiringly and trying to ignore the pain at the place where his cock met his balls.

"I feel so hot, I think I need some water," she blurted, moving toward the door.

"Don't go, *chérie*. Please stay. I'll ring for some." He pulled the cord that rang the bell and went to her, putting his hand to her forehead, and then replacing it with his lips. She seemed to relax instantly at his touch. "You do not feel feverish to me." *You're hot? I don't think you can know the true meaning of that. Christ!* "Let us sit here while we wait for your refreshment to come." He led her to a couch and caressed her hand.

She blinked at him. "I fear I am not in the mood for writing in my journal just now."

"No?"

"Not at all." She closed her eyes, shrugging one shoulder up to her ear and stretching her neck.

"What would you wish to do, *chérie*?" he asked in

anticipation, hardly able to stand the vision of her as she stretched, without pouncing on her. Oh, how he wanted to pounce. He wanted to peel that gorgeous dress off her slowly, and touch every inch of her beautiful body. He wanted to kiss her and touch her in places—his thoughts were cut off abruptly by her words.

"I think I should like to recline here and drink my water and look at you while you write."

She is wickedly clever. How did she just do that? How did she turn everything around like that?

The door opened then and the water was delivered and poured. Imogene relaxed back onto the cushions and took a sip. "You may return to your correspondence, my love; I do not wish to keep you from it."

Graham narrowed his eyes a little but did not leave the couch. She took another sip. This time a small drop remained on her lip. She licked it off with her tongue and rubbed her lips together, her eyes resting on him. Graham's carefully mastered self-control evaporated at that instant and he lunged for her. Water and glass tumbling onto the carpet was of little consequence.

To either of them.

Imogene met his kiss with equal passion after an initial squeak of surprise. He needed to feel her touch, even if for a moment. All day they had been looking and looking and now he just needed to feel her. Her hands went immediately into his hair. His hands went to her waist and pushed up slowly, smoothing over every inch of her bodice, caressing over her breasts until he reached her collarbone. It felt divine to have his hands on her, covering her, but then he stopped and pulled her up to sitting again.

Imogene looked unhappy as he drew away. She gave her

head a small shake as if to clear her thoughts.

Hell, my cock can give you some thoughts, my beauty.

"You are very scampish, *chérie*, distracting me so. I find myself quite unable to resist you."

"I am sorry, but I just felt so hot and I could not concentrate on my journal. Should you like me to leave you in peace?"

"No…no, no." He shook his head. "Nothing so drastic as that." He leaned down for a long, soft kiss to which she gave him sweetly.

"What shall I do, then?" she sighed onto his neck.

"I think the original plan is sound. I'll get you a new glass of water—sorry for pouncing on you before—and you can rest right here. I will go back to my desk and finish my letters, and you will be a good girl and watch me. Every now and again, I will look up from my writing and we can exchange a lover's glance. Then, in a while, we shall go into dinner and look at each other some more, over our plates. How does that sound to you?"

She nodded her head contritely, her eyes wide.

You'll never know how hard it is for me to write these damn letters right now. I want you so badly. You belong to me now, my sumptuous beauty. I want to be with you, upstairs in my bed. I want to be making love to you all night long. And I am going to.

They were true to their words.

Graham returned to his writing, and Imogene was content to look at him—for a time. In a short while though, her eyes grew heavy, she listed to one side, and settled into slumber. It was the first time he had ever seen her asleep. She looked so enchanting and peaceful on the couch he was loathe to disturb her. He watched her for a few moments, allowing himself to imagine how she would look when he was making love to her tonight. *Now it is my turn to be wicked. Get some rest, my love. You are going to need it…for later.*

IMOGENE woke to the most delectable feeling of Graham kissing her neck and speaking softly. "Wake-up, my beauty; time to go down to dinner. You've had a sleep."

"Mmm…what? Oh, did I? I am so sorry, how careless of me. Did you get your letters done?"

"What are you sorry for? You were obviously fatigued and needed to rest. I quite enjoyed the view of you, and yes, my correspondence is complete for now."

Imogene sighed, closing her eyes for a moment, trying to collect her wits. "I must go and refresh myself. I'll meet you at the dining room in ten minutes?" She moved to sit up on the couch, and Graham immediately offered assistance in rising. She tried to gauge his feelings at the moment, sensing he might be trying to put her at ease, giving her some space.

"I'll await you there…and you are beautiful in your sleep, Imogene." He held her fingers and kissed the fingertips.

His words made her blush. *He is teasing me a little about falling asleep. He imagines sleeping with me tonight, I think.* "Thank you."

"Oh, before I forget, your things have been moved into the suite—the one that adjoins to mine."

She nodded, understanding his meaning clearly. *I am such an inconsistency of emotions right now. Part nervous and part desperate for him to touch me. He was so…so unwavering and determined when he touched me on the couch. He had the look of a pouncing cat…and I was the mouse!*

WHEN she arrived at the dining room, Graham stood and held out his hand. He seated her at her place, at the end of the side of the table. He moved to his place opposite of her, at the same end.

"I like our seating arrangement," she told him.

"Yes, *chérie*, especially for our first dinner alone together I don't want you miles away. I can feast my eyes upon you and upon my dinner at the same time."

"How do you do that? I find it very distracting to look at you and continue with my tasks at hand."

"Practice, *chérie.* Remember, I have had many more years to practice than you have," he said, winking saucily.

Dinner proceeded slowly in Imogene's opinion.

"How was your sleep? You looked like Sleeping Beauty from the fairy tale."

"It was…restful."

"And how do you find your dinner?"

"I find it…perfectly…adequate."

"I cannot help but notice that you are not eating very much. More like you are doing battle, stabbing and poking at it. I assure you it is quite dead," he joked. "Are you not hungry?"

"Not very, not for…food." She lifted her eyes, looking boldly.

"What are you hungry for?" His breath seemed to leave him.

She whispered, "Your touch. I want you to hold me. I need to feel your arms around me."

Graham rose instantly from the chair, pulling her up, enfolding her into his arms. "Is this better?"

"Yes." She leaned into him. "I've only felt at peace today when you have held me. I've found this afternoon to be a very tiresome one, indeed."

"I know you have, Imogene, and you have born it very bravely, my darling." His hand came to her hair and face. "Thank you for staying with me today in the study while I had to write my letters. It was heaven having you close. Being selfish, I could not bear for you to leave my side."

"But I fell asleep. I am not very good at this. I fear I shall be a disappointment to you," she trailed off.

"Nonsense. How could you ever be a disappointment to me? You needed the rest, and I loved watching you sleep, I've already told you." He kissed her on the forehead and then pulled back to focus on her eyes.

The look he gave her was bold and burning.

It is time.

"Mrs. Everley, I should like to retire for the evening." He leaned down, whispering, "Are you of the same mind?"

Unable to voice a sound, Imogene nodded her answer to him. Heart thudding and mind racing, she knew both anxiety and relief in the same moment. *It's going to happen now. I could see it in his eyes—what Aunt Wilton talked to me about…*

"I'LL leave you to your privacy, *chérie.*" Graham caressed her hand, turned her palm up and kissed it. "An hour then? I shall think of nothing but you."

"An hour will be perfect," she managed to answer.

He backed away, but did not release her hand right away. He continued stepping backward until his arm stretched out all the way and their hands finally separated, falling apart. As a final gesture, he blew a little kiss.

Imogene loved how he could show his affection for her so easily, a romantic at heart. She continued to stare at the closed door for a long time after he was gone. The room grew quiet.

Nervousness rose up her throat, rousing her. She rang for the maid. Hester entered the room and took charge, much to Imogene's relief, chattering away about the beauty of her garments, her jewellery, and the excitement of the day, helping to fill the tense silence in the room. She assisted Imogene out of her wedding gown and into a quick bath, and finally into a filmy nightdress. Her hair was unpinned and brushed out. The bed was turned down. The fire stirred. A tray laid with refreshment.

"Will there be anything else I can do for you tonight, Lady Rothvale? And may I say, my lady, you look very beautiful."

"No, nothing. I am well. Thank you, Hester."

"Madam, on behalf of the staff here, we offer our sincerest congratulations and best wishes upon your marriage. If there is anything you need, anything at all, please ring so that I may serve you."

"My thanks, Hester, you have made me feel very comfortable here."

"Goodnight, Lady Rothvale."

The sound of Hester's steps now retreating down the corridor slowly faded away until quiet once again filled the room.

Lady Rothvale. I shall have to get used to being called that. She sighed at the thought and went to pour herself a glass of wine, hoping some spirits might settle her. She tried to sip the wine, but had little success because her stomach was a knot of nerves. *What will he do exactly? What am I supposed to do? I am nervous. I want to please him. Aunt Wilton said it might hurt the first time. Oh, dear God!*

IN his own room, Graham was pacing the floor in his robe, his hair unbound, swaying with his steps, contemplating his own anxiety as he turned the handle of the connecting door. *Gentle and slow. She's a virgin. Help me to do this without terrifying her. I hope I can manage to—*

The door swung open with a groaning creak, ending his absurd nervousness. It was time to claim his bride once and for all. The chamber was lit softly with candles and the glow from the fire when he stepped in, but he did not see her.

"*Chérie*? Where are you?"

"I am here," she answered, her voice tremulous.

He followed the sound to the dressing screen where she stood behind it, the outline of her shape showing clearly in shadow. "Do you need more time, *chérie*?"

"No." He plainly saw the shaking of her head.

"Then why are you still back behind there? Are you hiding?"

"No…I don't know," she whispered.

"Are you afraid, *chérie*? I hope not. You're so lovely. I can tell just by seeing your shadow through the screen." He saw her take in a deep breath. "I've seen you before in your nightdress, you know…and you were so beautiful then. 'Twas only a week ago, that night in the library, and you weren't scared." He heard a little gasp come from her. "Can you come out, *chérie*? I want to see you, and hold you in my arms. I love you so much, and I just want to show you, that is all."

Silence met his entreaty.

Patience… Give her what she needs.

"I'll wait until you are ready to come out," whispering the last part very softly, but knowing she heard, he saw her breathing get faster before she started to move out from behind the screen.

Glinting hair flowed over her shoulders and down her back; her gown had slipped a bit off one shoulder, the hem of it making a slight train. The shawl he'd given her was wrapped around her shoulders, but it had slipped down as well.

Glorious.

"*Chérie*, you take my breath away." He bowed to her first, and then held out his arms. It was the perfect gesture to break the tension, just what she needed apparently, because she came right into his embrace. To hold her, finally, after the long day's events was pure heaven. He tilted her chin up, "I do not have speech to express how beautiful you were just now, standing there for me."

"Your hair is loosed," she said in answer, reaching a hand up to smooth a portion lovingly behind his ear. "That I may see *you* like this," she whispered, completely unaware of the effect her words were having on him.

Graham bent and took her lips. Gently at first, he held her and kissed caressingly in the only way he knew how to be with her.

No more waiting to make you mine.

SHE felt his teeth graze her lips as the kisses grew stronger and more insistent. He pushed his tongue into her mouth and tasted. She followed his lead, but the pace escalated quickly, and soon all possession of her mouth was completely taken over by him. It was a conquering; there was no other way to describe what he was doing.

She stiffened a little in his arms and he felt her. Pulling back right away, he searched her face. "*Chérie*? Are you afraid? Does this worry you?"

"A little," she admitted. She took in a deep breath, trying to be brave. "I feel—I do feel your love, but I confess it is—" she swallowed hard, "I am unsure about how to—how to be a proper wife to you—"

He stopped her by gently placing his fingers over her mouth and whispered, "Let me love you. Never have fear of pleasing me, Imogene. If you were any more pleasing to me, I'd probably not be able to bear it." He brought his hands to her face; one stroked her cheek with his thumb, the other, her hair. "I want you to think back to the time before the wedding, when *this* had to be held in check for the sake of propriety?"

She nodded in remembrance, feeling her neck and shoulders flushing with heat.

Smiling admiringly, he remarked, "It is so very pretty when you blush for me." He feathered kisses along her neck and throat in between his words. "Now, we do not have to hold back. Things are finally as they should be between us, *chérie*. Please do not fear it…do not…do not *ever* have fear of me." Returning to her lips, he resumed the kissing, slower now, but just as demanding as before.

"Just relax, *chérie*, and let me—"

Being touched, surrendering to him in this way, did feel divine. She gasped in a deep breath of air at the touch of his tongue on her neck.

He moved back to look deep into her eyes as his hands

began slipping off her shawl. "I want…I want to see you, *chérie*?" It was whispered in the way of a request.

She nodded her agreement with the slightest movement of her head, and it was enough for him to proceed. Her shawl was laid on the settee, and his hands came to the ties of her gown. As he worked to untie them, Imogene met her husband's gaze and was mesmerized by the look of longing to be seen in his green eyes. She remembered Aunt Wilton's words: *'He will lead you in the ways of what he desires.'* He wanted to see her—all of her. And he was going to.

Oh, I cannot breathe. He is—he's taking it off!

The ties undone, he pushed it open to her shoulders. The fabric began to slip off and bunch at her waist. The weight of the gown caused it to continue to fall, slipping lower until gravity took over, sliding it completely off her body and into a pool on the floor. It required everything she had to keep her hands from clutching back her gown to cover herself.

She was bared to him and his raking eyes.

He stared, his eyes moving over her from head to toe. Graham studied her naked body as she tried to remain standing for him, and to remember to take in breaths of air.

"You are resplendent, *chérie.* You look like Botticelli's painting of Venus—'Venus Rising From the Sea' with your hair streaming down over you."

The next thing she knew Graham had swept her off her feet and was carrying her toward the bed. She felt so slight in his strong arms as he tenderly laid her onto the mattress, supporting her head before he released her, gazing down at her for a moment.

"I am undone by how lovely you are. Do not fear this, *chérie.* It is just me and I going forward together. I love you with all my heart." He said the words to her as he untied his robe. Slowly he shrugged it off his big shoulders until it fell down his back, and then he opened it and allowed it to fall away down to the floor.

His shoulders were not the only part of him that was big. Imogene knew what a cock was, but she'd never seen an adult male cock, and not in the condition which Graham's appeared at this moment, so rigid and…enormous. Dear God, how on earth would this work between them?

Imogene remembered the part of Aunt Wilton's advice about allowing him to lead her, and trusting him. The more she looked, the more she became unable to look away from the beauty of his body, so hard, and strong, and pulsing with need. For her. Imogene understood that much. He wanted her, but he was also asking her to accept him. He needed a kind of consent from her.

She opened her arms to him and he took her invitation swiftly, joining her on the bed, pressing his hard body up against her much smaller and softer one. As soon as she offered herself to him, an understanding seemed to fall into place, and Graham took the lead.

Hands and mouth moved over her, exploring, tasting, and giving pleasure to her senses. Especially when he put his mouth to her breasts and took her nipples into his mouth and sucked on them.

Imogene completely and utterly gave herself up to him and what he was doing. She yielded, mentally as well as physically. It was the only way for her to get through the experience, as she could hardly comprehend it. His touches were shocking in their liberty and all-consuming in their intimacy. He brought his fingers to her cunny and stroked the sensitive nub at the centre, making her sex wet and slippery. She could not imagine anything past the next second in time as she bore the pleasurable sensations his touch brought. Would it continue forever? How did it end? She trembled, moving under him, needing something, anything to complete this sense of teetering, but never falling. She became desperate. "Graham, please—"

He silenced her with his mouth. "I know…I know."

His eyes locked onto hers as he crawled up her body and moved her legs apart, bending them at the knees. Staring at her nakedness again, his eyes widened at the sight of her spread open and exposed no doubt. She could hardly comprehend what was happening to her—

"You're so perfectly beautiful, Imogene," he whispered as he lowered his hips to align with hers.

She started to shake, impassioned and nearly out of her mind when she felt the kiss of what was certainly the tip of his cock at her cunny. She closed her eyes.

"It is well, my beautiful *chérie*," he soothed her. "Please do not be afraid…you're ready for me…you are. You're so beautiful right now. God." His forearms rested on either side of her. His breath came quicker as he held her face with a hand. "Look at me. Look into my eyes. I want your eyes on mine…so you can see how much I love you when I—"

She opened her eyes and felt a great pressure pushing in at her sex.

Graham held her face to him and thrust forward with his hips, his green eyes flaring wide.

"Ohhhhh," she cried out as a sharp stab of pain broke through the waves of sensual pleasure she'd felt before.

Graham groaned over her but held the side of her face up to him, waiting for her to settle and become used to the feeling of him inside her. He remained still, but continued to stroke her hair and face, to kiss over her lips and jaw. "You feel so good, so perfect," he said lovingly.

After a few moments he began to move his hips, shallowly at first, sliding his cock in and out in a steady rhythm. The sensation was one of great pressure more so than pain for Imogene, but still overwhelming in feeling as well as mind, for she had to accept what was actually happening between them.

Bodies moved, lips kissed, pushing, pulling, sliding, stroking skin-on-skin at the most intimate of places. Captor to captive, husband to wife, lover to lover, they began the ancient rite. His movements started slowly, but then gained in strength and intensity as he took total possession of her. He claimed her body, plundered her, made her his. Time paused, didn't matter. She sensed his need and let herself go. It was her way of accepting this new experience. He was different than he had ever been with her before, uninhibited and utterly impassioned when she felt him grow even larger and impossibly harder inside her.

Graham cried out her name in a deep guttural groan, thrusting hard and deep one last time before shuddering over her, looking like a beautiful pagan god from a Greek myth.

GRAHAM collapsed down to his side and pulled her firmly, possessively against him, not capable of much more than just holding on to her. His arm and leg were strewn over her, his head nestled right in above her shoulder. For now, he just floated along in the ocean of her. *Heaven. Bliss. Love. Relief. Mine.*

He felt Imogene's fingers moving through his hair. She was quiet. They stayed like this for moments, hours, days; who knew, for time ceased to be. He kissed her shoulder and caressed. Then he opened his eyes. She remained on her back. Her profile was stunning in the firelight; her dark golden hair spread about wildly on the sheets; breasts bared for him to see and touch; brown eyes looking toward the ceiling; graceful lashes sweeping up; red lips parted and swollen from all the pillaging he'd done. He saw a streak of water reaching from the corner of her eye to her hair. With a stab to his insides so sharp it burned, Graham realized it was a tear. *She is crying? No! Please, no…*

He shot up, looming over her.

"Imogene, have I hurt you? I can't bear it if I have. Are you all right? Was I a beast? Why do you weep?"

Panic overtaking, he fired questions at her, dreading that his worst fear had come true: that he had given pain, and terrified her. She couldn't possibly understand how she affected him. He couldn't help it. He became completely crazed, a senseless creature who could think of nothing but possessing her. He should have gone slower, been gentler. It was her first time. He despaired, agonizing at the idea of her distress. *Damn me to the bowels of hell.*

She turned her face to look at him. "No. I am fine…and well. I do not know why I weep, truly, I cannot say. I felt suddenly overcome. Emotional. It stirred me and…it was powerful of sensation. I feel close to you. I am ignorant of this I know, but you did not hurt me, nor are you a beast. You could *never* be that, Graham. " She brought her hand to his face and reassured him. "I'll have to learn what you need to please you better. I am bereft for words to explain..." She pushed her face into his shoulder as if she might be feeling shy.

"And you believe that you did not satisfy me well enough just now? That I find you wanting in the experience?" He was incredulous.

Imogene nodded just a fraction, her face still pressed against him.

"That is not possible." Relief flooded through him that she was not offended by the fucking. He brushed his fingers under her chin, and forced her to look at him. "Let me relieve you of your anxiety, *chérie.* I was spent from the pleasure of you. I simply could not speak any words. Time ceased to be present, so lost was I…in you. I have dreamed of making love to you for so long. I was out of my mind with desire for you. We will learn together, but you must know, my lovely, brave Imogene, that you were perfect in every way, and I am *very, very* pleased." The thought she believed she did not please him enough was so absurd, he almost laughed. But he did not. Instead he kissed her gently, letting his hair curtain over her face; feeling her relax and melt into him was a comfort. He wanted her to know she was his precious treasure.

He relished the feel as her hand idly began stroking his hair once more, her other hand grazing over his skin. The warmth from the fire radiated throughout the room. Graham knew the cause of her worries. Imogene was feeling maidenly self-conscious to be sure, but she had not reached fulfilment, and did not yet truly understand what was possible between them. Thus the bereft feelings she'd tried to explain.

"*Chérie*, I think I understand. Now, you must trust me and allow me to help you. It is my duty as your husband to give you pleasure. Let me show you. Just me and me together, loving each other—that is all this is. No more worries or fears about anything. I wouldn't want you except just as you are. You are perfect, and have always been perfect to me."

"I do...trust you."

That was all he needed to go forward, and the next minutes were spent doing just that—trusting.

He urged her legs apart and slid two fingers between her thighs, up against the folds of her quim, now slick from the seed he'd spilled in her before. She gasped and jerked when he first touched her but seemed to accept the sensation once he started stoking the swell of her clit in a circular motion. She looked so beautiful submitting to him it was hard not to bury his cock deep into her again. He knew he needed to wait and give her this pleasuring first, but his beastly desires were raging nearly out of control.

"Just feel, *chérie*. Feel, and let the pleasure embrace you, let it take you over the edge."

In moments she was breathing heavy and panting his name. She rocked her hips and arched her back, thrusting her breasts closer to his lips. He took the beauteous offering and sucked on a dark pink nipple, loving the sound of her pleasured moan. Graham didn't stop working her slippery nub, pushing her closer toward a satisfying end.

Imogene's breath grew short, "I—I do feel something—"

He kept her going, in complete awe of her beauty and the sight of her body being overtaken and ruled by pleasure. Fulfilment that he gave to her. Her hands gripped his hair, anchoring him to her as she grew closer to her peak. Graham relished the power of giving her this first taste.

She cried out his name at the end, clenching her lovely tight cunt around his fingers. It was a beautiful thing to witness.

When she could speak, Imogene stared up at him, wonderment glowing in her expression. "Is that what it feels like for you?" Her brown eyes glittered with a passion and knowing that had not been there before.

"It would appear so, my beautiful lover…*mon bel amoureuse*. You are a priceless jewel; do you know that? Your pleasure is my pleasure, and my happiness is now totally complete."

Settling in next to her, he had a vision. It flashed forward many years. It was him doing this very thing—slipping under the covers with Imogene already there, waiting for him. A simple act, but powerful in its meaning to him. He felt guilty, like he did not deserve to be this happy. As he pulled her to him, he stroked her cheek with the back of his hand. "I love you so much…these words are not enough for what I am feeling right now. They cannot possibly do justice to this experience with you."

Imogene moved her hand over his body slowly. "I had no idea…no idea that it would be like this." Her hand traced his face and then his neck. She explored his chest and shoulder, moving down his arm to his waist, and across his ribs to his stomach, over the trail of dark hair that dipped down to his cock.

She appeared fascinated by his body. Her skin was so smooth and soft, so different from him.

"You are beautiful, Graham," she breathed. "You are magnificently made—"

He cut off her words with a deep, hard kiss. Imogene's open admiration of his body had inflamed him beyond his ability to rein in the desire for more.

He plunged his tongue into her mouth, taking her hands and pinning them to the bed before burying his cock into his beautiful wife for a second time.

And he didn't stop until she'd shouted out evidence of a second pleasuring…

They drifted into a half-sleep of contentment, just two lovers tangled in bed together when he asked, "How do you feel, *chérie*? How are you, right now?" He hoped she would tell him.

It was a moment before she answered. "Filled-up, possessed, loved…warm inside, so warm."

Her lovely words moved him. Pulling her up against his chest, feeling her breasts and skin meld with his, he was utterly gratified. "You warm me, Imogene. With you in my arms, I'll never be cold again, not in the whole of my life." He closed his eyes to sleep in the embrace of his beloved.

She murmured drowsily as she drifted, "I know. Nothing could ever come between us…"

His eyes snapped open.

The whisper of dread wafted past and brushed against the cocoon of peace that enfolded them.

No. Nothing will. I'll never let that happen.

Chapter 10

That I make poetry and give pleasure (if I give pleasure) are because of you.

Horace - Roman poet ~ Odes, 50 BC

Imogene woke. The room was darker now for the candles guttered low. Fire embers glowed in the hearth. Her husband slept next to her. *My husband.* Watching him sleep, she thought he looked younger, serene, and peaceful in his slumber. No trace of the burdens of daily life he must carry.

Thinking about their love making made her shiver, the images too new and erotic to actually picture in her mind. She had to admit his passionate demands surprised her, being both dominating and needful all at once. Graham's typical manner with her was usually easy and obliging, so experiencing this fervid, insistent side of him was an unexpected revelation.

It didn't frighten her, though. She felt secure in his love, and somehow understood his primal need for her. Aunt Wilton had explained it, saying he would take great pleasure in her. Thus Imogene was enlightened as to the power that her acquiescence would ultimately give her. It was an ancient understanding, a 'riddle' that women have solved about their men; the covenant between husband and wife.

Graham had certainly loved her thoroughly, his experience in these matters clearly evident. That thought produced a frown. Imogene didn't want to think too much on the idea of other women being with him, but she was pragmatic for all of her sensitivity; she knew that there must have been others. He was close to thirty years and had lived in Paris, as a painter. *Artists' models perhaps?*

She thought back on her aunt's advice that it need not be dreadful and giggled. *Definitely not dreadful!*

"Something amuses you, *chérie*? Pray tell, please share."

"Oh, I did not know you had awakened. Did I disturb you, my lover?" she asked with another giggle.

"Oh yes, you disturb me greatly. In my dreams you are cavorting about and producing for me the utmost of disturbances, for weeks and weeks now. What shall I do about it? Hmmm?" Reaching playfully, he tickled her.

Imogene shrieked from his tickling. "I never cavort about, sir! You must have me mistaken for another!"

"No." Graham frowned and wagged his finger at her. "I am positive it was you, and most definite about the cavorting."

"You cast aspersions to my character rather freely, do you not? What have you to say for yourself, sir?"

"It is an interesting question you ask of me. The thing is, I would much rather show you, than say for myself." He pulled her to him and pressed his hard cock against her hip, his message clear.

"Again?" she gasped.

"Oh yes, again. I cannot get enough of you." Graham

captured her mouth, took her face in one of his hands, holding her captive as he descended on her lips. "I need to be this close to you."

This time when he slid his cock inside her she welcomed the hard length of him filling her. It went faster, the feelings more intense, masterful. His domination of her was loving, but total.

He kissed her breasts and told her of his love as he moved, worshipping; adoring her body with his body. Telling her what she was doing for him and how wonderful her cunny felt wrapped tight around his cock. Scandalous words whispered in the heat of passion.

Graham's passionate need of her was still very new and almost frenzied in its expression. Imogene was completely in his power and feared she would lose herself entirely, in a spark of flame, as it ignited, burned and consumed her.

He consumes me, but it does feel divine to give myself to him in this way. He needs me.

Imogene fell asleep for the second time with this thought in her mind.

GRAHAM left her sleeping, looking like a goddess in the sheets. He thought she might need some time, some privacy for herself, so he removed himself quietly from the bed. To leave her, even for a moment, was unthinkable, but he did it anyway.

WAKING came slowly, until the morning sun had broken through the shades. Imogene became aware of her surroundings and blushed at the memories of the previous night. She stretched and turned, finding she was alone. Upon the pillow next to her was a note, and upon that, a hothouse rose. The outside was addressed to 'Mrs. Everley,' the handwriting his familiar script.

Imogene,

I hope you are well this morning and feeling somewhat rested. I went out to secure horses for our journey today onto Gavandon. I am anxious to present my beautiful bride as the new mistress of our home. The business that needed attending to is of a tedious nature and you were sleeping so soundly, looking so peaceful, I could not bear to wake you, even though, selfishly, I did contemplate the notion. Our first night together is a precious memory I will hold dear until the end of my life. Look to the breakfast tray, chérie, *and you will find a trinket, a love token if you will, from your adoring husband.*

G

Imogene pressed the letter to her chest as if to absorb some of him from it. She rose from the bed and found her gown still lying on the floor from last night. Heat filled her again from the memories it evoked. She donned it and located one of the gorgeous silk brocade wrappers that she had ordered in London, to wear over it. In truth, she did ache a little, but it was not bad. Graham had been so careful with her, considerate, solicitous even. She recalled how he had insisted upon allowing him to soothe her with a cool cloth last night, and blushed deeply again.

Don't bother yourself about being shy with him now for he's seen all of you and you of him.

Shivering at the thought, she went about her morning

ablutions.

When she went into the adjoining sitting room she saw upon the table a tray laden with their breakfast, and coffee and tea laid out. Peering down at the tray, she found a black jewellers' box. Imogene took in a breath at the sight of the 'trinket' inside. It was a pendant on a blue velvet ribbon. A puffed heart of gold, heavily engraved, rimmed with tiny pearls. On the back was the inscription: *I, You hold my heart, G.*

Imogene tied the ribbon around her neck, her hands shaking just a little. She put her fingers over the heart pendant and held them there. Feeling loved and cherished by her husband, she sat in the sitting room, sipping her tea, lost in thought, emotions welling up again and nearly causing her to weep.

"Ah, the beauty has awakened from her slumber." She heard his voice before she felt his strong arms wrap around her from behind. Lips grazed her neck, kissing below her ear. "Good morning, my lady. Does the trinket please you?"

"Oh, Graham." She reached a hand back and touched the side of his head. "It is so beautiful and precious to me, as are you. I will cherish it forever. You spoil me. But truly, it is hardly a trinket."

"On the contrary, *chérie.* Your beauty outshines that trinket a hundredfold. I fear you are not spoilt yet, just prone to a little reckless cavorting about in my dreams. I was blessed with the most satisfying dreams last night—probably the best I have ever known. And I can assure you there was a *great deal* of reckless cavorting involved."

"Ha, you devil!" She spun and leapt up from her chair, facing him. "If I am prone to reckless cavorting, the fault is all yours for imagining me as a cavorter in your dreams. The next time you find me there, cavorting recklessly that is, I hope I am wearing this pendant." She patted the heart lovingly with her fingers.

"Point taken, Mrs. Everley." He gathered her into his arms. "You are wise beyond your years, and quite onto me I fear." Graham kissed her deeply before pulling back to seek her eyes. His teasing put aside, eyes fiery with emotion, he whispered, "I love you, and thank you, for last night."

"As I love you, and it was my sincerest pleasure, my husband." She felt herself flush.

"Still blushing prettily I see." He stroked over her cheek. "Are you truly well this morning, Imogene? I was not too…demanding? If I was, I am deeply sorry. You create such a need inside me, to possess you, and to love you that I simply lose my self-control. On my honor, I will strive to be more of a gentleman in the future."

Imogene opened her mouth to speak, then closed it again as she composed the words to say to him.

"My questions have struck you dumb, I see." He frowned. "Not a good sign—"

She shushed him with fingers to his lips. "Stop. You are blabbering," she said very softly. "There is to be none of that. No more talk of offending me with your, ah, passionate ways. I am perfectly well and happy this morning." She tipped her finger at him. "I absolutely will not hear any talk of you striving to be *more* of a gentleman. Understand that you made everything perfect for me. Truly you did. And one more thing, my stormy lover," her voice lowering, "I love you, just the way you were last night, and the way you are right now."

Graham's beaming smile in response to her little speech reminded her of a schoolboy receiving praise from the headmistress.

"Will you join me for breakfast? May I offer you some

tea or coffee?" she asked him.

"Are you in need of sustenance, my love? I know I kept you quite occupied until late into the evening." He arched his brows.

"Yes, actually, I am quite famished."

"May I feed *you* morsels then? What foods would please you best?" He swept his hand over the table.

"You are very light-hearted this morning, husband. I thought your intentions were to get organized and moving along toward reaching Gavandon. Anxious to present the new mistress and all that? Am I mistaken in this, sir?" she questioned, archly.

"Thank God I wedded you, Mrs. Everley. You are the epitome of efficiency and organization. And a more beautiful task master could not be found anywhere, I am sure. Well done, my love." He reached for her again. "You are just what I needed in a partner because I am so easily distracted, you see." He teased, playfully kissing down her neck and shoulders.

"Really, my darling," she said with a mock sigh, "joviality abounding at every turn? Who would have thought it? The somber Lord Rothvale teasing and joking at all hours of the day and night. Hardly possible most would declare. Why, I daresay people would think you quite unhinged in your present state." She loved teasing him.

He touched the tip of her nose. "Of that I have no doubt, *chérie*, so it is good they cannot see me now." Sitting down, he pulled her onto his lap sideways, clasping his hands to hold her. "*Chérie*, please oblige me and let me tell you a little story, a fairy tale really. Will you hear it?"

"Yes, please."

"Are you comfortable before I begin? Would you like to

have your tea? A bun? Toast?"

"No more dallying, please. You've promised me a story, and now you must deliver."

"Very well…"

Once upon a time, there was a man, not so young, but regardless, came to be under a terrible curse. He was turned into a dreadful, ugly toad and found himself in a land of fools and leeches. The toad was lonely and unhappy and could not see how he would ever escape from his misery. His particular curse required a beautiful princess to love him without pretense and see through all of his toadiness underneath to the real man, and into his true heart.

Luckily, for this particular toad, he came to the notice of the most beautiful princess in all the land. She was not only beautiful, but also the wisest and kindest and bravest princess as well. Giving freely and generously of her kindly nature she accepted the toad as he was. The toad was desperate for the princess to love him, not because she would release him from his curse, but only because he loved her most ardently, and could not imagine life, any life, in any form, without her love in return.

The toad persisted valiantly to win the princess and made many mistakes along the way.

He embarrassed and pestered the princess, with his inappropriate, toad-like behaviours. He was a complete and incomprehensible idiot in love, subjecting himself to the amusement of others, but he never gave up trying to win her. Finally, one day, his joy was complete when the princess declared her love for the toad. The lucky man was restored to his human form, the ugly toad exterior gone forever.

As the man and the beautiful princess were married, he made a vow to himself that he would appreciate the blessings this life had bestowed upon him and to take joy in the things, great and small, that graced his life. He would pledge to spend his life loving the beautiful princess and her happiness would be all he would ever need to make his own complete.

Imogene had become very still during his story, her heart

filling with emotion. Unable to speak, she peered into his eyes as a big tear spilled down her face.

Graham took her face lovingly in his hands and kissed away every tear. He held her on his lap for a long time, their foreheads resting together. The emotion of the moment washed over her like a waterfall. He kissed her heart pendant where it lay in the hollow of her throat, whispering, "You do hold my heart."

"And mine," she whispered back.

A moment later, he asked, "Did you like the story?"

Imogene could hardly speak an answer. "I declare it is my favourite story, the best I have ever heard. I wish it was written down so I could read it over and over again and never forget the beautiful words."

"YOUR eyes…I get so lost into your eyes, Graham, and I always have. From the very first time I looked into them. I do love you so very much."

Graham held her, reflecting on the utter contentment at her profession of her love for him. He just wanted to revel in the sensation of knowing she loved him. He couldn't speak; he was afraid even, because now that he had experienced her love for him, he knew irrevocably, that if he ever lost it, or her, his life would be worth nothing.

But she wasn't done with her speech. "My darling, I am afraid you have married an emotional creature, given to fits of crying and laughter in an instant with all sorts of sensitivities mixed in. Try not to make too much of it though. We ladies are made thus, so as to complement the opposite extreme of impassiveness in the masculine character and," pausing, she looked at him in question, "you do realize that I am teasing you right now? The story you've just lovingly told to me being as far removed from impassiveness as anything could possib—"

He silenced her with a thorough kiss. "I know exactly whom I've married, and right now I fear I need you to complement *my* masculine character."

Murmuring the words to her, his hands and lips roamed freely. He untied her wrapper, pushing the silk off her shoulders so it slipped down all the way, her fine skin and breasts uncovered for his pleasure. Graham already understood Imogene's power over him and it was a potent drug.

He got quiet, tracing his fingers reverently over her breasts, circling the dark pink nipples that begged for his mouth. "These are so stunning, as I knew they would be," he told her.

"Well, I am relieved that you find them to your liking," she said softly.

"No. It is not just that." He sighed deeply before trying to explain. "It is that your body is so beautiful, and you are so generous and giving of yourself, and that you love *me* and want to give yourself to *me*. I can't even explain all that I feel. There are not words to express it." His eyes left her breasts and came to her eyes. "I want to show you, again. What say you, most beautiful princess of all the land?"

"I say yes, but you must allow me something first."

"What is your wish, *chérie*?"

"Stay very still." He felt her hands come behind his head to remove the tie holding his hair back. When it came away in her hand she brought his hair forward, to just behind his ears. He had to close his eyes for the feel of it. "Perfect," was the only word she spoke.

Graham was on his feet in an instant carrying her out of the sitting room, returning her to the bed. Clothes were stripped off frantically, as fast as he could manage. Imogene lay back and watched him. Her body was stunning, as real to being a princess as it was possible for her to be in his mind. She reached out her arms for him to come to her on the bed.

She gives me all of herself, every part, her body, her heart, her love.

He knelt on the bed and pulled her onto his thighs, holding her firmly. "I want to try it this way."

Her eyes flared wide and her breathing grew deep as she comprehended his words. Her surrender to his desires turned his blood to boiling in an instant. The need to possess her and take her was nearly uncontainable. He wanted to fuck her wildly, in every way possible, teach her everything there was to know about carnal pleasures all at once.

She was willing in his arms when he spread her wide and straddled her over his cock, guiding her downward and onto him. Her tight cunt sheathed his cock in burning heat all the way to his bollocks. She felt so good. He sucked on her nipples as he lifted her up and down on his length, slowly, dragging out the pleasure for both of them, taking her carefully, building the fire toward a climax in increments.

Imogene moaned and sighed and circled her hips against his movements.

Never had a fucking felt like this.

Because this wasn't just a fuck. It was making love for the first time in his life. He'd never loved a woman he'd bedded. Not before last night. Everything was different now. He'd been captured. His woeful heart had been captured by the beauteous creature in his arms.

How blessed was he.

"YOU never intended for us to start off for Gavandon today, did you? You planned to keep me captive here and ravish me. Do not deny it, sir, I know you did. You planned everything, the letter, the pendant, the fairy tale. Everything. And in doing so, secured my acquiescence with no trouble at all."

"Ah…yes, most definitely to ravish. I figured I should at least try to do a proper ravishment of you. Did I succeed?"

"I believe you did."

"Mrs. Everley, you are in possession of a most savage and brilliant wit, and it is with every trick and influence at my disposal that I try to meet the challenge of directing you without you knowing it. I can see now, that I have failed miserably in this. My plans exposed by your very clever deciphering of them." He smiled at her.

She laughed at him.

"Now I am remembering that last night you woke me with giggling and you failed to share the cause. Will you share it now? What made you laugh, *chérie*? I'll be miserable if you do not tell me."

"I was merely reflecting upon a conversation that Aunt Wilton had with me a few days before the wedding."

"Please continue."

"She wanted to prepare me for the demands that you would claim in the marriage bed. She told me that because it was evident you loved me, you would certainly be kind and gentle. She said I must not shirk away from my duty, and if I were to come to you willingly it would not be dreadful if done in the right attitude. She also said that I should expect you to be, ah…enthusiastic in claiming me."

"And you found that cause to laugh?" He frowned. *Dreadful? Surely not.*

She looked very naughtily at him. "I must say, my aunt was correct. I do not find it dreadful at all. On the contrary, I find it to be…just the opposite."

Graham thought that he must really appreciate Lady Wilton for the wise woman she was; mentally adding her to his list of most favoured persons in all the world. Sighing ruefully, he told her, "You do know, that when you say such things to me, looking like you do right now, that I am quite helpless to keep away from you."

She nodded slowly. "I know."

"You are a witch, my lady, a very beautiful and corporeal witch, who has me utterly under her spell. You seem to delight in vexation, but please, I implore you," he mocked, "do not turn me into a toad again."

"Oh, no, no, no, no, no," Imogene assured him, reaching a hand down his body and putting her small hand over his lengthening cock. "Never fear, my love. That will not come to pass as I need you in your *human* form, in *all* its glorious dimensions. I simply cannot—I cannot have a toad in my bed

She said it deliberately, her eyes dark and suggestive.

Graham was lost to the mysterious beauty that was his Imogene.

Utterly lost.

Chapter 11

To be totally understanding makes one very indulgent.

Mme de Staël ~ Corinne, 1807

"The master has sent these for you, Lady Rothvale." Hester handed her a velvet box with a folded note.

Chérie,

I understand you intend to wear a jonquil yellow gown this evening out. Please accept this item for dressing your hair. I think it would complement your mamma's pearls spectacularly. This tiara actually belonged to my grandmother just as your choker came to your mamma through her mother. Both pieces are older but created around the same time and should blend beautifully with the colour of your gown. I cannot wait to see you in them together. You will look just like the princess you are to me. I shall await you in the drawing room.

G

So, Hester dressed Imogene's hair for her and arranged

the tiara amid her up pinned curls.

Jonquil-yellow, currently at the height of fashion for the season, was indeed the perfect backdrop for her diamond and pearl choker, sitting just at the hollow of her throat. Long white gloves completed her ensemble for their formal evening.

Imogene was already learning of her husband's wishes to see her arranged artistically for his pleasure. Graham didn't make a great deal of requests of her, besides in bed, but he did seem to very much appreciate her willingness to indulge him in regards to her clothing and jewellery. He appeared to derive great pleasure from being granted these small kinds of requests, and since she loved him so much, and because he was always so good to her, Imogene gave him what he'd asked for.

AS she entered the drawing room, Imogene paused near the doorway.

Graham stood at her approach, loving the moment, assessing if his assumptions were correct in arranging her jewels and dress tonight. To others it might seem controlling, if they were even aware of it, but for him it was pure enjoyment to observe her beauty combined with objects of art. She would still be beautiful even if dressed in rags, but since he was artistically inclined and appreciated beauty in all forms, it gave him great pleasure to see her adorned in a way that he felt was her due. He directed with his finger that she should do a turn for him. Smiling, she obliged, completing her circle with a flourish.

"Perfection as always, my princess," he whispered, taking first one hand and then the other, kissing her palms. "Shall we?" He offered his arm. Once inside the carriage, he retreated back to thoughtful gazing.

"On what are you pondering now?" she asked.

"I am thinking of how beauteous you look and of all the ogling eyes that shall be trained upon you, of all of the grasping idiots who shall wish an introduction to you, and of having to share you tonight."

"That is very good information to have," she teased gently with a touch to his arm. "Graham, behave yourself tonight. Do not insult anybody on my account because you are jealous."

"A perfect gentleman I will be. On my honor, I will conduct myself with restraint." Taking her hand from his arm, he brought it to his lips. "At least…until later," he said wickedly, bestowing a gentle bite of his teeth upon her skin.

IMOGENE stood in the room waiting for Hester to come and help her undress after their evening out. She heard the door open, then soft footsteps.

The hands that reached for her were not Hester's, though. "I am to be your lady's maid this evening," he whispered into her ear. "Something I have long desired to do."

"How long has that been your goal, sir?"

"Honestly? Since the night of the Kenilbrooke ball."

"Such lecherous thoughts, Lord Rothvale, and upon the very same day as you laid eyes upon me. Shocking!"

"Guilty as charged," he breathed behind her, "but I have kept my word from earlier, when we were inside the carriage; I was a gentleman tonight, managing to fight through the throngs of grasping idiots trying to reach you. Nobody was harmed in word or deed, and now, I believe it is time for me to collect my reward."

"I see," she said, playing along. "As this is your first time acting as my maid, should you need any kind of instruction from me?"

"Please, *chérie*, that would be very helpful." He kissed the back of her neck. "But before we begin, I should like you here, standing before the mirror, and myself standing behind you," he told her as he arranged them both according to his wishes. "Now we are ready. What is the first step?" He faced and spoke to her into the mirror.

Imogene felt sensual heat fill her at the sight of him in the glass. Wearing only his trousers, his beautiful shirtless chest and unbound hair made speech nearly impossible. "F-first you m-must remove my jewels and return them to their c-cases."

In a low voice, Graham replied, "We shall be passing over that step. What is next?"

"You must remove my gown, being careful not to damage any of the fastenings for they are very delicate."

Graham pecked carefully at the fastenings one by one, seeming to grow frustrated by the stubbornness of some, and pulling a little too vigorously on others until a ravaged button ripped from its place and fell, bouncing and tapping along the floor. The sound of it garishly loud for such a small button. Looking up sheepishly, he spoke into the mirror again, "Whoops?"

Imogene burst out with a giggle, impossible to suppress, but controlled it quickly with a hand to her mouth. "Now you must help me out of it and carefully set it aside for repair."

Graham pushed the yellow silk down, off her shoulders slowly, feeling her body deliberately as he pressed the gown down lower and lower until it bunched at her knees. Bending, he held her hand for balance, aiding her in stepping out of it.

Gathering up the gown rather carelessly, he tossed it onto a chair, brushing his hands off for dramatic effect.

"My waist petticoat," she told him.

He tugged on the waist tie rather forcefully, causing her body to move along with his efforts. The petticoat fell in a heap, and again he assisted her in stepping out before gathering it up and pitching it over his shoulder. "This is going rather well, I think," he remarked into the mirror.

"My slippers will go next."

"Ah, yes, but we will skip that step as well, *chérie.*" Graham shook his head.

"I see, so I take it that since you will not be removing my slippers, then what of my stockings?"

He looked directly into her eyes in the mirror. "They will remain on."

Imogene swallowed. "My stays."

Deft fingers pulled the laces undone quite easily, his skill reminding her that he did have experience with ladies' undergarments, or in the removal of them at least. Imogene did not like pondering the idea.

She felt her stomach dip when he pulled the corset away, dropping it to the floor with a thud. "Next?"

"My hair should come down now."

She felt his breath falling on her neck, and then his deep inhale as he breathed in the lavender she used on her hair. "No. I shall leave it for now as it is. What is left?" His eyes lifted to look into the mirror yet again, with the intent to see her response.

Imogene was quickly losing her control, so arousing was this little dance he led her, but she drew in her strength and said boldly, "You must take away my shift and replace it with a nightdress."

He nodded thoughtfully. "Although a nightdress will not be needed, I have just the thing. It shall do very well." Imogene held her breath as he lifted the hem of her shift and pulled it up carefully over her body, gently over her hair, until it was gone. She stood bare before him, with the exception of stockings, slippers and her jewels.

Graham had turned away now, reaching for something on the back of the settee. It was her shawl. He returned to drape it upon her. She stood with one of her legs forward, her weight rested upon one hip. Graham moved her arms straight out at her sides where he laid the shawl over, swathing it in a drape across her back. Lastly, he brought her arms down to her sides with elbows slightly bent. Stepping back, he left her alone to view his creation.

Standing before him in only her jewels, her stockings, and her shawl, Imogene saw Graham's eyes go dark and sparkly.

"Let me look at you; indulge me," he whispered as he began to circle her. "I have to capture this particular image in my mind—it is very special, very special indeed."

Graham reminded her of a wolf, circling her right now. She felt the heat of his gaze and his whispered words, letting the sensations wrap around her. Power, lust, anticipation, control—Imogene felt all of those things.

After what seemed like an age of time, Graham swept her up, setting her upon the very edge of the bed, wolfish eyes drinking in more of the view. She started backing up, using her hands, not knowing why, just continuing to crawl backward until reaching the headboard and unable to go any farther. His eyes locked onto her wildly, head tilted—the wolf again. The air expelled through his teeth sounded like a soft growl.

Leaning in, he took hold of one perfect, stockinged,

slippered ankle in each hand, and swiftly pulled her right back to him, again to the very edge of the bed. His message clear—no escape—the wolf *would* have her.

And it was good, for escape was not her goal, to be captured by her wolf was…

He slid his hands up from her ankles and pressed one to the inside of each of her knees. Imogene knew what he was going to do and the anticipation made her swoon. The idea that she was on the bed already relieved her, for her ability to stand up for him on display had long passed.

It didn't matter.

Graham wanted her exactly where he'd put her. He wrenched her legs apart firmly, opening her up for taking his cock inside of her body again. She gasped at the thought.

She saw his eyes flare at the sight of her spread sex, his hands working at his breeches, tearing them open to free his cock. It sprang out fully hard and erect, pulsing and ready.

Graham didn't speak words. He didn't need to. His intent was very clear, and would end only when he'd reached his release and spilled his seed deep inside her. This would be after he made her fall apart with pleasure first. He was so good at pleasuring. So good.

Imogene was spellbound as she watched him put himself inside her. He did it slowly, with precision and total control, watching right along with her as his hard, hot cock burrowed into her cunny inch by inch.

The carnal sight of their intimacy, combined with the intense feelings of pleasure as he filled her up, quickly reduced her to incoherent. Nothing more existed in the universe than him and her striving toward the beauty of fulfilment, and that perfect instant in time before it blasted a body to the heavens, and back again.

Imogene put herself into her husband's capable hands and let him take her there.

Which he did with skillful attention.

Graham's big hands gripped her hips hard as he sank his cock into her over and over in long, gliding strokes, his hair whipping back and forth from his harsh movements.

"Look at me," he demanded as he thrust into her harder. "Look into my eyes, Imogene. Feel me in you. Know how beautiful you are to me when you give yourself like this. Feel how much I love you."

"I love youuuuu!" she shouted as she crashed over the precipice of a shearing climax, utterly lost to the fiery pleasure, and to the love she felt from Graham.

FACING his beauty in the bed after that explosive love-making, Graham was quiet. He didn't really have any words that needed saying at the moment. No words he could speak out loud in any case.

He'd just indulged in a fantasy fucking with his princess. He loved his princess with all of his heart, but *had* most definitely fucked her soundly just now. And the miraculous part was she hadn't seemed horrified or put out by his demands, either. She'd taken every bit of it and given back to him passionately. He did wonder why she'd crawled away from him right before he took her, though. The small sliver of doubt was replaced with the impression she'd been playing, and not really trying to get away from him at all. How in the hell could he ask her a question like that? Impossible. So, he just admired her beauty instead, and counted his blessings.

She held him in a spell of enchantment. This was his best

explanation of what Imogene was to him.

Eventually she broke the silence. "Although inspirational, these jewels were never intended to produce comfort while sleeping, I am sure."

He chuckled at her wry joke. "I agree. Though they served their purpose admirably, let me relieve you of them now." Carefully opening the choker's clasp, he lifted it away from her neck before fishing the tiara out of her tumbling locks, setting both pieces onto the bedside table. He stroked her luxurious hair, removing all the many pins until it flowed out free. "Thank you for indulging me my vision. I love you so much…*Je t'aime tellement.* You are a wonderment to me, Imogene. I shall have to work very hard to come up with new ways to show you how much I do love you."

"Do not work too hard, my darling, you are in top form already. Also, your skills as a lady's maid run to the profound, so you may always fall back on them."

Pulling her to him possessively, he murmured into her hair, "You are the only lady that shall ever benefit from my…skills."

"Tell me what you were thinking about just a moment ago, Graham."

"I am wondering how I managed to live without you for so many years." Again she surprised him with her keen sense of perception. She suspected he was self-doubting. Imogene could read him like an open book.

When she smiled softly and reached up to tuck his hair behind his ear he gained the courage to ask her.

"Why did you back away from me, *chérie*?"

"I do not know." Her lashes fluttered. "I—I wanted you to capture me."

I was right. "If you only knew how much I loved every

minute of capturing you, *chérie*."

She gave him a naughty wink. "I cannot wait to see the look upon Hester's face when she sees the destruction you have wrecked upon my clothing and this room."

He immediately began to tickle her. "You are quite the trickster, *chérie*, always thinking of some humorous bedevilment. Now be a good girl," he teased, tickling her some more.

Shrieking and laughing, she tried to wriggle away. "I will be good! I will be a good girl for you," she shouted before clapping her hands to her mouth, mortified at the noise. "Oh Lord, the servants. What will they think of me? Of us?"

"It does not matter what they think. Besides, you are so endearing to everybody; nothing would ever cause you to receive their disdain."

"I'm pleased to see I've blinded you to my faults."

"You have faults?" he teased. "How is that possible, *chérie*?"

"Mmmm, a great many faults I am afraid."

"Highly unlikely," he murmured.

Graham continued to watch his wife for a time. Not quite believing his great fortune in securing her love and awakening her passionate nature, unable to comprehend how he had found her, but so very grateful nonetheless.

Chapter 12

Knock off the chains
Of heart-debasing slavery; give to man,
Of every colour and of every clime,
Freedom, which stamps him image of his God.

James Grainger ~ The Sugar Cane, 1764

The miles of road between London and Gavandon were swallowed up by the coach as Imogene watched Graham dozing in the seat across from her. They had been married barely a fortnight. Much of that time spent in the master's suite of Brentwood. Emerging from their passionate lair, they had, on occasion, ventured out to the opera, and once to the theatre in the evenings. They had managed to ingest some of their dinners while staring at one another over their plates. One Sunday they had even attended church at St. Martin-in-the-Fields, and reminisced about their wedding day. An entire day had even been given up to stroll through The British Museum, arm-in-arm, viewing the recently acquired Elgin Marbles, or Parthenon Marbles as they were also known. The carved bodies were stunning in execution, but it was also disconcerting to see such beautiful and ancient works of art cut apart and lying on the floors. Both of them had to wonder as to the correctness of taking the marble masterpieces from their native Greece.

The journey over winter-ravaged roads was definitely no leisure spree. But last night—last night had been very pleasant. Imogene smiled, remembering their stay at the inn.

They stopped their travelling for a night of rest at The Lion's Crown, a fine establishment that Graham said he had used many times. He'd notified the proprietor in advance to prepare for their arrival, and who greeted them personally at the entrance.

"Lord Rothvale." He bowed. "The Lion welcomes you and your lady."

"Ah, Jacobson, hello. Your place is a welcome sight after the inside of a carriage on these blasted roads." He turned to Imogene. "Allow me to introduce Mr. Jacobson, the proprietor of this excellent establishment, and the most devilishly talented of cooks as you shall see." He winked at her. "Jacobson, my bride, Imogene, Lady Rothvale."

Mr. Jacobson was younger than Imogene expected him to be for a proprietor of such an establishment.

Smiling at her with kind, dark eyes, he bowed again in welcome. "Lord and Lady Rothvale, congratulations upon the occasion of your marriage, and may I say, you honor us here at The Lion."

"Thank you for your gracious welcome, Mr. Jacobson. My husband assures me he wouldn't consider staying at any other establishment aside from yours while travelling this way."

Jacobson flashed a quick look toward Graham before tilting his head in acknowledgement. "We are ever here to serve you, my lady."

"See there? In the space of just a few words and a smile, my wife has secured another admirer," Graham teased good naturedly. "I am constantly amazed at how easy these things are for her to accomplish."

Mr. Jacobson laughed in easy conversation as he showed them inside.

Once settled into their room, they gratefully sat down to a lovely dinner of venison and potatoes, and the most delicious bread Imogene had ever tasted. "Mr. Jacobson is indeed a talented cook. I should like to have his recipe for this bread. Do you think you might get it out of him?" Imogene asked.

"I'll look into it for you, *chérie*." His eyes twinkled at her. "You enchant people without even realizing it."

"You enchant me, and I am fairly sure you are well aware of it," she answered.

After the wonderful meal, while readying themselves for bed, Imogene thought Graham looked a trifle mischievous and sneaky standing there in his robe, like butter wouldn't melt in his mouth.

"What are you up to, husband?"

"Nothing really." He tapped the book he held in his hand, grinning.

"What have you planned? With you, there is always some sort of concocted plan."

"I thought I might read to you for an hour or so." His answer surprised her.

"How lovely. And what shall my ears be attending to?"

"Oh, just a volume of verses I stumbled upon." He shrugged. "Let's see," he said, making a show of reading the cover, "it is entitled 'Childe Harold's Pilgrimage,' and by a poet, perhaps you've heard of him? He is called Lord Byron."

"No! You got a copy of Byron's latest book? How on earth? It sold out immediately and nobody can buy a copy."

"I did indeed, and it was not easy. I procured it in Town

for the sole purpose of entertaining you upon this trip, that is, if it will not offend."

"I am sure my sensibilities can handle it. I like a challenge, remember?"

"I never forget it, *chérie.* But if the words are anything like the man, you should brace yourself to be in the least, shocked. He does nothing in half-measures."

"You know him?" she asked incredulously. "You know Lord Bryon!"

"Well, yes. I have had occasion to meet him through the connection of another. And he was also at Cambridge while I was still at my studies.

"What is he like? I have wondered if there is a possible connection in our families because we share a surname."

"Yes. I've speculated the same. About Byron I can tell you he is a conflicted person, delving into all manner of outrageous behaviours publically, which probably will be his downfall one day. But, that aside, the man *can* write a poem." Graham helped to settle her into bed next to him, fished out his glasses, put them on and began to read…

Adieu, adieu! my native shore
Fades o'er the waters blue.

Imogene loved the sound of Graham's intonation as he read aloud. She soaked up the image of him reading to her as the pages turned one by one, the beautiful words falling from his lips. As he read another part, Graham's eyes grew wider. "Incredible! He is referring to the Elgin Marbles. Listen to this stanza."

Dull is the eye that will not weep to see
Thy wall defaced, thy mouldering shrines removed
By British hands, which it had best behoved…
…And snatch'd thy shrinking gods to northern climes abhorred!

"It seems as if Byron did not care for their removal any more than we did." Graham continued his melodious reading and Imogene relished it, every word…

On with the dance! let joy be unconfined;
No sleep till morn, when Youth and Pleasure meet
To chase the glowing Hours with flying feet.

…He stopped reading then, and looked over for her reaction.

She couldn't help staring at him. "You are quite a contradiction of images right now, my husband," she said dreamily.

"How so?"

"Well, on the one part you look like an Adonis with your hair loosed and your skin showing with your robe open, just here." She touched her own chest evocatively in the place she indicated. "And on the other part, you have the look of a brilliant professor pouring over your book with your reading glasses and your dark robe." She whispered at him naughtily, "Professor Adonis."

Graham's pupils dilated and she saw him swallow hard at her teasing. He removed his glasses and gawked at her.

She kept at her merciless teasing, enjoying his reaction immensely.

"Professor Adonis, I beg of you sir to help me. I have need of your… instruction. Can you help me with that last stanza you've just read? You know the part about when 'Youth and Pleasure meet'? What do you imagine the author was trying to convey there? Could you tutor me on it and help me to see it with clarity, Professor Adonis? I *know* you can. You are *so* wise and *so*—"

Graham silenced her with his mouth and the book fell off the bed with a thud. There were other sounds too. Gasping, grappling, giggling, and the swishing of garments.

"Professor Adonis, you naughty man! Ah…your hands…ah…oh my…your hands are *very* wayward. What *is* that, Professor? What is that hard thing you have pressed against me? Do you carry a weapon under your scholars robe, sir? Oh! Professor! I do believe you mean to stab me. Oh dear me, am I in danger?"

"Great, grave danger," the Professor replied hoarsely.

GRAHAM awakened from his sleep in the coach to find his wife observing him and grinning like a devil. "What?"

She giggled. "I was remembering our tutoring session of last night, *Professor.*"

Graham stared at her with such longing, it pained him. He would remember her merry little game of professor and student until he drew his last breath. Imogene had made his life enjoyable again. She alone had accomplished that remarkable feat.

He slowly shook his head back and forth and wagged a finger at her. "Tsk, tsk, my lady. You are a most wicked creature, teasing me when I can do nothing about it while we are in the damn coach. But you know that already, don't you? You are very aware of your effect upon me. My God! Being married to you is going to be so amusing and diverting. I hope you keep me in this state of complete bewitchment for the next fifty years or so."

"But of course, my lord, I intend to take my charge seriously, to keep you so, with the upmost integrity." She blew a kiss at him.

"I have just one word for you, *chérie.*"

"What is the word?"

"Repayment." He rolled it off his tongue with a salacious drawl.

"Fine," she purred. "I'm bored. How about you read me some more out of Byron's book?"

"WE are almost there, truly? I cannot wait to see it—your home." Imogene peered out the window of the coach to see if any landmarks were visible she could ask him about.

"It is your home as well. You are mistress of it even now," he reminded her. "I have a surprise for you. Very soon now. I imagine you will be happy with it, and I can't wait to see your reaction. There you go. Look now," he told her.

Imogene saw rolling pasture, but just on the edge of the road stood a very large boy of about fifteen, an African with black skin. He held the reins of two horses, a lovely brown mare and a dark bay with a white splash.

Imogene shrieked as understanding dawned. "Terra! You have brought my Terra here to Gavandon. And is that Triton with her? Oh, my God. Graham, please stop the carriage. Please!"

He rolled his eyes dramatically. "Of course, all part of the plan," he said, as he rapped on the roof to signal their driver. "I love to see your face when you are happily surprised. It is priceless to me. Triton and Terra are quite taken with each other, you know. When I thought to bring her for you, I found I could not separate the *earth* and the *sea*. Hargreave agreed to let him go. He owed me anyway."

Imogene clutched him in a tight embrace. "Thank you. Thank you for bringing them. You are the most wonderful, generous man. You do make me so happy, every minute. I love you."

Graham assisted her out of the coach, leading her to the horses. "Ben, meet your new mistress," he addressed the groom. "Lady Rothvale is very fond of Terra here, and you must take extra care."

"Yes, my lord," Ben replied. "Lady Rothvale." He bowed to her solemnly.

"Hello, Ben. How is my beautiful girl?" Imogene stroked Terra's neck lovingly.

"She is well, my lady. I have taken special care of her just as the master asked me to," Ben replied, his devotion to the horses evident already.

"Yes, I can see that you have. Well done. She is perfect here in this place."

Imogene looked to Graham with weepy eyes she could not control. "Tears of joy," she whispered to him.

He smiled at her indulgently and offered his arm. "Onward then, Lady Rothvale?"

Once they were settled back into the coach, Graham returned to the contemplative gazing she knew so well, searching her face intently.

"What are you thinking, Graham?"

"Just realizing that I am learning to know your habits. That you get tears when you are most happy, and ironically, it has become the standard for my success. In order to give you the greatest happiness, I must have you in tears."

His answer was lovely but she had questions for him, and wondered if it was proper for her to ask. She hesitated, unsure how to even broach the subject at all.

"Imogene, do you want to ask me something?"

"Do you—is Ben a slave?" She hated even saying the

word.

"Dear God, no! I abhor that institution. Ben and his family are freemen. I sponsored their journey here from Antigua, arranged for their emancipation and papers, and offered them sanctuary and work on the estate. His father tends to the grounds at Gavandon. They are paid for their labour same as everybody. A better family could not be found anywhere. They will be there to greet you today and you will meet the rest of Ben's family."

His answer relieved her, but still, Imogene was struck with how much there was to her husband that was still a great mystery. The idea was daunting when considering she had fallen in love with, and married a man she didn't truly know very well, nor had she known him for very long. What if he had answered in the affirmative to ownership of slaves on his estate? What then? She had no say so in how he conducted his business or in forming his beliefs. If she was honest, it scared her, and filling the role of Lady Rothvale scared her too.

"How did your sponsorship of them come about?"

"Ah, you have not yet met the Reverend and Mrs. Burleigh, my good friends and good people besides. You will soon, and then you'll understand."

"I…love…you." She mouthed the words silently to him because she could not utter them and keep her composure. He tilted his head and gave her an indulgent half smile that spoke volumes.

"And we are here, *chérie,*" Graham announced a little while later as the coach pulled into the gravel drive.

Imogene could say her new home was a countryside vision. Gavandon manor had been beautifully designed. Light stone in an early seventeenth century style but improved upon over the years. Two round towers filled with windows flanked either side of the front which had a rather barbican feel. The massive ancient doors were remarkable in a rustic way. But Imogene felt the formal gardens laid out along the drive and the fountain pool at the front, were even more stunning.

"It looks like a castle," she said.

He tilted his head at her. "Appropriate for the princess to have a castle."

She tried to judge his countenance. He wore an expression of pride she thought. Was it because he had finally taken the first step in fulfilling his duty as heir? Imogene had been raised for such duty and she knew she must not let him down. He had married her, and now it was her responsibility to bear the heirs to carry on his lineage. Many people depended upon her husband for their livelihood. Vowing to do the very best that she possibly could, Imogene wanted to make him proud of her, too.

The workforce had assembled in the front to greet them as they exited the coach. A huge group of people encompassing staff of every portion of the estate, from house, to kitchens, to the gardens and extensive grounds, to stables and the farm fields, and more beyond that she was sure.

Graham addressed the entire group at once. "Your new mistress, Imogene, Lady Rothvale. I bid you to do your duty to her, welcoming and honoring her as you would me."

Several of the members received a personal introduction and a handshake. The steward, Mr. Duncan, who had been with Graham's father before him, she was told, of an age of about five and forty, and very earnest in his greeting. The property manager, Mr. Hendrix, seemed a quiet sort of man of around forty years. Imogene was struck by the kind demeanour of Mrs. Griffin, the housekeeper, and felt they might work well together. Her brother, Mr. Katz, was the head gardener. Ben's father was introduced as the groundskeeper and she could swear she heard Graham say his name was Hiram Everley. She didn't have time to contemplate this as she was introduced to Ben's mother, next. Her name was Antonia, much lighter in her colouring and strikingly beautiful.

Imogene made an express effort to greet the staff, personally, with respect and kindness. There were so many of them, and trying to remember all of the names was a challenge. Graham's valet, Mr. Phelps, the head cook who was introduced simply as 'Cook,' and a slew of others she would probably forget in a few moments. The whole experience was overwhelming for her.

While Graham led her through the line, Imogene was sure she noticed some shocked faces and even heard some gasps. She was not imagining it. It was not disrespectful, their reaction, but not what it should be, either. Not at all. Looking to Graham, she saw the hard set to his jaw, stormy eyes, and a resigned expression. She felt a sense of foreboding. *What is going on here? This is very unseemly. Why are they reacting to me in such a way?*

Graham led her into the foyer of the house first, but then turned back. She heard him say, "Mrs. Griffin, a word please?" She saw him speak quietly but firmly to his housekeeper, and observed the nod of her head in answer, but Imogene couldn't hear their conversation.

While Imogene waited, a lovely brown and white greyhound approached, claws clicking over the marble floor. She dropped down to meet what looked like a friendly dog. "Who are you, lovely girl?"

"Imogene, meet Zulekia."

"Zulekia. What a gorgeous name for a gorgeous dog."

She ran her hand over the dog's short, sleek fur and knew she had made her first new friend at Gavandon.

"She is called Zuly, and is our resident guard dog."

"Is that so?" Imogene asked archly, thinking that Zuly was too sweet natured to be a guard dog.

"No, not really," he joked, "but she is the house pet. Zuly was my mother's dog, and I have to say she seems quite taken with you." Helping her to stand, he then smiled, reassuring her with his eyes. "Imogene, there is one place in particular we must go first before I show you anything of the house. I wish to take you there now, and you will understand." He held out his arm.

"All right." Determined to be brave, she swallowed her nervousness and took his arm.

"Don't be afraid, *chérie*. It is nothing bad, just uncanny. You will see."

Graham brought her through one lovely room after another until finally reaching his destination—the portrait gallery. Without hesitation, he led her over to a giant portrait of a young woman, standing next to a dark horse. "My mother, Isabelle."

Imogene studied the portrait for several moments, taking in the image of a woman with very green eyes, knowing where her husband had gotten his.

Graham watched her, saying nothing.

Imogene looked back and forth between Graham and the portrait of his mother, analyzing and then understanding what she imagined to be the reason behind the odd behaviour of the staff earlier.

She held out her hands to him.

He reached out to take them instantly, bringing both to his lips at the same time.

"She was lovely, your mother. Am I correct in understanding that many people see a resemblance between us?"

He nodded solemnly, still holding her hands to his lips.

"Graham, I do not care for what the servants think, but I do wish to know your thoughts. Before you answer me, I ask most respectfully, that you be completely honest in your answer. I should not like something this important to come between us. And know this…I love you, but I would like the truth only, please."

GRAHAM let her declaration of love wash over him. It was all he really wanted in return, all he really needed. Knowing that *she loved him* was enough.

He led her to a marble bench in the middle of the room, sat down next to her, and took a hold of her hands again. He looked right into her eyes before he spoke. "I do see a resemblance, and I'm sure I saw it right away. My cousins, Jules and Elle, and even Colin, all mentioned it to me. It was evident to them most when they observed you riding. She was an avid rider like you. I give that your colouring and figures are similar, but that is where it ends for me. This portrait of her was done soon after she came to Gavandon as a new bride, years before I was born." He pointed to another portrait, "This is my mother and father, done about six years ago and this is the woman that I remember."

Imogene looked over at the portrait he'd pointed out for her, of his parents outside under a tree. She didn't say anything, just observed quietly.

"When others in the house know you, your similarity will

not strike them so, I am sure. You are so much different in your manner. They will be able to see that when they know you better. It has certainly been so for me. You are not the same person. You share a resemblance—not a body, and not a soul. That you take her place as mistress here, *and* share a likeness is uncanny to be fair, but I like to think it was that likeness that gave me the initial notice of you, helped me to find you. And whatever good fortune or fate or plotting of heavenly parents intervening, I'll accept every bit of it gratefully, if it's what brought us together. I love you, and I know that you are definitely not my mother. You are my Imogene." He took her chin and lifted her lips to his for a kiss, letting her know what he felt. "It gives me joy to bring you here and to install you as my wife, as *my* Lady Rothvale," he whispered against her lips.

She sighed and placed her head on his chest. "I feel a great burden of expectation, Graham. That your staff will compare us and find me lacking. That their scrutiny will surely cause me to stumble, and I fear I'll shame you somehow."

Graham felt guilt stab him. Was he failing her in his vow to protect her already? *Have I?* "No. Never, will you shame me, Imogene. What happened at your introduction just now will not repeat. I charged Mrs. Griffin with the duty of seeing to that particular matter a few minutes ago. Anyone who engages in such familiar behaviour with you again will be dismissed immediately. I promise you, we will weather this. You have been raised a lady, and you will be magnificent I know. I can tell from the very little I have just seen at our entrance. Make them bend to you, in your own approach and tactics. Take charge of what you wish to do as you did with securing Hester. You fancied her for your personal maid and approached her and offered her a place here. You did that all on your own. You can do this. If there are challenges to your authority, well, staff can be replaced, but you cannot."

He stopped talking and kissed her instead, letting his lips do the convincing for once. When he could pull away from her sweet lips, he took her face in both of his hands and whispered, adding in some dramatic desperation, "You must—you must stay here with me. I need you, and I cannot live without you now."

He felt her relax a little, but she stayed quiet, searching his eyes for understanding.

"Since we are already here, would you like to meet the rest of my family?"

"Yes, of course I would. And Graham, I need you, too. Sometimes I don't think you truly believe that of me."

Pulling her to him tightly, he let the feeling of relief wrap around him. "I believe you, *chérie*, and I am so very grateful that you do." *More than you will ever know.*

He began to lead her around the gallery, stopping first at a single portrait of Jasper at twenty years or so. Slighter in build, with darker hair, cut shorter, Jasper's gaze had been captured as slightly irreverent in the painting. A portent of his brother's demented character yet to develop done in paint and canvas for all to see if you knew what you were looking for.

"My brother, Jasper," Graham said stonily before moving on. Next, he stopped at the large multiple portrait of the cousins. "My great aunt Mary commissioned this one."

"Is that all of you as children? Tell me about it, please."

"Aunt Mary never married, but doted on us all like grandchildren and wanted to have all of us together in a portrait, so she arranged to have this one done. Jasper is about ten and five in this image. I am next at ten and three years old. My hand is on Colin's shoulder, who is about eight years. The boy looking down at the baby is Jules of course; he is twelve, and Elle, the baby, not even one year."

"Oh, my God, what a treasure for your family. Your Aunt Mary must have been so forward in her thinking to have this created. Look at you. You're just a boy. It is very special and so unique, Graham."

"Yes, it truly is. I am so happy you understand the importance, and before you say another word about it, you must know that I have every intention of continuing this family tradition. There will be many family portraits for us. Our little ones, when they come, will have to learn to sit for them, and you will too. I must have a whole roomful of just you." He touched her hair, and whispered, "Do you feel a little better now?"

"Yes, much better. You always make me feel so."

"In that case, let me show you just one more for today. This is a new addition and I find it stunningly beautiful in execution and in subject. It was painted by a great master, and features the current Lady Rothvale and her sister, as young ladies."

"What? How? What did you—?" Imogene drew up to the Opie portrait of her and Philippa that had been commissioned four years ago. The one that hung at Drakenhurst. She looked at him to explain.

"I had to have it here so I threw myself upon the mercy of your uncle and cousin Timothy, begging to borrow it so a copy could be made. This is the original and it will go back to Drakenhurst as soon as the copy is finished."

"I thought it unusual that it was supposedly having its frame repaired the day you took me to Drakenhurst. I am pleased to have a copy of it here in your gallery. It reminds me of happy times in my life."

She reached out her hand.
He embraced it tightly.
They did not speak. There was no need.

Chapter 13

...Her hair was long, her foot was light
And her eyes were wild.
She looked at me as she did love
And made sweet moan...

John Keats ~ 'La belle dame sans merci', 1820

"You will come to me in my chamber, when you are ready. You remember where? Just through those doors," he indicated with his head, a barely perceptible grin underneath his typical serious gaze.

His words were devastating, cutting into her, hurting her fragile foothold of familiarity with her new home. It must have shown on her face because he was quick to ask, "What is it, Imogene?"

"Do you wish to—do you wish to sleep separate from me?"

"Never. Why would you even think such a thing?"

She dropped her head. "Because you always come to me in my rooms and you have never asked for me to come to you in yours."

"Do you not wish to come to me?" There was an edge to

his voice.

"I was mistaken. I wish to come to you. I will come." She nodded. "It's just so new and different. This house—I must be out of sorts or something. The day has been a long one. I was not sure of what was expected…"

He drew her into his arms. "Please forgive me, *chérie.* I fear I have not been as open with you as I should have. I've been distracted and I apologize. It *has* been a dreadfully long day. But you have been magnificent." He pressed his lips to her forehead. "I'm so glad you're here with me, and I merely wish to sleep in the master's chamber tonight, with you. To see you there in my rooms, to have you come to *me* there. I promise I'll see you pleased," he said suggestively with a squeeze of a hand on her bum. "That is all, *chérie.* You see, I have never taken the master's chamber before this night. This is the first time *I* will sleep there. I never wish to sleep apart from you. Never. Imogene, do you believe me?"

"I believe you." She nodded into his chest. "But why did you never claim the master's place for your own?"

"This is the Lady's chamber—my mother's room. She was installed here. After my father passed I did not desire to remove her from her place. She was to be the dowager Lady Rothvale in any case and I could not take the master's chamber, with her in this one. It was a small thing and it meant little to me. I have been away in Ireland since she died anyway, so it was never claimed, until now." He touched her face, stroking with the back of his hand. "One more thing before I forget. I want you to remodel the Lady's chamber in any way that pleases you. Spend what you wish and make it your own space in the style and manner you would like it to be. It is yours, for you. Your retreat. There are to be no ghosts here."

"Thank you, Graham. You are very generous."

"When you are settled then? Come to me. I will be waiting for you," he said, before leaving her alone in her new rooms.

Imogene rang for Hester, and was overjoyed to see her maid. "Oh Hester, it is so wonderful to see a familiar face. I fear I am quite worn out. Tell me, how do you find it here at Gavandon? Are they being kind to you?"

"Oh yes, my lady, this is a kind house. I am happy to be here, and, madam, I know you will be as well."

"I know I will be." She sighed.

Imogene did not hurry in her preparations for sleep. The urge to laugh was suppressed because she wasn't alone, but really, she wouldn't be doing much sleeping right away. Graham would make sure of that.

Hester brushed out her hair and helped her into a nightdress with no wrapper. Imogene guessed he would not care for it, and she would not wear any of it for very long, anyway. He liked her scandalously naked in bed.

She cleaned her teeth meticulously and took a huge swig of wine to settle her frantic pulse.

What is he up to? He has me all worked up, and he knows it! I suppose I am destined for 'repayment' due for the teasing I doled out earlier in the coach…

Once Hester had finished her tasks, Imogene bid her a goodnight and slowly crept toward the doors of the master's chamber.

The door groaned upon entering the room. Her stomach lurched at the sight that met her eyes. The room was fairly well lit, enough light for her to see that he was sitting up in the enormous bed. Shirtless, he leaned against the headboard reading a book, wearing his glasses, hair unbound, the way she loved it.

"You are beautiful. A beautiful man," she told him, hoping words would calm, her racing heart a little.

"Come to me." He closed his book, removed his glasses and set them both on the bedside table, thoroughly prepared to enjoy the view of her as she moved toward him.

Her watchful Graham.

Imogene walked slowly to the edge of his bed. "I love your hair this way."

He nodded slowly, a hint of a grin present. "I know you do."

"Is this another 'indulge-me' game?"

He nodded again, this time with a full naughty grin.

"What must I do?" she asked, still whispering.

He looked her over before answering deliberately. "I want you to remove your nightdress and you must look into my eyes the whole time while you do it."

I was right on both counts. My nightdress off in less than one minute. And this is most definitely 'repayment.'

Imogene swallowed, her breath coming faster. Moving her hands to the neckline, she slowly untied the fastenings one by one. She did it by feel because he did not want her to break their gaze. One shoulder was bared, and then the other as the silk slid apart and off. As soon as the gown fell to her waist, it was as good as gone.

She realized then, his objective. He was still watching her face, her eyes. His intention was not to look at her body, but to look at her reaction to what they were doing, through her eyes. It was all very controlled and ordered.

"Now what must I do?" she whispered, never taking her eyes off him.

Steepling his fingers together, he set them on the edge of

his lips, still looking at her. He pointed his hands, enunciating each word with them. "I want you to come and sit on me, and face me, and look at me. Don't be shy. Just look into my eyes, and don't turn away or look down."

He held a palm out to assist her.

She kept her eyes on his, but didn't know how she could move her legs. Her heart was beating so fast she thought it might break out of her body and kill her where she stood. His request affected her so strongly, she began to shake uncontrollably. At first just a little, but then the trembling accelerated in intensity quickly as it took hold of her.

Graham held out both palms. "Take my hands, Imogene. I will help you. Just look into my eyes. That is all you must do, just look at me."

His voice calmed her a little. Enough to get her stone-pillar body to take a small step.

Move! Take his hands and go to him.

She stepped again, taking a hold of his hands, letting him pull her forward, onto him in the bed, her legs folding over him and settling on either side of his hips. When she sat down on him she could feel his cock hot and hard lying flat on his stomach and pressing into the folds of her sex. More involuntary shudders racked her through and through.

What is happening? I cannot breathe…

"Good girl. Now take a breath and relax, *chérie.* Just keep looking into my eyes and breathe. I am looking at you, into your eyes. I love you so much. You know I do."

He did not ask anything more, for a time. He just continued to look into her eyes as she calmed, and until her breathing had steadied. "I am going to touch you now…get you ready for me. I want you to keep looking at me, *chérie,* into my eyes only, and feel everything. That is what I want to see.

I want to see the fire in your eyes when you take your pleasure…"

She did not lose the hold of his eyes.

Not when he sucked on her nipples and bit them with gentle scrapes of his teeth.

Not when he slid his fingers up inside her and worked on her nubbin until she was slippery wet and aching for more.

And not when he urged her up so he could position her back down onto his erect cock and bury himself deep.

Imogene did as he asked and held onto his burning gaze throughout everything. She knew he saw what he had wanted to see in her. Imogene knew it because she was looking at Graham, into his eyes, when it happened to him.

JUST the feel of her quim clenching around his cock was enough for him to come with her. But feeling it, and then seeing it happen through her eyes was so powerful, and took him so fast, he was barely able to control the experience. He had to work very hard not to close his own eyes and break their gaze when the orgasmic blast fired through his cock and the spunk shot out.

He heard her.

"Do not look away from me, Graham. I want to see it in your eyes, when the pleasure takes you."

Imogene had become the watcher.

She sat on him, his cock still twitching inside her, the look on her beautiful face, triumphant and victorious. Finally she spoke, "I believe we are done here."

For this moment we are.

He pulled her down to his lips for a passionate kiss,

plundering her mouth until he was ready to let her go.

"Why this?" she asked.

"I don't know. I just wanted to try. You know of my secret passion. I am a watcher. I like to look and see many things, and this was one of them. But mostly I just want to watch you at simple times. I even watch you when you sleep. I do know I will never tire of it. I know that to be true. I will forever want to look at you."

She grew still, her eyes filling with tears. One spilled down her cheek.

He brushed it away with his thumb. "Tears of love and joy—my truest standard of success."

They stayed quiet for a time, sensing the powerful bond between them.

"I must say, *chérie*, you were quite transformed through the experience. You began it as the captive, but ended it most definitely the captor, and I know you know it. You are quite the fighter, facing your fears bravely because you are so valiant."

"Can a woman be valiant?"

"You certainly are. *Mon amoureux vaillant*…my valiant lover."

He squeezed her side in a ticklish move that had her shrieking and laughing and trying to wriggle away.

The happy sounds of laughter and joy, absent for so long from Gavandon had finally returned, and it felt as if the ancient place rejoiced in their happiness, blooming anew.

Later, as she slept beside him, he pondered her earlier distress at believing he would wish to sleep apart. Imogene had no idea of the real truth and he had not shared it. He did not want to appear to be so needful. It was very hard not to reveal the almost unbearable necessity to be close with her and he didn't wish to be suffocating. The simple truth was that it would be near impossible for him to sleep anywhere, but at her side. He adored sleeping with her. The sound of her breathing, the scent of her, her warmth against him, filled his brain and soothed his ravaged heart like a balm. Knowing she was right next to him, and that he could reach out and find her soft, warm body, and that she would be there all throughout the night, was tranquilizing.

Graham craved her, couldn't live without her, didn't want to imagine it, and he would not.

THE next morning Imogene woke late and alone in the master's chamber. Stretching and peering around the enormous room, she was able to see things clearly in the morning light. The painting was huge. It hung opposite the bed so as to be the first thing to view when you opened your eyes each morning.

It was of her.

Her in the Kent countryside, standing at the entrance to Kenilbrooke. Terra was there, perfectly depicted. Her hair as it was that day, blue riding habit, carrying the lamb in her arms. The entire scene recreated as it had happened.

How does he manage these things? Will I stumble upon one surprise to the next for our whole lives together? I don't know if I can bear it…

Imogene found her nightdress and donned it, exited his room and entered her own. She attended to personal needs first, braiding her hair into one long braid, and dressing into a green brocade robe before wandering into their sitting room. The first thing she looked for was a note.

There was no note.

Pouring herself a cup of tea from the breakfast tray, she took it with her and marched right back into Graham's chamber to look at the portrait again.

She studied it thoroughly while sipping her tea, trying to compel its secrets, but couldn't for the life of her understand how on earth Graham had managed this painting commissioned.

"I see you have found it this morning; you did not notice it last night," he whispered into her ear from behind.

Imogene sputtered into her tea and nearly dropped the cup. "That would be a fair statement, sir, as I could not have possibly given my attention to anything in this room last night apart from you…and the bedsport."

She looked him over thoroughly. Noting he was dressed for the day, waistcoat and cravat in place, hair neatly tied back.

"Always correct in your assessments, *chérie.* I did quite monopolize your concentration last night, I know, but it was memorable, was it not?"

She nodded once and took another sip of her tea.

"There is some business that needs attending to in here before we can start our day."

"Is that so?"

He took her tea cup away and set it on a table. Then he pulled a winter rose in blush pink from his pocket and tucked it above her ear.

"First, good morning." He kissed her forehead. "I love you." He kissed her left ear. "I adore you." He kissed her right ear. "You look beautiful." He kissed her lips and held her chin up to him ever so gently. "There, business done now. Did you have something you wished to ask me?" A wicked grin graced his face.

"Oh, my God, Graham! How do you manage this kind of thing? I am beginning to think you delve in the occult. The constant plotting and planning, doesn't it exhaust you? Because it exhausts me."

"No, not at all. I find it very invigorating." He reached for her. "Now do you understand why I want to sleep in this room?"

"Yes." She touched his cheek. "But how *did* you manage it?"

"I have a friend, an artist who conspires with me."

"You do? And have I met this person?"

"You have not met him." Graham shook his head. "He is a more mercurial sort. Not someone who would display himself with the staff for the new mistress's arrival."

"He is here at Gavandon then? Who is he?"

"Tristan Mallerton, an old friend. We met many years ago at school, at Harrow. I went on to Cambridge. He went on to Paris, painted and lived large. I joined him there for a short time before—"

Graham stopped abruptly, a look of wistfulness coming into his expression.

"Before?" she asked.

"Mallerton has lived the life I might have lived under different circumstances. He returned to England just before the time I inherited. While he was poor, I was not. I had need of a painter at my disposal, so I offered to be his patron and he accepted my offer. Now he has a home and money enough to keep him supplied in paint and canvas and other wants, and the exposure to people of wealth who will probably eventually steal him away from me one day. He is about the place. You will meet him soon I am sure. I hope you like him for I want him to paint portraits of you."

"Interesting, but how could he have painted this one? I have never met him and we, you and I, have only known each other for a few months. Paintings like this take time and sittings. How could he have possibly painted my likeness so perfectly?"

"Oh, he was busy to be sure. I had him working on it immediately after you accepted my proposal. I described the Kent scenery and sketched it out for him. I sent off for the Opie portrait from Drakenhurst as soon as we were engaged. He used the camera obscura to get the image of your face from it, and transferred it to this portrait. Terra arrived here some weeks ago, other horses stood in at first; he filled her in once she got here. You gave me your hair, which was so perfect. I was able to describe colours the way they should be, and your hair and figure, and was able to lay out the canvas for him. I think it skillfully done. He has captured the moment for me, the first moment I spied you and was pierced through the heart with Cupid's Arrow. I can remember with clarity the moment. There was pain in my heart when I first saw you. But instead of it killing me, I was awakened." His eyes had grown very dark green, drawing her in, as he retold the moment when he first saw her.

Could it be possible for any man to love her as Graham did, she wondered. Why was she so blessed in love?

I need him again.

Imogene reached for his shirt buttons to open it, but found that first she must deal with his knotted cravat. "I find these to be most devilishly inconvenient," she hissed, struggling with the offending length of fabric. Finally pulling it free, she opened his waistcoat and then his shirt wide to expose his heart. She then pressed her lips to the place where she could feel it pounding inside his chest.

The moment her lips touched him, Graham gathered her up and took her back to bed where he loved her ravenously. The carefully orchestrated control of their encounter from the previous night was nowhere to be found in this one.

AT breakfast Imogene was thoughtful as she sat across from him. She'd admitted she was still in shock at finding the portrait of her carrying the lamb. It made him happy to surprise her so he imagined she would have to get used to it.

"So many secrets. How many secrets do you have, Graham?"

"I don't have any secrets from you."

Liar. You know that you lie.

She gave him a hard look. "When you were a little boy, did the parson not tell you that all liars will go to hell?"

He laughed at that, amazed again at her skills of perception in reading him. "I am sure he did, but I do not count them as secrets or lies. Rather, they are surprises, gifts, arranged with love for you."

Graham simply smiled at his wife and changed the topic of their conversation. He'd decided that he would not allow any ugliness to invade upon his happiness of bringing Imogene to Gavandon. He would deal with those problems later.

"You know, these robes or wrappers you have are very beautiful. I especially like this green one you're wearing today. It is very elegant. You quite remind me of a wrapped package with the bow just here. The image is so…so emotive. Quite perfect." He continued to enjoy his view of her for a moment until she narrowed her eyes.

"I know what you are doing right now." She held one

finger up. "I know exactly what you are thinking and it is shocking."

He laughed again. "Please tell me, *chérie.* I want to know if you are learning to read my mind."

"Fine. You are thinking that you wish to arrange a portrait of me, in *dishabille*…wearing one of these robes, and looking—looking like you have just loved me. Don't you dare try to deny it. I could see right into your mind just now as if I had a mirror. And before you ask, you must know it is out of the question. I could not possibly sit for such a thing, even with your friend."

"Your mental power is razor sharp, *chérie*, and I confess you have routed me out. So, I will have to work very hard to convince you then?" He gave her his best hopeful expression.

"For now I think I shall keep the idea of it stashed away, my darling. A bargaining chip for me. A wife would be prudent to gather a few." She winked at him. "Maybe we could do a trade. I would not mind having a *Professor Adonis* portrait of you." Her eyes opened wide and she clapped a hand up to her mouth. "I cannot believe I've just said that to you. You see how you have quite corrupted me?"

His heart was happy.

"It is so wonderful to have you here, finally. You definitely liven this old place up, and a little corruption would probably do some good for all of us."

"Hester told me last night that this is a kind house." Imogene got up from her chair and came to sit on his lap. She put her hand to his cheek. "I am happy to be here, and you must know, that for me it is not the place. It is that I am with you, and we are together."

Graham nodded his affirmation to her wise words and kissed her. "What would you like to do today, *chérie*? I am completely at your service."

"I should like to see my sister."

WHEN Philippa Brancroft received the note from the messenger that Imogene and Lord Rothvale would call upon them later in the day, she quickly dashed off two notes of her own. One was a reply to the Rothvales anticipating their arrival, and the other to her husband at his surgery to get himself home by the arranged time.

She was finally to see her sister again after months of being separated. Philippa rubbed her belly and spoke to her unborn baby, "Today you will meet your aunty."

They lived at Harwell House in the cathedral town of Wellick. Her husband, Dr. John Brancroft, did not see patients in his house as some physicians did, rather, he ran a surgery for that purpose and it was not far from home. There was a hospital at Wellick, very new and modern, having been built less than a decade earlier. It was a teaching hospital as well, and her husband, one of its founding fellows. So, he divided his time between the surgery and instructing students at the hospital. John saw the more affluent patients directly in their homes.

She was thrilled at the prospect of reuniting with Imogene. They had last been together at their father's funeral. At the time, Philippa had desperately wanted to bring Imogene to Wellick to live with her and John. But Aunt Wilton had resisted the idea, feeling Imogene would rebound faster if she were in a more lively environment, full of young people and activities. She had proved correct in the end. The more robust home-life of Wilton Court had served Imogene well. It *had* been the better choice. It had brought her sister to her husband, Lord Rothvale, and for that, she could never feel anything but grateful to their aunt.

AS they pulled down the drive Imogene spied Hiram out working near the fountain and she was reminded of their introduction the day before. "Graham, did you introduce him to me as Hiram Everley? It sounded as if that was the name you said."

"Yes. Their surname is Everley."

Imogene looked at him inquiringly. She tilted her head a little asking the question without words.

He looked reflective as he explained. "When their papers of emancipation were prepared, a surname had to be chosen. As slaves they had none. No name of their own, nor any rights to a name, either. They wished to take my surname for their own. I tried to dissuade them to choose another name but Hiram was determined. They were very grateful for the sponsorship, and I know they wanted to pay their respects to me, and taking my name was a way in which they could do it. Hiram, Antonia, Ben, and his sister, Eva, were all emancipated from Antigua. The baby was born here at Gavandon. A free soul." He smiled at her.

"And the baby, what is he called?" Imogene asked ever so softly.

He lowered his eyes humbly before answering. "They call him Graham."

"They honor you, and in a way of value to them. You are so good—so benevolent. To give them such a life as they have here, and freeing them from a hideous existence." Imogene looked at her husband in awe. There was much to him that she did not know. But she knew with certainty that the man she had married was not the typical English aristocrat. There was substance in him. He was a gentleman who had been born to privilege but was not content to simply sit back and squander it. He would do things—good and worthy things, and her heart caught at the thought.

"Graham, are you involved with it? The abolitionist movement?"

"Yes. Well, I was, before I left for Ireland. It was the subject of my maiden speech in Parliament."

"How was it received?"

"Well enough, I suppose. I am in good company, as there are many that share my view. I think it will not be long now, before we have total success on the matter. Within ten years to be sure."

She nodded thoughtfully. "Did you ever meet my father? He was involved with the abolitionist movement as well."

"I think I must have, *chérie*, but I'm sorry I don't clearly recollect. It was a very hectic time in my life. My father had just passed and I had taken up my seat. I was five and twenty and trying very hard to meet my obligations here at Gavandon and in government. And not doing well with any of it. It is all a blur, that time for me." He paused and looked down at his hands. "I'll have to return to Parliament and face my responsibilities—soon I'll have to go back." He lifted his eyes to her. "I wish that I had known him, *chérie,* he was respected and served honorably."

"I wish he could have known you…known how good you are…known you would be my husband."

He placed both of his hands crossed, over his heart in thanks of her praise.

"You look so gratified and happy right now," he said. "It makes *me* happy to see you so. Tell me about you sister. What is she like?"

"Well, you have seen her portrait so you will recognize her. I have been told we resemble each other my whole life. It will be interesting to see what you think. She is three years my elder. There is a twelve year age difference between her and John. But it suits them just fine. Well, you know John. He has thoughtful demeanour in a brooding sort of way, but not when he looks at her. Her youth and sweetness complement the serious scientist in him. She has entranced him completely. Her colouring is a bit darker and her hair is a deeper blonde than mine. We have similar figures but I am slightly taller by an inch or so. And that is where the similarities end."

"What are you not telling me then?" he teased.

Imogene shrugged slowly. "She is wise and even-keeled. She is ever so patient and self-controlled. She is accomplished at the piano forte and wickedly skilled at handwork that I could never, ever do. Philippa is a perfectly gracious, charming woman. The consummate gentlewoman—always a lady. When you meet her you'll see what I mean."

"Do I detect a sense of inadequacy next to your sister, *chérie*?" he inquired.

"Yes! You absolutely, positively do. But no matter, I adore her anyway for all her perfectness."

"So, are you saying she rides expertly well? Can she make a target at fifty paces dead on? Does she rescue helpless creatures lost on the rocks? Is she wickedly competitive at games and the bravest woman I have ever known?" He paused in his questions and looked at her with solemnity. "Well, I would not want to be ungentlemanly and take anything away from your sister's obvious virtues as I am sure she is lovely and all you say she is, but know this, *chérie,* no lady could ever outshine you at perfectness in my eyes."

Imogene smiled at him gratefully and blew him a kiss. "I knew there was a good reason for marrying you."

Philippa and John greeted them on the steps when they arrived. Imogene took great pride in introducing Graham to her sister, but seeing Philippa full into her pregnancy brought a mix of emotions for Imogene. She was very happy at the thought of a precious little one to love, but very sad at the thought that their mamma would never know this baby or any Imogene herself might bear someday. Observing Philippa also caused her to ponder her own pregnancy. Could she be, already? It was possible she guessed for the amount of times she and Graham had been intimate, but her body felt just the same inside. Would she be able to tell? Did a woman know if she was expecting by how she felt? Imogene resolved to get some private time with Philippa today so she could ask her about it. Who better than her own sister and the wife of a doctor?

They stayed for a long visit and a late luncheon. John took Graham down to his surgery for a tour of the place. With the men gone, Philippa asked Imogene how married life suited her and Imogene was frank in her response, and in her questions. They made plans for Imogene to come again and sorted out a visiting schedule that would work for Philippa.

As she looked around their lovely, sedate, home, Imogene pondered how different her life might have been had she come to live here without ever meeting Graham. She wondered if their paths would have eventually crossed, a mere ten miles of distance between them. Strange was fate. She could not see herself living here in this home with them, though. She loved her sister and John dearly, but she simply couldn't see it now.

Graham had changed everything. Now she could not imagine being anywhere that he was not. Her life was completely and utterly entwined with his.

IN the carriage on the way home they regarded each other from their seats opposite one another. They usually situated themselves in this way. It provided the best setting for looking at the other. From the day of their very first meeting, this was something they had always reverted to easily without even knowing what they were doing. Others had noticed and would remark upon this particular behaviour they exhibited for the rest of their lives.

Graham looked out the window at the rolling scenery and then back at his wife. Sometimes when Imogene did simple things, such as blowing him a kiss or whispering an *I love you*, he felt overcome with emotion. The effect was usually to silence him, rendering him unable to speak or to respond in a way that made any sense. So he just remained silent and smiled at her, and revelled in the radiant glow of her love that suffused him.

Imogene broke the quiet. "Thank you."

"For taking you to see your sister? You do not have to thank me for that, *chérie*."

"Not for that."

"For what then?"

"For finding me. For loving me. I realized today that I would not have been happy living there with Philippa and John even as much as I love and adore them. So thank you. Thank you for giving me this beautiful, lovely life."

For the second time that day, Graham closed his eyes and just let her words float over him for he knew he would not be able to speak a response.

Chapter 14

He that would be a painter must have a natural turn thereto.
Love and delight therein are better teachers of
the Art of Painting than compulsion is.

Albrecht Dürer ~ Third Book of Human Proportions, 1512

It had been easy, really. So easy. All he'd had to do was slip the drug to them by way of the maid, with whom he'd been dallying. Flattery was a skill he possessed in abundance, along with his charm and good looks. He knew how to use every advantage where he might gain the most benefit.

She slept in the carriage, appearing peaceful and completely unaware in her slumber. The years had worn well on her for she was still very pretty. He perceived the tightening in his loins, remembering her lush body from before, what he had forced her to do then. But he didn't need to do that now. Generally, he liked his women willing, unless forcing them gave him an advantage. In this case, the advantage lay asleep in his lap, and would be ever so more effective in inducement.

SHE felt as if she were clawing her way out of a fog.

Opening her eyes, she saw a face she had hoped never to see again in her lifetime.

"Hello, Agnes. It's such a pleasure to see you again."

"No!" She cringed in fear until she realized that Clara was lying across his lap. "Clara. Give her to me. Please, I beg of you, give me my child," she implored, reaching out her arms.

He gave a slight shake of his head. "No, dear, not yet. You have something that I need."

"What do you want from me?" She tried to quell the bitter fear screaming to the surface.

"Just your signature, my dear." He waved a document at her and she took it.

She scanned it hastily. "I cannot sign this. We'll have nothing, no way to live!" she cried, looking at him in horror. "You can't do this. He said I would never have to worry, that we would have his support for life."

"Tut, tut, dear Agnes." He shook his head at her. "We men are so…fickle. He simply cannot be bothered with you anymore. He has married. A lady of rank, a politician's daughter. My dear, that's changed everything." Cocking his head, he lifted his chin. "Now you must see how any connection to you and your child would bring shame down on upon their noble name." He paused. "Can't have that, Agnes," he whispered.

"I won't sign."

"Ah, yes you will. You *will* sign, Agnes. You will sign because you wouldn't want *anything* to happen to the sweetling lying across my lap." He moved his hand to gently stroke over Clara's cheek before resting it against her neck."

Agnes broke then, giving in to the despair. She knew what he was capable of, and that he would have no qualms carrying out any evil he might devise. After another moment of anguished misery she relented. "I'll sign."

He grinned repulsively, looking back down at her daughter. "She is such a beautiful child. You know, I believe she inherited the best of both of you in her looks. Your colouring and his noble features, and those eyes, so fine…and green."

IMOGENE had so much to learn, but lucky for her, Graham was her enthusiastic guide. When the weather was dry they rode over the estate so she could learn its boundaries. When the weather was wet she explored the house and learned its secrets. It snowed one day and was a very pretty sight, but it didn't last. By morning it was gone.

There were many people to meet and names to learn. One new acquaintance shadowed her everywhere; the dog, Zuly. The elegant creature had taken an immediate liking to Imogene, attaching herself to her new mistress with utmost loyalty. It was absolutely no trouble to quickly grow affectionate of her new four-legged friend.

They settled into the habits that suited them. For instance, Imogene preferred to take breakfast in their sitting room except for the weekends or if they were having guests. Graham rose earlier than she did and would be up and about, and then come back to breakfast with her when she arose. For now they slept in the master's chamber and would continue to do so until Imogene's rooms were done up. Her things were still kept in her room and she bathed and dressed there, she just did not sleep in there. This caused some concession in regards to Phelps, Graham's manservant, but they worked it out. When Graham first woke in the early morning he saw to himself. Later, after breakfasting with Imogene, he would have Phelps attend him in his chamber for bathing and preparing for the day whilst Imogene had retreated to her chamber by that time, to be assisted by Hester.

Graham preferred to concentrate on estate business during the first half of the day. He often rode out with his steward, Mr. Duncan, attending to tenant issues and matters relating to crops and livestock. If not riding out, he conducted meetings in his study. Imogene used this morning time for her work as well. She met with Mrs. Griffin each day, and Cook, a few times each week. For now, she was busy learning the workings of the house and the names of the servants. By and by, she would have more decisions to make, and accounts to manage, but she wasn't in a great rush to take charge of everything. She made plans to begin tenant visits; as the new mistress of Gavandon, it was now her duty. Mrs. Griffin would help her in the beginning, until all families were known to her. The housekeeper seemed sensible. Imogene liked her for being so approachable.

After luncheon, correspondence took priority for both of them as the post had arrived by that time, and responses usually required their attention. Imogene preferred working from the library. It was housed in one of the front towers, and thus was a round room. There were abundant windows, which afforded a most lovely view of the formal gardens and fountain out the front. Graham arranged for work spaces set up for both of them in the library and started joining her there for the purpose of writing his letters.

The later afternoon was for recreation. They might go for

a ride or a walk if it was not raining. They both liked to read and had other interests to fill the time. Sometimes they played cards. Graham worked on his ancestry project and Imogene wrote in her journal regularly. He read the paper and she embroidered as a last resort if she had to stay inside. She knew that when spring arrived she'd definitely be spending more time outside.

Graham took her around the village at Whichford, introducing his new bride to the inhabitants there. Whichford was situated only three miles from Gavandon, having been a market town since medieval times, dealing in the wool trade for centuries. The entire village was built of red brick and very picturesque. They attended church there and Imogene found the parishioners to be welcoming and friendly. There had been instances of awkwardness with some persons exclaiming on the likeness between her and the previous Lady Rothvale, but it was soon forgotten. A few had paid courtesy calls on them, eager to become acquainted with the new mistress of Gavandon. Imogene sorted through the invitations that arrived for them, and Graham helped her with the responses.

There was one surprise when Graham showed her the fencing studio that he had created in a lower room, below ground. It had beautiful wooden floors, and because of its basement location, he explained how it was kept cool in summer and warm in winter. The windows were set along the ceiling, which opened out at ground level, at the base of the house. They afforded light and fresh air aplenty. Imogene was impressed by how well apportioned it was. Racks of equipment; foils, sabers, masks, gloves, padded jackets; everything was all organized and arranged along the walls. She looked forward to watching him and wondered at his reaction should she ask him to teach her to fence. She didn't ask him, but the idea was definitely kindled when she was shown that beautiful fencing room.

SHE did not recognize the man on the path. As she approached the house, he appeared to be leaving it. He carried some fine linens in his arms; shawls, runners, throws, a rug, were all draped over his arm. As they drew near to one another he slowed, stopping on the path, smiling at her, slowly dipping his head in a bow. "Finally we meet in the flesh."

Imogene was surprised by the familiarity of his words. "I beg your pardon?"

"I said, finally we meet in the flesh."

"I heard what you said, sir, but have we met in any other fashion?"

"Officially no, but I certainly feel as if I've known you for quite a while now."

Imogene took in his appearance; his stained hands, the linens draped over his arm, his Bohemian appearance. She knew who this man was. "Mr. Mallerton I presume?"

"Graham said you were very quick. Guilty as charged, Lady Rothvale. It is an honor to meet the lady who has captured his heart so absolutely." He bowed again, this time with more of a gallant flourish.

Imogene suppressed a giggle. This man was most unconventional, and irreverent, and utterly charming. She liked him. "Thank you, Mr. Mallerton. 'Tis a pleasure. I imagine we'll be seeing quite a lot of each other."

"Yes, well, that could be an understatement. I've just come from him you see, and he has quite a lot of portraits planned for you, milady. I hope we don't get sick of each other," he replied archly.

"Ah, time will tell, Mr. Mallerton. Time will tell on that score, won't it?"

"I would like to start tomorrow and set up a schedule of sittings for the first portrait. Tomorrow at one o'clock? Will that suit you?"

"It will. Where do I find you?"

"Graham will show you the way the first time. I paint out of my home studio for indoor portraits. Outdoor portraits require the outside, obviously, and he does have a suggestion for one of those as well. So, tomorrow then, Lady Rothvale?" He tipped his head at her once again and then moved to pass and be on his way.

Imogene watched him go. Tristan Mallerton was tall, over six feet without his boots. He had dark, unruly hair and was quite thin. His face was handsome in a tortured sort of way. He wore a grimace-like expression as if he were concentrating very hard on something. He was interesting, different, and she knew without a shadow of a doubt, that she had just met someone significant.

"I met your friend today, Mr. Mallerton," Imogene announced over dinner.

"I know."

Imogene looked at her husband inquisitively. "How? And why didn't you say?"

"I saw you meet him through the library windows and I didn't say anything because I wanted you to make your own assessment of him. I thought that if I introduced you, if I were present, you might feel obligated to like him more than you want to. I don't wish to force him on you, but what was your impression? It's been killing me not to ask."

Imogene chose her words carefully. "He is unconventional, I give you that, but he remained a gentleman in my presence. His comments to me were a bit irreverent, but not insulting. I found him charming and amusing in a slightly demented kind of way. I take it that you trust him completely? He is not some monster who will terrorize me?"

"Absolutely not a monster. He holds my complete trust. You relieve me, Imogene. He is gifted, and I know he will paint you beautifully, creating the kind of portrait I wish to have. All gifted persons, no matter their talent, seem to have that touch of creative madness in them, as does he. Not everyone can stomach him, and I would hate for you to dread his company, as you would have to spend a great deal of time in it. Are you willing to give it a go, *chérie*?"

"Yes," she said firmly. "He wishes me to come to his studio tomorrow at one o'clock. He said something about setting a schedule for the sittings."

"The first meeting will be about arrangement and the setting. You will discuss what is envisioned for the portrait, and he'll organize everything and explain what he needs from you."

"You will not come? I am to go on my own?" she inquired anxiously.

Graham looked at her lovingly before placing his hand over hers and clasping it. "I must be away tomorrow," he said softly. "Mr. Duncan and I must go to the eastern portion of the estate and I won't be back in time to take you. Ben will drive you, and await you. When the weather is fair you could even walk there if you are up to it. And take the dog along for company if you wish."

Imogene felt unsure as she absorbed his words.

"Oh, *chérie*, I love you so much." He caressed her hand on the table. "It is for the best this way. Many do not understand the creative process. No artist could do his best work with others peering over his shoulders and distracting with questions or guarding the sitter. I trust him utterly. He is a professional. His task is to paint your image, and he will best accomplish it if he is allowed to work in private with just you and him together—artist and subject. You have nothing to fear from him. All proprieties and discretion as to modesty will be observed."

Graham squeezed her hand and nodded his head, seeking to reassure her.

"All right. I understand then. I will be fine," she said.

"You are so valiant, remember? I adore that about you." He searched her face as if he was looking for any sign of fear or anxiety. "It will be glorious, and I can hardly wait until it is done."

Dinner continued quietly for a time before Imogene recognized the sweet bread. "Is this the bread we had at the inn? Wasn't it Mr. Jacobson's?"

"I believe it is the same recipe," he responded elusively.

"You got the recipe for us then, and gave it to Cook?"

"Not exactly. I am sure he got the recipe initially from his mother, *Mrs.* Jacobson."

Imogene was puzzled, but just for an instant before realization dawned on her. "Cook! Mrs. Jacobson is our cook and she is *his* mother?" Imogene just stared at him and shook her head. "You keep an inordinate amount of secrets, my husband. You delight in teasing me with these things. I daresay I shall not have even the slightest twinge of guilt about any secret I may ever contrive to keep against you, current or otherwise. You are *very* naughty!"

He charmed her with a humble smile. "I await my punishment with valor and leave it in your most capable hands, *chérie.*"

"Humph," she sniffed. "How does Mr. Jacobson have an inn such as The Lion's Crown? He is young in years to be proprietor."

"My father was fond of his comforts. He liked a good meal, and he hated the fare served at coaching inns along the road. He went back and forth to Town so often for Parliamentary votes that he quickly grew impatient with the poor meals and unclean beds. So he acquired The Lion's Crown, and figured if he owned it, the standard of service would be assured."

Imogene was surprised. "You own that inn?"

"We do, yes, *chérie*, and it is the only place our family has ever used since. It is exactly midway between Gavandon and London. Jacobson is a good man. He grew up here and found cooking to be his talent. Father was happy to set him there as proprietor, and it was a good choice too, for he has run the place profitably for about seven years now. Word of The Lion's quality and excellence has spread, proving it to be a successful venture."

"Truly amazing is all I have to say about that," she said in wonder.

IMOGENE and Zuly stood at the door of the stone house after having lifted the knocker. She was surprised to have the door opened by Ben's mother, Antonia. "Lady Rothvale. He awaits you in the studio. Follow me?"

"Is this your place of work, Antonia?"

"Yes, my lady. I am housekeeper for Mr. Mallerton during the days."

"I had no idea. I have much to learn about the workings of the estate as of yet. Ah, Ben has driven me here today." Imogene looked at her respectfully. "He is a good boy."

Antonia's face brightened before she gave a slight dip of her head. "Thank you, my lady."

Mr. Mallerton was waiting for her in the middle of a large, bright, nearly empty room.

"Will you allow my dog?" she asked him.

He inclined his head in a nod to indicate approval.

There was a great elegant chair in the middle of the floor and he indicated for her to sit. He then stepped back to an easel set with a canvas prepared, sat on a stool and faced her.

Imogene had some thoughts about Mr. Mallerton right away and she felt she was dead on accurate, too.

He is only a trifle bit beastly, and I think it is all for show.

"NERVOUS?"

"Yes."

"What are you nervous about?" he asked drily, thinking she would say something about the impropriety of being alone with him. She surprised him instead.

"Of disappointing my husband. He has high hopes of a successful, working relationship between us, Mr. Mallerton. It is for him that I do this."

That got his attention. *A fighter.* He regarded her intently, his impression turning to one of respect for this young intelligent woman. He saw the flicker of a smile creeping up one side of her mouth.

"Then we must make sure that we do not disappoint him, Lady Rothvale, as we share a common goal."

Her response was to nod in agreement at him, and so they began.

He asked if she would turn to the left and then to the right. He asked this several times of her, explaining that he was comparing her profiles to determine her best side. Then he adjusted the height of the easel and took several measurements from the floor to the top of her head and then her shoulders. While she sat, he marked the measurements right onto the canvas.

This done, he sat back down onto his stool and asked if Graham had discussed with her what he had in mind for this portrait.

She shook her head. "He did not."

"He indicated to me that he would like to have you in a formal gown, wearing an ensemble of pearls and emeralds. Do you know of the set of jewels?"

"Yes. There are a choker, earrings and a wrist cuff all matching."

"Bring them next time when you come. You will have to take them back and forth as I do not have a way to secure them here in this house. I would also like you to bring a selection of gowns that you like and feel would complement the jewels. On no account will I put a sitter in clothing they do not like. It never works in the end. We'll be able to decide which gown suits the best. Antonia will always be here when you come and can assist you with your wardrobe. Now, for your hair. I suggest you have it done for the first sitting in the way you would wear it for a formal occasion, so I can sketch out the general idea of it. You will not have to have it done so ornately each time, until I get to painting that part. When I get to that section of the portrait you will need to have your hair done up in the exact same fashion each time you come for a sitting, but I'll let you know when you need to do that."

She nodded in agreement to everything he'd said, but didn't speak.

"Do you have any questions for me, Lady Rothvale?"

"How long will a sitting be, and how many sittings will you need for a portrait like this one?"

"A sitting is never longer than two hours, and for this image, I'd guess no more than ten sittings will serve adequately. Now, tell me of your schedule. Graham mentioned you have arranged to visit your sister some days."

She gave him her free days and they both marked down the arranged dates and times in their appointment books.

"Ah, our business is concluded for this session. I must compliment you on your nerves of steel. You bore up very well under my onslaught. It bodes well for our future work together, milady." He gave her a grin.

"Thank you for the compliment, Mr. Mallerton, but please do not hold back anything on my account. I would have your true demeanour. I daresay I can handle the challenge, even of one so prickly as you." She smiled graciously, curtsying to him. "Until Wednesday. Goodbye now."

He watched as she walked regally out of his studio, her equally regal dog following at her side.

What a lovely, lovely, creature, and it shall be heaven to paint her.

IMOGENE was dressing for dinner when she realized it.

There was no start of a child. No baby this time. She was disappointed and dreaded telling Graham for the embarrassment, and the failure. The familiar cramp took hold in her abdomen. Maybe there was something wrong with her. They had been intimate nearly every day since the wedding and some days more than once. What did it take to start a baby? She knew they had to join together and she knew he had to spill his seed in her. Well, those criteria had certainly been met, numerous times! She needed to ask Philippa some more questions. Maybe the timing was wrong. They had been married for just four weeks. That didn't seem like very much time. She was completely ignorant of the biology of pregnancy and further embarrassed by that ignorance.

Her appetite faltered at dinner and Graham noticed. He noticed everything. When he asked her about it she told him her stomach was unsettled. She saw him frown at her reply. He was, however, eager to hear about the meeting with Mr. Mallerton.

"It went well. He was not so terrorizing as I thought he might have been. I think I earned his respect today, and do not foresee any problems between us." She tried to ease his anxiety. "I saw that my earlier concerns were for nothing—being alone with him in his studio. Why did you not say Antonia was his housekeeper and that she would be there?"

"Oh, that's right." He frowned. "You know, *chérie*, I honestly forgot about it. Remember, I have been away for a long time and have to relearn this estate, in a sense. I am glad that you have no reservations, and especially that you feel comfortable with him. It eases me."

"I will need to bring the emeralds and several gowns to the next sitting. Would you like to help me select some gowns to take? I welcome your opinion."

"I would love to help you choose, *chérie*."

LATER, when Imogene came to his room dressed for bed, Graham was already in it, reading a book.

She sat on the side of the bed and peeked at him through her lashes.

"You are all wrapped up like a package," he remarked, eyeing her wrapper. "All the better to unwrap you." He reached for her.

She stilled his hands. "We must not…"

Graham froze, shocked at her denying him. He inclined his head a little to get down to her eye level, waiting for her to speak. When she did not, he whispered, "Are you not feeling well, *chérie*?"

She kept her head down and mumbled the words, "It is my woman's time and we cannot…"

It took a moment for him to puzzle it out. "Ah. 'Tis all right," he soothed. He tried to get her to look at him but she kept her head down. He knew she was not comfortable sharing such things but she looked so stiff and unhappy he couldn't resist the question. "Are you in pain?"

"No." She shook her head. "It does not really hurt me, mostly just an inconvenience."

"I am glad you are not hurting, and I daresay that though it will be hard, I will survive a few days without you." He tried to lighten her a little with some teasing. "You'll survive it as well, *chérie*, but you'll have to be brave as I know how difficult it is for you to keep your hands off me."

She gave him a half-smile but it didn't reach her eyes. She then nodded before putting her head down again and said,

"I'm sorry, I know of my duty to you and I *will* do it."

Graham was perplexed. "You are sorry for what? What are you talking about—your duty to me? I don't understand you."

"You know, my duty to give you a child, an heir."

Understanding of where this conversation was going dawned and clarity finally found him. "Hmmm. You are disappointed you are not with child? I now understand, *chérie*." He took her hand and kissed it. "We have not talked about this and now it seems is the time to do so. Come here and let me hold you." He reached for her and pulled her down next to him in the bed where he could see into her eyes to guess her thoughts and feelings. He put a hand up to her hair and stroked it. "Do you wish to have a baby very badly? Is that what you want?" He searched into her eyes again.

She seemed astonished by the question.

"Of course I want it. I must give you an heir. You have much to lose with holdings such as you possess." She looked up at him resolutely. "It is the one thing I must do as a wife. You have remarked upon it more than once, Graham."

"I have?" He frowned. "I do not think so." He shook his head at her.

"Yes. Once with my uncle, when we discussed the dowry, and another time when you showed me the portrait of all the cousins as children. You said our children would have to learn to sit for portraits."

"Imogene," he admonished, "I merely referred to our children as a future reality. I am sure we will have them, most every couple does. You are not to worry about this. I understand that society expects it and that you bear the burden of giving me an heir, but I do not care about it at all. I don't care, truly."

"You don't? Why don't you?"

"Because it is not why I wanted to marry you. I did not want you for a broodmare. I wanted you because I wanted to live a life with you, because I love you and need you with me."

"But you have so much to lose if I do not give you an heir, a title even." She seemed so amazed at his declaration, unbelieving. "I cannot believe you. Losing Drakenhurst was a shame for my father in having no direct male heir. I think he was pleased in the end that Timothy would be the heir but I know he would have preferred his own son."

Graham shook his head firmly. "Gavandon entails differently. It is not a worry for me in the slightest. Even if we were to have only daughters, it wouldn't matter because the eldest grandson could take it. I do not plan on dying anytime soon, *chérie*. Remember, you owe me fifty years." He held her close and kissed her forehead. "Even if we had no children of our own, it would still pass to Colin and his descendants, and thus stay in the family. Gavandon is safe. You have nothing to worry about." He squeezed her a little. "Your competitiveness has got you into a bit of turmoil, and with your family history I can understand how you might feel pressured, but please let go of the idea." Tickling gently, he made her squeak. "Besides, we've only been working at it for a few weeks. It might take a little longer than that." He winked. "And when it does happen—and it will—we will take great joy in its blessing."

She snuggled into him. He could feel her smiling even though he couldn't see her face. "I feel so much better," she sighed. "You are wonderful in every way."

"Well then, since I am so wonderful, would you like to play cards for a while?" We can play right here on the bed. What do you say?"

"All right. *Vingt-et-un?*"

Later, after losing eight straight hands to her, Imogene could no longer hold in her giggling when he asked, "Twist or stick?"

"I think the better question for you, my darling, is to ask yourself if you can count." She laughed with a mocking grin, biting her lower lip and shaking her head at him.

Graham snorted at her. "Remind me to take you around to Almack's when we are next in Town, *chérie,* you could win us a fortune. The male players would be so befuddled by your charm and beauty; you could destroy them with just the slightest effort on your part."

She raised her eyes and shook her head slowly at him. "How do you fare at the game of chess, my lord?"

"You play? I had not thought of that, *chérie.* A most excellent choice for me as it goes very slowly between moves and would provide ample time for me to watch you as you puzzle through your attack. I'd like that."

HE dreamed of the monster again. It was the same dream—always the same—the crying, the tormenting, and the maniacal laughter. The young mother, the child, his parents, and the evil one, were all present and accounted for.

But this time when he hurtled awake, she was in the bed next to him.

Imogene stared at him in horror. Worry and concern showing clearly, even in the dim fire-glow. "Darling, I think you were having a bad dream." She smoothed over his hair with a comforting hand. "You were mumbling and thrashing about in the bed. What is it?"

Hearing her gentle words brought him careening up from hell and back into reality. He was instantly soothed by her presence and terrified by it at the same time.

What did I say? What did she hear?

He pulled her to him and held on. Imogene was goodness and light. Truth and virtue. His lifeline. He allowed himself the soft warmth of her to comfort and ease his racing heart.

"Graham?"

"Sorry, *chérie.* Sorry to wake you," he murmured into her neck, holding her close.

"What were you dreaming of?"

"I—I cannot remember." He felt guilty for lying to her.

I hate you. Stay away from me…and from her, you evil bastard.

"YOU cannot mean to leave us here. We've nothing!" Agnes cried in panic, holding her sleeping daughter.

"Oh Agnes, are such dramatics really necessary? You're a clever woman, you'll find some way to make a living…I just know you will."

The carriage was pulling to a stop.

"What is this place? We have no money. Please have some mercy!"

He rolled his eyes at her in boredom.

"I think it is called Stapenhill," he drawled, tossing some coins onto the floor of the carriage. "There. I have addressed both of your concerns." He eyed her valise. "At least I had your maid pack you a bag. Now get out."

She stared at him unbelievingly, thinking she must be trapped inside a nightmare that would end at any moment, restoring her life to normalcy. Numbly she picked up the money and her valise and got out of the carriage.

He peered out at her, the evil devil that he was, stabbing her with cold eyes. "And, Agnes, remember what I said. Don't you go squealing to him. It will do you no good—he doesn't want to be reminded. If you force his hand, we might have to get rid of the evidence…" He looked knowingly at Clara asleep in her arms. "You have my promise on that." He slammed the door, and she heard his rap on the roof. At his signal, the carriage pulled away and down the road.

Agnes stayed there watching until it was out of sight. Standing on the side of the road, her sleeping child resting on her shoulder, she looked up into the beautiful blue sky and tried to find something to hold onto. Something good and happy. Some kind of hope.

But there was none to be had.

The only thing she felt was ruined, and wronged.

For the second time in her life, Agnes cursed the fact that she had been born a woman.

Chapter 15

When I play with my cat, who knows whether she isn't amusing herself with me more than I am with her?

Montaigne ~ Essais, 1580

Today was the fifth sitting. Sitting in the elegant chair, she wore a pearl coloured gown, hands absent gloves, per Graham's request, her jewels in place. This portrait would be full length, her pose a three-quarter profile, one hand on the arm of the chair, the other in her lap. Her head was turned slightly as if she were about to stand and go to someone off-canvas and out of view.

Imogene was pleased to find Mr. Mallerton was quite chatty while he painted. They had quickly fallen into easiness and had no trouble discussing all manner of topics. As long as she remained mostly still in her pose, the conversation greatly helped to pass the time.

Breaking through the sounds of his brush on the canvas, Imogene asked, "How did you know you wanted to be a painter?"

"My father was a draper at York. There were just the two of us, as my mother died when I was young. He took me along with him all the time. I always liked to draw even as a very young child, quite the novelty for I could sketch out a profile in minutes and was a source of amusement at gatherings. Visiting the stately homes and manor houses with my father as he went about his business, was my inspiration. I was in awe of the paintings that were displayed. The more I saw, the surer I was of my path."

"Did your father support you in your wish to become an artist?"

"He did. Very early, providing the materials and lessons for me to paint at home and later when I was sent to Harrow for my formal schooling. Graham and I met there. My father wanted me to continue on to university, but that was not what I needed. I knew I had to go to Europe and paint. It was a struggle at first. The starving artist lifestyle is not easy or conventional, which worried my father. For me, that life was part of the education. At the time I knew it was necessary for me to live and to learn in that way."

"Is your father still a draper? I have need of a good one."

"My father passed a year after I left England. His legacy allowed me to continue in that life for several more years, enough to improve my skills that I might make a living."

They were quiet as Imogene absorbed his story. She could feel pain in it but also acceptance. There was a lonely quality about him. Something that set him apart from others. He was guarded, but there was kindness too. She was finding that she enjoyed the sittings. It was calming, and the inoperative time allowed her to reflect upon her new life with Graham.

"Why do you have need of a draper?" he asked after some

minutes.

"I have been charged to have the lady's chamber redone in the style of my choosing, but I've not started in on the project as of yet."

"Do you know what you would like?"

"Hardly. I really do not know where to start. Other than the colours I prefer, I fear I am no expert in decorating."

"I am sure Mrs. Griffin can put you in contact with a draper. What are your preferred colours?"

"Greens and blues with some browns put in."

"Ah, the cool colours. Cool, the green and the blue, but very calming. The brown is a warm colour, but earthy. They are excellent complements of each other. You have good taste."

Accepting his praise, Imogene explained, "They remind me of the outdoors, the grass and the sky and the earth. I should like to try to bring the feel of the outdoors to the inside. Those colours have always been my favourites."

"I have knowledge of fabrics and textures from my father and would be happy to give opinion on your choices if you wish, or if you want some guidance."

"Very kind of you, Mr. Mallerton. I may just take you up on that offer, not wishing to step wrong in my selections."

Returning to painting, he concentrated on his work for a time. "You know, Lady Rothvale, I do more than portraits of people. I could paint a landscape, or your horse, even. If you would like a portrait for your new rooms, I would be pleased to do something personal for you." He offered so easily, as if they had known each other their whole lives.

Imogene was touched by his proposition. "Oh yes, I would love that. A portrait of Terra and Triton together would be dearly cherished. I would have them standing at the front of the house with the fountain in view. Having such a portrait would be a treasure, and perfect for my rooms, I think. If you would do that for me, I would be most obliged."

"Of course, my lady. And since I am paid for my work, you do not have to be obliged to me in any way. I'll make sure your husband gets the bill, and I know he'll happily pay my exorbitant price just to keep you smiling and pleased." His eyes twinkling wickedly made her laugh out loud.

"Mr. Mallerton, would you oblige me further and join us for dinner tonight? The Burleighs are coming this evening and I would like it if you would join our party."

He gave her an odd look and then erased it just as quickly. "I will be there, my lady." He bowed.

He has already received his invitation to dinner and Graham did not tell me.

GRAHAM watched Imogene as she came up the drive with Zuly, having a clear view of her through the library window. Gleaming in her portrait finery, he was unable to do anything really but stare at her. Her face flushed with a joyful glow. She was absolutely radiant. He saw her say something to the dog and Zuly looked up at her. Their exchange, so full of affection and trust, he felt like a voyeur once again, remembering the time he had watched her reunite with Terra at Kenilbrooke.

Mine. She is mine.

He was lying in wait for her. Graham found he craved her return from the portrait sittings at Tristan's with illogical intensity, supposing it was simple instinct, male possessiveness of his woman. Tristan was trustworthy. Graham *knew* absolutely, that nothing improper would ever happen between them, but nevertheless waited anxiously for her whenever she was at a sitting.

Standing in the library doorway, he called to her as she would have passed through the foyer, held out his hand and motioned for her to come to him.

Flashing a lovely smile, she greeted him. "Are you waiting on me again, my darling?"

He wondered if his desperation for her when she returned from a sitting had caught her notice. Probably had. Imogene possessed a sharp mind.

She glided over to him as if she was well aware he needed a little soothing, and wondered where it might lead. He wouldn't mind a little soothing right here in the library. The door did possess a sturdy lock, after all.

Pulling her to him, he took in her heavenly scent. "Guilty as charged, *chéri*. But I am fine now you are returned to me." He gazed at her in all of her mystery. "Give us a kiss," he said to her, feeling a little of his tension let go now that she was in his arms again.

Imogene put her hand on his face and tucked a strand of hair back behind his ear. "I love you. I love that you wait here for me to come home. What have you been up to while I was away?" Her words, gentle and sweet, tumbled off lips he wanted to kiss.

He shrugged. "Nothing much. The post arrived and we have letters from Jules and Mina at Everfell, Wilton Court, and from your friend Jocelyn, I think." He paused for a moment before asking, "Why did you look so happy when you came in just now?"

"That is easy. I am happy because I am returning to you."

He rolled his eyes. "Very good diplomatic answer, *chérie*. Now try again," he scolded with mock sternness.

She grinned at him as if she was sharing an exciting secret. "Mr. Mallerton is going to paint a portrait for me. A portrait of my own choosing, for my rooms. I wish it to be of Terra and Triton in front of the fountain. It's a lovely vision and it pleases me. That is probably why you see me as happy today. Oh, and I invited him to join us for dinner with the Burleighs."

"What was his reaction to your invitation?" he asked with a grimace, remembering he'd forgotten to mention it to her.

"Well, he looked at me oddly now that you ask. He said, 'I will be there' when he accepted. Why would he say it like that, Graham, unless you had already invited him? No wonder he looked at me so strangely." She pushed at his chest. "Why do you not tell me things? Secrets, secrets, all the time. You make me appear an idiot." Her eyes sparkly with irritation, she folded her arms as she waited for his response.

Graham closed his eyes for a moment. "I apologize. It was my mistake, not a secret, I promise you. The invitation was last minute, sent over this morning. I forgot to tell you. I get so damn distracted with all of…everything," he sputtered, feeling very exasperated. "Being a bachelor for such a long time, I am not used to thinking about how I might get you into trouble, *chérie*. I am so sorry. I promise I'll get better." Leaning into her neck, he whispered, "I am at your mercy."

"Well, you do look remorseful," she said wryly, "and pathetic. And what is so distracting for you anyway?"

He gaped at her.

"Are you inferring that *I* am the source of your great distraction, my darling? How is that possible?"

Graham gave her a thorough, salacious sweep with his eyes before saying, "It is very possible, I assure you."

"Hmmph," she sniffed. "I'm going to go up and change out of this gown now."

"I will help you." He took her arm to go with her.

"Oh no, no. I don't think so, not today," she said, imperiously, removing her arm from his hold. "You will stay here and get yourself...*undistracted.* 'Tis your punishment, Graham. When I return, you can tell me how you intend to solve your little problem." Her lip curled up on one side; and he could tell she was enjoying this exchange with him immensely.

He felt his eye start to twitch, and began tapping his hand on his leg.

Inclining his head slightly, he said, "Do as you wish, *chérie.*"

He watched Imogene leave the library, a disobedient smirk on his face, and a quickly hardening cock in his breeches.

Both he and Imogene realized he had agreed to nothing.

Moving his hands up to his throat, he began to unknot his cravat.

IMOGENE fled quickly, knowing she had very little time as she raced to her rooms. He would come after her within minutes. She started pulling off the emeralds on the way to her chamber. Once inside, she dumped the jewels onto her dressing table, drew off the pearly dress, laying it over her bed, taking a white collared blouse from the wardrobe, buttoning it, her fingers flying, then she chose a soft grey jumper and smoothed it down. She was breathing heavily when she dashed out into the hall for a quick look. Moving hastily down the corridor, she stopped just past the corner and waited, her heart pounding so hard, she shivered.

It didn't take him long. She heard his boot steps come determinedly down the hall. Her bedroom door was opened, and then footsteps into that room were sounded.

Imagining him taking in the sight of her gown tossed on the bed, and the magnificent emeralds thrown on the dressing table, gave her such a thrill. The instant he saw them he would know she was hiding, and he would start hunting for her.

He called out her name one time, and then she heard no more.

He was moving on through her rooms, into their sitting room, and from there probably into his bedroom to search, she decided.

Imogene held her place and waited.

GRAHAM knew what she was up to the minute he stepped into her rooms. He saw the haphazard drops of gown and jewels and figured he was in for a game of cat and mouse. He searched the other rooms for good measure but didn't really imagine he'd find her so easily. Very carefully, he retraced his steps, walking lightly so his boots did not clink on the floor. Moving quietly back out into the hall, he stopped for a moment. He breathed in the air, catching the whiff of her honeysuckle scent and knew she was near. "Imogene," he hummed, "I know you are close by for I can scent you." He took a step in her direction, listening for any sounds from her. "You can run, *chérie.* Go ahead…run. I will just chase after you, but you know that." He took another step. "I will catch you, *chérie.* You know I will. And you *know* what will happen when I do…"

That last part did it.

He heard her tiny intake of air, and then the sound of scrambling feet. Pure animal instinct took over as he lurched toward the direction she was going even though he had not sighted her yet. He spotted the back of her skirt as she turned the corner at the end of the hall before pounding up the narrow staircase leading to the third floor. When he made it to the landing he could see many doors opened on both sides of the corridor.

Graham had a very good idea of where she might be hiding as he stalked her methodically, carefully, and patiently. "You are very clever, *chérie,* opening all these doors, trying to throw me off your trail. But it is hopeless. I *will* find you. It's just a matter of moments before I catch you. Isn't that right, *chérie?*"

He stopped chasing and decided to wait her out because he was actually standing in the doorway of the room where she was hiding. He knew she was in there because he could see a swath across the threshold where the dust had been swept away by her skirt as she'd crossed it. The other doorways all had their dust intact.

He felt the thrill of the chase, and her imminent capture, with great relish.

This is tremendous fun. Oh, Imogene, I am thinking of a word… A very bad word. A word I would never say to you, but I can think it. Nevertheless, the word expresses exactly what I want to do to you. And right now, you need it done to you. You need it badly.

He stepped into the room and swept it with his eyes. Not very many places to hide; under the bed, wardrobe, drapes, there was nowhere else. Walking over to the wardrobe, he opened it—empty. He spun at the sound of her squeal and the shuddering of drapes as she left her hiding spot and tried to pass him.

Imogene made a run for the door and she was quick, but not quick enough. She made it as far as a few paces down the hallway before he snaked an arm around her waist and dragged her back.

She screamed.

He clamped a hand over her mouth immediately. "Now we can't have any of that, *chérie*, and you mustn't upset the servants." Graham panted the words into her ear as he pulled her backward into the room, closed the door and locked them in. He removed his hand, managing to pick her up and drop her onto the bed, breathing heavily from all of the exertion.

Her elbows propped her up in the bed and she breathed hard, her breasts heaving, her eyes growing dark and smoky in challenge.

"I told you I *would* catch you." He leaned against the door, pulled off one boot, and then the other. "And you know what's going to happen now, don't you?" He asked her in a whisper, raking over her with his eyes.

Imogene nodded slowly, looking very sensual, and if he had to guess, very aroused.

He pulled her to her feet to stand at the side of the bed. "Your clothes are coming off now."

The jumper was pulled over her head, and then the white blouse. Her petticoats and corset were quickly unstrung and pushed down to the floor. He lifted her shift off, and she was there before him. His prize. His reward for all his efforts. Graham pressed her down onto the bed naked and enjoyed the sight of her body as he made fast work of pitching his own clothes to the floor to lie beside hers.

The instant he touched her on the bed she became like a feral cat, writhing underneath him, arching at every touch, every lick, every kiss, every bite, and every stroke. It was stirring and untamed, raging and tempestuous, and undoubtedly, a mutual ravishment. They worked at it very hard, and when it was time, and she could wait no longer for him to join her, she said the words, "Fill me."

"What?" he rasped, "what did you say?"

"Fill me!"

He served.

And as he did, he pondered what she'd said. *Fill... She said 'fill.' An interesting word choice. Same beginning sound, and the same number of letters as my word. Fuck, fill, take, need, have, mate, love—merely connotation. Words. Words change nothing about my feelings for her, or what I do right now. Ooooooh, fuck! Never let this end.*

THEY lay together under the covers. Graham had her pressed right up against him, her back to his chest. Nuzzling at her neck, he tried to wake her slowly. After their wild coupling, he'd dragged the blankets over their bodies to hold off the winter chill, and they had slept. He felt her stir and knew she was waking. "You are like a sleepy kitten now. Quite a transition from the wild, untamed feline of before."

"Mmm, which do you like best?"

"They both have their merits, *chérie*, and there was also a playful pussy in the mix as well, when you led me on this merry chase. I love all of your feline personas."

"Do you know what today is?"

"I do, *chérie*."

"Well, do you like your Valentine surprise then?"

"You planned this?" He rolled her to her back so he could see her eyes. "I don't believe it."

She laughed at him. "I was going to do it tonight, but your little omission, which got you into trouble, was too perfect of an opportunity to pass up." She shook her head at him. "If you could have seen your face when I told you to stay in the library. I will never forget it. You got a little twitch in your eye." She touched the corner of his eye and grinned.

He raised his brows at her. "I got a twitch somewhere else as well. You have that unique effect upon me."

"Yes, I know," she replied wryly. "I had no idea where I was going or what was even up here. I could hear you coming and closing in fast, so I ran by several doors and opened them all. I *knew* you would come after me and I would have no time, so I flew faster than I have ever done before. You can thank me that the spontaneity of the moment led us here to this little love nest," she reminded him. "Very appropriate for St. Valentine's Day, too. Is that not the day that birds are supposed to choose their mates?"

"Let's see if it qualifies as such." He purposefully looked around the room. "It has four walls, a locking door, a bed…and you." He tickled her. "Yes." He nodded. "I believe it qualifies as a love nest, but it is rather dusty." He sniffed the air. "Maybe we should get someone up here to clean it before we try to use it again."

"So you are assuming that this situation might repeat itself?"

"But I loved chasing you, *chérie,* so I dearly hope so. All you have to do is bolt and I'll come after you straight away and we'll see where we end up." He winked. "I don't know how I'm going to get through dinner tonight with our guests. Every time I look at you I'm going to think of this afternoon and people might suspect what we've been up to."

"You'd better not look at me then," she scolded.

"Impossible," he whispered as he dropped down for a kiss.

"THIS is a lovely colour on you." Graham admired her claret coloured gown, his eyes lighting up when he saw that she was wearing the heart pendant he had given her. He kissed the heart nestled at her throat and then sweetly on the lips. "Shall we go and greet our guests, Lady Rothvale?"

"Yes, my lord, I believe we should." She took his arm and sighed.

"What is it?"

She hesitated before she spoke. "The formality of the title is so—so ostentatious. I find it a little uncomfortable. I know I am to address you as *Lord Rothvale* in company, but it just sounds so affected. I feel the same way about my own title. I would prefer to be Mrs. Everley or just plain Imogene."

He squeezed her arm. "I know exactly how you feel, *chérie*, as I share your sentiments precisely. I am afraid there is nothing for it though. When we are in public, we will have to observe convention, with the servants as well. I have found that staff cling to the rules most steadfastly, never giving up the formal address of a title. When we are alone with our friends, we can do whatever we like, addressing them in the familiar if we wish to."

"Yes, all right."

Later, at dinner, Imogene enjoyed visiting with Charles and Jemima Burleigh, finding them a very interesting and engaging couple. She felt a connection with Jemima immediately and was fascinated to hear of their life at Biddenton where Charles held the vicarage. Charles and Jemima had been married for more than five years and had two children, Samuel and Clementine.

Jemima was still young at five and twenty, very busy with

her children and the emancipation work. They spoke a little about it. Jemima had gotten involved when Charles's family felt it prudent to pull out of their Antigua interests. They maintained their contacts however, and this enabled them to provide for sponsorship from English families of beneficent means. Jemima praised Graham for his example to the landed families of Warwickshire as he had been the first in the area to take a family. She also informed Imogene that Mr. and Mrs. Everley of Everfell were in the process of sponsoring a family from Antigua as well, and eagerly awaited their transport.

Imogene could see how the Burleighs did their good by example, and that this was how such acts of kindness and charity were passed along.

During dinner it became apparent that the Burleighs and Tristan Mallerton were already well acquainted and good friends. Imogene was content to sit back and enjoy the conversations around her when Graham addressed his friend. "What's this I hear about a portrait for Imogene that you are going to paint? She was quite thrilled by the idea."

"Lady Rothvale has commissioned a portrait of her horses and the grounds of Gavandon for her redecorated chamber." Tristan looked at her conspiratorially. "A tribute to her new home. Isn't that right, Lady Rothvale?"

Imogene smiled back at Tristan. "Please call me Imogene." She looked at everyone at the table. "Graham and I just had a conversation about the formal address of the titles and how off-putting I find it to be. When we are in private, among friends, I would wish to be called Imogene, please."

Tristan looked mischievous. "As you wish, Imogene, but would you feel slighted if I insisted you continue to call me Mr. Mallerton?"

"Not at all, Mr. Mallerton," she said smoothly and with

great understanding. "It would crush me to think I had made you uncomfortable by my familiarity, *Mr. Mallerton.*" She gave him a generous, serene smile.

Tristan burst out laughing. "Nothing rattles you. I have tried and tried, and you remain as cool as a cucumber despite my most vigorous efforts. I am teasing you, of course. I would be honored for you to call me Tristan. Mr. Mallerton was my father, the draper from York, remember?" They laughed together in sharing their private joke. "Does nothing rattle you, Imogene?"

"Oh, I am quite certain something rattles me." She looked to Graham. "And he's sitting at the head of the table."

Everybody laughed at her joke. Graham gave her a quick wink.

"Well, since we are all good friends now, I have a question for you, Graham," Tristan challenged wryly.

Graham waved him off. "Yes, yes, I know. Why did you get two separate invitations to dinner; one from me and one from Imogene? I will tell you. I am befuddled and distracted, apparently, now that I have taken a wife."

Imogene cut in. "And I saw to it that he was soundly punished. I doubt if such a problem will present itself ever again." Absently moving her hand up to her neck, she fingered the heart pendant as they shared a look over the table.

James glanced at Jemima, and then at Tristan. They all smiled at each other, and then James spoke, "Graham, you assessed it true, my friend. Befuddled and distracted, indeed!"

The men separated to have their port, leaving Jemima and Imogene alone after dinner. "Imogene, I cannot say enough how changed Graham is. We have never seen him so happy. It is apparent that you are very well matched. It's as if the events of last year had never happened."

"What events do you refer to, Jemima?"

"Well, his mother's death. It was very hard on him." Jemima seemed to realize her mistake right away, steering the conversation into another direction. "Graham has shared that you are a rider. I would love to ride with you. I don't get to go out as often as I'd like, but would love to arrange some time with you. It would be good for me to spend some time in the fresh air. Let's plan a date, shall we?"

Imogene didn't push for more explanation, but that didn't stop her from wondering of the circumstances preceding Lady Rothvale's death…

WHEN Imogene got into bed that night there was a book lying on her pillow. It was a thin volume entitled, *The Princess and the Toad.* Her heart stuttered at the sight. It was the story Graham had told to her the morning after their wedding night. He'd written the words out in a fine-looking hand and had coloured in some illustrations to accompany the story pages. Somehow, he had taken it to be bound in leather, the title embossed in gold lettering. It was an object of beautiful art to Imogene. She was utterly speechless as she poured through the velum pages and read the beautiful story.

"My darling Valentine, I hope you like it."

"It is priceless to me. Priceless. Thank you for such a beautiful gift. I treasure it as I treasure you."

He saw the tears welling and smiled, for he knew she was deeply touched by his gift.

"MAMMA?"

"Yes, love?"

"I'm hungry and I want my dolly."

"I know, Clara. We're just on a little trip and we'll have to get you a new dolly. You must be brave, darling. Can you be brave for Mamma?"

"Yes, Mamma," she sniffed.

"It's just a little farther." They had walked about a mile after receiving directions from a farmer driving an oxcart. The inn was just coming into view and Agnes pointed it out to Clara. "When we get to the inn, you may have your supper, and when we get to our room, we can lie down and I'll tell you your favourite story."

"The one about Dick Whittington and his cat?"

"The very one and the same, Clara." Agnes sighed.

The inn looked finer than her meagre budget could withstand, a sign identifying it as 'The Lion's Crown.' There was a small garden in the front and some benches. Clara found a tiny frog and immediately became distracted, following it in the grass. Agnes sank down onto a bench wearily and summed up their situation. Not very good. A single woman with a child of five years, very little money, and abandoned on the road. She had no idea where the village of Stapenhill even was. From the looks of the topography, she thought she must be many miles south from Gladfield.

It felt like thousands of miles away.

HE saw her walk into the courtyard. She was lovely. Very well dressed and the child too, in beautifully stitched clothes. It struck him odd that they had walked here. *From where?*

She looked bereft—so lost—on the verge of tears, even. Their situation was not right. It smelled of misdeed, most definitely. He let her be at first, watching from the window. He waited another hour before he couldn't stand it any longer.

His shadow fell over her as she sat on the bench in front of his inn. "Madam," he spoke gently, bowing. "Mark Jacobson, proprietor of The Lion's Crown. May I offer my assistance to you? I'm sorry but you seem to be in distress. It will be dark soon." He looked over at the sun, dipping low on the horizon. "Do you want a room?"

His offer seemed to unravel her. A sob escaped.

"I apologize, sir, Mr. Jacobson. I…I lost track of the time and have been distracted sitting out here. Yes. I'll take a room, the smallest you have. Thank you."

Her little girl bounded up then. "I found a tiny frog," she announced, holding out her hand to show him.

He bent down to view her impromptu pet. "He looks like a fine frog to me. I wonder though, since he is so tiny, that if he were changed into a handsome prince, would he be a tiny prince or that of a normal sized man?" He viewed the child earnestly, awaiting her opinion.

She seemed to ponder his question with all of the seriousness that one of her age could possibly give. "Well, a prince that tiny wouldn't be much good, I don't think."

He smiled widely at her firm logic. "A good point, I daresay." He bowed to her. "Whom do I have the pleasure of greeting?"

"I am Clara, and this is Mamma."

"Well, Miss Clara, welcome to The Lion's Crown. I am your host, Mr. Jacobson. Shall we see about showing you to your room?"

Clara nodded at him. Clara's mother rose up from the

bench to follow. She looked about on the verge of collapse. He wanted to help her. Hell, he *needed* to help her.

After they were settled and supper sent to them in their room, he returned to the register to study her entry.

'Agnes Schellman' was written in a clear, fine hand.

Chapter 16

Affliction is enamoured of thy parts,
And thou art wedded to calamity.

William Shakespeare ~ Romeo and Juliet, 1595

Ambling up the path toward the house, Imogene hoped Graham might be finished with his work. Her ride with Terra had been lovely, and after exploring some new places on the Gavandon estate, she had plenty of questions for him. Learning everything about her new home was her first priority as the new mistress, and she had every intention of doing her duty as Lady Rothvale.

Up ahead, she could see her husband at the front of the house, waiting for her. Several of the grooms as well as Mr. Hendrix appeared to be hovering as well. Imogene could tell that something was off, especially when all of the servants cleared off, leaving Graham standing there staring as Terra brought her closer to the house with each step.

The sight of her husband with his boots planted in the gravel, arms crossed over his chest, and looking furious, was not what Imogene was expecting to find upon her return.

Graham's face was hard, his jaw clenched, and his eyes narrowed, but those were nothing compared to the blazing anger rolling off of him in waves. Imogene had never seen him like this before. She didn't even know he had such an extent of the expression in him, and she was afraid.

As she pulled Terra to a stop, he wasted no time in snatching her down from the saddle. His method was rough…fraught, as he grabbed her and clutched her hard against his chest. His breathing ragged in and out as she felt his chest move from the effort.

His manhandling shocked her, and she pulled back questioningly. "What? What on earth is the matter?"

He stood there glaring at her, hard and unbending. "Excuse me, madam, if I cannot speak. I am very, very angry with you, and barely able to spit the words out right now."

Imogene felt her spine grow stiff. "Why are you angry with me? And why do you address me in such a way?" She was indignant.

"Oh, please!" he barked. "You pretend not to know? Fine, then. I'll play at your game but I know you are very aware of what you have done." Stabbing a finger in her direction, he shouted. "You rode out solitary! Nobody knew of where you'd gone! We did not even know of which direction to begin a search for you!" His voice went low and acrimonious. "You broke your promise to me, never to ride alone. You promised me, Imogene, and you—and you did it anyway." His eyes looked possessed by a demon, he was so angry. And his behaviour was so bewildering to her she hardly knew how to calm him.

"Graham," she spoke gently, "the promise I made to you at Shelburne was, I believed, for my riding there, while you were away from me. We are together now and this is my home." She stretched her arm out over the land. Am I not free to ride here on the estate? You have shown me the lay of the land and I know the way now. Surely you can't mean to keep me from riding—"

"Oh, I do mean it, madam, and my word is law here. I forbid you to ride solitary. I forbid it. This behaviour will not be repeated. Believe my words as I assure you I do mean them, every word."

Imogene recoiled in shock, utterly crushed by his poisonous words. "You forbid me?" Incredulous at his demeanour and tone with her, she gaped at him in wide-eyed shock. *Who are you? I don't recognize you at all.*

Graham leaned in then, close and tight, his mouth next to her ear, his words slicing into her painfully. "I do. And just so we are completely clear on this matter, understand me now. If you should wish to leave the immediate grounds in any manner other than your own two feet upon the earth below them, it had better be in a conveyance or in the company of another rider."

Imogene straightened her back, pulled herself together, and forced calm words from her mouth. They sounded calm but were really a mask for the outrage that roiled inside her. In deference to him, she lowered her head. "My lord, as you wish." Then she flashed him a cold stare, turned from him, and walked toward the house with her head held high. *At your command, my lord!*

Imogene had purpose to her step and knew what she was going to do. She went straight to her rooms and packed a valise, throwing her things together quickly. She called for a carriage before changing out of her riding clothes and dashing off a quick note for Graham.

It was a very short and terse note.

And she made a particular point to address it to *Lord Rothvale.*

She could feel her anger flow out through the pen as she abused it upon the paper, explaining she was going to Philippa at Harwell House and would stay overnight at the least. Mentioning nothing of their quarrel, she preferred her husband to glean his own meaning from her actions. He knew exactly where she would be. She was going there in a carriage, as per his command, and he could not fault her. It was decided and she was going.

Just as she came out of his study from leaving the note, she heard him walk into the foyer. He was looking for her, and had obviously passed right by her awaiting carriage out the front. So be it, she thought as she boldly came down the stairs with her bag.

He stood at the bottom and ogled her. "Where are you going? Hendrix said you called for a carriage." His voice was no longer as it had been before.

"I am going to my sister's," she said flatly. "I left you a note in your study, so you would know." She looked down at the marble floor, unable to meet his gaze.

"When will you return?" he asked softly, willing her to look up at him.

She kept her eyes down. "I cannot say. My sister will want me surely, and I must avail myself to her at this time of her need." She hoped her lame attempt at justification didn't sound as shoddy to him as it did to her. *This is dreadful, utterly horrifying. Please don't let me cry. I am not going to cry.*

"You mean you will be gone overnight? You will not be here?" He seemed stunned. All of the earlier spirit had left him.

"That is my intention, yes." She looked up at him then, and coldly asked, "Do you forbid me? I wish for your clarity on this matter, so we both know I am understanding you completely, my lord."

He winced as she used his earlier words against him. "Of course not. You are free to see your sister at any time that you wish," he said stoically. "Imogene, you do not have to leave. You are upset from our disagreement."

"Yes I do. And yes I am. You know where I will…be," her voice broke. The tears were coming hard and fast. She moved around him, rushing outside to the waiting carriage. As soon as she was in, she hit the roof hard with her hand, telling the driver to move out. Imogene held her composure for as long as it took to pull away from the drive. She did not look back to see his reaction to her leaving, so she did not see Graham break. She didn't see the panic in his eyes or how his shoulders dropped or how he stumbled upon the step and nearly fell. She was too occupied holding herself in the seat until she was far enough away from view and could safely fling herself down and weep her heart out.

GRAHAM watched her go. He almost reached for her and stopped her. Almost. He detested how he had spoken to her. It was not in his nature to use such harsh words. *Imogene, I was so terrified. Everything came back to me all in an instant. If anything happened to you, I don't know what—* He couldn't even finish the thought. Scrubbing his hands over his face in frustration, he had no idea what to do next. *Let her be.* He would give her some space for now and then later he would make amends. Explain his madness. Knowing he had hurt her terribly, and even as painful as the knowledge was, it was far better for her to be safe than to risk any danger to herself. He was right about that. He *was* right, wasn't he?

As her carriage disappeared from sight, he felt the anger draw out of his body as if he'd been stuck with a dagger. *She left. I was harsh, but only out of anxiety and concern. My anger caused her to flee me. She wanted to get away. From me. She has left.*

Graham barricaded himself in his study with a double brandy. The fact that he had poured such a drink was a testament to his state of mind. He avoided such excesses as a rule; hard drinking, tobacco, and gambling held little allure for him as they were painful reminders of his brother's weakness, and what it had wrought. There was one compulsion though, a vice of sorts. An addiction he could not, and would not curb. It was for Imogene of course, and he felt the withdrawal symptoms acutely.

He found her note and read it before casting it away like a piece of rotted meat. Imogene had up and left him. She didn't want to be with him. He poured over the events again and again, until he had stewed everything into a painful, boiling brew fit only for his wallowing in it.

The fault is all yours. You should have told her. You know she does not know. She is too considerate, and would have never gone alone if she knew. You are an ignorant fool.

True.

Graham gave his conscience plenty of fodder to throw around; enough to feed his inner beast for many hours.

IMOGENE cried the whole way to Harwell House. She regretted leaving him as soon she had cooled off. Now she was so miserable, and she didn't know what to say to Philippa and John when they asked her why she'd come. *Graham got very angry with me for riding out by myself. He felt that I had broken a promise I'd made to him, and forbade me to ride solitary ever again. My pride was hurt and I left the house.* Well, it was the truth even if it sounded petty and asinine now. Something else was bothering her as well. His reaction was so out of character, she knew instinctively there was some sort of explanation. Jemima Burleigh had alluded to something. If only Colin were here, she could ask him.

Trembling badly, she arrived at the door, actually considering returning to her carriage and ordering it back home.

A maid admitted her, and showed her into the parlor. John got to her first. The look of concern on his face was so sincere that Imogene fell apart at the sight of him. He pulled her into his arms as she cried and tried to explain why she'd come.

"Philippa will be down in a moment. She was resting before dinner," he murmured.

John's words brought on a fresh bout of tears when she came under the realization she was intruding upon them unannounced, with Philippa in her condition. Imogene crumbled, very ashamed of her actions, her manners, and for surely upsetting her pregnant sister.

Philippa arrived into the room then and pulled Imogene to the couch where she held her and listened as the whole terrible business was spilled out to them.

John and Philippa were quiet when she was done explaining. They shared a serious look together before Philippa said, "I have to tell her, John. I take full responsibility. Graham won't bother with me. Women who are eight months gone are quite fearsome indeed," she remarked wryly. John solemnly nodded his agreement to his wife.

"What is it? Please tell me before I lose my mind."

"Imogene, there is something you need to know about Graham, about his mamma. I do not know why he has not told you, but regardless I am going to tell you now. Her death was tragic…gruesome, Graham alone left to deal with it. I believe he was so affected by the circumstances, that her death was the driving force of his staying in Ireland for so long. His mamma loved to ride, as you do—"

Imogene stopped her sister from speaking. "No! No, no, no. I can guess what you are going to say next. He told me once, that his mother was a great rider." She felt cold, bitter fear grab hold of her heart as she resigned herself to hearing the rest of the story. Imogene squeezed Philippa's hand for strength.

"Lady Rothvale rode nearly every day and often alone, and one day she did not return. Graham found her. She had suffered a bad fall, was gravely injured, and made worse by lying in a cold field for hours, never regaining consciousness, and lingering for weeks before dying. Graham suffered and bore the entirety of it as his brother was not even in England at the time and she was gone before he could return. It was very sad, very painful. So you can see how Graham has a justifiable fear of your riding solitary. Imogene, he acted through fear because he loves you so."

Imogene dropped her face into her hands and cried some more. Her heart broke for Graham and her part in hurting him afresh. "What have I done? I am a terrible wife. I must go home and beg his forgiveness, now. Right now. I have to return home right now!" She tried to rise from the couch in her panic.

Philippa and John both said, "No."

"But I must go to him," Imogene wailed.

Philippa gently held her arm. "You must stay here for the night. It is getting dark and you cannot travel at night alone. It isn't safe."

"If I left now I could be home in an hour. It's not that far."

"No, Imogene. Philippa is correct, you must stay for the night now," John admonished.

"But why?" she sobbed.

"Because I value my life!" John exclaimed. "Imogene, your husband would string me up if I allowed you to leave alone in the dark of night. Think, Sister. The same reasons that caused your quarrel today would bring about the same fears in him if we let you go back tonight. I am sorry, but you will have to stay. You can return home early tomorrow if you wish. I'll go see to your driver and set him up for overnight."

Then Imogene stopped resisting and accepted her fate. She guessed it was appropriate punishment for her spitefulness, and would have gladly borne it if she didn't know that Graham was suffering as well, all by himself, at home, without her. That thought alone pierced her with the most acute pain she had ever felt. It was worse even than the immeasurable pains she had felt over her parents.

Philippa pulled her gently. "Come. Let's go in to dinner."

"No, I am unable to eat a thing. You go, darling. I've made myself ill and I should like to just go to bed. Perhaps some tea could be sent up if it's not too much trouble. I apologize for bringing this here into your home. I am wretched, a horrible wife, a terrible sister, and a selfish person. Please forgive me, Phil. Forgive me."

"You are none of those things and there is nothing to forgive. We love you and are here to support you in any way that we can. This will sort itself out, you will see. You and Graham have been through a great deal. Be easy on each other." Philippa kissed her on the forehead. "Go up to bed. I'll come see you after dinner."

Imogene went up to her room, dressed for bed, and washed her face. The cool water felt good. What she really needed was a literal baptism of water to soak away all of the sins she felt on her. Imogene did feel truly ill. Her stomach lurching around in her gut was most unpleasant on top of her emotional state.

A maid delivered tea, which Imogene gratefully accepted.

She sipped her tea and thought about what she would say to Graham tomorrow when she got back home.

GRAHAM decided he would give her this one night away. If she did not return in the morning he would go and get her. Yes, he was decided. One night without her would hurt to be sure, but he told himself he could stand it. He kept telling himself that as he went through the motions of the late afternoon and resolved to endure her absence. Trying hard, he really thought he could do without her; that is until it was time to go to bed and she was not there.

Wearily leaving his study to head upstairs, the dog passed in front of him. Zuly looked at him as if he were a pile of dung in the middle of the room. Graham and Zuly stared at each other for a moment.

It was just the impetus he needed.

Turning, he grabbed his coat, dashed to the stables, and found the determination to do what he should have done hours ago. Triton was saddled and racing down the road before the clock had passed the half-hour.

He was desperate to get to her, desperate to tell her why, desperate to hold her.

Just desperate.

When Graham arrived at Harwell House John greeted him warmly, "Ah, Graham, you actually arrived sooner than I expected you. Be of ease, man, I will not harass you too much as I can see you've your hands plenty full." He grinned and slapped him on the shoulder.

"John, hello. She is safely here then? I should have never let her go," he said, twisting his gloves mercilessly in his hands.

"Imogene is here and she is safe. Very, very distraught over hurting you, but she is fine."

"She knows then. Did you tell her?"

John shook his head. "Philippa did. And before you get upset with my wife, I must ask why in the hell didn't you tell her?"

Graham held up his hands in surrender. "I am not upset with your wife. How did Philippa even know of it?"

John sighed deeply. "Well, I think from a servant or something. Remember, it had not been a very long time in happening when I married her and I think a maid came from Gavandon to work here. Regardless, she knew. In fact, when we heard the news of your engagement, Philippa spoke to me of her concerns about this very matter. She worried that Imogene's riding might cause a patch of trouble for you."

"She did?"

"Yes, truly she was worried about it. The Byron-Cole ladies are not lacking in their mental faculties, Graham, as I am sure you have found. Philippa knows of Imogene's riding predilections, and knowing the circumstances of your mother's death, thought there might be some bumps along the way between you. God, man, why didn't you tell her? I don't wish to put you down lower than you feel now, but you do know you could have saved yourself a lot of trouble if you'd just been open with your wife. I know Imogene is emotional, but she is very considerate of others, and reasonable. Except for tonight. God!"

"What? Tell me. What did she do?" Graham feared what John would say.

John shook his head. "The poor thing was desperate to get back to you. We had to force her to stay. She was determined to return home tonight, in the dark, alone on the road. By the time she finally accepted she must stay, she'd made herself so ill she could not even take her dinner, and had to go up to bed."

Graham hissed through his teeth, "What a bloody cock-up I've made of everything."

"I won't disagree with you, Brother, but I'll let you work that out with your wife. You will stay tonight as well." John was adamant.

"I don't know how to thank you, John. I am indebted to you and Philippa."

"Nonsense." John clapped him on the back hard. "We are family now. What good is family if not to share in the misery, eh?"

"You are a good man." Graham thanked him again.

"Go to your wife. Upstairs, third room on the right."

Graham let himself out of John's study and made his way up the stairs, meeting Philippa at the top.

"Philippa," he greeted gently. "Please forgive me for the mess I've made of everything. I am so sorry for bringing this down on you and John, and your household."

She took his hands in hers, smiled and shook her head at

him. "Graham. You know, Imogene said almost those same exact words to me? So I'll tell you what I told her. There is nothing to forgive, nothing at all. We are your family and this is our right. I know you would do the same for us." She tried to lighten him just a little by teasing. "Now, if you had not come tonight, then maybe there would be something to hold against you."

Graham closed his eyes for just a moment, her words cutting right to his heart. He squeezed her hands. "You are extraordinary, as is she."

"She is just there in that room." Philippa pointed. "Very sad for hurting you. I have never seen her so heartbreakingly sad. Even through all of the other tragic business she has borne. But I know you can fix it, Graham. Only you can. Goodnight."

Philippa left him there, walking slowly away, one hand holding her back, the other on her belly. Graham thought she looked beautiful. He wondered if Imogene would look like Philippa did right now, one day, when she was heavy with his child.

He knocked softly on her door. When there was no answer he slowly pushed it open.

She was sitting at a writing desk composing frantically. Her back was to him, so she did not see him, but she heard him. He saw her stop writing and slowly turn her head.

Her feet hardly touched the floor as she launched herself at him.

He was ready and his arms were open to catch her.

They held on to each other for a long time, the same words coming from their lips in unison, "I am so sorry—"

Graham interrupted, "Me first, please?" Carrying her over to the bed, he sat and faced her. "Imogene, *chérie,* my love, I have wounded you appallingly. I spoke to you cruelly and harshly, hating myself for doing it, but I was so, so terrified beyond imagination that you were hurt or worse. I think I lost my mind while I was looking for you, ceasing to be myself. This is not an excuse, I realize, and I alone must accept my actions. Now, I am aware that you've been told of the circumstances of my mother's death. It was wrong of me to keep it from you. Even now I cannot talk about it much because I believe I have laid her to rest, truly. Those feelings of terror, dread, and panic, came screaming through me when I discovered you were out alone—I was transported back there to that time with her all in an instant. But this time it was *you*…and the pain and fear was many times worse. There is no one that I love more than you. I have not loved, and cannot love anyone more than I love you. Now, I must say the last part and I fear to say it, but I must anyway. Even with everything that has been said today and regretted, I still must insist that you do not ride solitary. I cannot risk you. If you go alone you put yourself at risk, and I cannot allow such a situation. I love you more than my own life—"

Imogene stopped him. Putting her fingers to his lips with tears pouring down her cheeks, she shook her head. "You need not worry. I vow to you I will never ride alone again. Graham, I would give it up. I would give it up freely and never ride a horse again if you asked it of me. Nothing is more important in my life than you. Nothing. If you are not happy, I cannot be. Hurting you today left me empty and filled with pain. I am embarrassed and disgraced for leaving you in anger. I regret that one thing more than anything else and I will never do it again, I promise. It is my hope that someday you will trust me once again." Imogene put her face in her hands, her eyes glistening at him over her fingertips.

Graham pulled her in closer. "Shhh. I trust you, Imogene. You have never been in danger of losing my trust. Even today, I understood you did not intend to deceive. You believed the promise to be a different one than I thought it to be—a misunderstanding. I would never wish to take your riding away from you either. I couldn't do that. Maybe Ben can trail you? He is a fine lad and very trustworthy. I'll go with you, make time for you. When Elle comes or Cariss or Jemima, they can join you. We will work it out. It is my fault for not being open with you. Hold me accountable for everything, no fault or blame fall to you. We will put this ugly experience behind us, yes? What do you say, *chérie*?"

"Yes…please. I never wish to feel like that again. I have been ill because of it. You are here now and I am so grateful."

"I should have never let you go in the first place—I should have begged you to stay, it was stupid of me." He put his cheek to hers and caressed her back, holding her. "What were you writing when I came in?"

"I was trying to organize my words to say to you tomorrow. I wanted to come home, but it was too late and Philippa and John said I'd have to stay the night. Knowing sleep would have eluded me in my wretched condition, I was writing out what I wanted to say to you."

"Let's get you into bed. I want to lie down next to you, and hold you. I want to know you are here beside me the whole night long."

She pushed out a heavy sigh. "Those are the best words I have heard this whole day."

IMOGENE woke the next morning in Graham's arms with

deep green eyes staring at her. "Good morning, my beauty," he whispered.

She took in the sight of him lying next to her in his clothes—and his boots? He was fully clothed, same as he had been last night when he'd come. Imogene had to ask. "Did you not come to bed? You've slept in your boots?"

"Well, I came to bed; I just don't think I slept really. I watched you sleep."

"You must be joking. Why would you punish yourself so?"

He shook his head firmly. "I had need of my wife. I needed to hold you and reflect upon things. I had everything I needed in this world. It was not a punishment. I have told you before I can never tire from watching you. It is not possible."

"Take me home," she whispered.

"Thank Christ!" He moved off the bed and held out his hand to assist her, needing no further encouragement. "How do you feel this morning? Are you still feeling ill?"

"I am completely well today." He looked relieved and kissed her gently.

"I am going down to see to Triton and the carriage while you dress. I'll meet you there as soon as you are ready."

Imogene nodded her agreement and smiled at his very evident eagerness to get away.

The carriage ride was slower than usual. Triton had to be tethered and led along as he was not a carriage horse and Graham would not consider riding him home. He sat in the carriage with Imogene, her body pulled right up against his side.

They were quiet, content to just be beside one another.

Soon though, Imogene felt Graham's head list her way.

He had fallen asleep, the side of his head resting upon her breasts for a pillow. She held him there, relishing the giving of comfort to him. *He needs me. Just for today I wish we lived fifty miles from Philippa and John…*

As the carriage pulled up the drive to Gavandon, Graham awakened. He stretched a little, took in his surroundings and lifted his head.

Imogene spoke reproachfully, "You need sleep."

He grinned at her. "But I did, and it was very pleasant." He directed a knowing look at her bodice. "I would like to continue the *sleeping* in our bed," he said darkly.

"Sounds perfect."

As they entered the house Imogene sensed a change in his demeanour. They were home, in their place now, and Graham was no longer the repentant husband of last night.

HE was in desperate need of his woman. He'd gone for her and had collected her back home. They were back in his territory now, and he was frantic to reconnect their bond, to repair the damage of yesterday's disaster.

On the way to their rooms Graham stopped to direct the staff. In no uncertain terms were they to be disturbed unless he or the mistress rang for something. He ordered breakfast sent to their sitting room, and then dashed after her, up the stairs.

Imogene was in his chamber, standing there, waiting for him.

He locked the door.

She watched him approach, her eyes clear with understanding of what was about to happen. She knew what he wanted, and that was part of her magnificence. She knew him better than he knew himself sometimes.

He stopped before he reached her. He said, "I love you. You know that."

"I know that you do."

"I need to be with you now. To heal this…thing…that came between us." He paused for a moment before saying, "Take off your clothes." The words were spoken softly as a request, but his need behind his words was anything but soft.

Graham needed her. Badly. He needed to connect with her, get in as close as it was physically possible. Sex was his instrument for meeting the driving need to repair their bond. He needed to feel her soft, beautiful body underneath his hard, insistent one. He wanted to fill her up, possess her, and get inside her head and her body.

Imogene undressed as he watched. Removing her garments slowly, she deliberately looked at him the whole time, except when presenting her back so he could unlace her.

Graham took off his own clothes quickly, roughly, everything but his trousers, but he left them fastened. He was hard all over with muscles tense and straining, his cock twitching, his bollocks painfully tight. His need for Imogene was desperate.

She was soft, and lovely, and beautiful, standing before him with nothing but her chemise. Hesitantly he reached out to touch her.

"You tremble, Graham."

"I have such need of you, Imogene, I am afraid of myself right now, afraid of handling you too roughly and hurting you." Even to his own ears his voice sounded ragged and anxious.

"You will not. I am not fragile. I am here for you and I

will not break."

Her words were just enough encouragement to push him past his hesitation.

With a hiss, he crushed her down on the bed and took her.

He seized and she gave.

He dominated and she submitted.

She opened and he entered.

Hands and mouth firm and potent on her skin, he compelled her pliant body to surrender to him. It was only as he melded into her, that Graham felt the broken link in their bond mend itself. He felt himself shatter apart and then reform, anew, restored, and whole.

IMOGENE actually thrilled at Graham's rough need of her. It gave tremendous satisfaction to know she was the only one who could fulfil his raging want.

He gripped her hips as he mounted her from behind and took her in that position. Pounding strokes that drove him so deep inside her passage she felt him at her womb. His teeth nipped in between her neck and her shoulder, holding her in place as he worked himself deeper still. The angle of the penetration dragged his cock back and forth harshly over the edge of her swollen clitoris each time he thrust, driving her into a pummeling climax.

Graham didn't stop as the sensual pleasure washed over and through her.

He continued to use her body, taking from her what he needed. When her knees buckled and she collapsed forward, he still moved within her—slower now—but still fierce and purposeful. Face down and beneath him, the intense plunges of his iron-hard cock forced from her a shocking second climax almost instantly, rendering her utterly undone.

Pleasure, feeling and sensation took over. Nothing else existed in those moments. Any thought or action beyond the act of his body and her body coming together in the most primal of ways was impossible.

Near the end of it Graham choked out a gravelly roar—something she had never heard from him before. He sounded so agonized, but yet so vitally complete.

She floated away with him and time lost all reference…

GRAHAM clutched her close and Imogene felt entirely replete. But her glorious state didn't last very long when the good feelings were soon replaced with trepidation. Not from her, but from him. She felt his guilt play out in a kind of time delay as he realized what had just passed between them.

He bolted up in bed, looming over her, inspecting her body with raking sweeps of his eyes, the expression in them frantic. "Imogene? Are you all right?" he asked, not waiting for her answer. "I've marked you all over. I'm sorry. Please, please forgive me," he demanded in anguish.

"What are you talking about?"

"Look at yourself. There are marks on your beautiful skin where I've touched you too roughly. There are love bites, too." Gently, he touched the places where he had sucked hard enough and long enough to leave a mark that would be there a good while. "I am a goddamned beast. Look at what I have done to—"

"—Graham, you really must stop this."

"I know I must. I don't know what comes over me. I become demon possessed and I can't say why. I am so very sorr—"

"—No! You misunderstand me. Look at me, Graham. Listen to me, and listen carefully."

She waited for his eyes on hers before she spoke. "I refer to your recriminations, after. I do not care for them and have no desire to hear them ever again. Do you understand?" She paused for a moment, staring. "When you love me, fiercely, as you have just done, there is no shame in it for me. I know that you do it with love in your heart. You have not given me pain or harmed or frightened me. You have shown how much you need me. When we are together it is not always as it was just now. Sometimes we are gentle and tender and slow. It is a balance of expression, and all of the ways of our loving are right, as they should be. As for your love bites, I revere them and hope they remain visible for a long time so I can see them and remember how you loved me on this day."

Graham's eyes grew greener, if such a thing was possible. Imogene would swear she could see it happening as he took in her words. He gave a cry of sorts, almost like a sob, full of emotion, and spoke to her in French. "*Je t'aime plus aujourd'hui que moi ai fait hier et je vous aimerai plus demain que je fais à ce moment.*"

Imogene's school French was not as proficient as his fluent prose, but she caught the gist of it. Something about loving her more today than yesterday, and that tomorrow he would love her even more than he did at this moment. The words were beautiful, and they sounded better in the French anyway.

Graham leaned over her, whispering, "Stay right here, I'll be back in a moment, *chérie*." Shrugging into his robe, he left the bedroom. When he returned, he'd brought back with him an enormous plate of food, a cup of tea, and a wrapper for Imogene.

"I know you did not eat dinner last night and you have to be starving. Although you would never ask me, I want you to have some food. And I want you to allow me to feed it to you. Please?"

Imogene gave him a little nod. It made him very happy, she could tell, and it made her happy to make him happy. Reverting easily into silent communication, it was no difficulty to converse with just nods and facial expressions. The words were thought and exchanged somehow, they both understood.

Graham draped her into her wrapper first, and then helped her to sit up in the bed. He took great pleasure in feeding her bites of egg and bacon and toast, sips of tea, and gently touching her mouth with the napkin when he needed to.

Imogene could feel love radiating from every part of him and for some reason it made her tears resurface. Graham saw.

He got back into the bed, gathered her close, and settled them under the covers. They slept for a little longer.

"WHAT did you plan to do today, *chérie*?"

"Honestly? I was going to wash my hair, which is quite a task and takes a long time, but I can do it tomorrow."

"No. You will do it today and I will help you. I have no intention of leaving your side this day, so you are stuck with me for a lady's maid, yet again."

"You have no other work or obligations about the estate to attend to?" She seemed so surprised.

"Nothing more important than helping you to wash your

hair. And since I am ignorant of how the process works, I think I should like to learn," he stated matter-of-factly. "Everything about you is interesting to me."

Imogene shook her head at him slowly, her brown eyes glowing up at him. "You are the most extraordinary man."

You are the most extraordinary woman.

"Don't you see? It does not matter what we do. I just need to be with you today. I truly do not care however we spend the hours. Wash your hair, stare into the fire, eat chocolate, read Byron, it matters not."

She smiled and touched his cheek with her small, fine hand. "All right then, I'll order a bath. What do I say to Hester?"

"Give her the time off. Tell her to take the day for her amusement, go to the shops, whatever she likes." He drew her palm to his lips and kissed it. "If this goes well, Hester may be having a great many days off."

She laughed at him. "First, I'm going to order the bath, and then we'll wash my hair. Should you like a bath as well?"

"Yes, please," he mumbled, mouth wandering leisurely down to her neck. "The day's activities are shaping up quite nicely, indeed."

Once their baths were complete and they started in on Imogene's hair, Graham was astonished at the amount of labour involved. After dragging up buckets and buckets of water for their baths, the servants had to then come back to clear everything away. They'd returned with more water and basins for the hair washing. He was finding that Imogene was correct—the washing of lady's hair was, indeed, a complicated undertaking.

Helping Imogene to rinse away the hair soap for the second time, he tipped the pitcher of lavender water over her head slowly, massaging as he poured from where he stood outside of the tub. A beautiful image of her began to form in his mind.

But he did not share it right away, preferring to keep his vision to himself. And it was so lovely.

He handed her a towel, watching as she pressed the dripping water from her hair. "Now I have to comb it out. I usually sit in front of the fire, so it will dry faster. It takes hours to dry completely." She was apologetic as she explained.

"I don't mind helping you to comb it," he told her. But he continued to observe as she took one section of her hair at a time, combing from the bottom, working her way up slowly until it was free of tangles. It was so long that when holding sections out from her head, she had to extend her arm completely to comb through its entire length. The sight of her mesmerized him as the vision took definitive form in his head.

"You look like a mermaid," he said. "Sitting as you are on your knees to the side, your blue wrapper about your shoulders the same colour as the sea, your silver comb flashing through your wet hair. You look otherworldly right now, Imogene. I want to sketch it out—my vision of you—right now. May I? Will you allow me?"

At her soft nod, Graham got up and dashed to his closet to retrieve what he needed.

AFTER rummaging around in his closet, he returned carrying paper, a drawing board, and charcoal pencils. He sat on the floor opposite to her, leaning his back against the foot of the bed, getting right to work as she continued to comb through her wet hair, section by section.

"Does this make you uncomfortable, *chérie*?"

Imogene shook her head very slowly before she whispered, "No, not at all, my darling."

He looked at her thoughtfully for a moment before asking, "Are you warm enough in front of the fire?"

She did not answer because she knew exactly what he wanted her to do. She just knew, so she decided to do it for him. Carefully, she set down her comb and opened the top of her wrapper, pushed the fabric off her shoulders, allowing it to fall to her hips where it bunched and rested. Deliberately she picked up her comb again and resumed the work of combing her damp hair.

Graham said nothing. The only sounds were the scratching of the charcoal upon the paper, the fire crackling, and the soft swish of the comb, for a long, long time. An aura of complete trust swirled through the air in the room, enveloping the both of them.

Finally he put down his materials, and crawled over to her. He came right up to her face, and looked at her deeply. "I am in awe of you, that you would allow me—you are so giving, *chérie*, you amaze me." He carefully found the top of her robe, drew it up from her waist, and wrapped her back up. He kissed her softly and sweetly.

Imogene felt the pull of tears again. "What will you do with it?" she whispered.

"Nothing. It is private, just for me. No one will see it, and it will never become a portrait. You have given me a great gift, *chérie*. I try to remember my visions, but with so many in my head, details are lost. To be able to get this one down on paper was so very special. Now, I may take it out when I wish and look at it and I will be able to remember how you looked as a mermaid, and that you did it, for me."

"Will you show it to me?"

He reached over for the sketch and slid it back toward them over the floor. It was an outline sketch; it was definitely her. He had placed her on rocks, sitting to the side, the sea behind her where the fireplace should be. Extending her right arm, combing out a section of hair, her left arm bent at the elbow, securing her hair close to her head. The swell of her left breast showed under the elbow. Her face in profile, the rest of her hair fell over her back, shoulder and down her stomach. Where her legs bent underneath her, were replaced instead with a single fish tail that went all the way around the back of her, ending at her side.

"That *is* a mermaid," she spoke softly. "It is…beautiful."

"That is you, Imogene."

She looked at him, unconvinced. "Do you really see me like this?"

"At that moment, in my vision, you were a mermaid, yes. But your beauty is unchanged. Your beauty would be conveyed as this in any drawing or portrait done of you. You are beautiful." Graham looked at her intently for a moment, questioningly. "Imogene, you are an extraordinarily beautiful woman, and not just outwardly." He put his hand over her heart. "You are beautiful inside also, inner beauty does radiate and can be expressed through art, and that is what I saw while sketching you." He smiled and arched his brows. "And you want to know what the best part is?"

"What?"

"*Vous êtes la mienne.* You are mine."

GRAHAM ordered dinner sent up for them into the sitting room of their chamber. They spent the entire day locked inside together as he'd said he wanted to do—and it had been perfect. Imogene's hair was now dry and braided into one long, thick plait.

She observed him as he thoughtfully scanned the walls around them. "Imogene, I had a notion about something we could do with your rooms. Having the baths in here and washing your hair today inspired the idea. It is such a tedious amount of labour for everyone, including you, having to wait on water being carried up here. What if we made you a bathing room, with water pumped up through pipes, hot and cold, and a drain to take it away? You could have your baths easily, and washing your hair would not be such a chore. I know people have such things already, it's just a matter of modernizing."

He showed her where the pipes could go and how the space could be closed in as a separate room, taking away very little of the generous space between sitting room and bedroom. The pipes would go down along the outside wall of the house and bend in where a boiler could heat the water down below.

"What do you think, *chérie*?"

"It sounds wonderful and convenient. I think I would love it."

"I could use it too. We'll order a bathtub so large we can both fit. I am going to call the carpenter up here to get some measurements straight away."

"You amaze me with all of your modern thinking. Is there anything you cannot do, my darling?" She tilted her head at him.

"Absolutely, there is. I cannot be without you. As it has been made abundantly clear to me in the past four and twenty hours."

She reflected for a moment. "When did you decide to come and get me?"

"When it was time to go up to bed and you were not here. Zuly stopped me on the way up and gave me a look of such disgust I turned on my heel and headed straight to the stables. Triton and I were flying down the road in minutes." He gave a little smile at the remembrance.

"What now?"

"That horse is fast, Imogene. He is gentle, I know, but I have never owned a horse so fast. He has been misnamed surely. He should be Pegasus rather than Triton. I've half a mind to enter him at Newmarket. I should talk to Gravelle about him. He is a veritable expert on all things racing and Newmarket. If Triton were to win, I'd have to settle with Hargreave, though. He has no idea what he has given up."

Imogene shook her head in amusement. "Bathing rooms and racehorses…what a great lot of ideas you've got rolling around in your head, my darling."

"And they all come back to you, *chérie*."

Chapter 17

A sweet disorder in the dress
Kindles in clothes a wantonness…
Do more bewitch me, than when Art
Is too precise in every part.

Robert Herrick ~ 'Delight in Disorder', 1648

Their money was almost gone after staying at the inn for a week. Mr. Jacobson was always very kind to Clara, indulging her with sweets from the kitchen and stopping to listen to her childish chatter. But Agnes was at the end of her rope because she had no connections here. The will to protect her child went before anything else. She must find work of some kind right away. But she knew not what sort of job it could be.

Mr. Jacobson walked through the common room right then, smiling kindly. She suspected he was cutting the rate of their room for it was far superior to the paltry sum he charged her for it. She wondered why he would do such a thing, too. The possibilities bothered her.

"Mr. Jacobson, may I have a moment of your time?"

"Of course." He stood with his hands clasped behind his

back and gave her his full attention.

"Sir, I am in need of—" she swallowed hard, "—employment." She felt her face flush in embarrassment. "I can sew. I have been in service, in the past, as a seamstress. Do you know if I might find work in the area? Are there any great houses where I might inquire?"

"No great houses—not close by. No."

Her hopes dashed, she tried to keep her dignity intact by nodding her thanks for his time to speak with her. "Well, thank you for your kindness of this past week. We must be leaving tomorrow to search for a permanent situation."

Mr. Jacobson frowned at her news and Agnes got the idea that maybe he didn't like her news very much. Interesting.

"I do know of an opening for a housekeeping position, though. It would require management of accounts—are you good with numbers and figuring?"

Agnes felt her immediate future had just brightened considerably. "Yes. I did the accounts for my father's tailoring shop. It's been some time, but I *know* I can do it, Mr. Jacobson. And you definitely know someone in need of such an assistant?"

"Indeed I do." He smiled genuinely.

"Oh, Mr. Jacobson, that is wonderful." She dipped her head at him in deference. "May I inquire who is this person?"

"'Tis I."

"I must commission another portrait, Tristan. It is important and I need the thing completed by his birthday at the end of April. You can halt on the portrait of Terra and Triton for my chamber if that might help you with your time schedule. Can you do it for me?"

"Why the urgency I hear in your voice? Does it have something to do with your little overnight trip?"

Imogene was now a disciplined sitter but at his words she quickly lost her pose. "This is so very difficult for me to ask of you. Please bear with me. Yes, it very much does. I hurt him deeply and this is a way to make amends."

"He came here looking for you, nearly out of his mind." Tristan put down his brush and regarded her seriously. "I understand his fear, but he *should* have told you about his mother. You did not hurt him consciously, Imogene, and should not feel you must make amends."

Imogene felt physical pain at Tristan's words. Imagining Graham in his panic and terror was not something she wanted to relive. "He does not expect this portrait. It is something I wish to do for him. To show him how much I love— This is not easy to put into words, Tristan. It is not proper or considered acceptable in any part. I hope you are not offended by me. I beg your indulgence in hearing of what I ask of you."

"Now you have piqued my curiosity, Imogene. What type of portrait do you have in mind?"

"It is something Graham would like to have. He mentioned it…once. But I told him it was impossible for me to sit for such a thing. It was before I knew you though. And now that I do know you, I think I would be able to do it." Imogene felt herself flush and swallowed hard. "Can you—would you be willing to—oh God, Tristan, this is so awkward!"

Tristan did not speak or try to help her along, rather he tilted his head slightly and just waited for her to tell him what she was after.

Imogene took a very deep breath and stiffened her back.

"I want for you to paint me in *dishabille* for him." As soon as the words were out of her mouth, she slumped and lowered her eyes, afraid to see his reaction.

He surprised her for he didn't really have a reaction.

"Lounge attire then." He looked thoughtful as if his mind was at work already. "Any particular elements to the scene that you have in mind?"

She nodded. "There are some items in particular: a tiara, a shawl, a book, a robe." Imogene closed her eyes then and felt the tremors start. "There is one more element, but I don't know if you can possibly put it in." She put her hand to her head and leaned into it. "I want it to suggest love—intimacy. Oh God! I want to hide." She was amazed she had actually spoken the words out loud to Tristan.

What must he be thinking of me right now? Imogene sat and waited for a response, knowing she was incapable of anything else.

"You must love him very, very much. I hope he knows what a treasure he has won." Tristan gave her a gentle look before he spoke of what it would entail to create such a portrait. "I can paint you in such a way, and I am willing to do the portrait, but it will be unsigned. You understand I cannot put my name to it. It will have to remain private as well. People of your class do not commission such things, my dear. At least they do not do so and flaunt it to the world. I suspect you knew that before, and I know Graham is well aware."

"Without question, it would be private," she whispered, barely audible.

"As for the last element you mentioned, it can be included, but is not something I can just paint in as an expression. You will have to create the intimacy for me, Imogene. You will have to show me in your face and in your pose what you feel. You will have to think it in your mind—of what that feeling is like. Do you think you can do that? Do you even want to try?"

"For him, I can do it."

TRISTAN was surprised at her candor. He could tell it had cost her greatly to ask him. There was not much that would shock him in reality, though, and he found her mortification innocently charming.

It will be magnificent. His mind started spinning with plans. "There must be a bed. I cannot very well install one here in this room, though. That would definitely raise questions. We will have to use mine. When Graham is away I can zip up to his chamber and retrieve the camera obscura to get all the details to match his bedroom."

Imogene seemed to find some courage, enough to enable her to speak once again. "When do you think you can start? How do we keep it a secret? I do not want him to suspect, it must be a surprise."

"When you come, we'll split the sitting into two parts. He might wonder at this formal portrait of you in the emeralds taking longer than it should, but I'll leave it to you to distract him from the idea. And further, if he is called away for much of the day, you should send word to me and we will get in a longer sitting on the *dishabille* and that should speed it along." Tristan regarded her and watched as she blushed deeply again. Her expression was hesitant now, as if she was unsure. "Imogene, are you having second thoughts? You look uncertain, now."

She averted her eyes and looked slightly down. "No. I

am decided. It's just, that you said we would have to use your bedchamber for the setting. How can you—would it not be uncomfortable, or difficult for you to have me—to have me there in your private room? What would I disclose to the staff? Wouldn't they find it terribly improper and scandalous to say the least? She shivered. "I cannot believe I am here asking such a thing of you, Tristan. I feel as if I am out of my body right now. I could not have possibly just asked you that question!"

Tristan spoke gently but with confidence, "Imogene, be of ease. It will not be an imposition for me to paint you as such. You know, I am probably the only painter in England who could execute such a portrait and *not* be tempted by you." *Such an innocent you are. You have no idea about me do you?*

"Oh. That is a good thing then, Tristan." She nodded modestly, biting the inside of her bottom lip. "Please accept my apology for all of this uncomfortable bumbling about. I am dreadfully embarrassed, but you have been so easy and kind about everything. You are a true friend."

"I didn't say I'd paint it for free, you know." He teased away the awkwardness between them. *I probably would paint it for free, though…just to create it…to see your image in it.*

"Right! And don't you dare send the bill to him when it is done. You will give it to *me*," she commanded. "I can well afford you all on my own."

GRAHAM was waiting for her to return as he often did, but not in his usual way.

Today he met her on the path as she walked home from Tristan's house. He was all smiles.

"This is a most lovely surprise," she greeted as she drew up.

"A note has just arrived for you by messenger. From Harwell House. I believe it is in John's hand."

Her heart stuttered as he passed the note to her. She took a deep breath before tearing it open and scanned the words hastily. Imogene joyously reported that Philippa had born a healthy daughter this day. John's scrawl proclaimed both mother and baby well and beautiful. "Graham, they have named her Gwendolyn, after Mamma. How perfect. Oh—"

She launched herself into his arms and felt tears coming, but before he could ask, she told him they were absolutely tears of joy because she was so blissfully happy for this little miracle. Her only regret was that their mamma was not here to share in the joy.

She felt him kiss the top of her head.

Graham knew her so well already. And Imogene was happy, truly she was. But that part of her that fought to contend, niggled at her conscience. If she was honest with herself, she could admit to being a little jealous of them. And that was all right, too.

"Your turn will come, *chérie*," he said, his chin still resting on the top of her head.

"You mean *our* turn will come," she countered.

She felt him nod his head.

"John says we can visit on Thursday if we like. They probably need a bit of time alone first. I should like to stay for a day or two. Will you wish to join me?"

"Of course. I want to meet my little niece. I want to see how you might have looked as a baby. I'll lay a wager you were captivating even then," he teased with green eyes dancing.

"I love you so much."

"Do you now?" A look of desire emerged on his handsome face. "So, I was wondering, were you planning on going up to change out of those clothes?"

"It just so happens that I was going to do *just* that," she said.

"Well, I think you should go on up straight away." He nodded seriously at her. "You may expect a lady's maid to join you very shortly."

"That is good to know. Although, I wonder which maid I will get today?" She mused out loud. "Hmmm…I rather like that tall one, hair pulled back in a queue, green eyes. Fairly expert—a bit mercurial perhaps—but quite disciplined and competent. He seemed to take the task seriously." She kept going, teasing him mercilessly, "You know, you may find that I'm not even in my rooms. I might have decided to hide…somewhere."

Reminders of that session broke the teasing banter, had him reaching for her, and tickling her until she shrieked. "Now go!" he ordered, sending her dashing toward the stairs without an instant's hesitation.

Where to hide this time? I loved hiding from him and I want to do it again.

Imogene turned back on the stairs and saw him take out his watch to check the time. "Ten minutes is all you'll get, *chérie*," he called out as she fled.

AS luck would have it, Graham was called away from the estate the next day. Imogene wasted no time in sending a note off to Tristan in hopes they might start on the *dishabille* portrait. She busied herself with gathering all of the necessary props. She still had to dress in the pearly gown so as not to alert anyone into suspicion. Tristan replied straight away and told her to come 'round as soon as she was able.

Imogene definitely knew she was not in her body as she sat on Tristan's bed wearing the green brocade wrapper over a nightgown, both garments loosely arranged. Her shawl was spread next to her with a corner across her thighs. Two other items were incorporated and Imogene had thought carefully about their inclusion: The *Princess and the Toad* storybook, and the pearl tiara and choker. They were, of course, all suggestions of the intimacy that had been shared between them, and Graham would understand as he had orchestrated those encounters. The jewels and the fairy tale story also served to give an intimation of fantasy to the image. She thought he might like that as he seemed ever compelled to evoke dreamy visions of her.

"Is this all right, Tristan?" She could scarcely meet his eyes. This was much harder than she'd thought it would be.

"You need to relax, Imogene. The props are fine, it is your expression and pose that need some attention. Remember what I told you before? You must think of what you are trying to convey or it will not be present in the painting. Clear your mind of everything else and find a memory you can replay in your mind. The more you practice, the easier it will be to feel yourself inside with the image around you."

"I am trying to," she said in frustration. "I have to keep telling myself that I am not in your bed wearing only my nightclothes!" She shook her head unbelievingly.

Tristan gave her a patient look. "Imogene, you must let go of the bindings of propriety or you will not be able to reach your goal. I do not tell you to shock you, or to coerce you, or even to persuade you into doing this, but simply to disclose that if you do not let go of society's constraints you will never have this portrait for Graham."

She sighed heavily. "You are right of course."

"You already know this portrait would be considered indecent and completely improper for a baroness. So, that being said, I suggest you accept what you are doing is scandalous, and go ahead and do it, or not. No one will ever see it except for Graham. It won't hang in the gallery or be sold off." Tristan let his words sink in for a moment. "I am going to step out for a short while and give you some privacy. When I return, we'll know if this is going to work or not."

Imogene took a deep breath, forcing her mind to think of Graham and only of him, concentrating on their love for one another. She thought about when they were intimate, they were as close as it was physically possible to be, pondering how the act of love itself was divine, but for her, only because it was done with Graham, and only because she had ultimate trust in him. She felt the love she wanted to give to him, and thought of one time, one special moment that defined them and focused on it, willing everything else to go away, and just pretended she was in that moment. The time she recalled was the morning she discovered the portrait of her leading Terra and carrying the lamb.

His ingenuity at creating such a painting without her ever sitting for it had been a shock. Graham had re-created the moment he'd first seen her, and she remembered being dumbstruck by the depth of his love for her. He had told her, that in that moment, the pain of Cupid's Arrow piercing his heart was a tangible feeling, and instead of killing him it had awakened him. He wanted the painting of her in that moment so he could always remember.

What Graham had explained to her was love—deep and unconditional love.

Before Graham, she had not been awake either. In offering himself, he had awakened her. Giving all of herself back to him in return was the most sacred thing she could give, and was her way of showing him she had committed her soul to him. The complete trust they shared was the most precious part.

Graham had also shared that morning how he would love a portrait of her in *dishabille*. Imogene had been innocently shocked at the time, but not anymore. No, she wasn't worried about the impropriety of such a portrait at all. Imogene wanted to give this to him more than anything.

She realized the gift of the painting to Graham had nothing to do with propriety, nothing to do with posing in Tristan's bed, dressed as she was. It was nothing more than wanting to give everything you could to the one you love, if it could bring them some joy.

Focusing her thoughts, she arranged herself, sitting on the bed in profile. Her gown and wrapper loose, slipped down, baring her shoulder. Legs were bent at the knees, one bent more than the other, her feet peeking out. Her hands were together, buried in her robe between her legs. The shawl draped over the bed. The book lay on the shawl, title to be visible. Her hair was left styled as it was for the emerald portrait, but taken down as if the pins had just been removed. Tiara in place and choker on her neck, her head was in profile, lips just barely parted. She posed herself to look like she was waiting for him to come to her, and that she would turn her head at any moment.

When Tristan came back into the room he said nothing. He just went straight to work. Imogene knew then she had her pose and expression correct. She didn't know the reason Tristan did not speak. He didn't because he was incapable of audible speech when he saw her.

The sitting proceeded quietly.

"I am getting tired, Tristan."

"I know, almost finished. You have done very well, Imogene. This has been an excellent start."

"I don't know when next I can sit for you. Tomorrow we go to Wellick to stay at my sister's. The baby was born yesterday."

"Boy or girl?"

"Girl. Named Gwendolyn after our mamma."

"Well enjoy her, then. While you are gone I can work on your horses' portrait."

"You are amazing, Tristan. That you can create these things."

He did not respond to her compliment directly. "Graham will love this, Imogene. It is going to be very special."

AT dinner, Graham thought she looked exceptionally pleased. "How did you fill your day, *chérie*?"

"A little of this, a little of that."

"Are you keeping secrets, *chérie*?" His eyes twinkled.

"I really couldn't say, my darling."

"You're up to something, my beauty, I can smell it. But it is of no matter. I am confident I can get it out of you in a more, private setting." Her eyes darkened at his suggestion.

"You are welcome to try, certainly," she trailed off with a challenge as was becoming so familiar to him. He loved her competitive teasing.

"On a more serious note, *chérie*, we need to choose rooms to move into, temporarily. The work on your chamber and the bathing room is set to begin in a few days. I thought we could choose tonight and while we are away visiting the baby, our things can be moved over. I could show you my old rooms, if you would like."

"I *would* like that, Graham. Seeing the place where you rested your head each night as a lad would be inspiring indeed. All the dreams you must have dreamed there," she mused out loud.

Dreams can be a curse too.

Graham escorted her through the possibilities of rooms they might use while the work was being done. Imogene was non-committal as they toured, until they reached his old bedroom. She swanned in, announcing, "I like this room." Gracefully, she stroked along the edge of the bed and the pillows. She sat down on his old bed and bounced a few times. "It is good. What do you say?"

"I suppose it could work, *chérie.* It opens to the next room." He led her into the adjoining area which was set up as a lounging space, thinking out loud as he looked around, "Might it work if we brought up a sideboard table and rearranged furniture so you could continue to have your breakfasts up here?"

"I really just need a place to keep my clothes and to dress, so maybe a vanity could be added for now? Make it more of a dressing-sitting room combination. We can use it for our breakfasts in the mornings and for our lounging in the evenings." Looking decidedly around the space, she nodded. "'Twill be fine for me, Graham, and it's only for a short while."

He thought about how unique she was as he pulled her into his arms. "You are an enigma, *chérie.* I am amazed at how easy you are in regards to these womanly concerns. You are a perfect lady in your grace and style of feminine beauty, but you never seem to fuss over the details like clothes, and rooms, and the inconveniences that make most women vexed and displeased. How do you manage it so effortlessly?"

"Manage what?" she asked innocently.

"To put yourself together so magnificently without seeming to work very hard at it?"

"Thank you, my darling, for that lovely compliment. But I have everything that I need as long as you are near." She grew serious then and lifted her eyes. "You give me everything that I need."

THEY stayed just two days at Harwell House. Imogene delighted in the baby and in all her sweet, pink, softness. She was amazed at the change in Philippa, as well. Her sister was a mother now and the look of abounding love Philippa had for her daughter was precious to behold.

"What's it like, Phil?" Imogene asked as she gazed down at the sleeping Gwendolyn, she was cradling in her arms.

"It is like nothing I've ever known. The love I feel for her, the need to protect her and care for her is indescribable. The transformation happened instantly, the moment I first held her. It is miraculous. I cannot explain it really. We created her. She grew inside me and now she is here. A complete, perfect, little person that I love more than my own life. I would do anything for her to keep her safe."

"I am so happy for you, and for her. She has the two best parents in the whole world." Imogene sighed.

"Tell me about you. Do you think you might be?"

Imogene dropped her eyes back to the baby. "I suppose it's possible but it is much too soon to know. How did you know for sure?"

Philippa laughed with a snort. "I am married to a doctor and in his practicality, I am sure he knew before I did." The sisters laughed together at the thought of John trying to figure if his wife was pregnant or not. "It is wicked of me to tease him behind his back, he does not deserve it. He is so wonderful and good to me. He is the best husband and father, and doctor. He will attend you, Imogene, when your time comes. You will be in the finest hands."

"I know. Graham has also spoken so highly of him. I know he has the utmost respect for John. But really, I need information, Phil. How did you know for sure?"

"Well, you have to have been… intimate…consistently during the time midway between your cycles. You know, two weeks after it comes. That's the time when you might conceive."

Imogene gave her sister a tolerant look. "I think we've got the consistent part down adequately enough." They laughed again together.

"I cannot say I am surprised. The way he looks at you. The way you look at him. I am happy for you, little sister. You have a husband who loves you most dearly and is not afraid to show it."

"And I love him in the same way. I cannot imagine my life without him now." She shook her head and reverted back to their previous topic. "So did you feel different? I've heard that some women are sick."

Philippa smiled. "You are nothing if not persistent, Im. Well, you know your cycles will stop. That's the best sign. For me, after about six weeks or so, I started getting sick in the mornings. Having dry toast and tea first thing, will help settle you. The sickness lasts about a month or so until it fades away for the most part. Your breasts will get fuller and they'll be tender, and you'll notice that right away. You'll want to sleep and take naps. John says your body gets tired from growing the baby so you need more rest."

Imogene nodded her understanding as she took in the information, thinking that soon, she might actually know something.

FOR the two days they were with the Brancrofts, Graham and Imogene took amusement in John's enchanted grin that remained fairly plastered upon his face and carried with him wherever he went. The change in John was just as astounding as the one in Philippa. Entranced by his wife and daughter, the scientific pragmatism in him was getting some much needed tempering with love and devotion.

Lounging atop the bed and propped up against the pillows, Imogene attempted to read more of Byron's poetry to Graham. He rested his head in her lap as she toyed with his hair absently, reveling in the touch of her fingers and in just being close together. "John looks like he's been bashed to the side of the head with a board," he said.

Imogene put down the book. "He most certainly does and I think it's good for him, too. They are a most perfect and happy little family and I think we have intruded long enough. What do you say to returning home tomorrow?"

"I think you are wise and wonderful, *chérie*," he answered. "As much as I enjoy their excellent company, I find I am anxious to get you back home, all to myself. I am most selfish when it comes to sharing you."

Imogene pursed her lips together, smiling down at him. "You could not have kept me away from the new baby, but now we know she is arrived safe and well, we could return home. She has two parents who love her and it is their life to live. This is not the place for us. I have the most loving husband in the world, a beautiful home, and *our* life to get back to."

He took in her words, closed his eyes for a moment, and quite simply counted his blessings. The blessing in finding her.

Imogene quietly gazed down at him. "What are you thinking about, my darling?"

"Fate."

"Will you share with me?"

"I was pondering what might have happened if we had not met in Kent at Jules and Mina's wedding. Or if we might have had cause to meet once you came to Philippa and John, just a few miles away from Gavandon. Of how long it might have taken to discover you. Imogene, it almost hurts to think on it. I cannot imagine—do not want to imagine a life without you."

"You sound melancholy," she said. "You know you do not have to live without me so you should never have to imagine it either. Funny, I said the same words to Philippa today, that I could not imagine my life without you. I am just grateful we didn't have to wait years to find each other. You are very generous in showing your love to me. Everyone remarks how much you love me. Apparently, you are an open book, my darling."

"Come here. I need to hold you." He moved his head off her lap and drew her down beside him on the bed where he could bring her close. He breathed in the lavender scent of her hair before dropping his lips to the silky strands.

Graham knew he needed her more than she needed him. He did not doubt Imogene's love. She was as generous and open in bestowing it as she was in unknowingly wielding her power over him. He was thankful for her kind and affable spirit, as another woman might deem to use such power to subjugate. He knew he was blessed. Rather, it was an instinctual understanding that in any relationship there was one person who *needed* more than the other.

In their relationship, that person was him.

Chapter 18

For ne'er
Was flattery lost on poet's ear:
A simple race! They waste their toil
For the vain tribute of a smile.

Sir Walter Scott ~ The Lay of the Last Minstrel, 1805

As Imogene and Zuly made their way back toward the studio, a commotion broke out in one of the rooms, expelling a very flustered Tristan, bursting out through the entry. "Oh God, Imogene! My dear, I apologize deeply for this. I will not be able to accommodate you this day. I have received an impromptu…guest. Quite unexpected, and will not—"

Tristan was cut off by a rakish looking man with long, curly hair, following close on his heels, a pronounced limp showing in his step. Imogene saw his eyes widen in surprise as he caught sight of her standing in her shining silver gown and magnificent emeralds. He smiled in appreciation as he looked her over. "What have we here, Mallerton? Who have you got there that you're trying to hide from me?"

Tristan seemed frozen, unable to speak.

The newcomer did not relent. "*Very* nice," he said boldly in reference to Imogene as if she were not standing a mere three feet from him. "Where are you manners, man?" he barked at Tristan.

Tristan just stood there gaping at him, and Imogene was surprised at Tristan's lack of confidence for once.

"An introduction, *please*," the rake drawled impatiently.

Tristan seemed to snap out of his astonishment enough to speak, "Lady Rothvale, may I present George Gordon, Lord Byron."

Did he just say Lord Byron? Imogene was sure her eyes were popping. She remembered Graham's words to her when she had been surprised he and Lord Byron were known acquaintances. *'I have had occasion to meet him through the connection of another.'* Understanding emerged. Lord Byron was *Tristan's* friend! Graham had met him through Tristan.

But Imogene could see that Tristan was clearly agitated by his friend's presence, probably because he was known to be uninhibited and immune to the limits of propriety. Judging by his bold assessment of her, Imogene could see how the description of him was indeed accurate. He was behaving in a manner far too familiar.

"Lady Rothvale." He bowed. "It is a divine honor to meet you." He swept over her with a thorough, admiring gaze. "So, it seems Rothvale, that gentleman farmer, who once fancied himself an artist, has taken a bride, and a diamond at that. No wonder he keeps you hidden away up here in the wilds of Warwickshire."

Imogene felt the flush creeping at his words. "Lord Byron." She curtsied. "Sir, I assure you my husband has—"

"—Commissioned a portrait of Lady Rothvale and this is her sitting appointment that's been inconvenienced, Byron," Tristan interrupted.

"How intriguing. I should say he is quite justified in his desire to have your likeness preserved on canvas. I know I would." He smiled at her. "Have you been married long, Lady Rothvale?"

"Just over two months now, my lord." *His boldness is unsettling. He is just as scandalous as they say.*

"Newlywed. Wherever did Rothvale find you, my dear?"

"In Kent. I had come to live with family there after the death of my father, Lord Wyneham."

"Wyneham you say? I remember him. We met in the House. He was very complimentary upon my maiden speech, and I was greatly appreciative of his kind treatment. My condolences on your great loss, as well as England's." He seemed reflective for a moment. "I recall there was something about his name…" he trailed off. "What was your surname, Lady Rothvale?"

Imogene smiled. "Byron-Cole. My father was Philip Byron-Cole." *What will you do with that I wonder?*

But Lord Byron just laughed out loud, obviously delighted at their common name. He glided over to her, taking up her hand to kiss it. "How fortuitous to meet you, *Cousin*, and I insist that you think of me as such. I know that is how I shall think of you."

Imogene smiled at the audacity of him. He was everything she had heard him to be. 'Mad, bad, and dangerous to know.' She had to agree because it seemed to suit him. *Unbelievable. I am standing here conversing with Lord Byron, and he is claiming me as family within five minutes of an introduction. I wonder what Graham will say.*

"What brings you to Warwickshire, my lord?"

"I am visiting friends on my way to Devon." He noticed the dog then, and bent to pet her affectionately. "What an elegant dog you have, Lady Rothvale." He then walked over to the unfinished portrait of her and surmised it, thoughtfully.

"Mallerton, you are most gifted. The portrait is striking and it is appropriate that you have included her dog. I would love to watch your sitting, if you would permit me." His gaze rested on Imogene with open admiration.

Imogene looked to Tristan in panic. *What should I do?* She knew she must not allow herself to be placed in such a compromising situation, unsure how to extract herself gracefully without offending him. She saw Tristan shake his head slightly and mouth the words, 'go now.'

"Mr. Mallerton, Lord Byron, I fear I must take my leave. I am sorry to have intruded upon your visit. Maybe another time, we could arrange something—"

Byron interrupted, "Before you go, Lady Rothvale, please enlighten me as to the meaning of the *other* portrait of you I found in Mallerton's closet." His eyes looked positively predatory now.

Imogene thought she might burst into tears. Tristan looked angry enough to draw blood. "Snooping does not become you, Byron. That portrait is private and no concern of yours! Have you no shame, man? What in the hell are you doing dredging about in my closet anyway?"

Imogene cut in, "My lord, please—it is a gift for my husband. He does not know and it would break my heart to expose the surprise now. It is a private portrait, just for him, for his birthday." She crossed her arms and challenged him. *Stay strong. Something tells me he will respect strength and defiance more than pitiful tears.*

He regarded her in her anger for a moment before a curl of a smile began to lift his lip. He bowed gallantly. "As you wish, Cousin. I would not dream of exposing your secret. In fact, I applaud you. It is just the sort of thing I would consider doing. We are of a like mind. We must be related by blood, after all."

Somehow, Imogene trusted him. She knew he was unorthodox, yet she believed he would be true to his word to keep her *dishabille* portrait a secret. Thus she was powerless to stop the next words that tumbled from her lips. "I would like to extend the invitation to you both for dinner up at the house this evening. Seven o'clock? You are most welcome."

"I graciously accept on both our parts," Byron said smartly.

Imogene inclined her head in acceptance. "Zulekia, come," she commanded Zuly who had laid down in repose in her usual place, next to the chair.

"What did you call her?" Byron inquired.

"Zulekia. She is named Zulekia, but we usually call her Zuly."

"A most beautiful and striking name. *Zulekia. It is beautiful. It would suit, say, an Arabian princess. I may use it in a poem.* "Until this evening then, Lady Rothvale." Byron bowed again and scrutinized as the stunning Lady Rothvale and her elegant dog glided out of the sitting room, and out of Mallerton's house.

"My God, Byron, you are disreputable!" Tristan was aghast with him. "I am here at Rothvale's pleasure and I have no wish to lose my situation. I will remind you not to jeopardize it by terrorizing his beloved bride. You are a devil to torment her so. Her face—her face was stricken with fear and I know you were well aware, man. Have you no compassion?"

"She is an angel, my cousin. Rothvale is a lucky bastard to have discovered such a treasure." Byron regarded Tristan thoughtfully before musing, "What could have been if I had found her first."

"God, man, she is his wife! Remember that at dinner, would you? I cannot imagine what possessed her to extend an invitation," Tristan muttered. "Rothvale will not tolerate you lusting after her. He is of a liberal mind in most things, but where she is concerned, he is nothing of the sort. He is very protective, and a man utterly devoted to, and in love with his wife. Don't think for a moment that you have any chance with her, Byron."

"Relax, Mallerton. I will not impose on her. I simply wish to admire her up close. We are family, after all."

Tristan's response was to roll his eyes and shake his head in exasperation. Something Byron was well used to.

IMOGENE approached Graham's study with trepidation. *I have invited him into our home, for dinner. Why did I do that?*

She knocked first, but opened the door quickly. Graham stood abruptly upon her entrance, concern filling his face. "*Chérie*? Why are you back so soon?" She went right into his arms, burying her face in his chest. He brought fingers to her chin and drew her face up. "What is it? You are trembling. Tell me, please."

The words tumbled out before she could frame them calmly. "I invited Lord Byron to dinner tonight! He was there with Tristan and I met him. He thinks I am his cousin and wanted to watch the portrait sitting. Tristan told me to leave and come home…"

Graham's look of confusion first and then understanding as he made sense of her rambling explanation was telling in its simplicity. Graham didn't trust Byron either. "You mean he is here at Gavandon, with Tristan?"

"Yes! I believe he took Tristan by surprise, and to his credit, he tried to keep Byron from meeting me, but Byron just pushed his way forward and demanded an introduction, and then he wanted to watch Tristan while he painted me, and I don't know why I invited him to dinner. I am sorry," she wailed.

"It's all right now," he soothed. "Thank God Tristan has some sense and got you out of there. Do not worry about it." He smiled gently. "It is fine that you invited him. What else could you have done? I will protect you from him, and you will get a firsthand glimpse of England's most famous poet, *chérie,* in all his disreputable glory at your table."

Imogene relaxed into him. "He is rather alarming and quite forward in his manners. He seems a little mad actually."

"I am not surprised. Remember what I told you about artists? Poets are artists as well. Their creativity and talent is often expressed to the rest of us mortals as a kind of madness. I have seen it time and time again. In order to express the art, the mind must be freer and more open to experimentation, and often in direct conflict with society's limits. Byron is more outrageous than most, it's true." Graham gave her a look of wonderment. "Does he really think you are related to him by blood?"

Imogene nodded. "He called me *Cousin* and said he would think of me as such, insisting I do the same." She shook her head in disbelief. "He also told me he had met my father in Parliament and that Papa had complimented him on his maiden speech."

"You are unsettled, *chérie.*" He kissed her forehead. "Why don't you go on up and have a rest. All is well, and I'll not have you worried over this for even one moment. 'Twill be fine, you will see." He led her out of the study, blowing a smiling kiss at her as she left him.

Walking away, she felt weak. Graham was, of course, easy in his manner with this difficulty, as was his way. She felt guilty in sharing the secret of the *dishabille* portrait with Byron. *If he says anything about that portrait in front of Graham I will give him a limp in his other leg, I swear!* Still, something in the back of her brain told her that worrying was for naught. She could trust him with the secret. He would keep her confidence. Imogene had to believe that he would because she didn't have a choice in the matter.

GRAHAM came up to check on her later. The work on her chamber and the bathing room was progressing, and they were now settled in their temporary rooms. Imogene was having a soak in the bath when he entered. "How is my bewitching mermaid?" he whispered from behind as he drew up close, kneeling on the floor. "Are you feeling more settled, *chérie*?" Resting his hands on her shoulders, he slowly began to caress downward with searching fingers. She relaxed her head backward to rest on his chest and allowed him the pleasure of his hands on her. "You certainly feel more relaxed," he breathed into her ear, bringing his head around the side of her face to kiss her deeply. He could feel her passionate response to him and it spurred him. He really didn't come upstairs with the sole intention of having her. Rather, it was just usually the culmination of his visit. One look, one touch, one kiss, and he was lost to the passion she ignited in him. Her beauty and loving nature caught him every time, making him helpless to refrain from showing her how much he loved her.

"Mmm, I was hoping you would come to see me."

"Really? So my visit is a welcome one then?"

"Your visits are always welcome."

"Now you are feeding my ego, *chérie.* I wonder if you know what you do to me," he asked glumly. "I am powerless against your charms."

"I know," she purred. His eyes met hers, sparkling in all their rich brown brilliance. They communicated silently with just their eyes, both imagining what they might be doing in the next moments.

"Are you ready to leave your bath?"

She nodded and held out her hand. Graham reached for a towel and assisted her out of the tub, wrapped it around her slick body and carried her to the bed. Laying her down, he smiled slowly but determinedly while stripping out of his clothes. When he was as bare as she was, he pulled her towel away and joined her on the bed, holding her close for a while. He adored the feel of her next to him with no barriers, nothing to separate the touch of his skin against hers.

He trailed his mouth over her in a slow languorous sweep of kisses that started with her neck and moved on down. He kept going, in a pathway down her ribs, over her belly and lower still to the top of her thigh. His mouth moved toward the inside of her thigh. He heard the intake of breath at her understanding of his intended destination. "Imogene…I want to taste you… pleasure you. Please, *chérie*? Let me." He pressed her legs apart gently before feeling her give way, allowing him to do that which he desired…

He licked at her nub and buried his tongue inside her soft quim, learning her taste and relishing the tightening of her muscles in response to his actions. He pleasured her to the brink, and then over the other side on sobbing moans. All of it music to his ears—as was the shuddering of her thighs against the sides of his face when she climaxed, shouting out his name.

Imogene rolled onto her side, pulling her knees up and panting through the pangs that lingered. Graham sidled up behind her. Kissing along her neck now and resting a hand over her pounding heart, caressing her nipple. "You are so beautiful when you take your pleasure. I love giving it to you. Spiced plum, you tasted like a spiced plum."

His words provoked her, and she gave a little cry, burying her face into the pillows. "Oh Graham," she moaned. "What you do to me!"

He laughed softly, trying to roll her so he could see her eyes, but she resisted, keeping her face buried in the pillows. "Oh, *chérie*, do not be shy with me," he teased. "Have I shocked and embarrassed you?"

"Utterly!" She continued to resist his efforts to turn her.

"What? Are you not going to look at me now?"

"I doubt if I shall ever be able to look at you again," she cried, still speaking into the pillow.

He spoke confidently. "So, it was dreadful? You do not wish for me to repeat that, ever again, then? Pity, I thought you were enjoying yourself. It seemed like you were…"

With a squeal she flipped herself over and pushed him back down into the bed. She hovered over him with a challenging smile. "Lord Rothvale, you are most shocking, and outrageous and scandalous and—"

Snaking his hand behind her head, he brought her down, cutting her off with a hard kiss. "Let me guess. You have thought about it, and have decided that you might like me to do it again after all?"

"Perhaps. But you are still wicked, and very, very—"

Imogene paused, looking down at him thoughtfully. Teasing put aside, her mind appearing to be working. "I shall have to punish you now. You know, an eye for an eye?" She smiled at what had to be his look of complete astonishment as understanding of her intent dawned on him.

Oh, fuck yes.

Dropping her head down quickly, she settled herself right over his cock, taking the base in her small hand and stroking it a few times slowly. She studied him for a moment before opening her pretty mouth and covering his cock with her warm wet tongue. She explored him, learning how far she was able to take him down, sliding his shaft up and down. She licked up the sides and tip and simulated the act of a fuck.

The sight of his cock piercing and then retreating from within her pink lips sent him up to the heavens and back again.

His beautiful princess did for him what he had done for her. She took his prick into her sweet mouth and sucked until he couldn't hold back a second longer and spilled his seed down her warm throat. As he rode out the intense feelings of pleasure he had pause to observe his wife. If he had to assess her feelings about what she'd just done for him he'd say Imogene seemed fascinated by the experience, in a kind of wonderment at the whole thing. She looked up shyly at him and licked her glossy lips…

It was a long time before he was able to say anything.

"So you turn tables on me yet again, *chérie.* I am no match for you, of that I am sure."

"I told you. An eye for an eye. It is only fair." She said saucily, "Please say if I was too shocking or if you do not want me to do that to you again. I will abide by your wishes."

He rewarded her teasing with a thorough tickling to which she shrieked and laughed. "You may have my complete cooperation should you wish to repeat that particular performance, *chérie.* I assure you, I can accommodate you, any time." He kissed her slowly until their mood changed back to relaxed and languid. "Now, when you must tolerate Byron this evening in his trouncing of convention, and his boorish attentions, I want you to remember this afternoon and know that nothing he does can touch us…what we have together, Imogene."

She looked up at him in amazement. "Is there a purpose behind *everything* you do?"

"Not at all. This interlude was, most assuredly, a complete surprise for me as it was for you. But I will admit that in everything I do, my purpose is to show you how much I love you."

"Did you ever think you'd be doing any of *this* in your old rooms?" She looked around the room decisively.

"Now who is being naughty?" he clucked at her. "Who would have thought that underneath all that innocent beauty is quite an intrepid seductress?"

"You can definitely take all credit for my transformation, husband. For I *know* I was not like this before you!" She gently pushed at his chest with her hands.

He grasped her hands, pinning her playfully onto her back as he loomed over. "Credit I will gladly accept, but still, I want you to think of our encounter today and know that nothing Byron says or does can shock you anymore." He gave her a smirk that broke into a wide grin. "The expression on your face is priceless, *chérie.*"

"I won't forget, Graham." And she wouldn't forget their encounter this afternoon for a long, long time. If ever.

IMOGENE dressed carefully for dinner with Hester's expert assistance. She wanted to equip herself with as much armor as possible to help her survive the evening with Byron. She even devoted part of her afternoon to reading the rest of 'Childe Harold's Progress' in an effort to have topics of conversation to draw from. She chose a long sleeved, low-cut, blue silk gown. She wore the heart pendant from Graham with its sparkling sapphire border and selected sapphire earrings to complement it. Her presentation was simple and elegant, and she intended to portray herself as confident and composed, at all costs.

Graham arrived to escort her down and paused in a courtly bow, sweeping his eyes over her with a dramatic flourish. "You are far too beautiful for your own good, *chérie*." He offered his arm. "I was hoping you'd have dressed yourself in a sack and have dirt on your face," he admonished. "I fear it is my fate to be forever fending off the throngs of avaricious fools who admire you and seek your favour. You know you do not help me when you look so beauteous."

She smiled at him gratefully. "I know you are up to the task. I have every confidence in you, my darling."

They settled in the parlor to await their guests. Graham was reminded of the letter that had arrived earlier from Everfell and realized Imogene had not yet had an opportunity to read it. "We have been invited to Everfell. Jules and Mina insist we have been left on our own for long enough, and must grace them with an extended stay. They are having a ball in our honor, celebrating our marriage since they were not able to attend."

"How generous."

"I don't see how we'll be able to do less than a fortnight with them," he said tentatively.

She nodded and then at seeing his quizzical expression, "What? Are you asking if I want to go?"

"Yes, *chérie.*"

"Why wouldn't I? Of course I'll go." His hesitation surprised her. "Graham, forgive me for saying so, but it seems as if it is you that maybe does not want to go to Everfell. Am I right?"

He shrugged. "No. I *do* want to go. I want to take you to Everfell. It is so fine and grand, architecturally significant. I think you will enjoy it, and you should definitely see it. And I wish to see my family. It's just—"

"What is it, my darling?" She rested her hand on his forearm.

He sounded melancholy again. "It's just that I wish I could take you away. Just us. Away from everyone, away from duties, and responsibilities, and requirements. I really want to take you to Ireland, to Donadea, but it is not fitting to return there so soon after being away from England for a year."

Imogene put her hands up to his face. "I love you. I know you will get your wish sometime, and I am sure it will be all that you hope for. It gives us something lovely to look forward to. In the meantime you can tell me all about Donadea and I will cherish hearing your stories of what must be a most magical place if you love it so much."

He did not speak, but rather nodded his acceptance. It did give Imogene some comfort to see her sensible words had earned her one of his rare, but shining smiles.

Their guests were announced at that moment by a footman, and they moved greet them.

Imogene observed Graham in his role as congenial host, able to accommodate the tastes and interests of his guests. He welcomed Byron warmly and proceeded to engage him in conversation about his travels to Greece and Arabia. To her surprise, Byron's manners were irreproachable in Graham's presence, and she was pleased to know he could follow decorum when it suited him. Maybe Tristan had schooled him before their arrival.

Imogene sat back, content to observe and listen to Byron regale them with stories about his travels. Over dinner, the topic turned to Greece and the Parthenon was mentioned. Graham remarked that he and Imogene had toured the British Museum and had opportunity to see the Parthenon Marbles.

"Lady Rothvale, you are very quiet tonight. What have you to say about the marbles?" Byron inquired.

"You wish a woman's opinion on the whims of government?"

"Yes, I do," he challenged.

"Well, the carvings themselves are remarkable, one of a kind. Most of them are friezes so they are not carved in all of their dimensions, but flat on the back where they were attached to the Parthenon. I will confess, that seeing them cut apart and lying on the floors was bothersome. I dearly hope the final presentation of the marbles will be done with dignity as befitting works of such importance. They should be mounted on the walls in their display, I think." She paused to gauge reactions to her definite opinions. "But all of this is just superfluous to the fact they are here in England and most likely will stay here." Bestowing a tentative glance at Byron, she guessed, "I think you are asking me, did I agree with their removal from their place of origin?" She saw his slight nod of agreement. "While I can comprehend the argument for preserving priceless artifacts from within a country whose political situation is unstable and that the risk of losing said artifacts is possible. Even so, I am not sure I can condone

Lord Elgin's transference of the marbles to England."

Graham beamed at her from across the table with a look of pride as they awaited her view on the matter. He encouraged her with a quick wink. She forged on, "My reason is that the Parthenon is a temple, an ancient place of worship, a shrine. The manifestation of the gods themselves preserved in exquisite sculpture encircling it. 'Twould seem profane to desecrate a shrine by dismantling it, even if the religion is an ancient and pagan one. I cannot deem it was righteous to take them. Even if the Greeks have fallen upon hard times, and cannot preserve what is theirs, the fact remains that the Parthenon friezes *are* the property of the nation of Greece. I wonder at the concept of them being available for sale at all. I can only imagine what the ancient Greek philosophers would have to say about England, in her presumption to rob away from Athens, her history, her art, her sacred temple gods."

The three men stared at her after she finished her argument, but Byron was the first to chime in. "Lady Rothvale, my dear cousin, it is refreshing to meet a woman who is not only endowed with beauty, but a working brain as well. You make an eloquent argument, but I agree with you in that nothing so sensible will likely come into the minds of those in government. They must feel obligated to dither and argue, and in their way of delaying action, so wrestle control and permanent possession of their loot." I am sure it is as you have suggested, and that the marbles are unquestionably here to stay."

"I thank you for the compliment, your lordship. I do not know you well enough yet to gauge your sincerity in claiming kinship with me. Do you really and truly believe us to share family blood, or are you merely bestowing flattery?"

"Yes," was his maddening reply, "and I insist that you call

me George, *Cousin* Imogene."

He turned his attention on Graham then. "Rothvale, how did you ever secure her? The gods surely favoured you with providence in finding and winning such a wife," Byron said admiringly.

"I asked her to dance at a ball, and she, in her benevolence, agreed to it." Graham looked reminiscent. "Your comment about the gods showing favour is accurate, Byron, because I can remember that exact sentiment flying through my mind when Imogene graced me with that first stunning smile."

"I wish I had spied her first."

Imogene thought Graham was generously tolerant in his response. "Oh come now, Byron, you do not strike me as a man quite yet content to settle into marriage. Your prodigious fame and celebrity must make great demands on you. How could a wife possibly fit into all of that?"

"You are probably right, but still, maybe I would have considered it just the same if my cousin had been known to me," he sulked.

"Now gentlemen, I should say I do not care for you speaking of me as if I am not right here with my ears attuned to every word you say." Imogene ended the topic for them.

"Please forgive us, *chérie,* it is very boorish behaviour on our parts. Our society is sorely lacking of ladies tonight and all eyes are turned on you I am afraid." Graham smiled down to her.

Imogene inclined her head in acceptance of his apology and returned his smile. They shared an intimate glance for just a moment. Both of them remembering how they had spent the afternoon, and the pact they had made to be impervious to Byron's gauche attentions. Tristan had to grin at Byron's arched brows, his annoyance at Imogene's obvious devotion to her husband clearly readable.

In an effort to change the topic of conversation, Tristan broached a new subject. "Byron, how do you weigh on the notion of a gallery of portraits, for the nation, for England? Graham and I have discussed it often, and keep abreast of any news of action toward that goal. The idea has been much weighed about since the government let slip away that treasure trove of paintings that eventually went to the Hermitage and the Russians. I dare to say it was a tragic loss of opportunity to found such a worthy institution as well as a loss to the nation," he said regretfully.

"Hmmm, a national gallery you say? What kind of portraits would go into it?"

"Famous individuals, historical figures, landscapes, anything really as long as it was quality, and worthy of representing England to her citizens," Graham interjected.

"Mayhap a portrait of me could be included," Byron suggested with a smirk.

"Ah, I know you are jesting, Byron, but your portrait is exactly the kind of work that should be included. You are an English poet of note and your likeness should be preserved and gifted to the nation for prosperity. Some day you will not be here on this good earth, and there should be a record of your likeness, so future generations can feel that they knew you in some small way."

"Such the philosopher you are, Rothvale."

"I am serious, Byron. I would gladly commission a portrait of you." He turned to Tristan. "Tristan, if you are of a mind, and he is willing, please consider my offer sincere and paint a portrait of him, by all means."

"This talk of portraits reminds me I should still wish to

watch Mallerton at work. When will you next sit for him, Cousin?" Byron directed the question at her quite firmly.

Imogene could see his mind working, knowing he had no intentions of letting the matter go. He wanted to coerce her because he was keeping her secret about the other portrait. She wracked her brain for a solution, knowing that Graham would never allow Byron to observe an intimate portrait sitting. *You are a devil of gargantuan proportions, Byron!*

"Ah, George," she said charmingly, "I have a proposition in regards to that. Will you hear it?"

"Of course," he replied, his face alight, thinking he would get his way after all.

Imogene took in the countenances of all three men as they trained their undivided attention on her. Byron wore one of deceit; Tristan, one of amused anticipation; and Graham, one of foreboding. She honored Byron with an enthralled glance before presenting her plan, praying he would accept it. "Since you have expressed a sincere wish to observe Mr. Mallerton at his talent, what if *you* were to sit for *your* portrait during your stay here? We could come and keep you company while you sit. It would be for a worthy cause. I believe it might benefit all of you in the end." Imogene looked at all three men individually before continuing. "George, you will have the opportunity to learn about the prospect of seeing Mr. Mallerton go about his excellent work, and he will get credit for it. My husband will have a superbly executed painting, with which to gift to the nation for the portrait gallery when it is ultimately founded. And lastly, your likeness will be preserved onto canvas for posterity and future generations, securing your contributions to the literary world as worthy of the highest honor."

They all watched as Byron's demeanour changed from

interest to one of self-satisfaction. He really did think quite highly of himself, falling easily into Imogene's trap. Extolling the importance of his image being preserved in honor of his literary talent, she snared him. "I think it is an excellent plan and I will agree to it, but only if you keep your promise to stay with me throughout the sittings—you know, ease the boredom of it."

"YOU have my word," Imogene replied serenely to Byron, looking down the table at Graham, whose expression was at that moment, filled with utter amazement at the genius of his wife. *Unbelievable…my precious Imogene has captivated the most famous poet in England, if not the world. Thank God I found her before Byron ever did.* Graham could not hold back the involuntary shudder that coursed through him at the thought of what Byron would have done with an innocent like Imogene.

And combined with her earlier questioning as to why he didn't want to go for an extended visit to Everfell made him ache that he couldn't tell her the real reason.

I am afraid and I wish I could take you far away. I want to shield you from the ugliness that is brewing. So you cannot know, and will not turn from me.

Later that night in the privacy of their bed, both of them pondered the interesting conversations they had shared with Byron. "Well, thanks to you and your sharp mind, *chérie*, all survived the evening without great insult being thrown. You have gifts and talents that astound me, Imogene. The way you dealt with him was miraculous to behold. He could not have refused you if he had wanted to, so securely you ensnared him. Are you over the strain of it, my sweetheart?"

"Oh yes. But before you thank me, please remember that

we will still have to bear his company through the sittings. And what is it about him that is so different? I cannot put my finger on it, but strangely there is something about Byron that is atypical. What is it do you think? And what of he and Tristan? They are close friends?"

Graham sighed. "I knew this day would come eventually."

"What is it? Have you kept something from me?" She looked hurt.

He pulled her close and kissed her hair. "Just trying to protect you. You are so innocent, and the world is not."

"Tell me please! Trust me, Graham."

He sighed again and squeezed her a little. "They are good friends and have known each other since our school days at Harrow. Byron is a few years younger but school is where they met. Tristan was always different from the other boys and his difference had to be kept secret."

"Why ever for?"

"To keep him safe. There are those who would cast him out, shun him for his predilections."

"His predilections? And they are what, exactly?"

"He does not love women, or rather he is not attracted to the fairer sex for companionship. He is attracted to men in the way that most men are attracted to women. It is the reason he is a bachelor and will remain as such." He raised his eyebrows, looking to her reaction.

She was quiet but nodded her head in a way that suggested she finally had a complete understanding of Tristan.

Graham continued to wait for her to respond. When she did not, he asked gently, "What do you have to say about what I have just told you?"

Imogene worded her response carefully. "It certainly

explains some things, his situation and some comments he has made. I think I understand him now."

"What comments has he made?"

"Once he told me that he was probably the only painter in England who could not be tempted by me. I believe it is also the reason why you trust him to paint me without a chaperone present. Is that correct, Graham?"

"Correct. And do you feel differently about him? Do you still wish to call Tristan your friend?"

Without hesitation, she spoke assuredly which relieved him greatly. "Of course I still consider him a friend. He is the same man I knew before you shared this information with me. A good person and a true friend to you and to me. Even if I could not accept his *preferences,* the fact you trust him and value him as your friend would be enough for me. I trust you and know you to be honorable in judging character. You would not put me in his path if you did not think him worthy." She pondered it some more. "Are there many men like him?"

"There are, and even though society reviles such practices publicly, in private it is tolerated as long as discretion is applied. You probably have the acquaintance of others with such predilections but you would never know of it. I don't believe they can help it. It is just the way that they are born."

"I had no idea."

"You have been sheltered from such things, as you should have been."

"What of Lord Byron? Does he love men? He looks at me like he wants to…most improper, flirting outrageously…and there is talk of his many female conquests." She looked confused.

"Byron is not exclusive to men. He indulges in debauchery and his weakness is his lack of discretion. It is well known that he went to Greece to have encounters with young men. Even so, he still pursues women and could not be trusted in any situation with a beautiful woman alone. I could *never* leave him with you alone. He knows I would not. Byron simply cannot be trusted. He is not evil, but regardless, a complete libertine who does not apply restraint of any kind. He does as he wishes and the consequences be damned."

"What is his relationship with Tristan?"

"They are friends of long standing. Beyond that, I am not entirely sure, *chérie*, and quite frankly, I do not care to know. Whatever they do in private is none of my business just as what we do in private is nobody's concern either."

"I agree with you. I have no wish to think about such things in regards to others. I will be relieved when Byron is gone, but what a story we'll have to tell our grandchildren, hmmm?"

"Yes we will. You are exceptional, my dearest. A definite diamond in a sea of glass. You are so wise and clever. How did you ever think to ask Byron to sit for his own portrait instead of watching your sittings? You were brilliant and I thought I would burst with pride for you tonight, seeing you catch up Byron at his own game. It was a delight to view as the whole business unfolded."

"You do not give yourself enough credit, Graham. It was you who suggested the idea to Tristan and inspired me. What I did could never have been accomplished without you there for encouragement and support, and let's not forget your most noble protection and defense."

"*Je toujours ici pour vous mon chérie*…I will always here for you, my darling." He whispered the words against her beautiful lips as he descended.

Chapter 19

...Or like a fairy trip on the green,
Or, like a nymph, with long disheveled hair,
Dance on the sands, and yet no footing seen:
Love is a spirit all compact of fire...

William Shakespeare ~ Venus and Adonis, 1593

In the end, Byron stayed just a week with them. It was enough time for Tristan to get his likeness onto canvas, and gratefully to Imogene's relief, her secret was not divulged.

Busy with preparations to depart for Everfell, she had two important things to accomplish before they made their journey, however. One was to get in the final sittings for the *dishabille* portrait and the other was to secure the plans and preparations for Graham's birthday celebration at the end of April. Only a week would remain whence they returned from Everfell, and she wished to have everything in place for the event before they left Gavandon.

The celebration of Graham's birthday was meant to be a surprise so Imogene enlisted the help of Mrs. Griffin and Mrs. Jacobson, to ensure success. There were many letters to write and responses to receive, and she worked diligently on her tasks.

Imogene looked forward to seeing Elle again, and the great house of Everfell, and hoped Graham came around in his feelings about the visit. Imogene sensed something was not right within his business or possibly a family matter she'd not been privy to, nor had been shared with her. She could tell he carried the burden of worry about something, and he had bad dreams in the dead of night sometimes. He always apologized for waking her and claimed not to remember.

The prospect of going to London for the Season was discussed, but after baring their hearts in all honesty, both were delighted to find that neither one of them desired to go. Graham felt that the pressures of running the estate to be demanding after so long an absence, and Imogene saw no purpose for her to go at all. Graham suggested they could go to Somerset at Kilve in late summer if she might enjoy a holiday by the sea. He told her of the lovely seashore cottage there, called *Marlings*. It had been his Aunt Mary's house. He spoke of how he had enjoyed visits there as a youth, had ridden along the beaches, and of viewing the beautiful sunsets over the ocean. He told her that he would dearly love to take her there. It had been several years since he had visited, thinking it might make a lovely substitute for Ireland until they could manage a trip as far away as Donadea.

As her daily meeting with Mrs. Griffin was winding down with the usual business concluded, Imogene broached a new topic with the housekeeper. "Mrs. Griffin, now that I have had time to know our tenants, I intend to continue with the visits, regularly assisting where it might be needed in households facing illness or other troubles. I know from experience that if you do not have a personal relationship with the tenants, you will not know of their needs until it is too late, and by then the seeds of resentment have set and situations deteriorate."

"Your insight is extraordinary, Lady Rothvale, but then you were raised understanding these matters, weren't you?"

"Yes, I suppose so. My mother had high expectations for my sister and me, and she was an excellent teacher until her illness prevented her. That is another area where I am well experienced, Mrs. Griffin. My mother was ill for years and I attended to her every day. There is little of the sickroom to offend me. I have seen and touched all of it. It will not bother me. If I can give some relief and comfort to the sick, I am glad to do it."

"My lady, your attentions will be very welcomed and appreciated I know. We have been without a lady's presence here, and also since we have no rector, or more importantly, a rector's wife to see to visits of this kind, there has been no one to call upon. I must admit your disclosure this morning is a bit of a relief."

"Thank you. Do you think everything could be organized while we are away at Everfell?"

"Yes I do, my lady. We will be ready for you upon your return from Everfell, with this matter and also the other of the master's birthday." She smiled conspiratorially.

"Thank you again, Mrs. Griffin, you are most accommodating and easy. I feel very blessed here at Gavandon. I know I am fortunate," she offered sincerely. Mrs. Griffin smiled at her kind words of praise. "You mentioned the rectory. How long has it been vacant?" Imogene was curious.

"Oh, it has been more than five years now at least. The old rector passed on before Mr. Jasper even," she said quietly.

"And the post was never filled?"

"Not to my knowledge, no." Mrs. Griffin was not forthcoming with any more information than that, so Imogene let it go. She would investigate and get to the bottom of it later.

"I must ready myself to attend my last sitting for the portrait with Mr. Mallerton. Please inform my husband if he should return home before me."

"Oh, before I forget to mention, my lady, a package has arrived for you. I've had it sent up to your room."

Imogene hurried to dress quickly into the silver gown, which was annoying really when it was merely a sham to throw everyone off of her real purpose in posing for the other portrait. As soon as she was dressed she passed through and spied the package Mrs. Griffin had mentioned. Her curiosity was piqued and so she quickly opened the thin parcel after checking for a hint of the sender. There was nothing on the outside, which she found to be very odd.

As the brown paper was removed a smaller bundle wrapped in tissue paper was revealed. Inside was a pair of finely crafted ladies gloves. Buff coloured leather ones. Exactly like the gloves she'd discussed with the man in the modiste shop in London before her wedding—

Imogene felt the hair on the back of her neck raise up when she noticed a slip of paper peeking out of one of the gloves.

A note…

Dear Lady Rothvale,

My congratulations on your marriage. Consider this a wedding present from a grateful friend who you may call upon if ever you find yourself in need. I am an excellent listener, and could provide you with answers to some questions you will have cause to ponder in the near future. Apologies for being cryptic, but know that I am ever your servant.

Ralph Odeman

She dropped the gloves into a drawer and buried them deep with the note tucked back into the left one.

Imogene didn't know what to make of the mystery, for it was certainly that, and a very disturbing mystery on top of. Something wasn't right about Mr. Odeman and his…gift. And it was completely inappropriate for him to send her such a personal item when she didn't even know him beyond his name. How did he even know where they lived? Did Mr. Odeman know Graham? Imogene remembered how she'd spotted him on the London street in front of the shop staring at her through the window of her coach. Even remembering the look upon his face then, made her shiver now. Graham would not like this news. He would be outraged in fact. Imogene knew this much and she didn't want to shatter their peace when she could tell her husband was already burdened with other matters.

So she decided to say nothing for now.

GRAHAM was grateful the journey to Everfell was a relatively easy one, the distance being only seven and twenty miles from Gavandon. He'd watched Imogene take in the wild scenery from the window and was pleased she appreciated the stark beauty of it. The past week had been very full with preparations for this trip, and he could tell she was feeling a little weary as she rode in the carriage. He watched her getting drowsier and drowsier until she finally succumbed and fell asleep with her head against the seat cushion.

It gave him time to think about what he needed to do. As soon as the opportunity presented itself he needed to speak with Jules about his *problem.* Time was running out and the dread of stone-cold fear was getting the upper hand.

Watching Imogene so peaceful only made his worry worse. If she found out he couldn't say what she would do or how she would feel about him—

She stirred and lifted her head, blinked and rolled her neck as she woke up from her nap. "Oh! Did I sleep the whole way? I cannot imagine why I did that. Sorry, my darling, for not keeping you company."

He smiled lovingly, "You were out cold, *chérie*, so you must have really needed a rest. How do you feel now?"

"I am well." She glanced out the window as she attempted to smooth her hair and dress. "Can the house be seen yet?"

"If you look to your right, you will just start to see the house as we come round this next curve… There." He pointed as the grand estate came into view. "Now before you is all that is Everfell," he said silkily, observing her reaction.

He saw her eyes widen at the sight of it. "Oh! I—I can see why it is so celebrated. Why, it's positively palatial! And the grounds—and the lake!" She looked at him quizzically, her brows furrowing just a little. Opening her hands, she lifted them in question.

He took delight in her confusion. "You look as if you'd like to ask me something, *chérie*."

Flustered, she replied, "You obviously relish vexing me with mysteries, but fine, I'll humor you. Why does the Barony of Rothvale hold Gavandon and not Everfell?"

"Ah, so you notice the inequity of the houses," he said dramatically, "are you disappointed that you shall never be mistress of such a grand residence?" He paused. "You've got a title instead."

She seemed to choose her words carefully. "Everfell is magnificent indeed, but I assure you I am well suited to our home, or rather it is well suited to me."

"How is that, *chérie*?"

She continued to take in the view of it through the carriage window before she answered. "Well, for one, I am a country girl and I like a country house. Everfell is, as I said before, palatial and would be wasted on me. No, I am very happy as we are."

"What a relief. Here I have been worrying that you would be jealous of all the splendour and be discontented with Gavandon once you saw Everfell, but I can see now I worried for nothing."

"You teasing man. You know I do not care about such things. My question is merely one of curiosity. How did such a grand house slip away from the barony?"

"Sorry for the teasing, *chérie*. I know I am wicked to do it, but I cannot help myself sometimes. You are so unspoiled." He admired smugly. "I will submit to *any* punishment you deem fit for me…later." He raised his brows suggestively before answering her. "My great-grandfather was the one who made the vast fortunes, in wool mostly. He acquired the house with some of that fortune, and made sure it was not entailed with the barony for he wished to gift it to his second son. My father inherited the title and the family estate and his cousin, my Uncle Jameson got Everfell, sans title. Uncle James went further and married *very* well in distinction and in money, with the Julian family, which garnered him the means to make

Everfell flourish and to increase the lands. Jules has had a burden of responsibility in taking it on at such a young age, but he has done admirably. Everfell is unique and he enjoys all of the advantages of wealth and connections, but not the title. I have the wealth and the connections *with* the title, but not such a magnificent house." He grinned. "But *I do* have a magnificent wife." He blew her a kiss from across the carriage. "And she assures me that she prefers our bucolic country home to this one. For me, I care not about the houses, just the wife," he finished neatly. "And there you have it, *chérie*."

She smiled at him adoringly, mouthed a quick 'I love you,' and made ready to alight as the carriage pulled to a stop at the steps of Everfell's entrance.

They were greeted with the enthusiastic embraces and kisses of welcome from Mina, Elle and Jules. It had been four months since they had last been together. Ushered into a beautiful parlor where tea was being served, they were all afforded a chance to visit a bit before settling into their rooms. They were to meet downstairs for a tour of the house in three hour's time; the tour being for Imogene's benefit alone, as she was the only one unfamiliar with the stately halls of Everfell.

"I think I'll lie down for a bit before I go back down, that way my stamina for the tour will be restored. I can only imagine it will take a long time to get around the whole house. I am feeling unusually tired," she said, stifling another yawn.

Graham felt her brow in concern. "I hope you are not becoming ill, *chérie*. Let me unlace you, so you can rest comfortably." He moved to help her out of her dress and to unfasten her stays. His hands roamed a little over her as he divested her of her outer garments.

"Is it your intention to bed me in your cousin's house so soon, my darling? We have only just arrived," she cajoled.

"Hmmm." He put a finger to his lips, playing along with her teasing. "It is my intention to bed you *well* and *often* in my cousin's house, but not just now." He kissed her forehead. "You need a rest, and that is what you must do." He helped her into bed, leaning over for more kisses. "I'll send Hester up to you about a half-hour before the time so you can dress, and then I'll come escort you down. How does that sound to you?"

"Perfect."

"I cannot even comprehend to imagine how magnificent your ballroom will look on Friday in all its splendour and filled with guests. Graham has shared with me his love for Everfell. I must tell you it is wonderful to be here, to finally see it, and to be with all of you, our family." Imogene offered the sentiment over the elegant dining table.

Jules replied, "Thank *you*, for accepting our invitation. We wanted so badly to be at your wedding, and since we were not able, thought this would be the best way to honor your marriage. We are grateful to have you so close in distance and it is high time we celebrated in happiness together as a family. It is a good thing, is it not, Graham?" Jules asked him.

"It is a true thing, Jules. I find it deeply comforting to be back here. And all the better for it now with our lovely brides gracing its halls and paths," Graham remarked. "Have you heard from my brother?"

"Colin wrote to us and expects to arrive the day after tomorrow I believe," he answered with a knowing look to Graham. "And, Imogene, your sister and Dr. Brancroft have accepted our invitation as well. They are to arrive on

Thursday. My uncle and aunt, Sir Thomas and Lady Hargreave, have also accepted," Jules said with a pointed glance at Mina. "Let's see, Mr. Gravelle and the Burleighs are coming. My cousin, Colonel Nicholas Hargreave, will be here as well. Those are the ones you would know. Mostly everyone else, you would not know, but are the families that we have known all our lives."

"I am so looking forward to seeing everyone again and of course, meeting the people of Warwickshire."

Elle spoke up then. "Imogene, I would love to ride with you again. Would you like to go tomorrow?"

"Very much," she replied eagerly. "Mina, are you riding yet? I know you are a great walker, but you told me it was your intention to learn to ride. You said at the time you feared it would be the only way to get around to seeing Everfell for all its vast and remote locales."

"I did have the very best of intentions it's true, but alas I have not had more than a few lessons as of yet." Mina looked to her husband with a smile and a tiny nod of her head.

Jules beamed at them all. "We have happy news to share. We are expecting. He *or* she should be gracing us with an appearance sometime in the early autumn."

Congratulations were shared, and Graham felt a gladdening inside his heart. For the first time in years really, he was finally able to approach his life with optimism. There had been so much loss for both sets of Everleys, and it was uplifting to know that the tremendous loss and despair was finally succumbing to the joys and comforts of happy family life. Heartened by their glad news, he had pause to wonder if he and Imogene would soon be following them down the same path. He was good with details and had kept track of the weeks. She had been indisposed just the one time. But

Imogene had said nothing and he would not bother her with questions, however he did speculate at the possibility she was already with child.

Mina continued, "We agreed that it would be best to resume the riding lessons after the baby comes just to be safe. No, I won't be able to join you in your riding tomorrow but do not give it another thought, Imogene. You *must* ride with Elle. She has been anticipating your visit for such long time now."

"But what will you do while we are away, Mina?"

"I have plenty to busy myself with, I assure you," Mina replied. Then turning to her husband, she teased, "Are you going to beg an invitation to join them, Julian?"

"I thought I might," he said meekly. "Would you mind if I tag along with you ladies?" he asked pointedly to Elle and Imogene.

"Not at all. Please join us, Brother," Elle responded, but then turned to her cousin, "Graham, would you like to come along as well? I remember a time not so long ago when you were quite keen to go riding with me." Eyes sparkling, she reminded everyone of his collusion in arranging time to be with Imogene in their first days of acquaintance.

"Oh, and I am keen still! I would love to join in your riding party and go with you, dear, sweetest Elle. It will be so relieving to go with you and just enjoy the riding, with no angst about winning the affections of a certain lady," he joked, flashing a quick wink at Imogene.

IN the predawn hour, Imogene quietly settled herself back into bed, but not quietly enough because Graham stirred awake and asked sleepily, "*Chérie?*"

"Nature called is all, go back to sleep."

He pushed against her instead. "But *I* am awake now and so are you." He breathed into her ear, nibbling the soft flesh of her neck.

Arching into him, Imogene felt the involuntary shiver of arousal brush over her. "What are you going to do about it?" she whispered back.

"By all means, let me show you…"

After peeling away her nightdress and making her completely bare, he pulled her atop him, splitting her legs wide over his hips and settling her down onto his cock. She descended slowly until he was buried deep and tight. The fullness of his thick shaft filling her made her weak from pleasure. Graham took over gratefully, urging her to move up and down, helping her find a rhythm by gripping her bottom and lifting.

"I love it this way, seeing you, admiring you from below…so beautiful," Graham told her breathily as the thrusts of his cock grew faster and stronger.

Her body moved with his, her breasts swaying from the jolts of his cock and her cunny connecting and separating over and over again. Imogene felt the walls of her sex grow tighter as his cock swelled inside, preparing to spill. She strained toward the feeling of release, so close she couldn't control the desperate moans that escaped from her throat.

Graham knew what she needed and he gave it to her. He put two fingers over her slippery clit and pinched. That did it. The climax burned through her and took over her body, stealing her breath, making her incapable of anything else but giving into the frenzy. Graham thrust up hard and deep one final time on a feral growl and held himself in her as he released his seed.

Their eyes locked together as did their bodies, allowing the pall of peace to chase the rush of exquisite pleasure…

Finally Imogene dropped down, arranging herself next to him, wrapped tightly to his side. He combed his fingers through her hair while their breathing levelled out. "You just indulged me another of my fantasies, *chérie*," he whispered against her ear.

"I did? Tell me."

"One of making love with you at Everfell."

"When did you fantasize about that?"

"Oh, you would be quite surprised at how soon after meeting you I thought it."

"Really? How soon?"

"Right away," he admitted, gripping her a little tighter. "You must know that I had nothing to do but wait between the times I could be with you in those first days. I had to fill the endless hours with something nice or go mad. Imogene, I was adrift in my life, truly. Meeting you taught me to hope that I might find a reason to rejoin the realm of the living. I knew I had to win you, and marry you, and bring you to Warwickshire. That eventually we would come here, to Everfell together, and it would be very special."

"It is." Imogene stroked his cheek lovingly.

"The reality was far superior to the fantasy, I assure you."

She stirred awake in the morning when he got caught looking at her naked perfection. Graham was ready and propped on his elbow, just enjoying the view as she threw off the mantle of sleep.

"This is a pleasant surprise," she remarked. "You are always up before me so I rarely get this view of you when I wake."

"Well, we are on a kind of holiday I suppose, and there is

nothing I would rather be doing right now. And how are you on this fine morning, *chérie*?"

"Most excellent. We are to ride this morning with Elle and Jules and cannot lie abed." She leaned over to greet him with a kiss. We must bathe and dress in our riding clothes before we go down to breakfast." She moved to rise from the bed but he stopped her by snaking his arm around her and drawing her back.

"Not so fast, *chérie*, I need a little cuddling before I am ready to release you from the bed."

"Oh, well I suppose I can give you just a *little*," she teased, "but only a very little mind you, no more than that."

"Why only a little?" He pretended to pout.

"Because I have caught you at naughtiness again. Peeping at me whilst I sleep bare in the bed. I felt the covers lifting. I know you did it. I daresay you will need a sound punishment."

He had the grace to look guilty. "Oh, *chérie,* peeping at you, that is not naughtiness. It is reassurance, that you are not a dream for all your otherworldly beauty. But please, feel free to indulge yourself in carrying out my punishment. I wait on your deliverance." He raised his lips to receive her kiss, eyes closed.

She delivered a clout to his face with a pillow instead, along with the sounds of her most satisfied giggling as she scrambled off the bed. "You said I was to carry it out," she reminded him. "And so you admitted to your guilt at the same time. Come retrieve me in an hour, my husband, and I might be ready with some new *punishments* for you," she called over her shoulder as she quitted the bedroom for the dressing room.

Graham let her go, wickedly imagining several 'punishments' he might enjoy.

On time, one hour later, he took in the view of her as she exited the dressing room attired for their planned equestrian activity. "That is my favourite one of your riding dresses. The colour is so rich and suits you perfectly. You certainly know how to choose an outfit, *chérie,*" he said admiringly.

Imogene had chosen her brown velvet habit this day. It was a deep reddish brown, reminiscent of shimmering bronze, embellished with teal blue enhancements. The top sported a white false shirt underneath the tightly fitted bodice. The matching hat was trimmed with a teal blue veil and her gloves also dyed the same colour.

"Thank you, my darling, I am glad you fancy it." She peered at him with bedevilment. "You look quite smart yourself, but then I have always been captivated by your outward charms. Those green eyes, that long hair, those burly muscles, your manly visage—"

He hushed her with a kiss and some silent laughter. "All right, all right, no need for sauciness or I might have to take you back to bed."

"I am sure you would like just such an excuse." She pushed at him. "But now, we must go out into society and you will have to behave yourself," she said, wrapping her arm under his, "and so will I."

"You are quite right, Lady Rothvale, as always. Shall we sally forth?" Graham's heart was light as he walked her down to the breakfast room of Everfell.

"The weather is quite perfect today for your riding. I shall miss being outdoors on such a fine day," Mina remarked over breakfast.

"Darling, I feel that we should not all abandon you. I will stay," Jules told his wife decidedly.

"Oh no, you will not. I wish you to go. I know you want

to ride with your cousin and I will not have it any other way. I am firm in this, Julian. You are going!"

The others shared looks all around, feeling somewhat discomfited at leaving their hostess behind, when Imogene found sudden inspiration. "Mina, have you ever shot targets, with a bow and arrow?"

"I confess I have not."

"Would you like to? I could teach you if you wish. It is so lovely out today. It would make for excellent sport and is quiet enough not to tax you physically. I thought ahead and have brought my bows. I have been waiting for good weather to start up again. Elle, what about you?"

Mina beamed, "I would love that, Imogene. It sounds most enjoyable to be outside, and I would be eager to take a lesson in shooting from you. We'll see how I do."

"And, Elle, would you like it?" Imogene asked.

"I would. I did a little target shooting at school and it *was* good sport. I'd like to give it another try."

"An excellent proposition, Imogene, thank you," Jules said warmly. "I'll speak to Falcon before we head out and have him fashion some targets for you. He might even be able to rummage up some equipment from the carriage house. He'll know if anybody does."

"Old Falcon is still with us?" Graham asked. "The Gamekeeper of Everfell…he was old when we were boys," he reminisced.

"Oh yes. He's still with us. Refuses to give up his post. Knows I would give him a free cottage and maintain him in retirement, but will not hear of it. Graham, remember when we used to help him gather the pheasant eggs for setting under the hens? He would always call us out for the hatching of the chicks so we could see what our efforts had wrought."

"I do remember, Jules. Falcon was always so proud of us if we could find the eggs and get them in without breaking any." He looked at Imogene. "We used to compete for who could bring in the most eggs."

"Who won?" All three ladies asked at the same time.

Jules laughed at their eagerness. "That's an easy question to answer. Graham, for certain. He would find more nests than I, and was far more gentle and patient in transporting the eggs. I always broke a few in my enthusiasm. I can't recall you ever breaking any," he remarked wistfully to his cousin.

Graham shrugged. "I don't know about that, but I should like to say hello to Falcon while I'm here. He was good to us, tolerating our irritating childish presence. I hold very happy memories of him." He was thoughtful before looking to Imogene, a smile appearing on his face.

"I know, when we grow tired of target shooting, we can go into the wood and hunt eggs! It sounds ever so sporting. This is the time they'd be laying, isn't it? We can see who gets the most!" Imogene suggested excitedly.

Everybody laughed. Graham remarked to their hosts, "Did you know that my wife is very competitive? She likes to win."

"Well you'd better let her then, if you know what's good for you," Jules told him.

Graham did not favour his cousin with a reply. Instead he turned to Imogene and said, "I would love to hunt eggs with you, *chérie*. It sounds perfect."

And yet again, Graham and Imogene achieved the look the others were growing accustomed to. They shared a look between them, just for them, and were, as always, unaware of the bemused glances of the others at the breakfast table that morning.

MINA was a natural with a bow, taking to it most enthusiastically. Elle put up a great effort as well. Imogene was a patient instructor and seemed delighted in sharing her knowledge of the sport with her friends once again. Old Falcon fashioned targets for them and even managed to dredge out a few more bows from somewhere. He had them oiled, restrung and ready for use when the riders returned.

"Thank you for this, Jules," Graham said as they sat on the lawn and watched the ladies take to their sport. "It feels most satisfying to just be here with Imogene. I'm grateful you insisted on a visit. I did not realize how much I needed to reconnect with my family." He was quiet for a moment. "For the first time in a great long while, I am happy."

"It's most evident, Graham, and everybody is happy for you. I am glad you are here with us, as well. And even better when Colin arrives for Elle does so adore him."

"Is she completely recovered from her trauma at the hands of Odem—ugh—I cannot even say the blackguard's name, he is so low."

"Yes, I think so. I worry though of her exposure to him again, and of being reminded of her hurt. It is bound to happen eventually. Odeman has wreaked more disaster since you've been away. He ruined a girl in Kent, caused her death. She was from a good family, a distant relation of Mina's. I tried to help, but there was little I could do. I still shudder to think that it could have been Elle."

"Poor girl." Graham sighed. "Poor you. I am so sorry, Jules, it must have brought back such dreadful memories. I cannot imagine having to bargain with that miscreant."

Careful…you may have to bite back those words. This latest concern has the full stink of Ralph Odeman all over it.

Jules said pensively, "It is amazing what you'll do for the ones you love."

"True…so true." Graham had to agree.

THE following day the weather proved finer than the day before it. Another round of target shooting for the ladies, and a picnic luncheon was enjoyed on the lawn. "It was so engaging to hear your music last night," Imogene remarked. "You both play and sing so well," she complimented Elle and Mina. "It is one thing we are sorely lacking at Gavandon I fear. I never learnt to play or sing. And Graham does not sing as far as I know. He has never sung any songs to me in any case. He has read me beautiful poems—but no songs," she said adoringly, placing her gaze upon him.

"Would you like for me to sing to you, *chérie*? I could make a concerted effort just for you," Graham said cryptically. "I don't know if you would like it though. What do you say, Jules? Should I sing for my wife?"

"Probably not. Listening to you croak out a tune might cause her to lose some of her affection for you, or at the very least, abandon the picnic." Jules leaned toward Imogene. "He has no musical ability whatsoever. To that I can attest. In our school days Graham would always stand betwixt Hargreave and me during the hymn singing. After suffering the poisonous glares of the choir master, we finally convinced him to just move his mouth and keep quiet. Worked like a charm and there were no more problems after that."

Imogene laughed out loud at the thought of Graham

duping the choir master. She adored hearing about his boyhood and was grateful for these little windows into his past. "Oh, my darling, I promise I will not abandon you if you should suddenly feel the urge to break out in song. I *will* stand by you, on my honor. I feel I must defend you in any case as I have no more musical ability than you do."

"But you make up for it in other ways. Isn't that right, Imogene?" Jules asked.

"Oh, absolutely she does. Imogene rules the drawing room in after-dinner conversation, most assuredly," Graham attested.

She was puzzled by their comments, thinking herself to be usually quiet and rather prone to listening more so than talking. She looked at them both questioningly.

Jules continued, "You know, charming and manipulating depraved but celebrated poets, be they blood relation or merely deigning to flattery."

"What is that you're saying, Julian?" Mina inquired, her curiosity piqued.

"Tell us what you mean," Elle implored.

"Well, Graham was telling me that our poet celebrity, Lord *Byron,* descended upon them at Gavandon quite unexpectedly, claimed kinship with Imogene, and sat for his portrait," Jules said.

They gasped and Imogene blushed, shaking her head as Graham regaled the ladies of the tale of Byron's visit. "She had him eating out of her hand. It was a delight to watch the whole scene unfold. I am convinced she could charm the skin off a snake. It certainly was so with Byron, and he never even knew it." Graham finished with an admiring look at Imogene.

"And the portrait? How did it turn out?" Mina asked.

"Magnificent. Mallerton is very gifted. He is painting

Imogene's portrait right now and it's nearly done. Everyone has seen it but me."

Jules interjected, "I should like Mina's portrait painted. Do you think—?"

Graham cut him off abruptly. "Absolutely not, Jules. You cannot have Mallerton. I have far too many projects for him in progress right now. If I allow precedence and let him leave Gavandon, he might never return. No," he said decidedly, "you must find your own artist, you cannot have mine."

"So you won't let him off the property even?"

"I might concede he can paint Mina, only if you come to stay with us at Gavandon. He can paint her there. That's as fair a bargain as you will get on the matter, I promise you."

"Is that an invitation, Cousin?"

"Of course. You are welcome to come anytime you wish. We are decided against a London Season this year. I'm just not ready. We may take in the seaside and go to Marlings in the late summer, though."

"I love Marlings. I haven't been there since Aunt Mary was alive."

"Please feel free to join us if you'd like. There is plenty of room—the house is huge for all that it's called a cottage." Graham asked quietly, "Will you take in the Season? Are you heading to Town for any length of time?"

Jules shook his head in the negative. "We would only go for Elle's coming out, but she does not wish a big pother." He looked over at his sister pensively.

"And I am grateful in having a brother who takes my wishes into account and listens to me," Elle replied. "I do not want a presentation at court. That practice is starting to fade anyway—it does not suit for me."

The conversation lulled as each fell into quiet

contemplation after Elle moved to take up her bow and resumed to target shooting.

"IMOGENE, over here," Graham called. She approached where he knelt in the shadowy grass, the trees overhead blocking the light of mid-day. He parted the grass with his hand and showed her a clutch of pheasant eggs. They were the softest dove brown ranging from tan to nearly palest green.

"You found some," she said as she leaned her chin on his shoulder from behind. "Oh, how lovely they are. Graham, you are amazing." She counted quickly. "I count twelve eggs."

"Help me gather them up. They are fragile." He took out his handkerchief, unfolded it on the grass and placed six of the eggs in it to carry them. Imogene got out her handkerchief and did the same with the other six. "Come, let's take them to Falcon. I want to say hello." He leaned in to give her a kiss. "And introduce you. You'll like him."

Graham led her along the path, farther into the wood until they arrived at a timbered stone cottage. "This is it. I loved coming here as a boy. It seemed a magical place to me then, maybe still is." He looked around wistfully before rapping on the door and then grinned as they waited.

"Coming, coming! Who's that then?" a gruff voice grumbled from within.

"Egg gatherers here, Falcon," Graham shouted.

The door opened and a grizzled face appeared in the doorway. The dark eyes registered surprise first and then recognition as a great smile cracked forth on the wizened features of the old gamekeeper. "Bless me!" He put his hand up to his heart. "Master Graham, 'tis really you?"

"Aye, it is me, Falcon, and I bring gifts." He held up his handkerchief.

"What have you got for me then?" Falcon asked.

Graham carefully opened his handkerchief and showed the eggs. Imogene held hers out as well. Falcon peered to look. "Those are right perfect. Here, come in, would you?" He ushered them in and shuffled over to a shelf, returning with a basket lined in downy feathers. Falcon watched as Graham gently transferred first his eggs and then Imogene's eggs into the basket. Falcon spoke with remembrance, "Not a one broke, just like when you were a boy. I'll set them under the hens later." He moved the basket back to its shelf. "What's got you out to gather in eggs for me after all these years, Master Graham?" he asked pointedly.

"I wanted to say hello, and I've brought someone to meet you. Falcon, I am here with my wife. This is Imogene, Lady Rothvale. My cousin has told her how we used to hunt eggs for you and she asked if we might get the chance to do it again." He indicated to Falcon. "Imogene, may I present Mr. Falconer of Everfell."

"My lady." He bowed low for an elder gentleman. "You honor me." Falcon looked to her admiringly, then back to Graham with a nod of acknowledgment.

"Mr. Falconer, how do you do?" She smiled gently at the old gamekeeper. "Thank you for arranging targets for our shooting yesterday. It was the first time in a long while, and it was good to fire a bow again."

"Your devoted servant, my lady. Glad to be of service, and always happy to make things useful again. Will you sit to tea with me?" he extended sincerely.

Imogene did not hesitate. "We would be delighted to join you."

He served them tea from stout mugs and sliced some cake. "The cake comes from the big house by way of Mrs. Lake," he said with a twinkle in his eye. "Not to worry, my lady."

"It is delicious cake, Mr. Falconer. I cannot remember when I've had a more delightful tea, or shared it in such good company," she remarked archly looking at both of them. She meant it too, every word.

The glow coming off Graham taught her he was happy here, visiting with his old friend and mentor. He seemed lifted of his burdens for the moment somehow, relaxed and content, and it filled her heart.

Graham spoke, "Oh, Imogene does not stand on ceremony, Falcon. She is a country girl, and appreciates the bounties of nature. My wife assures me she is most typical in this regard." His green eyes betrayed the hint of sarcasm in his voice.

"I'd not say she is typical, more like a rare bloom. You have chosen well, my lord," Falcon replied. "Your mother, rest her saintly soul, would have approved. But you know she would have. I know that you know…" he trailed off, offering condolences silently to Graham for his great loss.

Feeling impelled to give them a moment alone, Imogene rose from her place and wandered over to a wall draped in tail feathers. Pheasant tails of the most glorious hues: rich and changeable, the brilliant quills shading from a deep red to violet, to green, and to bronze. "So many feathers. They are absolutely beautiful, Mr. Falconer."

"Falcon, my lady—please just Falcon. I save the tails from the shootings. Mrs. Lake likes them for arrangements and adornment for the house at Christmastide especially. Now that Master is married, 'twill probably be more festive at

Christmastide than before." He reached up to pluck a magnificent tail from the wall with teals, greens, russets, and bronzes gleaming in glorious iridescence, and handed it to Imogene. "With my compliments, Lady Rothvale. 'Twould look fine on a hat perhaps, or to use as you wish."

"Thank you, Falcon. I will cherish them as a remembrance of this lovely afternoon upon my first visit to Everfell," Imogene said while looking into the luminous green eyes of her husband.

Chapter 20

Then press into thy breast this pledge of love;
And know, though time may change and years may roll,
Each floweret gathered in my heart
It consecrates to thine.

Percy Bysshe Shelley ~ 'To Harriet' dedication for 'Queen Mab', 1813

Colin arrived the next day, and he brought with him a surprise guest—Imogene's dear cousin, Cariss Wilton. All of it arranged by Graham of course, with some of the logistics worked out months ago. Colin had agreed to fetch Cariss from Kent and then escort her safely to Warwickshire for the spring visit Imogene had dearly hoped for. Graham was gratified to give yet another gift to his wife, and delighted in witnessing the joy she felt at reuniting with her cousin. It was also good to have Colin back with them. Their brotherly bond went very deep and Graham realized how much he'd missed the companionship of his brother while he'd been away in Ireland.

Mina informed everyone that the night's entertainment would be dance instruction in the Viennese Waltz. Since the gentlemen all had previous experience of actual practical knowledge, having done it in Europe on their tours, the task fell to them to teach the ladies the steps as there were to be three waltzes played at the ball.

All retired to the ballroom following dinner. Elle and Cariss agreed to take turns playing the music so each of them could have a chance to learn the dance steps. Jules demonstrated the proper position of the hands with Mina as a model, and slowly walked through the steps, which were quite simple really, with just a basic one-two-three rhythm.

Graham held out his hand to Imogene, "It's all coming back to me, *chérie.* I know it has been a long while since I waltzed, but I believe I can muddle through." He bowed. "Will you do me the honor, my lady?" At her agreement, he situated them into place, settling his right hand on her waist, her left hand on his shoulder, while clasping opposite hands together. "What do you think, *chérie*?"

"I think I shall enjoy dancing with you again," she responded.

"But we have never danced the waltz before."

"I know." She frowned at him as if she didn't care for being reminded of it.

"I will endeavor to enjoy this practice dance because I am pragmatic enough to realize I'll probably get no more than a single dance with you in the entirety of the ball. I know I'll be jealous the whole night," he said resignedly.

"Oh well, my darling, I am already jealous that you have danced the waltz with scores of women before *me*."

"Hardly scores of them," he insisted, "and I remember nothing of any of those women."

She rolled her eyes and huffed.

"What? You don't believe me, *chérie*? I don't lie." He

pulled her a little closer—possessively—as he led her through the lilting steps.

"Yes, well we've had this conversation before," she said the words with scorn. "Your interpretation is more of keeping things *from* me, rather than lying, I suppose." She continued on relentlessly. "So even if you had waltzed with scores of women you would just keep silent about it and I could not know the truth, no matter what you'd said."

Graham registered shock for an instant before narrowing his eyes. "You wound me. What have I done to deserve your contempt here tonight?"

She cast her eyes down. "Nothing. You have done nothing to deserve my derision. I beg your pardon, darling. I—I am out of sorts, and not good company right now. Quite frankly I am weary. It has been a full day."

He nodded to her in acknowledgement; hurt still lingering from her sharp words.

After a few more minutes of awkward dancing she spoke again. "I think I've got an understanding of the steps now. If I may, I'll beg goodnight early." At her declaration he stopped them and moved to lead her out of the room. "No, please, Graham, do not end your evening because of me. Stay. Stay and teach Elle or Cariss the steps so they will know them for the ball. I'm just going to tuck in early. I am tired." She put her hand on his arm and was insistent.

"All right then. As you wish, *chérie.*" He leaned in to kiss her goodnight. But she turned her head at the last second, causing his lips to land inelegantly on her jaw. Surprise opened his eyes at her rejection, and he stood there stupidly for a moment as she fled the room. A stab of pain hit him in the chest. He had not felt like this since their misunderstanding about the solitary riding. His every urge was to chase after her and demand to know what was bothering her. But, no, he would not. She did not want him right now, that fact was more than apparent when she insisted he stay and teach the steps to Elle and Cariss, so she must be needing her privacy.

The men separated from the ladies after the dancing practice exhausted itself.

Thank bloody hellfire.

Graham's mood was no longer light. Brooding and nursing Imogene's rebuff with a stiff whiskey, he sought the companionship of his brother and his cousin. They played billiards, discussed the current military campaigns abroad, and of course politics. Graham also shared a troubling concern with them that had recently come to light.

He told them of his solicitor's most recent letter and what it most likely meant coupled with the disappearance of Agnes and her child. The men discussed the plans already in play and Graham accepted their offers of further support. He knew the time was coming that might force his hand to share with Imogene his responsibility for them—and his relationship.

He didn't want to even entertain the idea of telling her now. The worry about how she'd react to the news was not a pleasant notion, especially based on how she's just been with him—showing jealousy over phantom women he'd danced the waltz with years ago and soundly forgotten. How in the hell would she take to news of his connection to Agnes? Not well, he predicted, and yet, he clung to the hope that somehow he could escape the eventuality of his wife having to know about Agnes at all. Would the spectres from his past mistakes haunt him until his dying day?

Just the thought of it sent him over to the decanter of whiskey so he could top off his glass.

The drink continued to flow through the earnest chatter,

and when their party broke up much later all three were deep into their cups. Even so, they arranged to ride out together the next day to look over an estate that had come up for sale. Jules wanted their opinions as to its suitability, having put about the idea that the Hargreaves might like to relocate to Warwickshire.

Stumbling up to their room, Graham was good and drunk. The effects of the drink notwithstanding, he was leery of Imogene and still confused by her unease and rejection of him earlier. He figured she would be asleep, and not wishing to bother her further, tried to be quiet as he put himself into the bed next to her.

In her state of sleep Imogene sensed his presence and rolled over to settle her body facing his, her head coming to rest just below his chin. Graham breathed in the intoxicating scent of her hair and knew he was helplessly and undoubtedly lost. His resolution to leave her alone evaporated the moment she nestled her body into his. *You should not...* was the last rational thought to register in his muddled brain before he reached for her.

IMOGENE was roused from her sleep by caressing hands and roaming lips making free with her curves. "Graham?" she mumbled.

Her voice only seemed to inflame him more. "*Chérie*, you smell soooo good. You're soooo soft and beautiful," he muttered, kissing down her throat and opening the neck of her gown in an attempt to take it off her.

"What? Graham?" She smelled the whiskey on his breath and could hear his garbled words. "Are you foxed?"

she demanded.

"Yes, *chérie,* but I love you…soooo much," he purred, pushing her gown down to her waist. "I know you are vexed with me, *chérie.* I don't know why you are." He kissed her mouth, demanding a response, his tongue preventing her from speaking. "What did I do? Please, *chérie*?" His hands began to claim her. "Let me…please, Imogene, I *need* you." Caresses growing more urgent, his mouth devoured the flesh of her breasts. "Tell me you want me too. Please tell me." The words tumbled out of him, the desperation in them clearly audible.

"I do," she assured, moving against him, "I do want you, Graham."

Even in his inebriated state, Graham comprehended her willingness and forcibly tugged her gown off, before ditching his own garments. Once he pressed into her and felt the full contact of their skin coming together, he sighed a great relieved breath. "You feel so heavenly and soft, and I love you so much. You are my everything—I need to be inside you," he rambled, the words coming out breathy and disjointed.

Imogene felt his hands move over her, touching and penetrating with determined purpose. She wanted him, no question, completely aroused and yearning, her full attention awaiting on him. He had her splayed out underneath him, hands entwined. She relished the whole exquisite length of him covering her. "Ah…oh…Graham…" she moaned as he slid his cock into her hard and deep, and began to move.

He thrust into her with delectable intensity. *Just a little more. Almost…there…almost.* Imogene pushed herself toward that desired, glorious end of pleasure. But it was not to be, because he climaxed right then. Looming over her, she felt him stiffen. *No…not yet!* He groaned and spilled into her, shuddering out his release. *No…no…NO!*

Graham felt like a log on top of her, not moving. *You have got to be joking!*

"Graham?" She nudged him. *He cannot be asleep…leaving me unfinished like this.* "Graham!" she barked in frustration. Nothing from him. No response except the heavy breathing telling her he was indeed alive. Realizing the futility of her situation, she pushed hard at his shoulders and shouted, "Get off, Graham." Still nothing. She struggled and wriggled, eventually extricating herself out from underneath his limp, comatose form.

Her husband was out cold, sprawled on his stomach, looking quite peaceful and content.

She studied him ruefully for a moment before leaving the bed to clean the effects of him from her.

Imogene had much to ponder when she returned seeing Graham still snoring softly, unaware in his slumbering unconsciousness. She sighed heavily, feeling guilty for how she'd treated him downstairs.

He was hurt. I hurt him and I must make amends when he wakes. I don't know why I was so unkind and horrid to him.

But if she was honest she did know why.

Imogene was jealous and there was no getting around the idea. She was jealous of the women he had known in his past, the artist's models he had seen…and been intimate with. She was jealous of the life he had lived in Europe before her and she wanted to punish him for it, even as irrational as she knew that to be. Last night she'd been feeling emotional and a little heartless, she knew she'd been cruel but in the moment hadn't been willing to try to come to terms.

You cannot be angry with him. You caused the whole thing. Wounding with your words and turning away from his kiss until he was so anxious with worry he drank too much. When have you ever seen him drunk? Never! He came to you tonight begging for reassurance. Let go of your angst. He is nothing but honorable and good at every turn. You know he is the best of men. Whatever happened before cannot be undone and forcing guilt for his past is cruel and unfair. It has been very painful—his past—and he was entitled and likely to seek out comfort somewhere. You were wrong to treat him as you did. You know how much he loves you…and how much you love him.

Imogene's conscience told her what she needed to hear and she vowed to make amends to her beloved on the morrow.

The next morning when she woke before him it was no surprise. The spirits he had over-imbibed the evening before were still holding sway over his body. For now.

Imogene quietly removed herself to the adjoining dressing room, rang for Hester, and prepared for her day. It was early but she wished to get outside and take advantage of yet another blessing of pleasant weather. She met Mina at the stairs on her way down to breakfast. "You have arisen early, Imogene. Are you well?"

"Very well this morning, thank you, Mina."

"The men were deep into their cups last night I believe. Is Graham still feeling the effects of it?" Mina asked with a grin.

"I fear so," she remarked, shaking her head. "I have left him undisturbed. I wish to be outside on this fine morning. What are your plans, Mina?"

"I was just going in to have a quick bite and some tea. Then I thought to be off for a walk. You are most welcome to join me if you are inclined to it. I often walk early in the morning, although Julian does not thrill to my going off all on my own."

Imogene nodded her acceptance. "I would be delighted to join you. A good long walk would heartily do me good I think."

"I have just the place to take you—I think you might find it enchanting," Mina told her.

GRAHAM woke slowly. The cheerfulness of the morning sun belying the havoc being wreaked inside his head that all was well. He suffered through the pounding pain and began to sift over the events that had led him to this point: the rift with Imogene in the evening; the over-indulgence of drink with Jules and Colin; his agreement to ride with them today to view that estate as a possibility for Hargreave; staggering up to bed; Imogene in the bed…

It was here in the sequence of events that his memory betrayed him. He could not recall anything beyond that point, and felt the flicker of unease wrap itself around the cotton that seemed to be stuffed inside his brain.

It is late. I've overslept.

Realizing he had agreed to ride today, he moved to get up from the bed. Groaning at the pain that gave the impression of having merrily taken up residence inside his skull, he flipped the covers off.

He was nude.

The flicker of unease from before had now developed into a hammering panic. *Damn! What did I do? Did I force myself on her? I could not have…could I? Dear God. No…not that! She'll never forgive me.*

Graham willed himself to think and concentrate. He closed his eyes and tried to calm his escalating anxiety. He remembered a single thought from last night. He remembered thinking he should not do something, but wanting to do it anyway. The words *'You should not.'* rang true in his memory. There was also a vague but beautiful image of her splayed out on the bed. *Damn it all to hell! What does that mean…that I wanted to make love and I did, or that I wanted to, but I did not? Hell, I always want to. Did she resist? What did I do to her? Blessed Christ, please tell me I did not take her against her will.* He made an audible cry of anguish, "Imogene, I cannot remember!" He hit his palms repeatedly upon his forehead.

Graham prepared himself for castigation, accepting that it would surely be his fate. There was nothing for it but to face his wife and ask for the truth. He called for Phelps and made haste to dress so he could get downstairs and find her, and see about repairing the disaster in his marriage that had erupted overnight. Headache and malaise dissipated quickly in the rush of panic-laced fear that gripped him in totality.

MINA and Imogene had been walking for a good hour when their destination was finally revealed. She had led them to a hilltop glade covered in light forest. In the middle of the glade was a small circle of nine stones. The location was dreamlike and unusual in that the stone circle was surrounded by woods. The setting and the ancient stones presented an atmosphere of quiet and sheltered peace.

"Oh, Mina," she breathed. "It is simply magical, a fairy land. What is this place?"

"I thought you might like it. I know you favoured the ruins high above Kenilbrooke estate. Julian tells me the local people call it, 'The Nine Ladies.' They are ancient standing stones. Not very large as some are, but ancient indeed. They were set here before the Romans came even into Britain. It is said that Druids turned up to standing stones such as these and used them for their magical arts."

Imogene absorbed Mina's every word. "I don't care who set them here or why, I love this place. It is so captivating…pure magic, Mina. Do you not think so?"

"Oh, I think so. I am just glad you are so delighted with it and that you have an appreciation. I have not long discovered it myself as the weather was not fit for great walks such as this until recently. Shall we sit and take a rest? I do get more fatigued than usual, now."

"Yes of course, Mina. I am so sorry to have forgotten. You must rest and regain your strength. My sister Philippa told me your body gets tired from growing the baby and you need to take your rest often."

They both settled their backs against stones. Mina took out a flask of water and sipped. She offered it to Imogene who gratefully took a drink.

"I was thinking that *you* might be feeling some tiredness, maybe? You have needed to take your own rests, Imogene, I have noted," Mina said with a gentle smile.

Imogene blushed but could not suppress the excitement she was beginning to feel in greater measure as each day passed. "I admit I do have some suspicions, but I think it is still early to know for certain. I have said nothing to Graham or anyone. My last courses were the third week of February. It is now the third week of April and they are not come. Do you think I have the start of a child?"

Mina took her hand and patted it. "Honestly? Yes, you probably do have the start of a child. You have missed two courses and you are more tired than is normal for you. Other than that, do you feel well?"

Imogene nodded. "Very well, except…I have felt irked and provoked by things that should not be a bother to me. When we return I must beg pardon to Graham, in fact. I was discourteous to him last night, for no reason really. Is peevishness a symptom?"

Mina laughed lightly. "According to my dear father, it is. And he would know, having lived through three such events." At seeing Imogene's remorseful expression she reassured her quickly. "Do not fret, Imogene. Graham loves you so he would forgive you anything, especially at your joyful prospect. Do you not believe that he will be in high spirits at the thought of his child?"

"Oh, I believe he will be very happy. I am just not ready to tell him yet, thinking I could wait until his birthday. By then I could be more definite."

"That sounds very reasonable and sensible, Imogene. I am so glad you are here with us. I hope we have many, many visits such as this over the years. I can see how happy Julian is to have his dear family all together at Everfell."

"I know. I can see the same happiness in Graham and it is good for him to let go of some of his painful burdens." She had a pleasant thought and smiled at Mina. "And soon after this visit you will join us at Gavandon, and we will all be together again."

GRAHAM could not find Imogene anywhere. He inquired to Hester who could only tell him that Lady Rothvale had risen earlier than usual and had gone down prepared for the day. When he asked Hester as to her disposition she said, "My lady was as she always is—proper and elegant, my lord." *Thank you, Hester, for that thorough and insightful description as to Lady Rothvale's spirits this morning. I am so relieved!* He barely managed to hold back the sarcastic thoughts before dismissing the maid with a curt nod. *Where are you, Imogene? How are you?*

He encountered Jules and Colin in the breakfast room. Both of them nursing strong cups of coffee and possessing the blood-shot eyes fruitful of their particular indulgence of last eve.

"There you are," Jules croaked, looking him over. "God, Graham, you look quite stalwart, like a man single-minded in his purpose. Are you not feeling ill effects of our indulgence last night? I sure as hell feel it and Colin here could barely make it safely down the stairs."

"Appearances can be deceiving, Jules. I feel it all right, I can assure you. Say, I am looking for Imogene. Did she leave word with anybody?"

"Yes. Mrs. Lake tells me that she went on a ramble with Mina. Both of them up early this morning, awaking to a quiet house I assume. To be honest, I am grateful she went along. I do not like for Mina to walk so far all on her own. She loves it though," he said wistfully.

Graham relaxed a little, sitting down to the table with his own portion of strong coffee. He tried to push his anxiety down and away, but it was mostly futile. The gnawing pit of fear inside his heart gripped him fiercely. He nodded his head and grunted monosyllabic answers to the questions and comments directed at him but couldn't have recalled one word of what was discussed at breakfast.

Mina and Imogene had not returned from their walk when it was time to leave for the ride over to the estate. With a heavy heart weighing him down, Graham accompanied Jules and Colin on their scheduled trip, knowing it would be hours until they returned, until he could make right with Imogene.

MINA and Imogene made their way back to the house at a slower pace than they had left it. Both feeling a little worn but thought the walk to the Nine Ladies had been worth the effort. Mrs. Lake, who was charged with the essential duty to know where her mistress was at all times, greeted them upon their return. "Mrs. Everley, Lady Rothvale, I hope you enjoyed your walk this morning. I informed Mr. Everley you had gone together. I must say he expressed his happiness that you were in company," she said knowingly, to Mina. "Luncheon is set to be ready in an hour. Miss Vickering and Miss Wilton are in the music room, I believe."

Imogene wanted to speak to Graham. Her conversation with Mina had cleared away any doubts that lingered about what she needed to do, and she did not want to wait a moment longer. She turned to the housekeeper, asking, "Do you happen to know where my husband might be keeping himself, Mrs. Lake?"

"Oh, Lady Rothvale, they are not here. Lord Rothvale, Mr. Everley and Mr. Colin have all ridden out together late this morning. I am not certain of when to expect their return."

"Yes, that's right, Imogene. Julian wished them to view a neighbouring estate that has come up for sale. He seeks their opinion on the suitability, and to evaluate its possibilities for the Hargreaves. I cannot deny I am thrilled at the prospect of them coming to live in Warwickshire. But please say nothing for now, in case you should write to your family as no final decisions have been made."

Imogene smiled kindly and offered her hopes for a happy result for the Hargreaves. *I'll have to wait after all. Graham, my darling, can you hear me? I am very sorry.* Accepting that it would be some time before she could right her wrong, Imogene settled in to quiet indoor pursuits with her cousins and thought of all the things she had to be thankful for, and vowed she would not forget it again.

The hours passed slowly.

Imogene grew more anxious at being separated from Graham.

She hated having this friction between them without possibility of immediate repair. *It is all your fault. You caused every bit of it. Think of how he must be feeling. It will serve you right if he rebuffs your apology when he gets it. He would not do that…would he?*

Despite her growing despair, the exertion of the morning walk demanded restorative rest. Imogene excused herself and went up to the room intending to lie down with a book for some quiet reading, but within minutes drifted into a dreamless sleep.

THE long morning and early afternoon had stretched interminably for Graham.

The estate had been thoroughly viewed and evaluated, and the three men had lunched at a public house afterward. Now that the welcome view of Everfell was finally in his sights, Graham felt that he could not wait a moment longer to go to her. He veritably leapt from his horse and shoved the reins toward a waiting groom before dashing up the steps and into the house. He went directly to the day parlor where he knew the ladies liked to go. Entering the room with trepidation, he bowed in greeting, and was crestfallen to see that Elle, Mina and Cariss were there, but not his Imogene.

"You are back," Mina greeted him.

He tilted his head in acknowledgement, offered a weak smile and spoke, "I had thought …Imogene…might be in here with you."

"She has gone upstairs to rest. She was feeling tired," Mina told him.

Worry flooded him. "Is she ill? It is not like her to sleep in the day." He frowned.

"I do not think she is ill, just tired. Our walk this morning was quite vigorous," Mina answered.

"Ladies." Bowing first, he indicated his impending departure and quickly made his escape.

The girls shared humorous glances all around before Elle disclosed her thoughts out loud. "My cousin is the most besotted husband in all of England. At least it appears that way for others to see. He reads like an open book. I hope that when he finds her, she puts him out of his misery." They all laughed.

It would have been easier to cut off his own arm, than to keep away from her. He entered the room very quietly and found that she was indeed asleep. He stood and studied her for a moment: so beautiful resting on her side, her hands tucked under the pillow edge. The book she had been reading was next to her on the bed. Tilting to get a glance at it, he smiled, recognizing the volume of Robert Herrick's poems he had given her at Christmas. *That is a good sign.* Very quietly he stepped back and seated himself on the settee. He made himself comfortable and focused his eyes onto the form of his sleeping wife, content to stay there watching over her until she was ready to awaken.

He did not have a long time to wait. Observing her

involuntary movements, he saw the change in her breathing, the slight twitch of her eyes underneath her lids, indicating that she was waking. He tensed, unable to stop the fear from rising. *Please let her be willing to hear me out.* Lifting his head, he closed his eyes in silent, fervent prayer. When he lowered his head and opened his eyes he was rewarded with the very open and awake eyes of his beloved. She smiled. *She's smiling at me.* Imogene pulled her hands out from under the pillow and lifted her arms to him, calling him to her.

Not waiting for a second invitation, he lurched forward into her arms, settling himself on the bed facing her. He said nothing for a moment, just held on to her, absorbing her, savouring the moment. Graham could not have been more shocked than he was then, to hear the following words come from her lips, "My darling, I must beg your pardon for my abominable behaviour toward you last night. Can you possibly forgive me?"

She is apologizing?

"Wait, you are not angry and disgusted with me for last night?"

A look of confusion crossed over her features. She frowned slightly. "No, darling, why would I be? You are the one who should be angry. I was well out of sorts last night, nonsensical and ill-mannered, abandoning you during the dancing and turning from you. I am so dreadfully sorry for all of it. I do not know what came over me, but I do know you did not deserve such treatment. I have been waiting all day to ask for your forgiveness."

"You have?"

"I have." She cupped his cheek and rubbed with her thumb. "It has been torture waiting for your return."

He just continued gaping at her incredulously, saying

nothing.

"Please tell me that you can forgive me," she implored in a whisper.

You are begging my forgiveness? This is the last thing I would have expected to end this hideous forenoon. Thank the glorious heavens!

He pulled her close in a fevered kiss and began to laugh in silent shudders, nearly giddy with relief. "I forgive you, *chérie*...I love you...I adore you," he chanted between kisses.

"Graham? Are you laughing at me?"

"God, no. I am laughing at the irony of the situation, *chérie*. You see, I was very drunk last night and know not what happened or what I might have done when I came up to bed. I woke late this morning and you were gone on your walk so I could not judge your countenance. I found myself unable to remember anything at all and I was...nude in the bed. I had terrible fear that I had pressed you, forced myself on you, and that you would despise me."

A slow grin appeared on Imogene's face at his words. She arched her brows at him. "So you remember *nothing* of us last night?" Her words gave him the sure impression of details yet undisclosed.

"What? What are you not telling me, Imogene?" he asked in a low voice. "Did something happen between us? Did I...?" When Imogene continued to smile slyly at him without further explanation he felt the unease begin to creep in once again. "Imogene, please! Please tell me what I did," he begged.

"I am sorry, darling, but I must say it feels wonderfully satisfying to actually be aware of something you know nothing about." She brushed his lips with her fingers, smiling coquettishly.

He rolled his eyes. "Not that tired subject again. Please

tell me before I have an apoplexy! I cannot bear this uncertainty for another minute, Imogene." He grew cold. "I did impose myself on you, didn't I?" When she didn't deny it he realized the truth. "I knew it. In my heart I knew I must have."

"Stop!" she ordered, gripping his face with both hands. "Stop this worry you have. You are nearly hysterical. I'll tell you everything, I promise, but you must relax and take your ease. Do I look like I am angry, or frightened, or offended by you? No, I do not because I am none of those things, Graham."

Her words helped him to relax a little.

"You came to bed and did awaken me with your loving attentions. When I asked you if you were foxed you answered honestly that you were and told me you loved me very much. You also said you knew I was vexed with you but that you didn't know why, and wanted to know what *you* had done to upset *me*." She reached to stroke his hair. "You were amorous, it's true, but you asked for my willingness in it, and it was only when I assured you that I was indeed willing that you…proceeded. You would never force me, Graham. It's not in your nature to even be capable of it. Do you not know yourself better than that?"

He just stared at her unbelievingly. "This is bizarre. Having you telling me all of this and remembering none of it is the most disturbing feeling. So, now that we have established I made love to you in my oblivious state of drunkenness, how was I?" He threw the question out recklessly, knowing he was completely at her mercy by this point.

She appeared to hold back a chuckle, rolling her lips closed. "Let's just say you were more *self-serving* than I have ever known you to be, my darling." The laugh she had held back before now escaping in good measure.

"Ugh!" He actually felt himself flush. "It cannot possibly get any worse. So I did nothing for you?" he asked mortified.

Imogene laughed. "Darling you tried, most valiantly and I was very appreciative until—" Continued laughing stopped her words.

"I misspoke before, it is worse still! Please continue. You might as well tell me all of it and take it to the bitter end," he groused.

"You finished quite suddenly and…collapsed out cold. My greatest concern by that point was to get out from underneath you, for you had quite trapped me in your unconscious state and you were utterly unresponsive to my prodding and entreaties that you should move off."

"Sweet heavenly Christ! I am, I—I am without words—" He looked up to the ceiling and raised his hands. "Am I in hell?"

Imogene laughed and laughed and could not stop. The clear, happy sound of it assuring him that she forgave his drunken, tactless lovemaking of the night before and that she did, for some reason, find it *very* amusing.

It took a significant amount of soothing to convince him to let it go. Even so, he hoped she was left with the understanding that he would have gone to the ends of the earth to make it up to her. She told him she was just happy to be back in harmony with only love and caring between them.

"My walk with Mina this morning was remarkable. She took me to the most magical place. I am still entranced by it utterly. It is a fairy ring of set stones in the most lovely secluded glade."

"You went to The Nine Ladies. It *is* lovely there. I have not gone up to see it in years."

"Oh, Graham, it is the most enchanting place. My first and only thought was to bring you there. I want to go there with you and lie down in the grass inside that circle of stones and seek out shapes in the clouds."

"You love the rocks and ruins, don't you?"

"I suppose I do. There is something so peaceful and soothing about them. What I wouldn't give to have such a place at Gavandon for solitude and quiet reflection as The Nine Ladies. Is there such a thing at Gavandon?"

"No, I am afraid there is not. But there are similar stones at Donadea and other ancient edifices on that estate. Such stones are scattered far and wide in Ireland. It makes one wonder as to the people who envisioned such constructions in the first place."

"Graham, will you go with me tomorrow to The Nine Ladies?"

"Yes of course, *chérie*." An idea of inspiration hit him. "Wait, do you want to go now? Right now on horseback? We could take horses and it would be no time at all before we could be there."

"But you have just returned from riding all day. Surely you wish to relax at home now that it is afternoon."

He shook his head. "It is barely just two o'clock now and by taking horses we can be there before you know it. And I am not tired. Seeing you has restored me, especially now that I know you still love me," he reminded with a brush of his lips to her forehead. "And what can I care of being tired anyway? For in a short while I shall be lying in the grass inside that ring of stones next to you and searching out shapes in the clouds. What could be better than that?" He kissed her again slowly, taking his time with his tongue. "Come with me to The Nine Ladies, please, *chérie*?" he whispered into her ear.

In truth he had sensed her excitement and once she had revealed it, nothing could have kept him from giving that one thing to her which he knew would please her. It would not have mattered if he were exhausted, he would still go with her, simply because it was what she wanted. His happiness was inextricably linked with hers—despite him feeling a little overwhelmed with desire to please and appease her, Imogene's love also made him stronger. More the man he wished to be. It was contentment he felt with her. Not the concern of being crushed. And after the day he had endured, going to the ring of stones with her would be a blessed reward indeed. His mind was already working as to how he could make it a special outing for them.

"It sounds lovely. Very well, let us go then. I must first dress in my riding clothes."

"Call for Hester to help you, *chérie*. I'll just go down and see to our horses and will await you in the courtyard. You can meet me as soon as you are ready to go." He bussed her cheek with a soft kiss before dashing out of the room, leaving straightaway for the kitchens to procure the necessary accoutrements for their excursion, in short order.

WHEN Imogene stepped out into the courtyard, Graham was waiting for her as promised, looking quite smug standing by their ready horses. "What are you up to, darling? I see that look on your face. You've been plotting," she teased gently.

"Your horse awaits, my lady wife." He bowed gallantly, indicating with his arm.

She regarded him for a moment before shaking her head slowly back and forth. "You're up to something—I can smell it."

He raised an eyebrow. "And does your keen sense of smell indicate to you whether or not you will enjoy whatever it is that I am 'up to'?"

She didn't answer his question directly. "You must have been a very clever child, cunning and scheming secret surprises upon your playmates. You do have a mischievous bent, and I see now that the solemn exterior is merely a mask."

"My lady, I believe it is my duty to remind you that this excessive philosophizing into my childhood is doing nothing to assist you in reaching your goal for this afternoon."

She laughed at him but conceded that he was probably right as she approached the horse meant for her, unable to resist one last ribbing. "I reckon you used that charm and those gorgeous green eyes of yours to wheedle your way in and out of situations as you desired. Am I right, my sweetheart?"

"Yes." He tilted his head and widened his eyes. "And I intend to use them now to ensure that you cease and desist this blither-blathering of no account and—" he put his hands on her waist, gripping firmly, "—mount…your…horse." Easily lifting her, he dropped her atop the waiting steed.

She flashed him a wicked grin, leaned down so only he could hear her and whispered, "I love it when you take charge of me like that." She spurred her horse then, and bolted off at a gallop, leaving him gawping after her in utter surprise. The sound of her laughter must have jogged him out of his shock because he recovered quickly, mounted up, and followed after her.

When they approached the glade Graham turned to her, asking, "I have a humble request, *chérie*. When we dismount, I'll need for you to turn away for a moment until I have made ready. Do you think you can do that, my darling?"

"Of course I can do that for you," she agreed. He dismounted first and waited with hands ready to help her down. She reached for his shoulders as he took hold of her waist and lowered her. When she was down she raised her eyes and stayed in her position, her hands remaining on his shoulders…remembering.

"What are you thinking about, *chérie*?"

"When we rode out together in those first days, I would anticipate this. The moment you would put your hands on me to assist in mounting and dismounting. The feel of your hands on me was so wonderful. I craved it. It still is…and I still do."

He rewarded her little speech with a long, slow kiss, before gently turning her away from the stone circle. "Give me two minutes—and no peeking." She could hear him rustling around in the travelling pack she had seen on his horse. After a time she was aware of him standing at her back. "It is ready, my *chérie*."

She turned to see that a beautiful picnic tea had been set out upon a blanket spread in the middle of the stone circle. "It's lovely," she said.

"I believe your fantasy required 'lying down' as a critical element. It simply would not do for the elegant Lady Rothvale to return to the stately halls of Everfell with bits of grass in her hair. What would people say?"

"And the tea? So thoughtful of you."

"Well we would have missed tea-time being out riding so I thought we could have our tea here. I used my charisma and hypnotic eyes, as you've said, to beguile the cook into setting me up with jam tarts and flasks of tea. It turned out quite well, I think, considering I had no time at all." He offered his arm. "Shall we?"

They lay on their sides propped up on their elbows and

faced each other, feeding bites of tart and sips of warm tea to the other between caresses and giggling laced with liberal amounts of silliness.

"My fingers are very sticky."

"I have just the thing for it." He grabbed her hand and proceeded to lick each of her fingers clean, one by one. She watched him, her eyes growing dark from the sensual picture of her fingers in his mouth. "Delectable, and *very* sweet," he murmured, leaning in closer, "I see a spot of jam here at your mouth that must be seen to as well."

Graham proceeded to lick around the corner of her mouth with passionate attention until the welcome response from her demanded more loving treatment from him, which he was more than happy to bestow.

Chapter 21

O! beware, my lord, of jealousy;
It is the green-eyed monster which doth mock
The meat it feeds on.

William Shakespeare ~ Othello, 1602

Inside the stone circle, Graham and Imogene relished the magic of the afternoon.

"Well, that is now two remarkable teas I have enjoyed since coming to Everfell. The first, being at a gamekeeper's cottage, and this one inside a fairy ring. Tea in the parlor will be utterly uninspiring from now on I am afraid," Imogene joked.

"I see your point, *chérie,* but we have yet to complete your vision of searching out shapes in the clouds, though."

"For it to happen, dear husband, there must be clouds in the sky, and as you can see the sky is quite clear this afternoon so I imagine we'll have to save that part for another time. Perhaps we do have other unconventional teatimes yet to come." She was quiet for some moments. "I think this is the best gift you have ever given to me."

"It was such a simple thing to do this."

"Sometimes simple is best."

"I am glad you are happy. It is all that I wish for, *chérie*. I hope you know that." Lying together on the blanket, they played with their hands, twining and untwining their fingers, steepling them and rolling knuckles together, tracing lightly over the other's palm, quiet and reflective for a long time. "*Chérie*, can you tell me what it was that upset you? What caused your vexation? As much as I am relieved to know we are recovered from last night's disaster, I find myself unable to let it go."

"Nothing. It was nothing you did, Graham. It was only my emotional sensibilities getting the better of me."

"You are not telling me the whole truth, Imogene. I can tell. I would have the truth from you, please. I know you love me, but I also know there is something that bothered you and *nothing* should come between us, no matter how small you might deem it."

Shaking her head, she answered, "You cannot be hurt again. Don't force me to tell you," she begged, looking like she might cry.

"Now I am really concerned. Tell me, Imogene. You can tell me anything, *chérie*, even if it hurts. So be it. I trust you."

She was quiet for a long time before she answered him. "Last night when you, Jules, and Colin were teaching us the waltz it occurred to me, again, how you all have had past lives. You travelled, attended university, lived in Europe, and must have known many women, artist's models and others. You may have had attachments to other women with whom you have shared intimacies." She closed her eyes. "Though I am ashamed to say it, all in a moment I just felt so jealous of them—those other women before me—and wanted to punish you for having a past. I know that's a ridiculous notion. I'm over my jealous fit. Truly, I am. I know how much you love me." She regarded him solemnly. "There you have it. That is the truth, Graham."

He felt the stabbing pain of guilt but kept his eyes on her throughout the entirety of his response. He'd said for her to tell him even if it hurt. So it seemed he would be given that which he'd asked for. "There is one word you've said which is critical to this discourse. That word is 'before.' If I live to be a very old man, and look back upon my life, there will be one point at which to make a division…the time before you…and the time after you. The only part which will matter is the time that came after you, Imogene."

Graham watched her beautiful brown eyes turn glassy with tears.

He attempted to steady his racing heart. "Before you, I had been with others, it is true. But now that you are my wife there will never be anyone after you. This I *know* for absolute truth. I have never had an attachment, nor been in love with a woman before you. Innocent I am not, in the ways of physical love, but that first time with you, on our wedding night, it felt like I was…innocent. It was a new experience, the first time with *love* in my heart. You are the first to receive my love, and the only. I am not proud of everything in my past, but regardless it cannot be undone. You'd be hard pressed to find a man of my age who has not had such experiences. But understand that I believe myself a different man after you came into my life, Imogene, and I knew it with utmost certainty as soon as I met you. I knew nothing would ever be the same for me again. Because you saved me. Your love rescued me from that other very lonely and very empty life. Remember 'The Princess and the Toad' story, *chérie*. You are the only woman I can ever love like that, all I can ever want, and all I can ever need. There is no other for me. Only you. I hope you'll believe every word I've said is true because it is coming from deep inside my soul."

With tears falling she nodded. "I do believe you. Thank you for your honesty, my darling. We never have need to speak of this again." She drew close to him, nestling her head under his chin, simply holding on as he drew his arms around her. "But true love is a durable fire…In the mind ever burning…Never sick, never old, never dead…From itself never turning." She quoted Raleigh's ballad again. "My heart is full," she whispered.

"As is mine, *chérie.*" He held her against him and stroked over her hair for a long time after that.

Graham's decision had been made for him. Fate had come for him and he could not stop the forces at work. He had to find a way to tell her about Agnes or the torment of guilt was going to eat him alive.

Later that night, with tranquility and peacefulness between them, Imogene felt the pull of slumber when she heard Graham's words and was immediately roused.

"I have a trouble, *chérie.* I am loathe to tell you, but knowing how you dislike me not sharing all with you, I know I must. In truth I have never considered this *affair* to be of my concern and it is certainly not of my doing, but now it seems it is part of my inheritance. The ugly past is rearing its head, demanding its due and I fear there is nothing to impede it. I dread your exposure to it, and hate to have it touch you, fearing that you will regret marrying into my wretched family with all of its damn skeletons and suggestions of depravity—"

His voice came to her low and anguished.

"Graham, you must know I will be in support of you no matter what comes. I can never regret our marriage. And your family is not wretched; it is a lovely family. For better or for worse, remember?"

He squeezed her hand, exhaling deeply. "My brother Jasper was not content with destroying merely his own life—he dragged others down with him as well. He ruined a young girl, seduced her, and cared not a whit about what he had done. She bore a child. Her name was Agnes and she claimed Jasper was the father of her babe, and even worse, that he had forced her. My mother appealed to my father and all hell broke loose. Jasper was away on a flit somewhere, when Father attempted to locate him, to no avail. I have never seen my father so angry. The shame and disgrace completely overwhelmed him, contributing to his failing health. My parents agreed to support the girl and arrangements were made for her to have her child in a safe and decent environment. They must have believed her claim for they did not contest it. In truth I think they were surprised to have not faced the prospect of other by-blows from Jasper arriving at their doorstep before that."

"Oh, Graham, how dreadful. What happened to Agnes, to her baby?"

"The baby was born winter of aught eight, a girl she named Clarabelle. My brother died that summer and never acknowledged or saw his child." Graham paused for a time and Imogene did not press. She imagined he was trying to gather the right words to continue. Holding on to his hand, she stroked softly with her other hand, waiting for him until he was ready.

"After Jasper's death my parents grieved of course. For all his faults, he was still their son and heir. My mother wished to know her grandchild, little Clara being her only remaining link to Jasper. Father would not allow it. He forbade her to see the child and this caused a terrible breach between my parents that lasted right up until his apoplexy about a year later. He lingered on for a few months, having nearly daily audiences with me. My father was weak and it was difficult for him to speak. He was determined to counsel me and share his wishes and experience in handing over the barony to me. It was a difficult time—" Graham stopped abruptly, the painful memories too poignant to describe. He scrubbed his face with his hands, working to regain composure. "This is very hard to speak of."

"I know, my darling, it must be very hard. If you tell me everything you might feel better being unburdened. Carrying this weight upon your shoulders exclusively is wrong. Whatever we must face, we will do it together and it will be resolved somehow."

He closed his eyes and kissed her forehead. "Thank you, Imogene. Thank you for being as you are, so loving and sympathetic." He took a deep breath and resumed the history. "My father may not have wished for my mother to acknowledge Jasper's child, but he did make sure that Agnes and Clara would be supported for their lifetimes, securing my promise to see that it was carried out. After Father died, my mother was further broken down in grief, but still determined to know about her granddaughter. You see, my mother lost a baby girl, my sister, Vivienne, born between Colin and me. She died of a fever before her first birthday. Whether as a replacement for Vivienne or to connect with Jasper, my mother ached to know Clara. She was obsessed with her, sending messengers to spy on Agnes and her baby who later reported back with information. I couldn't stop my mother and didn't even try to. Apparently, little Clara has the green eyes that further confirmed her to be Jasper's child. Interesting, since they must have skipped a generation because Jasper did not have our green eyes—his eyes were brown."

Graham seemed very wistful as he brought up all that deep history to the surface. "I know my mother visited Clara and saw her at least twice. That's all I know. Learning my duties as master of the estate consumed every waking moment then, and that time is exceptionally foggy for me. I had to immerse myself in order to be competent. Mr. Duncan has been a rock of support. I don't know how I could have done it without him there. He saw to the regular payments of support for Agnes over the years and things continued as usual during my absence to Ireland. Agnes was set up in her own cottage in Gladfield where she went by the name of Mrs. Schellman, posing as a war widow. She takes in sewing as a seamstress; being a tailor's daughter she is good with a needle. Or at least she did, for we have lost contact and know not where Agnes and Clara are."

"Recently, Duncan informed me of an irregularity with Agnes's stipend. There were some suspicious withdrawals from her money. It seems she sent a letter requesting a change of address, for her stipend to be routed to Yorkshire. This raised further suspicions, and I sent Duncan to investigate. I got word from him the day before we left for Everfell and the information he passed along is not good." Graham wearily rested his forehead in his hand. "Duncan was able to discover that Agnes's cottage in Gladfield was visited by a man who it appears, was dallying with her maid. Within a week, the cottage was vacated and they were gone with no word to anybody. Upon inquiring as to the man's description, Duncan was told he wore regimentals. That fact, combined with the

Yorkshire address is now leading me to believe in the involvement of one nefarious, Ralph Odeman." Graham's lips curled in distaste when he spoke the name.

Imogene gasped the moment he spoke the name, feeling a shiver of dread overtake her whole body.

"What is it? Have you heard of him?" Graham gripped her by the shoulders and stared. "Imogene?"

"Oh, my God, Graham, do not be angry with me," she begged in fear. The look on her husband's face terrified her even more. "I met him in London at a modiste's shop a few weeks before our wedding."

"What did he do?" he shouted. "That lump of horseshit approached you, Imogene?"

She cringed at his tone and harsh language. "Yeees…he asked me my opinion on some gloves, and introduced himself as Ralph Odeman. He told me he was buying a gift for his sister," she answered in a timid voice.

"Why didn't you tell me?" he barked. The anger in his words and the expression on his face made him appear dreadful.

"I don't know," she replied. "He was just a man asking about gloves."

Graham loosened his grip and kissed her on the forehead. "I am sorry for shouting and scaring you, *chérie*, I am in shock at his boldness in approaching you."

"Graham, there is more," she said meekly.

"There is?" he asked dumbfounded, his jaw hardening again.

"I forgot about him completely, but then, right before we came to Everfell he sent to me a package—a pair of buff leather gloves exactly like the ones in the shop. There was a note inside one of the gloves. It said something like, "accept this wedding present from a grateful friend who you may call upon if you're ever in need. I can provide you with answers to some questions you will have cause to ponder in the near future. Your servant, Ralph Odeman."

Graham stilled, frozen in complete horror at what she'd just told him. She knew what his next question would be, too.

"I didn't tell you because it unnerved me. I didn't understand why he would send me a gift. I knew you wouldn't like it and I could tell you were burdened by other things. I didn't want to cause you any more worry." She lost the battle with her tears then and let them fall freely. "I am sorry, Graham. I should have told you."

"Yes, you should have, Imogene. He is dangerous and the thought that he was close enough to you to even dare to engage you in a conversation has me tied up in knots. I will see him hang for what he has done. First my cousin Elle, then Agnes, and now he dares to ensnare you, my wife, in his poisonous net of evil? He is a marked man."

"Graham, you are frightening me." Imogene felt herself begin to shake. The wave of dread she'd felt when she'd seen Ralph Odeman on the street staring at her in her carriage returned all in an instant, a hundred times more fierce than it had felt to her then. *What did Elle have to do with Ralph Odeman?*

He immediately softened and held her close, kissing over her face and hair. "I am sorry for scaring you, Imogene. The history with him is terrible and dreadful. I cannot bear that he has tried to contact you, that he has even looked at you and told you his name."

"He has done evil things? And to Elle?" She was almost scared to know.

"Yes. Ralph Odeman is the worst sort of man. Recently he came to Kent and seduced a girl—Emily was her name.

She died in birthing his child. Hargreave told me of how dreadful it was for her parents. They departed in disgrace. Emily was their only child and they are raising her baby, a son." Graham sighed heavily. "That is bad enough, but Odeman tried to do such before. He preyed on another young girl two years ago…my cousin Elle."

"No!"

"He did." Graham nodded sorrowfully. "Trying to elope with her to gain her marriage settlement. Gratefully Jules was able to stop him in time and retrieved her. Elle was completely terrorized at only sixteen years of age. Odeman threatened exposure and to ruin her reputation, making her unmarriageable. Jules paid off Odeman's debts, bought him a commission in the British Army, set him up in Yorkshire, everything. Jules was bled very deeply—thousands of pounds. Odeman is lower than a rabid dog. He needs to be put down. Any advantage he could gain, hurting anyone in the process, would matter naught to him. Nothing is beneath his daring."

"I cannot believe it. How horrible for Elle."

"She was hurt by him, an innocent child devastated by his treatment of her. Ralph Odeman is a poor relation of the Julian family, taken on in charity by my aunt and uncle as a youth. He grew up at Everfell and I have known him all my life. Jules and I had little toleration for him as children as he was always scheming some evil mischief in an annoying or cruel way, growing worse with age. For all that Jules and I could do without him, my brother Jasper could not. Jasper and Ralph Odeman got on *very* well, enjoying the same dissipations and carousing tastes. Being of the same age and attitude, they went off together at school and remained devoted through each step of Jasper's descent into his eventual demise. I know Odeman was aware of Agnes and Clara and I now suspect he might attempt blackmail on me. He has always been jealous of our wealth and his lack of it, although he has squandered every advantage he was ever given. Maybe expecting to be paid for his silence about Clara being Jasper's misborn is his goal. I now know he's heard of my marriage to you, a lady of rank and wealth, and determines he can use it to his advantage—threatening to expose the secret and bring further shame and tarnish to the family. I shared everything with Jules and Colin last night and they concur with my assessment."

"What can be done now?" Once again, her fortitude astounded him. She did not slink away from this information, but rather asked how to help. *Beautiful.*

"Well, we first must locate them. I am worried that some evil has befallen Agnes and Clara. Mr. Duncan is searching with other agents for them. Until then, we wait."

"Dear Lord, are you never to have any peace? Graham, I do not want you to worry about me in this. Even if Odeman exposes the child as illegitimate, he will still need your good graces to get his money."

"I have no graces for him. Not a one! And I detest to giving him money, Imogene. I cannot bear his hold over me. It feels like Jasper has reached up from the grave contriving to wreak damage and pain, as he did in life. I would rather deal with the exposure and the scandal if it comes to that. But that is just me, and I now have you to consider. What would you have me do, *chérie*?"

"What you know is right, and to worry naught about what others might think, say, or do. Those who rely on you for their livelihood and your friends know you. Their respect for you will not alter based on the claims of a scoundrel like Ralph Odeman."

"But what of you? What if you suffer for it? It's all my

fault—" Graham stopped abruptly.

"How might I suffer, and anyway, how is any of this *your* fault?"

"Some sanctimonious ass might cut you in public, just because they can get away with it. Bringing down our family in shame could be a thrill for those who'd love to see the golden wings of the Rothvales clipped by way of a 'bastard' child. I have wrought this, Imogene. Not…seeing to my responsibilities as I should have…running away to Ireland." He lowered his head, his shame and anguish apparent.

"Let them cut me then, if they are so inclined. I am not bothered by such intolerant behaviours. And you didn't run away. You were restoring your soul. There is a difference." She squeezed his hands. "Look up at me, Graham."

He lifted heart-piercing, sad eyes to her face, his hand moving of its own will, brushing her face, tracing her lips.

She spoke gently. "No more self-deprecating. Any reasonable person would know it is not the child's fault nor is it Agnes's if what you say about her being 'forced' is true. Your mother would want you to find them, and insure their safety, and see to their care."

He nodded again. "I know. You are right, she would want that."

He held her then, simply held on, as if he was drawing her strength and her love into him, and hoping that somehow, someway, he could make everything right for those who had been wronged.

Imogene hoped and prayed for the same.

IMOGENE woke the next morning to an empty bed, Graham

having risen before her as was his usual habit. As soon as she was up and moving she felt it. The nausea. It gripped her firmly and swiftly. She was hard pressed to make it to the water closet before her stomach unleashed. *It's starting, just like Philippa said. Sick in the mornings.*

Hester heard her and rushed in. "Lady Rothvale, are you ill?"

"I've just gotten sick," she groaned. "Hester, please bring me dry toast and tea up here. I'm just going to lay back down for a bit."

"Right away, my lady." Hester nodded with a knowing look and helped her mistress back to bed.

"Please do not alert Lord Rothvale. He will worry excessively. I'll be better as soon as I can take some tea and toast." She dropped back into the pillows.

"Do not worry yourself, my lady. I'll take care of everything. Just rest now."

IMOGENE gazed adoringly at her niece Gwendolyn's sweet face as she slept peacefully in her arms. *I'm going to have a baby of my own. A baby is growing inside me right now. We've started one. I'm going to be a mother. Graham's going to be a father—*

"She is beautiful, Imogene." Colin's words broke through her reverie as he peeked down to admire the baby.

"She is, isn't she?" she agreed, smiling up at him. "Colin, are you soft on babies? I had no idea."

"I'm afraid so, babies and puppies are a definite weakness," he joked.

"Philippa! Colin is admiring your daughter and has confessed to a weakness for babies and puppies," she called to her sister, cheerfully. "Quite unusual for a man to admit to such."

"Thank you, Sister, for exposing me," he teased back, still admiring Gwendolyn. "Mrs. Brancroft, your daughter is lovely and sure to break scores of hearts one day, I predict."

"Mr. Everley, you are very kind in compliments to my daughter, but for all that I am partial to her, I daresay I might get more sleep if she were a puppy," Philippa countered.

They all laughed at her joke. It was a mild day and the house party guests were enjoying a picnic on the lawn, with some shooting at targets, some lounging. Graham and Jules were off a ways from the group, deep in conversation. Imogene assumed it was about Ralph Odeman and the troubles he had related to her last night. Philippa and John had arrived earlier in the day. Jules's cousin, Colonel Nicholas Hargreave, arrived just before luncheon. The ball was tomorrow and the house was starting to fill with guests.

Mina joined in then, "Oh, my God! I am in disbelief." The letter she had been reading fluttered to her lap. She looked up with distress showing clearly in her face. "My sister Jocelyn has accepted an offer of marriage. She is to marry at the beginning of May, to a Mr. Calvin Thornton, a widower of five and forty years. I cannot believe it. I—I am utterly dumbfounded."

"I don't remember him. Who is he, Mina?" Imogene was also astounded. "Is that a letter from Jocelyn? What does she say?" Imogene wondered if she had her own letter from Jocelyn awaiting her at Gavandon.

"This letter is from Mamma. She says Mr. Thornton is recently widowed and without an heir. He has a profitable estate and a good income. She says he is from the neighbouring parish. He has been a regular at church and offered to Papa for her hand. Jocelyn has accepted him. He must have noticed her at church. Cariss, what can you tell us of him?" Mina sounded still disbelieving.

"I have seen Mr. Thornton a time or two. He is very solemn and quiet, a mature gentleman, who always comes to church alone. His comportment seems rather severe, actually. I don't recall him attending anything social, like an assembly or a gathering on a feast day. I think Papa tried to draw him out in conversation, but with little success." Cariss provided what little information she knew.

"But, Mina, he is more than twice her age! Why would Jocelyn agree to marry such a man, especially if he is severe and cold as Cariss says? How could she have an attachment, or feel obliged to accept him?" Imogene suddenly felt the twinges of her earlier nausea return to lick at her insides.

"I cannot imagine what would persuade her to do such a thing, only thinking that if he is in need of an heir, he has chosen her because she is young…" Mina trailed off and Jocelyn's situation hung in the spring air, for all to ponder. "He is well placed financially from what Mamma says. Perhaps my sister feels the need to be independent of them now that we are all married."

"Oh, dear God. It is unconscionable to me that she would sacrifice herself so. I cannot believe what I am hearing. She has settled for him, and now she has to live with that choice." Feeling very upset, Imogene complained, "I am sorry, but I think it's dreadful."

"I was thinking the same thing, Imogene. Oh, Jocelyn, what have you done? I pray there is a good outcome in this." Mina now had tears visible in her eyes.

Imogene's stomach was roiling wickedly now, the news of her friend making her well and truly sick. She leapt up out of her chair and thrust the baby toward the nearest pair of arms that happened to be Colin's. "Excuse me. I beg your pardons, I think I'm going to be sick!" Clamping a hand over her mouth, she ran, making it only as far as the hedge before everything came up.

Imogene was out of view, but certain everyone could hear her retching. The mortification distressed her further as well as the crying that accompanied her embarrassment. The calm voice of her sister and the soothing hands that held her hair back were welcome. "There now, Im, it's all right. Breathe and it will pass." Philippa rubbed her back and continued to hold her hair away. "Come, let me help you to your room so you can lie down."

COLIN was still holding baby Gwendolyn when Philippa turned back and called to him, "Thank you, Mr. Everley. I'll send the nurse down to take her. I'm just going to help Imogene up to her room right now."

"Not to worry, Mrs. Brancroft, I am delighted to hold your daughter. If we get into trouble I'll call upon one of the ladies."

Graham came striding right up, a frown darkening his features. "Why are you holding the baby? I saw Imogene running into the hedge. What has happened?"

"Easy, Brother," Colin admonished. "It was imperative. She got sick in the hedge and her sister is taking her back to the house."

"Sick?" he bellowed. "Good God! She has not been truly well the whole of this trip."

He made a move toward following them, but Colin stilled

his arm. "I think you should wait, Graham. Leave them to it for now. She received some distressing news about her friend Jocelyn Charleston and the shock of it made her sick. I saw the whole thing."

"I'm getting Brancroft. I want him to examine her right now." He stalked off to find his brother-in-law, Dr. Brancroft, who was shooting targets with Elle and Nicky Hargreave.

You, my brother, are a lovesick mess. Colin had yet to fully witness the complete personality change in his brother—and in such a short amount of time—and only since meeting Imogene.

But he was happy they had found each other.

Happy that Graham and Imogene could find something he didn't think was possible for him to ever know.

"WELL, Sister, I am confident it is as you suspect." John smiled at her. "Congratulations, little mother. Late November should be your time. You are to drink plenty of water and light on the wine, for it can bring on a headache. Rest as you feel you need to. The nausea should pass in a few weeks so until then try to avoid the foods that bother you. Your sister had a pretty easy time of it, so hopefully you will as well. If you have any bleeding, even just spots, or painful cramping, you are to get off your feet and call for me at once. Other than that, you may remain as you are in your usual activities, riding and such, at least for now."

"Thank you, John. We are so lucky to have you. I know I am in excellent hands." She smiled dreamily up at him. "I am happy."

"I can see that you are, and we are very happy for you as

well. Now, my dear, there is a beastly man just outside that door. He is growling and fussing something terrible in his worry over you. You ought to have some mercy on him before he does himself harm and then I have another patient on my hands. What do you say to letting him in?"

"Let him in, Dr. Brancroft!"

John stepped out into the hall and conferred with Graham briefly before the sound of his retreating footsteps told Imogene he had left them alone.

Graham approached her tentatively where she sat on the couch. He knelt at her feet and put his head in her lap. She stroked his hair. "How are you, *chérie*? Are you well now? John didn't tell me anything. He said you could tell me. I have been very worried about you." He brought her hand to his mouth and kissed her palm.

"I am well, my darling, and you have no need to worry over me for I am not ill."

"But Colin said you got sick in the hedge when you got some bad news about Jocelyn Charleston, and you have been very tired."

"Well, I am distressed about Jocelyn but I can do nothing about it. I hope she will be happy in her choice and I wish her all the best. As for the other symptoms, I am told they are perfectly normal." He looked at her questioningly, patient and calm, waiting for her to continue. "I am sorry for all of the dramatics of late. I fear you will be the one to bear the brunt of my sensitive, idiotic emotions." She put her knuckles up to his cheek. "Graham, darling, how would you feel if I told you that you were to be a father?" It was a joy to see the look of comprehension and then happiness take over his countenance and Imogene thought she would never forget it, as long as she lived.

"*ENCEINTE,*" he breathed out as his eyes widened. "My God. For truth, *chérie*?" He jumped up next to her on the couch, drawing her into his arms. "I am—we are blessed. You will be the best, most beautiful, most perfect mother to our child." He laughed, unable to control his emotions. "I am to be a father. Some little person will call me Papa. Extraordinary… Are you happy, *chérie*? I think you wanted this."

"I am deliriously happy, my darling. We have made a child together." She reached for his face. "You will be such a wonderful father. I can't wait to see you in the role."

He pictured himself as a father to their child, and it was a most wonderful vision. "Our child." He put his hand over her very flat stomach, bending to kiss her there. "Our baby is right here, sleeping and growing inside you. I feel filled-up with happiness and love, *chérie*. Please tell me everything that John has said to you."

She relayed John's orders. "He said my time will come in late November."

Graham smiled at that. Realizing that their baby would be born at exactly one year from the time they first met, he pondered the blessings being given to him. Knowing that even though he didn't deserve such miracles, he would grasp onto them anyway. He would take Imogene's love and the blessing of their child, and cherish his gifts in full measure.

Family…

His family was being restored, and nothing—*nothing*—not a person, or a curse, or a sin from the past, would be allowed to take his family from him again.

BUT the monster came for him in a dream that very night, not willing or able to leave him to his comfort in Imogene's joyful news.

...He tried desperately to fight it off. This time the monster slithered around his legs, trapping him, trying to bring him down to the ground. From behind, he could hear the mother screaming, and her child crying. He struggled in vain to get his feet free so he could help them. The monster had him around the neck now, choking the breath from him. Straining mightily, he could do nothing to free himself from its grasp. It was going to kill him—

Bolting awake, he breathed deeply attempting to calm his wildly beating heart and to avoid disturbing Imogene.

He would have to tell her all of it.

He knew he couldn't go on like this.

He'd go mad.

The guilt was going to kill him as surely as a draught of poison.

THE ball was the first formal occasion given by the Everleys of Everfell, and since it was a celebration in honor of the Rothvale marriage, it really served two purposes.

Imogene felt like a princess in the lustrous, silvery ball gown, adorned with the emerald and pearl jewels Graham had given her. She also wore the pearl and diamond tiara that had belonged to his grandmother, as it was reminiscent of a bridal wreath. He complemented her colours with a new formal coat in dark green.

Imogene was relieved to know that of the three waltzes

played tonight, two would be danced with her husband. They would lead on the dance floor to open the ball and would do so again for the final dance to close it. Both would give the other waltz to their hosts—Imogene would dance with Jules, and Graham with Mina.

"You look ravishing, *chérie*, and I am so happy right now, with you in my arms, dancing the waltz with you. No problem or worry is going to reach down into this night to cloud the moment for me."

"I am happy, too, so happy, so blessed. And you—you look just as ravishing, my lord, but then you have always looked so to me."

"And, *chérie*, are you well? I want you to enjoy the dancing, but if you start to feel the slightest bit unsteady or queasy, you are to tell me right away, so I can escort you out." He spoke with great concern. "Please tell me you'll say if you feel unwell."

"I promise, my darling, I absolutely will. Now *you* must promise me that you will not worry overmuch or succumb to fussing. I want you to enjoy the evening as well. Won't you take pleasure in the company of your friend Mr. Gravelle this eve? You have not had his companionship for a long time."

"*Chérie*, your concern for me touches my heart. I promise to enjoy the evening, but can honestly say it will be near impossible for me not to fuss over you when I know you are *enceinte*. How can I not? You are more precious to me than words can convey. And now that you carry our child, I know I'll not be able to keep from thinking about it no matter how hard I try. As for Gravelle, I'd like to invite him for a stay with us. What do you think?"

"I think you should invite him. It's always good to have your friends by your side."

CLIVE Gravelle and Colin Everley both watched dancing couples circling the ballroom.

"Look at Pellton ogling Elle. God! She is a young girl and he is an ill repute of the worst kind. I don't like how he is looking at her like she is something to be devoured." That Colin Everley was clearly not amused with any man looking at Ellenora Vickering was evident even to Gravelle's unpolished eye.

"Yes, well he is admiring her to be sure, but, Everley, you must realize she is as good as grown-up now and beautiful. It is to be expected that men will look at her."

"Bleh, Pellton though. He is not trustworthy. Have you heard some of the stories about him?" Everley snorted in disgust, his arms folded. "I cannot fathom why Jules even extended him an invitation tonight."

- "If you are so concerned about her maybe you should alert her cousin, Nicky Hargreave.
He kills men for a living, being in the Army."

"True, but he is busy at the moment dancing with Cariss Wilton, and from the looks of him, he is oblivious to everything else," Everley said dryly.

"I see what you mean." Gravelle frowned, watching every move of the smiling colonel dancing with the lovely Miss Wilton. The colonel looked a little too entranced for his liking. "And what of your journey together from Kent? I hear you escorted her, and she was a girl all alone," he charged.

"What? What do you imply, Gravelle? Her parents asked if I would. They know and trust me. Cariss is the best sort of girl and I consider her family, like a sister really. They couldn't send her up in a coach on her own, now could they? I rode outside the coach and saw that she was safely delivered. God! Why am I explaining all this ridiculousness to you?" He grew flustered. "Gravelle, I think *you* have an itch for Cariss Wilton. Do us all a favour and ask her to dance, would you?"

Everley stalked off, leaving a chastened Gravelle standing at the edge of the ballroom, his eyes never wavering from the charming Cariss. He moved forward, his mind decided. But before he could reach her across the room, that rakehell Edgar Pellton stepped up and claimed the dance.

Gravelle did not like that. His eyes narrowed and his frown deepened, and he clenched his fists as he watched Pellton dance with the most beautiful girl in the room.

No, he did not like it one bit.

ON the other side of the ballroom, Jules and Graham surveyed the dancing. "Did you know, Graham, how Nicky once told me he would have offered for Mina first, if she had promised a greater dowry? Sometimes the way he looks at her, like right now—God, I hate it. I hate the way he looks at her."

"Jules, he does no harm. You can trust him with your life, and your wife. This I know to be true," Graham admonished his cousin. "He is a hard-working soldier in the British Army. Nicky is entitled to a little diversion of a beautiful woman on a dance floor. I think you could give him that."

"Oh, really? Is that what you think? You know, Graham, you should count your blessings he did not get wind of Imogene before you did. With her fortune and rank, she is exactly the kind of wife he needs. My uncle, Sir Thomas, said as much to me. He is quite vexed you won her and not

Nicky—or me for that matter." He rolled his eyes and shook his head in disgust.

Graham scowled and his lip curled. "That is just out of bounds," he snorted. "You know, I've never cared much for your uncle. He is a pompous ass, most severe."

"True that, Graham." Jules had to agree.

IN the early hours of the morning as the ball quietly came to a close, and the many guests had departed, the family gathered at the foot of the grand stairwell to say goodnight.

"The ball was just lovely, Mina. You are sure to be hailed as *the* hostess of the shire. Thank you again for honoring us." Imogene expressed her gratitude.

"Our pleasure, Imogene. I had a fabulous time myself. And Elle and Cariss, how did you find the evening?"

"It was perfect," Elle answered.

Cariss announced, "I can't remember when I've had a better ball."

Mina glowed with satisfaction. "Well, we should do it again, soon, since this was such a success. What do you say, Julian?"

"Yes, of course." Jules lied to his wife. "Whatever you wish, my dearest."

Colin raised his eyebrows, thinking he could do without the slathering dogs after Elle.

God! Must we? Graham thought, as he gazed adoringly at his bride.

Chapter 22

Because the birthday of my life
Is come, my love is come to me.

Christina Rossetti ~ 'A Birthday', 1862

The return to Gavandon after a fortnight at Everfell was welcome. For all that they had relished being with family, it was good to be home again. Imogene delighted in having Cariss return with her and was happy Colin could stay at Gavandon for a month, which she knew, was easing for Graham.

There was also the additional appreciation of moving back into their old rooms. The renovations and bathing room addition were now complete. Imogene was more than satisfied with her redecorated chamber. The wall coverings, upholsteries and bed trimmings were reflective of her. It was now a soothing and peaceful retreat, reminiscent of nature. But the *piece de resistance* however, was the massive portrait Tristan had done of Terra and Triton on the grounds of Gavandon. To Imogene, it was breathtaking. On their first night back, Graham had come in to find her sitting on the floor hugging her knees, gazing up at it in rapt meditation.

"There you are, *chérie.* Ah, are you enjoying your new painting?"

"Oh, Graham, I love it. It is just what I like, and my rooms—they are perfect." She held her arms up. "All of this. It's so, so perfect and beautiful, a comfortable sanctuary I shall adore."

Graham sat down on the floor next to her, slowly perusing the finished room. "*Chérie,* I am thrilled that they are as you wish them to be. May I say that you have made excellent selections. The palette of colours is divine and suits you so well. You have created a space that reflects you, totally. The blues, and greens, the warm browns, the English oak, they all work wonderfully together. Corporeal. You've brought the sky and the grass and the earth indoors to be enjoyed. I love it in here now, and I hope you'll invite me in often."

She laughed softly. "You know you are always welcome in my rooms, and are to come in whenever you wish. Now what do you think of my painting?"

"It makes the room, for truth."

"I know it does. Tristan is so talented. I am amazed at what he can do," Imogene agreed.

"He is unique and we are fortunate to have him here with us, but it will not always be so. Some day he will want to go…and he should. Great distinction will be his one day, I predict. Hopefully he'll stay long enough for us to get more beautiful works like this from him."

"Graham, now that my rooms are done, we must really think about the next project. Can you guess what it is?"

"I know, *chérie*, for I have also thought of it. The nursery. And believe me, it needs attention for the last occupant to spend any time there was Colin. I suppose I must call the draper and the painters back straight away."

"Bravo! You're exactly right. How should it be done do you think?"

"Refreshed mostly. Maybe Tristan could do a series of paintings to go 'round the room. Fairy tales or something similar? Knights in armor, princesses, dragons, unicorns?"

"I love your ideas. You are so brilliant. My very own, brilliant Professor Adonis." She leaned toward him for a kiss. "Would you like to sleep here in my room tonight, *Professor*?"

"Most assuredly." The professor appeared distracted however, his thoughts no longer focused on the beautiful new rooms or their plans for the nursery. As he kissed into her neck, he had more engaging activities in mind, and for the very immediate future, Imogene guessed his plans did not involve sleep.

SHE arose hesitantly each morning, Hester with her tea and toast at the ready to help with the morning sickness. Thankfully, it usually passed by mid-morning and Imogene was able to attend to her duties for the most part. She found that the convenience of the bathing room and the ease of getting water up to her room a timely luxury. The baths were very comforting in lessening the discomforts of pregnancy.

Graham fussed over her terribly at first, and she had to tell him, quite firmly, that his over-attentiveness was most unwelcome. He took her criticism well enough, in his easy way, but she knew it pained him not to fuss. They settled back into their regular routines and looked forward to the warming weather of late spring.

A letter from Jocelyn Charleston was waiting when she returned home to Gavandon. Jocelyn stated that Mr. Thornton was a mature gentleman, and while he was older, he wasn't unattractive. She didn't think their age difference much of a concern. He was serious and sombre but had paid his particular attentions to her alone. His offer of marriage was honorable and respectable considering her dowry was not substantial, and he was well situated on a profitable estate, close enough to her parents that she would have opportunity to see them occasionally. She was anxious to make her way in a life of her own and figured that Mr. Thornton would suit as well as any other. She had no illusions of making a love match as Imogene had done. Her only regret was that she would not be able to visit Warwickshire this year and couldn't possibly know when she might ever. She promised to write often, hoping to see Imogene again whenever she stopped in Kent to visit her family possibly on a trip to London.

Imogene wrote back to Jocelyn straight away. She offered congratulations and shared her happy news of expecting a baby in November. She pledged to write and assured to visit on their way when they made the trip to Town, which would come eventually as Graham had obligations to Parliament. She still felt the pang of uneasiness regarding Jocelyn's choice when she posted her reply, realizing that by the time Jocelyn got her letter, her wedding day would have nearly dawned.

With the help of Mrs. Griffin and the companionship of Cariss, Imogene resumed the tenant visits. So far they had gone off smoothly and the tenants seemed honored by the attentions of the new mistress. It was clear they respected Graham. They were well pleased the master had returned from his sojourn to Ireland and further gratified he had brought back with him a kind and benevolent wife.

30th April, 1812

"I cannot find my watch," Graham grumbled at breakfast. "I took it off last night and set it in the usual spot at my bedside table. I am certain I did."

"I am sorry, my darling. I'll look for you when I go back upstairs." She grinned. "You are getting forgetful in your dotage?"

He narrowed his eyes at her. "What are you up to, *chérie*?"

"La! You didn't think you'd get away with it passing and no observance, did you?"

He looked sheepish. "I did hold out hope, I admit. But you didn't answer my question, *chérie*. What have you concocted?"

"Just a simple birthday supper tonight; a few friends will join us is all," she replied demurely. "So look sharp and wear your merriest face. That is all I am telling you."

"*Chérie*?" he warned.

"What? Can a wife not honor her husband on his birthday? I could not allow your birthday to pass without acknowledgment, now could I? Not when I have the best, most loving, handsomest, most gallant, and adoring husband in the world."

He drew her into his arms and gazed down. "I *am* honored. He kissed her lingeringly, bringing his hands to the sides of her face.

"Good. I have a special gift for you, but I'll give it to you tonight, when it's just us, in private."

"Ah, I cannot wait," he answered knowingly, eyes gleaming wickedly as his hands reached around to grip her bottom.

"It's not that, you scamp. It's not what you're thinking,

but you know you'd probably get that anyway," she said more quietly. "It is a tangible gift and I think you will like it. I hope so."

"Oh, *chérie*, I will love it, no matter what it is, but you should know that you have already given me the best gifts of all, your love and…this." He brought his hands to rest on her stomach. "How is our precious cargo this day?"

"Well, I believe, and firmly in place, still making me sick each morning, so he must be strong and stalwart like his father," she teased with a smile.

"That's the baby making you sick, and not me I hope?"

"I hope he is just like you."

"You think it a boy then?"

"I don't have any idea, really. And you?"

"I see a bouncing, blonde-haired angel, demanding a pony ride."

She laughed at that vision. "Why do I feel as if you are drawing up a fiction of me as a child?"

"But is it fiction, *chérie?* I bet I am spot on. I can see you bounding into your father's study and stamping your foot, telling him your need for an immediate ride on your pony. I am sure your entreaties worked quite seamlessly in gaining your desired end. He was helpless against you and did what any doting papa would do: dropped whatever he was doing and seeing to a pony ride with his princess." He smiled as if imagining it. "I would love that for myself."

"You're going to be such a wonderful father." His eyes sparkled at her as she placed her hands over his.

"GRAHAM darling, Tristan is arriving first. I think we should be ready to greet him."

"He'd better be bringing what I think he might."

She merely smiled at him. "You look smashing in your fine new jacket and waistcoat. Mr. Phelps has done a good turn with you tonight. I say, you grow more handsome with the passing of the days. I hope I don't have to fight off scores of admiring ladies for your attentions."

"I sincerely doubt that will be a problem, *chérie.* It never has, I would remember that," he said wryly. Graham clutched her hand tightly, wrapped over his arm. She could tell he was nervous.

"Now darling, I want you to relax and enjoy yourself this eve. No worries about anything. This is merely the companionship of good people who care about you."

He nodded at her solemnly. "Are you feeling well, *chérie*? Please do not overdo yourself in orchestrating your plans for the evening."

She had to laugh at his words. "I am excellent tonight, and I promise if I become fatigued, I shall take up a seat and sit back and enjoy the show."

"My God, woman. What have you designed?" He looked wary.

"I am only jesting. The look on your face. I could not resist, you were begging for a tease."

He grabbed her then and kissed her wolfishly. "No, not really. But I can think of something you are begging for. You need it badly and it is most definitely not a tease," he growled the words low and soft in her ear.

"Now watch yourself, my lord, you have a guest arriving at your doorstep as we speak. You can deal with me later." She flashed him her sauciest wink.

"Naughty, naughty, Lady Rothvale," he clucked at her. "I

intend to, and that's a promise."

The footman, Hicks, appeared then, announcing, "Mr. Mallerton."

Tristan came forward, carrying what appeared to be a portrait. It was covered with fine cloth and tied with string.

"Finally. Finally! I thought I'd never see it completed." Graham greeted Tristan eagerly.

"Yes, well I've worked as fast as I was able. I think you'll be pleased with this." He untied the string, pulled off the cloth and turned the canvas to face Graham.

Graham was stilled by the sight of the portrait, inspecting it reverently. Slowly, he expelled a breath. "You have a rare talent, Tristan. It is perfect, just as I might have imagined it. Thank you for portraying Imogene so magnificently."

"I am a realistic painter, painting the subject as it appears." He nodded at Imogene. "Thank you for the compliment and I am glad you are well pleased."

"Oh, I am, you can be assured." Graham was animated and excited. "Say, I want to have this on display here in the parlor, tonight. I must have an easel for it." He moved toward the door.

"Graham, are you going? Why not send someone to get one for you?" Imogene inquired.

"I must, *chérie*, they'd never find the proper one. I know exactly what I want for this—better if I go. I'll just pop up to my old studio and return in a moment." Bussing her cheek before turning back to Tristan, he said, "This pleases me greatly, Tristan. Thank you, thank you, my friend."

Tristan waved him off as he left the room in search of the perfect easel, sharing a giggle with Imogene. "Are you nervous?"

"Why should I be nervous, Tristan? Just because I've

invited half of Warwickshire for a house party and my husband doesn't know about it? I feel like I'm going to be sick again."

"Please warn me if that is the case, so I may step out of the way, my dear," Tristan muttered. "Before I forget, here's this." He handed her Graham's watch, which she placed on a side table.

"And the other?" she asked.

"Safely delivered with the help of Mrs. Griffin. She said to tell you it is under the bed."

She squeezed his hand in answer, mouthing the words, 'thank you.'

Graham returned then, the desired easel in hand. He smiled at them and set to work, arranging the portrait to his liking. "There. It can be viewed to the best advantage from over here. Magnificence. I love the expression on your face, *chérie*, as if you are about to say something very significant to an unknown person off canvas and out of view. It is evocative of ambiguity and mystery. I am glad Zuly is in there with you, as she fits in so elegantly. The three-quarter profile is a marvelous element, displays the jewels to their best I think. They came across so luminous in paint. It's just so—"

"Darling?" *Come up for air, my dear.*

"Yes, *chérie*?" He paused for a moment in his fussing over her portrait and gave her his attention.

"While you were gone, I happened to look down here and look what I've found?" She held up his watch.

"Thank Christ. I've been looking all day." He came forward and took the watch. "This watch belonged to my father—" his words cut off abruptly as he opened it. "Oh…" He snapped his head up to lock eyes with his wife. "It is so lovely. You've put a miniature portrait of yourself in my watch. Now I can take you with me always." He embraced her. "Thank you, *chérie*, it is the very best gift of all." Imogene could tell he was overcome. "I am afraid I am at a loss for words, I am so touched by this beautiful gift."

"It is not a gift from me, darling. It is from your friend here," she said, indicating with a tilt of her head toward Tristan. "My only part in the plan was absconding your watch for the day so he could set it inside for you."

Graham shifted his eyes to Tristan, who gave him a short nod and a grin. "Happy birthday, old man, glad you like it. I must say I am surprised you didn't think of it before I did, and beg for one. You would have had it long before now."

"Tristan. Thank you. Sorry, I am bumbling." He bowed to his friend. "A lovely gesture and it will be treasured always, my good friend." Tristan bowed his head in return.

Hicks reappeared and announced, "Mr. and Mrs. Julian Everley, Miss Vickering, Colonel Hargreave."

Graham, further surprised by the announcements, came forward to greet his guests. "Ha! I have been taken totally unawares. Welcome, welcome. God, it is good to see you here at Gavandon." He turned to Imogene. "You are amazing, *chérie*, and *very* good. I had no idea."

She just smiled at him and arched her brows in challenge.

Colin and Cariss entered the room then with Hicks following close behind them with another announcement. "Mr. Gravelle," he bellowed.

Graham greeted him warmly. "I hope you will stay with us for as long as you can, Gravelle."

Mr. Gravelle looked at him a little oddly. "I had planned to stay, yes. Christ, man, are you getting dotty in your old age?" he quipped.

Graham just shook his head and shot another look Imogene's way, now beginning to comprehend what she had orchestrated.

"Mr. and Mrs. Burleigh, Dr. and Mrs. Brancroft," Hicks announced more guests.

"How many have you invited, *chérie*?" he whispered as he moved to greet the newest arrivals.

"Surprise, my darling. I lied a little, but just a little, mind you. It's not only a supper party, you see, I've invited them all to stay with us. It's a house party! Happy birthday."

GRAHAM could not remember a more memorable birthday, nor a time when he felt so honored by his friends and family. It was heart-warming to enjoy the companionship with loved ones in the halls of Gavandon again. Imogene had arranged the additional entertainment, with Tristan's cooperation of course, to have him sketch miniature line drawings of everyone for a keepsake of the occasion. The musical talents performed, and the miniature portraits had delighted everyone. Elle and Mina were now quite accomplished at playing duets, apparently.

Imogene had shot a satisfied look at Graham when it was Cariss's turn to play for them, and Gravelle stepped up to turn pages for her. He had to agree that her suggestion Gravelle might like her young cousin seemed rather accurate.

During supper, the excellent staff of Gavandon had been busy settling the guests' luggage into their rooms. Mrs. Griffin, operating without a glitch in the arrangements, as if she organized a whole houseful of guests every day, was superb. Graham could not recollect the last time Gavandon had hosted such a large crowd.

He thought of his late mother and how she would

definitely have approved of their house party. The reminiscent notion brought feelings of regret though, regret his good mother would never know his wife. Oh how he would have loved for them to know one another. He was grateful Zuly was included in the emerald portrait with Imogene. Zuly had been his mother's dog, and now she was Imogene's, seemed connecting somehow. It brought them together in a way that was right and good. The passing of the torch from one Lady Rothvale onto the next.

When they retired to their room at the end of the night he was still amazed at what she had managed to plan without him knowing. "*Chérie*, you have outdone yourself in your attempts to make a magnificent birthday for me. I loved everything, and had a marvelous time tonight. I will never forget the occasion or the gesture."

"Oh well, I am not yet done, my darling."

"There's more? How could there be more?"

Imogene nodded knowingly. "Now, I want you to sit here on the couch and close your eyes." She kissed him on the forehead, then pulled back to hold his chin. "You know, you look boldly handsome with your hair loose, and lounging in that deep purple robe. I am a lucky wife," she admired. "No peeking now. Just give me a minute."

He heard her scrabbling on the floor, and something sliding, keeping his eyes closed while he listened to the additional sounds of string being pulled and rustling. He sensed her close, could hear her breathing…could smell the familiar scent of oil spirits and paint.

"For you, with all of my love," she whispered.

He opened his eyes.

She held it for him.

At first he was speechless, but then he found his voice.

"You did it. You had him paint you in...*dishabille*." The words came out of him like a cry he was so affected. "I—I—how did you—" His eyes found hers and then darted to the painting, back and forth. He brought his hand to his forehead. "Sorry, I am having trouble understanding; this is so, so beautiful. It is incomparable. I cannot believe you did this for me. I could stare at it forever, *chérie*." He continued to gaze at the painting, and then took it into his hands to hold himself.

"I am so pleased you like it. It was a challenge, but I see now that it was worth every bit of the effort. Happy birthday, my dearest husband."

He looked up at her in wonder. "I don't deserve you," his voice tremulous, "any of this."

"Deserve? What does that mean? Who deserves anything? The world does not work in such a way. Things just are as they are. We met and fell into love and that is just the way it is. We are together now, forever, and for today, this is something I wanted to do for you because I love you and want to make you happy. All the time. I am thrilled that you are happy. You have given me so much, Graham. It makes *me* happy to do this. I love you profoundly, to the depths of my soul."

Carefully setting down the precious painting, he got up from the couch, deftly lifting and carrying her to their bed where he made love to her as he'd promised he would earlier in the evening.

He did it slowly and with great care, the whole time whispering words of devotion and adoration, showing her how much he loved and needed her, and that it would always be so, for him in this way, with her.

Chapter 23

Not mine own fears, nor the prophetic soul
Of the wide world dreaming on things to come.

William Shakespeare ~ Sonnet 107, 1605

The monster was trying to kill him again. No amount of pleading and entreaty would dissuade it from its path of destruction and devastation. 'Please…please leave me in peace to be happy with her! Will you ever cease tormenting me?'

'Never! It is all your fault…all your fault…all your fault—'

"Graham darling, wake up. You are dreaming again." She rubbed his shoulder. "You were thrashing about and agitated like you were fighting something off."

Her gentle voice greeting him awake from the tortuous dream was almost just as horrifying. He tried to keep his voice level. "Sorry, *chérie.* I apologize for disturbing you. Go back to sleep."

"Enough of this. You must tell me about your nightmares. Why won't you tell me?" She was no longer soothing but angry with him.

"Because they are so horrible and I cannot have the filth touch you."

"I'll wait. I am a patient person, Graham. I'll wait here until you share all with me," she declared frostily.

The silence was deafening for long moments. Graham sighed deeply, and then finally he began to talk…

"Jasper, my brother. There was something wrong with him. Not always though. When we were children he was carefree and witty. He changed as he became a man, becoming something else—a misogynist—an abuser of women. My father tried to beat it out of him. I do not know why he treated women so badly. He held no regard or respect for them; they were objects to be used for his needs only.

"Father always instilled in us that gentlemen did not dally with the servant girls. It was low manners, beneath our station to do so. Furthermore, it was our duty to protect and preserve those who gave us service and depended upon us for their livelihood. But Jasper disregarded everything Father taught us. I cannot tell you how many times I came upon my brother *flagrante delicto* with some poor girl. He had no boundaries of decorum; he did it out in the open, blatantly. Dark hallways, haylofts, up against a tree, didn't matter. They went willingly with him, though, and I know he was depraved but I didn't think him capable of—" He took a deep breath. "I worried that Colin might follow his example, but he didn't. Colin is good."

He shuddered before continuing as he remembered. "There was a girl, a seamstress. She did the house sewing. It was…Agnes. She was a good girl, intelligent, and she could read. Her father had been a tailor but he died and she had to go into service. Father allowed the servants use of the library if they could read and had the inclination to do so. I got to know her a little when she would come in to exchange a book. I suggested titles I thought she might find enjoyable."

"Did you like Agnes?"

"I did. There was nothing untoward about it though. We were friends. I thought she was a decent person, admiring her efforts to improve her mind by reading. She was very pretty. I asked if I might paint her image after I came across her one day in the library. She was sitting in profile, holding an open book close to her face. It was such a perfect moment. I wanted to capture it. She agreed, and we started with some sittings. That was my great mistake."

"Mistake?"

"*Chérie*, please know I did not have designs on Agnes. She was not for me. I only wanted to paint a pretty girl for her image, nothing more. But it was poor judgment for me to ask her. Even so, I take responsibility for what happened." He felt his jaw tighten. "It's my fault. I should have known he would target Agnes as soon as he saw me give her even the merest look. I put her in harm's way. For that, I will always bear the guilt."

"Guilt for what, Graham?"

"One day I came upon them. Jasper and Ralph Odeman. Both of them at the same time using her, most cruelly. Rape. The most base, vicious, hurtful—" He scrubbed his face with his hands. "I went insane—I—I nearly killed them both. Colin pulled me off or I probably would have finished them. Agnes fled the estate. Later, I found out it wasn't the first time he had assaulted her. Father banished Jasper and he departed for his final jaunt, the last spiral of descent into his dissipative demise. I left Gavandon for London, living there for months, until Father called me back home. Agnes had arrived on the doorstep, heavy with child."

"Oh, Graham…"

"This was another reason I gave up my painting. Look what it had cost me, cost Agnes? My brother haunts me from his grave and Ralph Odeman does it in life. I cannot seem to get free from the past, Imogene."

"Was Jasper ever decent? What was required of him? He must have gone to university, surely."

"Father made him go but he didn't last even a term. They kicked his arse right out. Still remembering his foolery when I got there and it was not easy to overcome his legacy, short though it was. I have always had to bear his legacy. He would raise hell over the entire shire and delighted in giving my name instead of his own. So whenever he got into trouble the magistrates would come looking for Graham Everley. He thought it most hilarious to impinge my good name."

"Why was there so much animosity between you?"

"Jealousy I suppose, but I'm not completely sure. He knew he was weak in character—he had to have known. I was also larger in build than him and he could not best me. It bothered him, but I still had to keep my wits about me for he would try to ambush me whenever he got the chance. I also had to protect Colin, keep him safe, teaching him to fight." He looked into Imogene's eyes. "If my brother Jasper still lived, I would not even consider bringing you home to meet him. He would have gone after you just because you were mine. That's how his demented mind worked."

"How appalling to know such a thing about one's flesh and blood. Graham, I cannot imagine how you've suffered with this."

"On his deathbed, I asked Jasper how he could have done that to Agnes and not take responsibility for the child. He laughed in my face. Said I made him sick, the good son, the perfect, saintly son, who never did wrong. Sanctimonious, he called me. He said he hoped I'd enjoy inheriting what was his by birth. Said he'd haunt me from the grave. Then, in front of my parents, he gifted me with the perfect revenge. He told them the child could have been any of ours. Could be Odeman's, or…could be mine. He said that I had bedded Agnes many times, that I was painting a portrait of her in secret."

Graham's voice broke. "Jasper lied, *chérie*—it was a lie. I told my parents that he lied. I was never with her in that way. Not once! But he planted the seed of doubt for them. I could tell by the way my mother and father both looked at me, there was some small niggling part in their minds that thought I might have fathered Agnes's child because I had started the portrait of her. They never accused me, but I know they considered the possibility. For that, I cannot forgive…my brother, Jasper. And the child has green eyes like me. I told you before that Jasper's eyes were not green. Anyone who ever knows of Clara will always believe she is *my* child. Jasper is dead, forgotten. I am alive, and people will always assume the very worst. It tarnished me to our parents, and then they died." His voice dropped to a whisper. "Oh, *chérie*, that's all of it. Now you know everything." He rested his forehead in the palms of his hands. "She is of my blood, but she is not my child."

"Look at me. Graham, will you look at me?"

He turned away. "I am afraid, *chérie.* Afraid for what I might see in your eyes."

"Only love…love is all you will see in my eyes."

A cry came out of him—from deep inside his soul—a cry of relief, of thankfulness, and healing, before turning to face the woman he loved, and who loved him in return.

In the shelter of her loving arms, some of the pain of the past began to melt away.

HE was already up and off somewhere when she woke alone the next morning. Imogene wasn't surprised. It was rare for Graham to laze in the bed, being he was a habitual early riser. Indulging in a latent thought lounging in bed would be nice, she readily shelved it. As hostess to this house party, there would be no breakfasts in her sitting room for quite some time. Gingerly she got up, always anticipating the nausea, which usually didn't show its effects until she was mobile. Reaching for her wrapper, she saw that he had left her a note upon his pillow.

Chérie,

I could not leave you this morning without telling you what a generous, loving, and affectionate wife you are. Your gift of the portrait means more to me than words could ever convey, more than you will ever know. But your greatest gift is accepting me with my many flaws and burdens in your compassionate way. You are all that is goodness and light. The perfect partner. You have filled me up with joy and happiness. I am forever in your debt for giving to me such a life as this, with you, my beloved wife.

Ever in your devotion,

G

P.S. I am in my studio and would like to show it to you if you are of a mind. Upper east wing, end of the hall.

That he was so touched by the portrait made her jubilant. He was always giving to her. Always. She knew she was blessed beyond all imagining in her husband, and she took great satisfaction in bestowing something back to him. His invitation to join him in his studio was intriguing. To her knowledge, he had not used it since their marriage and though she was vaguely aware of its existence, she had never heard him mention it directly until last night when he went there to retrieve the easel.

She rang for Hester and proceeded to her new bathing room for washing. The baths were very restorative especially when her stomach was so fickle. She blushed at the sight of the love bites on her breasts acquired last night, recalling that Graham, too, would be sporting some on his own skin.

Their loving had been all consuming, both one for the other. She sighed as she remembered him touching her body in ways that made her tremble with the pleasure he forced from her. Her brooding lover was so different in the throes of passion, and she loved that aspect of him, too.

Imogene left her room in search of Graham's studio feeling quite triumphant, for she had managed to bathe, dress, and have her tea and toast without bringing it right back up. Thinking what a treat it would be if she could avoid being sick for a day, she wove her way to the east wing with Zuly at her side who faithfully waited for her mistress to emerge each morning.

She knocked and heard him call, "Come."

When she entered, she could see that the room was large and open, with many windows. One whole wall was a work area with shelves and a long table where he'd been apparently working.

"Thank you for the invitation to your sanctum, my darling. I am very honored."

"Thank you for coming." He held out a hand to her.

She drew up, clasping his hand with hers, greeting him with a kiss. "Is that a frame you're making?"

"Yes. For your *dishabille* portrait. Due to its subject matter I will not be sending it to the framer." He smiled. "I get to do it myself, and I must say it feels good to get my hands in this again."

"Will you show me?"

Graham spent the next minutes showing her how a picture frame was built, his manner quiet and pensive. "It is unsigned…"

"True. He was willing to paint it, but said he couldn't put his name to it. Tristan said you would understand."

"Imogene, I am so overcome, still. The image of you is beauty personified." He put a hand to her hair. "So special and very inspiring. Your gift has stirred me." He stroked over her hair. "I am feeling the desire to paint again." Looking into her eyes deeply, he said, "I want to paint you."

"Really?"

"More than you could know."

She thought she detected he wanted to ask her but was hesitant to do so. "I would love to help you to paint again. I'll sit for you if you want. It will be something we can do together, just us."

He pulled her into his arms and held her. "Thank you, *chérie.* I would so dearly love to paint you. I was afraid to ask. Are you sure you do not mind? You said the *dishabille* was a challenge and I don't want you to submit yourself to it if you don't want it."

"I don't mind at all, and we could enjoy the time together. The *dishabille* was a challenge only because it was new and strange, and it was Tristan painting me, and we had to keep it a secret. It was only a challenge at first, because the sittings became much easier, and by the end, no hardship at all. Having you paint me would never be strange—it would be special. How many women have an artist for a husband who could paint them?"

"You make me so happy, *chérie*." He stroked her cheek with the back of his hand. "*Mon trésor précieux*…my precious treasure."

THEIR house party lasted a good ten days. Some members leaving and returning as was necessary. There were ample opportunities to ride for the ladies. Imogene loved it and made a point to thoroughly enjoy herself while it lasted for she knew her riding would be restricted soon enough as her pregnancy advanced. Philippa and Mina did not ride, but it was no matter as the two connected instantly, taking pleasure in the other's company. Mr. Gravelle brought more horses from his estate at Kelldale, only five miles away. This insured enough horses for everybody to have proper mounts to select from.

The gentlemen enjoyed the usual manly pursuits, small game shooting, hours of billiards and cards laced with port and brandy, and to the delight of Imogene, many opportunities to fence in Graham's specially appointed studio. She was glad he could take up his sport again. Mostly she enjoyed seeing him bond with friends and family in a way he had not allowed himself for years. At her urging and request he agreed to a fencing display for the ladies benefit to finish out their house party.

The fencing match was to be held outside. Generally Graham participated in assaults, friendly combat between two fencers without attention to scoring. But this was a small tournament of sorts and each bout would be scored. Four judges would be needed—two judges per fencer—at all times to determine whether legitimate hits were made. The match would be played on a marked narrow strip of grass called the *piste*. They were to use foils specially fitted with a leather safety tip, or *bouton*. Each participant wore a metal mesh mask to protect the face and a special one-armed, heavily padded jacket called a *plastron*, which buttoned high up the neck, leaving the sword arm free of a confining sleeve. In foil fencing, the target area being the torso, excluding arms, legs and head, with the object to score a set number of hits in order to win. Hits must be made with the point of the sword, thus the need for safety measures. The first to score five hits would win the bout and advance.

Since Imogene was the most eager for the fencing display, Graham playfully made her the president. This honor allowed her to give the order to 'play' and 'halt' as needed. She could also outvote a tie between the judges. He had been schooling her on the rules and moves for she dearly wanted to learn. She would have begged him for lessons in using a sword if she weren't pregnant, just as she also knew that someday he'd succumb to teaching her. She loved sport and competitiveness made her yearn to try her hand.

"Take your place, Lady President." Graham indicated to her chair, set along the middle of the sidelines. He leaned in behind her, brushing a kiss at her cheek.

"Wish me luck," she whispered. "I am nervous I'll make a blundering mistake."

"*Chérie*, you're the perfect president. Just relax and remember what I've showed you and keep your eyes trained on them at all times." He grinned naughtily then. "Good luuuuck!" She watched him walk away to take his place, feeling both, immensely proud of him and the thrill of the impending fight.

"Play!" she ordered, and it was begun.

The men were ranked prior by their expertise and were eliminated in the best of three bouts between opponents. John surprised them by eliminating both Tristan and James Burleigh in turn, but was bested by Colonel Hargreave during their match. Colin won out against the colonel, and then Jules as well, which was unexpected. Elle's face was riveted in tension as she watched her beloved cousin and brother battle it out. She cheered wildly when Colin was declared the winner, much to the chagrin of Jules and the rowdy comments being shouted about.

Colin faced his brother. "Let's see what they've been teaching you at that school I pay so dearly for," Graham growled.

"Let's see how you hold against youth, old man," Colin retorted. They gave their bows and at Imogene's command, began their match. It went slow at first and dragged out over time for they were very evenly skilled, but Colin had been battling steadily as Graham was his third opponent. Colin won the first bout, but then lost the next two, eliminating him and advancing Graham.

GRAVELLE knew he was the highest ranked fencer of the group. He had worked very hard for his skills and would use them with no apology. Maybe he didn't possess as much natural talent as Rothvale, but he was consistent in his practice and training, while his friend had been away from it for more than a year while he was attending to family business in

Ireland.

Feeling the eyes of the others on them as they battled was a thrill for Gravelle. The thrill of competition that he craved. Rothvale was a large man and he moved well—with finesse—but Gravelle was bigger, and the added height gave him a longer reach, and thus a slight advantage.

Advance, retreat, lunge, parry, envelopment, this last being the act of sweeping the opponents blade through a full circle, was, in his opinion, a kind of clashing beauty. Gravelle won the first bout and Rothvale the second. For the final bout, whoever won it would be the champion of the tournament and winner of the purse. They had all contributed to the pot of winnings in good-hearted fun. But Gravelle did not care a whit about winning the purse. He had more of an affecting motivation to carry him, that being the art of performing well in the presence of a certain young lady.

They moved stealthily forward and back, and in time, both scored hits on the other. When they were tied with four hits each, the end was near and it could go either way. Gravelle thought he needed the win more than Rothvale did. Rothvale had already won his lady's heart and was relaxed in enjoying the competition of the fight without pressure to impress. Gravelle, on the other hand, was propelled to win it, and as most champions can attest, the mental will to prevail is just as important as excellence in technique and skill. Envisioning of the win is vital, and any hesitation to the fact spells certain failure. So in short order, an opportunity was offered to him for just that outcome. Rothvale slowed just a fraction. Gravelle pretended to attack, causing Rothvale to move to parry. By envelopment he controlled Rothvale's blade, catching it at the point where it was weakest with the third of his blade nearest the guard where it was strongest, rendering Rothvale's parry ineffective with a circular motion.

And in that final elegant flourish, the decisive hit was scored.

Everyone erupted.

He didn't hear Lady Rothvale's command to 'halt' nor did anyone else as they were all storming the *piste* to congratulate the fencers for a tremendously thrilling match.

"Godsblood, Gravelle, that was fine!" Rothvale acclaimed. "I can't remember a more exhilarating challenge. Well played, man." He clapped him on the back.

Gravelle bowed. "I had a worthy opponent. Well played *you*, Rothvale, for truth. I am so glad you're back."

Gravelle spared a look in Miss Wilton's direction to find her smiling widely and clapping for him, her eyes meeting his from across the *piste* in congratulations.

He felt a painful stab into his heart, too.

THE house party broke up the following day. Elle would remain at Gavandon as was the original plan, and Colin was still with them for another fortnight. Gravelle was invited to stay longer and it was thought he would, but he approached Graham with the news he was required in Town on business and would take his leave with everybody else.

Graham's shoulders fell a little before he answered, "All right, Gravelle, but you will be missed. I hope you'll come back to us when you are returned to Warwickshire. I have enjoyed your companionship and the fencing. It has been a long time. Too long…" he trailed off.

"Indeed."

"When you return, what do you say to a standing

appointment? Pick a day of the week and I'll make it a priority. Fencing with you is a reminder of how much I've need of it," Graham challenged cheerfully.

"I am in full agreement. Consider it done. I would not pass up the opportunity to baste you weekly," he laughed.

Graham asked his friend another question. "Have you heard word of your friend, Trenton? Do you know if he ever finished his orders? I told him to write to me, but he never did."

"I believe he did finish them. Last word was he was called back home. Family troubles or some sort. He has a brother who is a real problem. It is fair to say he is truly dicked in the nob." Gravelle indicated by tapping his head purposefully. "Causes all sorts of difficulties for their father and the family. Interesting that you ask, for I was going to search Trenton out when I got in."

"Well, if you see him, please extend an invitation from me again, to write. I can sympathize, a problematic brother. How uncanny Trenton and I should have such in common. I would like to have him here to spend time with us. Get to know him. I am inclined to offer him the rectory if it can be worked out to everyone's satisfaction. It is quite an excellent proposition, the rectory at Swandon. If he is of a mind to come, please bring him along with you when you return."

"I can do that," Gravelle agreed, grinning devilishly. "My God. The thought of Trenton a cleric and preaching on a Sunday is just—I am speechless really. I'll have to come to church regularly, if only for the sport of seeing him up there. I'll gladly drive the five miles to come to church at Gavandon."

"What? You're going to sit in my church and mock the rector? That won't get you any points with—" Graham pointed up with a finger, knowingly.

"That's a given, but worth it maybe." Gravelle grinned. "I'd thought Trenton being my good friend and having a line in might be my only hope, but then again, I'll have to actually attend and make some effort."

"Gravelle, you attend, we see you most every Sunday."

"When I'm here, yes. But more truant than not when in London, and I live there half the

year."

"Feeling some guilt then, eh? What does your good mother have to say about it?"

"Quite a lot actually. She's quite given up on reforming me into anything resembling respectability."

"It's never too late to change if you've a mind to it." Graham offered his hand.

"Farewell then. We'll be at a loss without you. Come back to us soon."

Gravelle took the offered hand and shook it, bowed in deference to Graham's rank, and turned away.

"Safe journey," Graham called after him.

Gravelle did not turn back, but simply lifted a hand in a wave.

WITH The Lion's Crown in his sights, Gravelle felt a welcome relief. A spring squall had been his unpleasant companion for the last few miles, leaving him cold and soaked.

"Mr. Gravelle, welcome." Jacobson eyed his sopping attire sympathetically. "I can put you in your usual room, and send up a hot bath to warm you, if you like."

"Saints yes, Jacobson. It sounds like heaven. It's pissing down something wretched out there, and caught me good and truly."

"Other than the rain, you have been well?"

"Yes, thank you." Gravelle remembered Jacobson's mother was Cook at Gavandon. "You'll be pleased to know your mother is still working her magical talents in the kitchen to perfection," he praised. "I've been two weeks at Gavandon for a house party. In fact I've just come from there. The old place is quite transformed now Rothvale has married."

"I had the pleasure of meeting the new Lady Rothvale. She is very gracious. And I am always pleased to hear my mother is well. It is rare I can get to see her, being so busy with the inn."

When Gravelle saw the blonde beauty at The Lion's Crown, he knew he had seen her before. He just couldn't think of where. Then he saw her little girl, or rather he saw the unique green eyes her child bore, and that pushed him to investigate. She bustled about busily, clearly employed in a position of no little importance. Maybe she was Jacobson's wife. Gravelle knew without a doubt she had not been here the last time he'd stayed overnight, though. He would have remembered.

She saw him staring, and he wondered if she might recognize him. He tilted his head. She responded in kind.

"Have you married, Jacobson?" Gravelle indicated toward the woman with his eyes.

"Ah, no. That is Mrs. Schellman. My account books are now in excellent order thanks to her. We are so busy here; it was time to take on more help. Liken it to the role of a housekeeper at an estate. The Lion was in great need, and she appeared at just the right moment, luckily for me."

Jacobson was unable to hide his admiration for Mrs. Schellman, of that Gravelle was certain. He looked nothing short of a man in love. "Good for you, Jacobson. And her husband? Is he employed here as well?" he asked craftily. He knew he was fishing for more information, but felt that the end justified the means.

Jacobson shook his head. "She is widowed with a young child to support."

While riding on toward London in the mist the following day, Gravelle had plenty of time to think. He remembered. It all came back to him in miserable, depraved detail. The devastation wrought at the time had been brutal, according to Rothvale, who had lived in Town for months after. Jasper Everley had been a heinous beast when he was alive. His cohort, Ralph Odeman, just as beastly. Mrs. Schellman, the object of their wicked attentions back then, seemed to be safe and secure for now.

Two questions remained though.

Why was she in Stapenhill employed as housekeeper for The Lion's Crown?

Did Rothvale know?

Chapter 24

The union of hands and hearts.

Jeremy Taylor ~ XXV Sermons Preached at Golden Grove, 1653

Graham's wish had been granted. The warm sun pouring into his studio, created a feeling of a blanket wrapped around her. "*Chérie*, you are so gorgeous in this setting. I regret that I cannot show this to the world. Not for my mediocre talent, mind you, only for the beauty of you."

This pose was like nothing Imogene thought she would ever do. She was nude. The shawl, draped strategically, was her only garment. She sat with one leg folded under the other, bent at the knee, supporting her resting head. Only the top of her hair showed, since her face was turned down. Her arms met with clasped hands, cradling under the knee, resting on the floor. Nothing blatant was visible—just her arms, legs, shoulders, feet and hands.

She smiled at Graham's words but kept her pose for him. "I find I enjoy these quiet interludes. It gives me time to simply think and reflect."

"What are you thinking about this day, *chérie*?"

"Our baby. What he *or* she will look like, whether he will have your eyes or mine, if she might look like me or you."

"I hope our baby looks just like you, but even if not, our child will be beautiful because of you. I've said it before, you are not only beautiful on the outside to me, your heart is beautiful. What child would not be blessed with such a mother?"

"Now you must stop, my darling. I am *enceinte* and very emotional. Understand I cannot bear too many compliments at once for you know what it does to me, and I don't think you want me crying in this portrait."

"All right, I'll stop. But you should know I can take your tears when I know they be happy ones."

"Tears of joy?"

"Yes." He changed the subject then. "I've had a letter from Gravelle, well if you can call his illegible scrawl writing, that is." Graham chuckled in amusement of his friend. "Anyway, he comes back to us next week, bringing someone with him, a friend. I met him in London just before we married. I like him. He is Lord James Trenton and has taken his holy orders."

"You think he might be for the rectory at Gavandon, then?"

"I do in fact. He would be perfect. However, I need to know him better. He'll spend some time with us and we shall see what comes of it. He knows you, your family, hailing from Essex. His father is Lord Langley?"

"Lord Langley. Of course I know him. He is the most charming elder gentleman, good friends with Papa. When at the funeral he spoke so kindly to me. Always smiling, Lord

Langley is witty and amiable to everybody. He carries sweets for the children in his pockets, delighting in passing them out. He is a Marquess so his younger sons would be addressed as 'Lord.'"

"So you know Lord James then?"

"I have met the Trentons. There are three sons and a daughter. Lord James must be the youngest from what I remember. A composed gentleman, very kind, easy mannered, a little like you, Graham. One of the brothers is very quiet, and the other one is rather rakish. My sister, Philippa, was dancing with that one once, and didn't care for the way he looked at her." She laughed. "I have trouble picturing Mr. Gravelle being good friends with a clergyman."

"You have no idea, *chérie*," he said, agreeing wholeheartedly. "When we are done, I'd like to take you riding. Do you feel up to a ride with me? We'll take it slow and gentle."

"Of course. I would love to go with you and I'm not even going to ask where, for I know it would do no good as you are obviously up to something."

"ALL right, I'll give you a hint, *chérie*." She'd let him enjoy his mystery ride to a destination unknown. It pleased her most when he was playful and delighting in surprising her as he was at the moment. Allowing herself to savor his gesture, she knew it would be good.

"When we were at Everfell and had our tea inside the fairy ring, we didn't have the chance to complete your vision that day, *chérie*. I distinctly remember you wished to lie down in the middle and look for shapes in the clouds. Recall how the sky was clear on that day and you could not?"

"I recall the occasion well, my darling. So you are finishing my fantasy for me then?" Imogene got only a flashy wink from him in answer.

"Let's stop the horses here. We'll walk the rest of the way—it is not far." He jumped down from Triton and assisted her off Terra. "Are you up to it, *chérie*?"

"Of course I am. Stop fussing, please," she commanded in a testy voice but tempered it with a kiss. He smiled in anticipation of disclosing her surprise. She thought he looked like a child, eagerly awaiting a sweet. Wrapping her arm around his, he led her forward.

"An indulgence, *chérie*. Please close your eyes for me? I'll steady you, it's just a bit farther." She knew they were coming to some trees for she recalled the light forest at the top of the rise. He stopped, turned her slightly, wrapped his arms about her so she could lean into him, and breathed into her neck. "You may open them now, *chérie*."

The gasp she uttered began loudly but ended barely audible as all of her breath escaped. "Oh… You made this? For me?" She turned up to him.

He nodded slowly. "Well, Hiram made it with Colin's technical knowledge. Does it please you, *chérie*? I tried to have it done up as close as possible to The Nine Ladies."

"Graham." Imogene knew she needed a moment to absorb what her eyes were seeing. "I—I do love it." She laughed and it came out as sobs, so overcome by the gesture that she had to drop down to the soft grass. Shaking from the happy sobbing, she held up her hands helplessly, completely stunned.

He dropped down beside her and wrapped his arms around her, propping her back against his chest from behind.

"You've made me a fairy ring." She looked around at the grassy glade they were in. "It's so lovely and peaceful here. It's private. I had no idea about this place." She looked up at him again. "Tell me about it? I cannot get up just yet—I want to sit here for a moment and take it all in."

"When you asked if there was such a place at Gavandon, I immediately thought of this site. It is similar, but even better for it is completely surrounded by forest. They did fell some additional trees so the flowers will have more light to bloom." He indicated where the trees had been removed. She saw that Bluebells had naturalized in the glade and would do even better now in the greater exposed sunlight. "I began thinking how we could get big enough stones to make a ring for you, and just couldn't see how it might be done. Then I remembered the stone cairns in Ireland. Instead of one large stone, they are built by piling small stones into a cone. They've built eight stone cairns in a circle."

"Why eight? And why is that cairn built with red stone and the others with black?" She pointed to the one, red stone cairn.

"That one is the north cairn, and opposite it is the south cairn." He showed her. "There is east, there is west, and the four mid-directions between them." He squeezed her arm a little. "It's a gigantic compass rose, *chérie*, like on a map. True in directionality—completely accurate. We, at Gavandon, mark ourselves at the centre of the world." His green eyes glittered in the sun as he explained it to her.

"The Compass. That's what we shall call it." Her voice trembled with emotion. "You built a fairy ring for me…a beautiful, lovely, perfect haven…and at the centre of the world." She leaned into him for support, the moment too poignant for mere words.

"Would you like to search out cloud shapes now, *chérie*? Today we have abundant puffed clouds from which to observe."

She shook her head for she still could not speak.

"No? What can I do for you then?"

"Just hold me…hold on and never let go."

She was rewarded with one of his brilliant smiles. The ones she treasured for all their rarity. "*Oui chérie.*" He kissed her lingeringly. "I'll get the blanket and bring up the horses."

"Can you be as happy as I?" Graham asked her a few minutes later as they lay together on the blanket.

"I believe I must be, my darling. I have you and your love so brilliantly displayed toward me." She pointed with her arm at the stone cairns encircling them. "I have our baby right here as proof," she whispered, pressing his hand to her stomach.

Graham moulded both hands over the fabric of her dress. "I can feel the swell now—it's not soft, but hard." He explored the burgeoning bump of their baby, and seemed completely amazed.

"Mmmm. I am going to get much bigger. I hope you'll still like me then."

Rolling his eyes, he told her, "You really don't have any idea of how beautiful I find you. Like you? I love you, and when you get very big, there'll just be more of you for me to love," he teased, tickling her gently.

She giggled and arched under his hands, causing her breasts to push up from her bodice.

He cupped them both, grinning roguishly. "These are changing too. Lucky me."

"Yes, and very sensitive so a gentle touch, please." Catching the look of alarm on his face, she saw he meant to release her, so quickly reassured him by pressing her hands on top of his to keep them in place. "But you are always gentle and I love your hands touching me."

"Oh, Imogene, I feel…as if we are in our own Camelot, a magical land where everything is perfect, surrounded by goodness and light." His words were joyful but did not come across that way to her at all.

"Why do you say it with melancholy in your voice?"

"Because I am afraid it cannot last, that nothing can stay this perfect. Camelot disappeared into the mist, remember?" He looked longingly at her. "I worry for you, when your time comes."

"Please don't. I will be fine. My sister had no trouble with Gwendolyn's birth, and I have the best doctor in all of England. You worry far too much over me." She kissed him.

"I am sorry, *chérie,* to vex you. I just—if anything happened to you, there would be nothing—no point in anything, anymore." He caught her look of frustration with him, immediately giving in. "I'll stop. Sorry. I realize I'm an idiotic fool and should not speak of such things. I just love you so much. Without you, I am no good. All of this happiness right now is because of you. *You* are my compass."

"As you are for me." She nestled into his side, breathing in his spicy scent. "Graham, you do not credit the many things you do and will do in the future. When you go back to Parliament, you will help get the emancipation bill through. Your signature will be on that document, someday. You'll get your national portrait gallery as well. Your name will be mentioned as a founder of that worthy institution. I know it, just as I know we'll have our fifty years, at least fifty, probably more than that. By then, I'll be grey and wrinkled and you'll be deaf and gouty, and we'll still be happy, here in our own little Camelot."

"Promise?"

"Absolutely. No more sad feelings or thoughts. You must relax and enjoy this time before the baby comes for you will be very busy once she is here."

"Now you think it a girl?"

"Oh, I don't know. I go back and forth. Some days I see a little girl and other days a boy. But either way, get ready to be interrupted in your work." She grinned and nodded.

"What do you mean?"

"Remember your vision? You said you could see a little blonde angel stamping her foot, demanding her Papa stop whatever he is doing and take her for a ride on her pony."

"I remember." He smiled. "I cannot wait for that."

"I like to imagine her with long, straight, dark hair and green eyes." She held his face and made him look at her until she could see the worry had left him.

"All right, *chérie.* You have cheered me. I am fine now. Sorry for my little fit of the blue devils." He kissed her several times, pressing his lips to her cheeks, eyes and nose. "Would you like your tea now? It probably won't be very hot though."

"Lukewarm tea, a fairy ring in the shape of a giant compass rose, bluebells blooming about me, a handsome husband—*my* compass—beside me. Yes, I believe I'll take the whole lot."

"Right, then. Allow me to serve you, my lady." He got up to retrieve the travelling pack from Triton so he could lay out their tea. "Why don't you search for your cloud shapes while I set this out," he called over his shoulder.

"I don't think so," she remarked boldly. "I'd much rather watch you prepare our tea. It is a far superior view than any old cloud shape could ever be." Her eyes tracked him.

"Watch yourself, *chérie.* Looking at me like that and I

doubt either of us will get any tea today."

"WELCOME to Gavandon." Graham greeted James Trenton warmly. "How excellent you are here, Trenton. Thank you for considering us."

"It is my pleasure, Lord Rothvale. Thank you for the invitation."

"Please, just Rothvale." He offered a seat. "Surely you know why you are here, so I'll get right to the point. You impressed me when we met in Town last winter, and I was struck by your sensible manner in approaching your calling."

Trenton tilted his head in acceptance of the compliment. "When it comes to God's work, I am not a fervent. I would describe myself as much more pragmatic. Other options are open—but this is the path I have chosen. I am a third son and have the support of my good father, yet I need to do something worthwhile with my life."

"Very noble, Trenton. We have a fine rectory here called Swandon, vacant for five years now. The house is lovely. As rector you would be entitled to tenant tithes as well as the living, which is substantial, for your lifetime. The chapel, The Church of Saint Clare, has been empty for far too long. I need someone to take it on and see to the needs of the people of the parish. Have you other prospects you are considering?"

Trenton shook his head. "To be honest, Rothvale, I haven't pursued it. My ordination is complete, but my family has had need of me recently. There were some troubles…" he trailed off.

Gravelle said there was a problem brother. I've been in your boots. "I understand. Family comes first. But what are you looking for, Trenton?"

"A place with good people where I can help those in need without a great deal of emphasis on sermonizing. I intend to make mine short; you'll not get long-winded moral lessons out of me for it is not my way. I do not seek to chastise persons for their mistakes. Rather I see myself as avowing to live a good life and to be a help to others in their pursuit of the same. I can foresee there are those who will not approve of me for that."

Graham grinned at him. "Well, I would approve for we are of a very like mind, Trenton, and that is exactly why I've asked you to come. You suit me. I would be honored to have you serve Gavandon Parish. This is a good thing. Since we have been vacant for so long, everyone has forgotten the old rector and you'll not be compared against anyone and found lacking."

"I must say, it all sounds very appealing, Rothvale. Having a patron who is of a like mind would be a relief. I have doubted one such as you would exist at all." He looked pleased. "I couldn't get into too much trouble for the short sermons if that is what my patron prefers."

"Exactly. And I must confess that the fact you fence is another mark in your favour. When I am in need of spiritual counsel I know how it can be attended to." Graham's eyes lit up. "Would you like to see my fencing studio?"

"Rothvale, I would be delighted."

A fortnight later they gave their goodbyes to Lord James Trenton on the steps of Gavandon. Graham and Imogene remained until his coach was beyond the main gate. "Do you think he'll accept your offer?" Imogene asked him.

"I greatly hope so, *chérie,* I really, really do." Graham was optimistic though. "James Trenton is the perfect man for the job. After two weeks in his company, I have no doubts about that. I knew it really, the night I met him in London at the fencing academy. That's how sure I am. He has asked for time to consider our offer and I am happy to oblige him for I don't want any other."

"What if he declines?" Imogene put her hand into his.

Graham reflected before answering her. "I'll be very disappointed, *chérie.* We must have faith, yes?" He took up her hand and kissed it.

"He will accept. I believe he will, Graham. I have good feelings about him and I can see how important he is to you." She touched his cheek. "So it must be so."

He nodded perfunctorily. "What are you going to do for the rest of the day, *chérie*?"

"You know, I feel quite lazy, I believe I'll sit in the solarium and write in my journal for a bit."

"What of Elle and Cariss? Where have they got to?"

"Riding. I don't think I am up for the kind of ride they had in mind. John said, 'nothing too vigorous.'"

"He's right, you know." Pulling her close, touching her belly, he caressed the swell. "You do an awful lot and are always so busy around here. Writing in the solarium sounds like an excellent plan to me." Neatly avoiding the appearance of fussing over her, he was learning, and feeling a trifle smug as he kissed the top of her head. "I'll come find you in a while, and if you like we'll take an easy walk."

"Sounds perfect." She looked him over carefully, probably not fooled at all by his veiled attempt to impel her. "My darling." She winked and blew him a kiss before gliding away.

Graham really looked forward to Trenton taking the rectory as it had been unfilled for so long. In truth, he felt guilty for neglecting to appoint someone but couldn't bear the thought of a pompous windbag up in the pulpit each Sunday, torturing him with moral fanaticism. He could picture the waving hands and pious chastisement with too clear of a vision for his liking. A sycophant was just as dreaded. The bowing and scraping some clerics performed for their patrons made him ill. He'd be unable to tolerate such behaviours. Trenton was nothing of the sort. Graham realized he was unique among the clergy. He also genuinely liked him, and knew had they met sooner, James Trenton would have been a friend anyway. His family troubles seemed to be monopolizing his time for the present but Trenton had agreed to give his answer by the end of summer. All they could do was wait.

Graham would always be grateful he entered the solarium quietly when he went to find Imogene an hour later.

For the sight that met his eyes nearly brought him down to the floor.

He was a painter in his heart and in his training. He knew that what he saw was significant. If there was ever a moment in his artistic life that moved him, this was it. He knew what must be done. Nothing could have stopped him.

Her image must be captured, preserved, as she looked in the moment. At all costs, this impression must be rendered in paint and canvas.

Forcing his body to calm, Graham made a mental picture of her form, sweeping slowly over each part, to record her in his mind. That done, he stepped quietly out into the hall.

And then he ran.

Ben was dispatched as quickly as he could be located.

"Ben, go to Mallerton's and bring him back here. Tell him he needs a canvas and supplies to sketch. Quickly! As fast as you can. Tell him it is most urgent!"

"Yes, my lord." Ben nodded perfunctorily.

"When you bring him, he's to go to the solarium, but tell him to enter very quietly. Lady Rothvale is sleeping and I do not want her disturbed."

Graham raced to his studio to get the camera obscura.

Imogene was still asleep when he re-entered the solarium, and gratefully, in the same position. The first step was to close the shutters to darken the room. Next, he lit the candle opposite the lens inside the box. The paper was moved slowly, incrementally, until her form appeared…in all its stunning glory. He barely breathed as he copied out her image, the draping of her gown, and the shadows. Graham was aware Tristan entered the room at some point, but they did not speak. Tristan set up his canvas, drawing right alongside his friend. They worked that way for an hour, until she awakened.

Both men blew out sighs of relief, understanding that enough of her pose has been copied, to recreate it faithfully for another sitting. "Graham?" Imogene was mildly surprised as she stretched out her limbs. "Tristan, what brings you in here?"

"Summoned to capture your image as you slept in the chair, my dear." Tristan eyed her thoughtfully. "I may do the painting, Imogene, but Graham is the master when it comes to contriving a scene." He shook his head in disbelief. "We've been frantically tracing you while you slept so we might recreate the scene. It is like nothing I have ever painted before."

"Tell me," she implored.

"I'll let your husband do the honors." Tristan bowed and

quitted the room.

Graham tried to explain but knew it was pointless. "*Chérie*, I hardly have the words…"

JUNE was swallowed up as the warm, idyllic days floated along. Imogene wore her jonquil day gown and sat for the sleeping portrait. It didn't even seem to be much of an imposition for her either. Many times, she simply fell asleep anyway, providing ample opportunities for Tristan to get it completed.

The significance of the portrait was Imogene's pose. Her left arm was bent and supported her head, while her right arm lay across her stomach. The shawl draped over her middle, obscuring the pregnancy. Both of her knees were bent, her left leg tucked underneath her so that her left arm could rest upon it. Her right foot pointed at the floor, supporting that bent knee. Zuly rested beside the chair. Her lap desk, pen and journal, abandoned on the floor.

Tristan pushed himself.

He had never painted draped clothing in such a manner.

He poured all of his skill into this composition, knowing instinctively that he must do so, and do it well.

Chapter 25

...Ransomed, healed, restored, forgiven,
Who like me his praise should sing?

Henry Francis Lyte ~ Hymn, 1834

For the first time in a long while, Graham and Imogene would be all alone in the coming days. Elle had already departed, returning to Everfell. Colin had finished at Trinity, and was now in Ireland at Donadea. Arrangements were made for Gravelle to escort Cariss to halfway at Stapenhill, delivering her to her father, Sir Oliver. Gravelle had offered eagerly, which was not much of a surprise, saying he was for Town regardless, and would be honored to ensure her safety along the road.

It was on Gravelle's return from London that he stayed once more at The Lion's Crown before heading on to Gavandon.

"Gravelle, you are bloody good for all your beastly size. You are agile, man," Graham complimented, breathing heavily.

"Keeps me fit so I don't run to fat. I'm grateful for you, Rothvale. The fencing is diversion from the boredom at least, if not your brooding company," he joked.

"Don't try to be clever, Gravelle, it's not where your talents lie."

"You speak true, we both know. And I jest of course. You're not nearly so broody now you're ensconced with your bride and playing house with her. To the outside world, you appear quite happy, my friend."

Graham looked thoughtfully at him before replying. "You know, there was a time I thought I could never be happy again. My brother saw to that." He sighed. "Gravelle, you remember what he was like. You were around enough to know of the disaster he wreaked."

"Ah yes. I've been forgetting to mention that I saw that girl, the one he took with Odeman…" Gravelle gave him a level look. "I am sure it was her. Pretty, blonde, and she had a little girl with her, bearing the same green eyes—"

"Where? Tell me where she is, Gravelle!" Graham bellowed at him, his heart pounding within his chest.

"What the hell? You're as pale as a sheet."

"The girl, Gravelle! Agnes. Where did you see her?"

"She's at The Lion's Crown with Jacobson. As his housekeeper. I thought you might know about it, considering your connections to Jacobso—"

"They are well?" Graham interrupted, almost afraid to ask.

"Quite well, from what I could tell. I think Jacobson's besotted with her from all indications."

Graham sat down shakily. "Praise God. Gravelle, this is the best news. Agnes and Clara, well and safe." He stood up abruptly. "I must tell Imogene right away. Will you come, and speak of all you know?"

"What must you tell me?" Imogene asked charmingly, standing at the studio entrance.

Graham rushed over, embracing her. "*Chérie*, Agnes and Clara have been found."

IT was decided that Graham would go to Stapenhill right away. Gravelle offered to accompany him in support, which was heartily accepted. Graham would have to be away from Imogene for a few days though. He didn't like leaving her on her own with no other family present. She suggested Tristan might be willing to stay with her, and that they could use the time to collaborate on the fairy-tale paintings for the nursery.

"Where will Agnes go now?" Imogene asked directly. "Is it safe to have them so far away, Graham? They need protection. Who is to stop some other disreputable from trying to take advantage of her again?"

He kissed her on her forehead. "You are so wise and kind in your heart. And you are right, of course. For now, I would like to propose for them to come and live at Wellick. I have spoken to John, and he has agreed to take Agnes for nurse training at the hospital. A new home can be arranged for them in Wellick, and a nanny to care for the child when Agnes is doing her nursing and be a companion to her, if she agrees to it." He tilted his head in question, wanting to know her true opinion. "What do you think, *chérie*? Does this all sound like a reasonable plan? I want your blessing in this."

"And you shall have it. Thank you, Graham, for sharing all with me. I appreciate your trust in allowing me to know about everything for I think you are doing the right thing." She touched his face. "My husband is the best of men."

He pulled her into his embrace fiercely, his voice breaking. "I will miss you so much. I want you to rest and not overwork yourself on the nursery. Please let Tristan entertain you. I've asked him to move into the house while I'm away. John and Philippa will visit on Thursday as well. Promise me you'll take good care of yourself, *chérie?*"

"Of course I will, and you must do the same."

He knew they were both feeling the pangs of parting on this, their first separation since their marriage. "I suppose there's a first time for everything, *chérie.* And so this is the first time I must leave you. I hate that I must." And he truly did hate it but duty called him and so he didn't have a choice. Life was built from duty as he had learned from childhood.

"As do I, my darling. But, the sooner you go—"

"—the sooner I can return to you," he whispered against her lips.

GRAHAM attempted to quell the dread weighing heavy on his chest. He had not seen Agnes for six years. His last image of her had been horrifying, with her traumatized and desperate to cover herself. He had been too enraged in his efforts to beat Jasper and Odeman down, and might even have killed them; he was so out of his mind. By the time Colin had pulled him off, Agnes had fled, and he had never seen her again.

Not a soul was in sight when they rode up onto the property and secured the horses. Entering the inn, Graham was surprised to find it so quiet. "Hello?" he inquired.

"Hello, sir." A beautiful child stepped out from behind the counter and stared stoically. "You have green eyes like me," she said as she looked up at him.

Graham's heart melted at the sight of her. There was no doubt in his mind that she was of his family blood. The resemblance was too strong. He bent down on his knee so he could speak to her close up. "You are Clara," he whispered in awe.

"How do you know my name, sir?"

"I know you because I am your uncle…your uncle, Graham."

"I don't have a uncle, just a mamma." She shook her head at him.

"Yes, Clara, you do." He nodded solemnly. "My brother was your…father." Graham gave her a sad smile and put his hand atop her blonde curls.

"Did my father look like you do?"

"In some ways we looked alike."

"You look sad."

"People tell me that all the time," he said wryly. "Seeing you doesn't make me sad, though, for I've been trying to find you and your mamma. For a long time I've been searching and here you are. I am very glad to finally meet you, Clara, very glad indeed. I want to see your mamma, and talk to her."

"Mr. Jacobson and Mamma are talking right now. They talk in his study all the time."

Gravelle snorted a laugh at that, directing a knowing look to Graham. "Told you," he said smugly.

Clara turned her countenance toward Gravelle then. "I have seen you before."

"You remember well, young miss. I was here but a few days ago," Gravelle answered Clara with a wink.

"This is my friend, Mr. Gravelle. He is the one who told me where I could find you and your mamma—"

"Clara! Who are you speak—" Agnes froze as soon as she came into the room and saw Graham. The colour drained away from her face and her bottom lip began to tremble. She held out her hand to Clara. "Sir…I beg you…do not hurt her. I promise I did not say a word. I have told no one, just as you required."

Graham's heart ached, knowing Agnes was afraid of him.

She stood trembling, silent tears trailing down her cheeks pleading for Clara to come to her. "Agnes. Please be of ease, I mean you no harm. I have come to help you, to restore your support. Whatever wrong has been done you, was not of my will or of my knowledge. I have been searching for you for months now. Please tell me what has happened to you. How did you come to be here?"

Jacobson entered the room.

His surprise at the persons assembled was evident and the air in the room crackled with cautious tension.

"I would like to know the same," Jacobson asked quietly, levelling a steely gaze. He was being careful, while at the same time, letting the men know he had an interest. "What kind of fiend abandons a woman and child on the highway?"

One Ralph Odeman I would venture a guess. "Jacobson," Graham greeted him. "Thank God it was you who took them in. I cannot express my relief at what you have done."

"Lord Rothvale." He inclined his head. "I have offered lodging and employment to Mrs. Schellman. With all due respect, my lord, why have you cause to be grateful to me? What is she to you?"

I deserve that. "How much do you know, Jacobson?"

"Very little, apparently." Jacobson looked to Agnes who was still silently weeping.

Graham looked at each of them with resolve. "We must talk. There is much to say and much to make right. It has been put off for far too long and cannot wait another moment of time…"

"TRISTAN, these are lovely. My favourite is the unicorn by the lake."

"I think I fancy Saint George fighting off his dragon best," he countered. "By the way, you're doing an excellent job on the sky. Quite the painter you are, Imogene."

"In truth I am enjoying myself. It is satisfying to do something creative for a change. Won't Graham be surprised?"

And he was.

Because he stood in the doorway unobserved, watching them as they worked on the murals for the nursery. Tristan was drawing in a landscape while Imogene painted in blue skies. From behind she looked just as she always did; nobody would even know she was with child. He'd missed her dreadfully this past week. Even now, he had to will himself to find restraint to keep from rushing over and grabbing her. All he wanted was to feel her against him, to breathe in her scent, to kiss her. She completed him, in every way. Now he was back with her was proof, for his body knew and reacted accordingly. The ache in his heart from being parted vanished instantly, replaced by the joy in seeing her well and happy.

"He is indeed, *very* surprised. My wife a painter? How was I to know?"

She turned at his voice. "Oh, my darling!" she cried, rushing into his arms, paintbrush in hand. "I missed you so much," she breathed into his neck.

He looked down at her belly, and touched it with both hands. "You've grown since I've been away," he said, suddenly feeling cheated by missing that time with her.

"Yes, I am growing huge. John said I was big for my sixth month. I dread to think how much bigger I'll get."

"You're beautiful," he whispered because Tristan was still in the room with them. "I am so happy to be home. Finding you well and enjoying yourself makes our reunion all the sweeter." He looked toward the door in silent communication.

"Tristan, that is all for me today," she stated, depositing her paintbrush into a jar. "I'll resume my part tomorrow." She smiled at her friend. "The pictures are perfect, Tristan, just lovely."

"Yes, they look excellent, Tristan. And thank you for being here with Imogene while I was away. You have kept her well, and for that I will be ever grateful, my friend. I am in your debt." Graham bowed his head.

"I'll be sure to mark that down in case I ever have need of money," he shot back cleverly, but returned the bow with his own and a grin. They all understood so words weren't really necessary.

"And know that you are welcome to stay on here while you are at work in the nursery, if it pleases you," Graham offered before turning away.

Graham heard Tristan chuckling as he and Imogene fled together, knowing that he wouldn't have bothered to wait for Tristan's response to his offer should he have even given Graham an answer.

WHEN Imogene felt the pull of a climax taking hold of her body she squeezed her inner muscles as hard as she could around Graham's cock. His eyes flared as he pumped into her from above. "You feel so good wrapped around me… I—can't—be—away—from—you—Imogene!" He grunted each word with a thrust as his hands gripped her hips, holding her firm and open.

Imogene relished every slick plunge and dragging pull of his hard cock as he made love to her. He was the perfect blend of careful mixed with desperate in her opinion. She loved having her man desperate. She loved that she was responsible for making him that way.

He told her in whispers and on kisses what she did to him, how much he loved her, and how much he loved to pleasure her.

Everything he did to her in bed drove her wild. He always had. She was a slave to needing him like this.

But Graham was mindful of her condition as he pulled her right to the edge of the bed and took her from a standing position against the side so he wouldn't crush her belly.

"I am going to—" She lost her words when she felt his fingers slide back and forth over her nub. That was all it took and she exploded.

"Ahhhh…Graaaaaaham…"

"Yes, my beauty, you are perfect when you shatter. I could watch you do this every day and never get tired of it." He kept going, thrusting harder as she crashed wave over wave with an explosive climax.

She felt his sex swell inside her and reached down between them to take his bollocks in her hand. They felt tight as she gave a squeeze to his male flesh and he moaned in pleasure.

"Yes," he shouted with one last powerful thrust as he found his release and his seed erupted, flooding into her.

Their eyes connected in that moment of intimacy, and all of the love they felt for each other was gifted and received. And it was so good. SO good. So right.

Later, when he'd crawled up on the bed so he could hold her, and had her cradled in his arms, did Imogene finally feel completely at peace.

"It's heaven to be back in our bed with you against me."

He stroked over her naked body reverently, his hand coming to rest on their baby.

"Mmmm, I was just thinking the same thing. I will get my forty winks tonight finally, because I've learned I am no good on my own trying to sleep in this huge bed without you." Imogene shifted to her back so she could see him. "You were greatly missed." She reached up to comb through his hair with her fingers as she loved to do, smoothing it behind his ears before bringing a finger to trace around his lips. "I love you."

"Those are the sweetest words I ever hear from your lips." Graham closed his eyes for a moment. "As painful as it was to be parted from you, I must say it does feel very fine to know I was missed, and my welcome home was most excellent too." He nuzzled her neck. "*Chérie*, how much longer can we do this? Is it safe for you and the baby?" She did not answer him, just flashed what she hoped was an alluring grin at him. "Acts of love—what did John say about it?" His expression told her he was clearly embarrassed posing the question.

She laughed at him. "Are you blushing, my darling?" More giggles escaped her. "John said nothing about that, and I did not think to ask. He said I was healthy and strong, and the baby thrives, kicking and tumbling about inside me. I know…why don't you ask John yourself? I would suggest you do it in a letter so that he cannot see your blushes."

Her words coaxed silent laughter from him. "You love to tease me, don't you, *chérie*?"

"I do so dearly love to, my darling, if only for the reward of one of your beautiful smiles, or to hear you laugh. Your smiles and your laugh are precious to me."

"Well then, you'll be happy to hear I'll have much more to smile about now."

"So your trip went well? Tell me everything, Graham. I

am dying to hear all of your news."

Imogene lay back in the pillows, watching her husband's handsome face as he retold the events of finding Agnes and Clara.

"...Apparently, he convinced Agnes he acted in my stead. Odeman, being Jasper's friend, told Agnes I had asked him to make her and Clara disappear because I feared the exposure of the secret now I had married. Agnes went along with it because he threatened harm to Clara." Graham looked freer as he spoke, as if a great burden had been lifted. And for him, it must have truly felt that way. Imogene could see he was lighter and feeling less fraught now the painful, gaping wound from his past was in the process of healing. *My wonderful husband, so caring.* The scar would always remain of course, but with absolution and wrong being put right for Agnes and Clara, the debilitating pain was decreasing.

"I left them well and happy."

"And they will now live closer, at Wellick?"

Graham shook his head. "No, *chérie,* they will not. Agnes will not come to Wellick."

"Why ever not? Where will she go?"

"Nowhere. Agnes will stay at The Lion's Crown," he said cryptically, "as Mrs. Jacobson."

At Imogene's shocked surprise, he happily told her the rest.

"As soon as I suggested Agnes and Clara be settled at Wellick, Jacobson immediately asked to speak privately with her. It soon became apparent he has found his lady love in Agnes and was most determined to keep her. He asked for her hand and she accepted. Clara has also ensnared his heart. I was most impressed by his affection for her."

"They fell in love," Imogene said dreamily.

"They did indeed and will be very well matched. I have a good feeling about them."

"And what of Ralph Odeman? Any trace of him?"

"No. He may have left the country for all we know. After he dumped Agnes and Clara on the highway, he probably went on to London, and from there, who knows? Formal charges were filed with the magistrates. If he shows his face he'll be charged with fraud, extortion, kidnapping and deserting his regiment. I hope the Army catches him first because they will hang him."

"And Clara?"

"Everything's settled. I went on to London and met with my solicitor to have the financials arranged. Clara will inherit a legacy, in her own right when she comes of age. It is their wish she takes the name of Jacobson, and that he adopt her as a daughter."

"How wonderful. What a remarkable man is Mr. Jacobson, hmmm?"

"Indeed. He is a fine man. To express my gratitude I have given him The Lion's Crown. He holds the title free and clear now. I told him to consider it a wedding present. Jacobson well deserves it for all he has done over the years, and most recently with Agnes. They will do well there, and make a good life together. And we will have connections with them for his mother is here, and we will see them whenever we stay at the inn as we travel to Town."

"Graham?"

"Hmmm?"

"You make me proud."

He kissed her lingeringly for a long time.

…HE was swimming. Swimming in the warm ocean that was Imogene. He could no longer tell where he ended and she began. And he did not care either. He just wanted to float in the sensation of being surrounded by her…loved by her…lost in her. This was his dream and it was perfect. But then everything changed. She drifted. He swam toward her, but just when he got close enough to touch her, she drifted again. Determined to get to her, he tried over and over to reach her, to pull her to him, to save her. But he never could. No matter how many times he swam to her, he was unable to grasp onto her to bring her back…

Graham awoke from the nightmare in a sweat. In panic he reached out his hand for Imogene. She was there. He felt her warmth and could hear her sounds of sleep. The unique scent that belonged only to her filled his head. He willed his heart to slow and breathed deeply to calm his thundering pulse, telling himself everything was fine, and as it should be. It was only a dream…

He remembered her words from earlier and contemplated all of the diverse emotions of the past days. The enormous relief. The gladness in seeing that Agnes and Clara were happy and well. The contentment of knowing Imogene thought well of him.

Graham knew he was blessed…in so many ways...he was a man blessed.

Chapter 26

And she forgot the stars, the moon, and sun,
And she forgot the blue above the trees,
And she forgot the dells where waters run…
And the new morn she saw not; but in peace
She had no knowledge when the day was done…
And moistened it with tears unto the core.

John Keats ~ Isabella, 1820

Imogene dabbed on the white paint delicately in places, thicker in other parts. Pleased with her efforts, she knew her skill at painting clouds was definitely improving. She had taken to studying some of the landscapes hanging in the house to observe the technique used by the artists to paint in the skies. Working in the nursery these past two weeks had been enjoyable. Graham had even joined in the fun, and was contributing a scene of a princess speaking earnestly to a toad. He had wanted the princess to have her colouring, but she convinced him to paint a dark-haired, green-eyed, beguiling beauty instead.

"Time for luncheon," Graham announced. "We all need a break I think."

"Sounds like an excellent plan to me," Imogene said, stepping backward to view her progress as she ruefully rubbed her lower back. "I can now appreciate the hard work you artists devote to a project."

"Are you hurting, *chérie*?" Graham frowned in concern. "You are finished painting for the day," he said determinedly. "I can see your back is bothering you. You need to be off your feet and I want you to rest after luncheon, agreed?"

"Tristan, tell him not to fuss, would you?"

"I will keep my ideas to myself, thank you. I think I am intelligent enough to know that staying well out of your marital rumblings is very much in my best interest," Tristan retorted wryly. He turned toward her and gave a smirk, but then gentled his expression. "You have been hard at your work for a long time though, my dear. I have to agree with your husband this time."

"Traitor!" She backed up another step and then turned to set her brush into a jar. As she did, her foot tangled in the drop cloth, setting her off balance. She flung out her arms to compensate, catching nothing but air as she fell backward.

Time slowed down excruciatingly as she saw everything move in slowed motion.

Graham and Tristan both lunged at her, intent upon catching her before she struck the floor.

The sickening sound of flesh hitting against a hard surface was horrifying, as was the involuntary groan that expelled from her throat. Both sounds telling them they were too late.

Imogene felt a sharp pain deep inside, almost like a rending, but it went away just as quickly. Shock at her situation caused her to suck in deep pulls of air. *I am all right. The baby is all right. All is well. It has to be!*

"Holy hell! Imogene!" Graham hovered, hands shaking, almost like he was afraid to touch her lest he do more damage. "I could not get to you fast enough. Are you in pain?" He brought a hand to his mouth in fear. "What can I do for you, *chérie*?" Tristan stared down at her, his eyes flaring wildly.

"Just one sharp pain but now it's gone," she panted, holding her belly. "I am fine. I *will* be completely fine," she said forcefully, willing herself to believe it. "I'm sorry, Graham. I lost my footing…"

Her resolve crumbled, fear getting the upper hand for a moment before she crushed it down. *No! I refuse to give in to fear. Everything is fine and will be well!* She chanted the reminders to herself over and over, unwilling to accept anything horrible would happen.

Graham studied her intently, his face changing through many different expressions of emotion. Imogene understood exactly, because she was feeling it right along with him. He seemed to gather his wits and took charge of the situation. "Tristan, go find Mrs. Griffin and have Brancroft sent for immediately!" Tristan was out the door before Graham even finished speaking. "*Chérie*, let me get you off the floor first. Will that be all right, do you think?"

"Yes. Help me up! I am going to be just fine. Everything will be all right." Imogene figured she must believe in it if she wanted it to come true.

Graham drew her up and helped her to a chair first where she shakily took stock of her person. She felt no pain or anything untoward, no broken bones or apparent damage. She felt normal. The baby kicked as if on cue to tell her everything was fine. Relief poured through her body, and she smiled at her husband. "I am well, Graham," she nodded. "The baby just kicked. I have to be well…and I will be," she told him in a quivering voice.

Graham pressed his lips to her forehead and held them there for a moment. "Yes, you will. I know you will be fine. Let me carry you to bed. You should lie down now, *chérie*."

"Yes...probably a good idea. Thank you, my darling." Imogene tried to quell her worry, forcing herself to relax and lean against the strong chest of her husband as he carried her to bed.

"I cannot find any sign of distress to the baby or indication Imogene is harmed. The next four and twenty hours are important though. It would be prudent for her to get as much rest as possible, Graham." John Brancroft spoke directly, but gently. "If she were to deliver now, the outcome would be bleak; the baby's lungs are just too underdeveloped to breathe properly. You understand?" Graham nodded solemnly. "I gave her a bit of laudanum and she is sleeping peacefully. I could sense she was very upset and worried and that is not good for her right now."

"Thank you, John." Graham paced in his study. "I just couldn't get to her in time. It was insanity to allow her to be painting like that!" He berated himself.

"Graham, she could have fallen on the way down to dinner. It is common at this stage for women to be unsteady on their feet. She must be more careful. No more falls."

"Can you stay tonight, John? I'd feel so much more at ease with everything..."

"Of course, you need not even ask."

IT happened in the middle of the night.

Their fairy tale ended in tragedy, their hopes and dreams shattered, and there was nothing they could do to change it.

Graham woke to the sound of Imogene crying out in

pain, their bed wet. Everything felt wrong and he knew fear, deep, paralyzing fear, the kind of fear that dripped down into the very core of his bones.

"What is happening, *chérie*? Tell me!" Bolting up from the bed, he lit the lamp and held it over them, pulling back the covers. The bed was soaked and there was blood as well. "No, no, no, Imogene. What—what? Are you—"

"Get John! It hurts. Ohhh, dear God, it hurts!" She held herself down low between her legs and sobbed. "No! No…nooooo! It's too soon! Too soon, too soon, too soon," she chanted the last, hysterically.

These were the words Graham would remember always with regret and sadness whenever he heard them. These were the words that would haunt him in his dreams, when he tried to forget. 'Too soon…too soon…too goddam soon.'

"Imogene dear, drink this. It will take away the pain and relax you. I am trying to stop the baby from coming." John directed her firmly, although Graham could tell she barely registered his instructions.

He told Graham his main concern was for Imogene. And he had very good reason to feel that way. She was in shock, hysterical from the fear of giving birth too early, well aware that her baby, if born now, would have no chance at survival. John explained he didn't hold much faith in the ability to stop the birth. Clearly, her waters had broken, and her body was readying for the inevitable. Even so, he dosed her heavily with laudanum, knowing that she would be spared from facing the worst of what was to come.

Graham stayed bravely by her side, even once she was unconscious. He watched all of it, his heart breaking for her, and for himself. Mrs. Griffin and Hester were also there helping and assisting John, but it was into Graham's hands that he placed the baby when it was delivered.

Even through the devastating reality of the sad outcome, Graham was still awed by the miracle of life. Thus, they were all surprised by the words John next spoke, "Twins! Another baby is coming. She is carrying twins…"

HOW would he tell her? How would he say the words to her that would annihilate her world?

How did he do that to the person he loved more than anyone on this earth—

But he did do it, because there was no one else who had the right. Even though his heart was breaking in two, he would tell his beloved. And he would mourn with her.

Graham was with her in their room when Imogene awoke for the first time. She took one look at him and he could see the ice-cold fear taking root.

"My baby, Graham? My baby?" She grabbed at her belly as she remembered.

Graham moved to hold her, and tried to whisper the words he knew she must hear, the most difficult thing he'd ever faced in his life.

Her anguished cries carried out of the room, down the corridor, through the house and to the gardens outside.

The pall of death was heavy like a fog, shrouding Gavandon and cloaking it in sorrow. Their bucolic realm retreated into the mist, as if even the house and grounds themselves could not face the pain of its occupants, and had to turn away from them in grief.

IMOGENE'S mourning was profound, and after the initial heartache over the loss of her babies was felt, fear turned alarmingly for her health.

She would not eat. On the third day she stopped speaking. In her sleep, she suffered terrible nightmares. Laudanum was given to help her sleep. Her melancholy grew, spreading like a weed that takes over and completely covers all in its path. She became unreachable, lost in a world not known to the rest of them.

Elle came to stay at Gavandon. Visits from Jemima Burleigh and Philippa were frequent, but for everyone who loved her, their worry grew with each passing day.

Imogene could not face the pain of her loss. She could not go forward until such a time had come to pass that she was able to face it.

Graham lived in a state of continual panic, the effects of which made him ill.

He understood his wife was slipping away and was frantic to stop its progress. He was afraid to let her out of his sight, reasoning that if he stayed by her, he could hold on and keep her from falling deeper into the darkness.

The dream he had dreamt of her floating away from him was now his horrific reality. Even so, he was reluctant to force her to face the painful events, fearing she would slip over the edge and be forever lost to him. Imogene did not ask him about that night and he did not speak of what he had seen or experienced.

Zuly was the one link that remained intact. She was able somehow to breach the fortress protecting Imogene, to move freely in both worlds. Imogene did not speak to her at first, but sought her company, stroking her soft fur, seeming to take comfort in her companionship. Zuly was kept with Imogene at all times, hoping she could draw her out of the iron grip the blackness held over her.

Eventually Graham had to cope with the panic. It was a primitive reaction—the body simply taking over in order to survive.

He became a madman possessed with physical, exhaustive work, and took to labouring in the fields on the estate. He dressed himself in tenant work clothes each morning and went out and dug ditches. He ploughed fields and brought in harvests, working most of the day, stopping only to eat enough to keep his body functioning.

In the evenings he came into the house, cleansed away the dirt and sweat of his labours, and went to Imogene. He sat with her. Read to her. Brushed her hair. He bathed her and agonized at the sight of her beautiful body so thin from not eating. It broke his heart. Graham painted too, staying up very late into the night to work in his studio after she slept.

Imogene was passive and unresponsive to most of what he did. She accepted his closeness, but was oblivious to all emotional interaction. Byron's books were read to her, as well as old letters. Her body was there with him, but her mind was entirely somewhere else.

Imogene allowed Hester to dress her and attend to her needs. She began to eat on her own after two frightening weeks of this behaviour. Finally, she began talking again but conversation had to be initiated since she did not volunteer to speak on her own.

Graham consulted with John, who advised him on the subject of melancholia in women after child loss. John felt sure it was the multiple pregnancy that caused the premature birth. The trauma of her hard fall had been too great to keep her birth waters from breaking with two babies adding stress to an already stretched membrane. He pronounced Imogene perfectly recovered from the birth, physically at least. John was optimistic her spirit would rebound in due time with the loving support of her family, when she was ready.

COLIN approached his brother's study carefully as soon as he arrived. He too, dreaded what would await him on this visit home to Gavandon. He knocked.

"Come in, Colin, I saw you ride up." His brother's voice sounded broken, reminding him of another time of loss and wretchedness.

When Colin stepped inside the study he could see how Graham just sat with his back to the door, brooding as he looked out at the beautifully manicured grounds sweeping up to the tree line. His older brother, who he'd looked up to for his whole life, was morose. "I can't reach her, Colin. She lives in a world of her own making," he said slowly without turning away from the window.

Colin put a hand on his shoulder. "She'll get better, Graham. She needs…she needs to face it." He said it gently, for he knew Graham was hanging by the merest of threads.

"You cannot understand the pain she feels. She's not able to face it yet. She is not ready, and I cannot allow her further hurt."

"I want to see her."

"She's in the solarium. I'll take you."

"Elle says she is greatly changed, and is very worried."

"We are all worried, Colin," Graham said sorrowfully as they walked. "Be gentle, Brother. She is fragile. You will see what I mean."

Colin nodded, alarmed at how changed Graham was as he took in his disposition. He looked like he'd aged ten years. For the first time in his life, Colin thought his brother looked…old.

"*Chérie*, look who has come to see you." Graham gently roused her from the chaise.

Imogene slowly turned glassy eyes toward the door. It took a moment for recognition to register. "Colin." She offered a lazy smile. "Shouldn't you be at Trinity? How could you get away?"

"No, I finished up at Trinity, remember? Now I just do research for Sir William Hershel." He sat down and picked up her hand. Her skin felt cold.

"You are so brilliant, Colin. You find stars in the heavens and give them names…" She looked wistful like she was miles away. "The stars are so very beautiful up in the heavens."

"But I've been in Ireland at Donadea. I wanted to come back to Gavandon to see you and Graham."

"Ireland? Graham loves it in Ireland. He wishes he could be there all the time. I know he does." Even Colin could tell she was trying to make an effort at conversation, but it was apparent she was only partially present within her mind. "Do you look at the stars in Ireland, Colin?"

"Yes, of course." He tried to get her to meet his eyes. "How have you been, Imogene?"

He ignored the daggers piercing into him at Graham's glare from across the room. Imogene simply ignored the question.

She was trying, though, trying to be attentive, and polite. Her face alighting with a smile, she faced Colin again. "Elle is coming. She is coming to stay with us, Colin. I know you adore her so. Is that not…nice?"

Colin flashed eyes at Graham. "But Elle is already here." He spoke gently. "She has been here with you for some weeks now. Don't you remember?"

"Oh." She shook her head slightly. "I forgot." Her eyes began to fill. "I'm so sorry. I forget everything." Some tears spilled down her face. "What is wrong with me, Colin?"

"Nothing." Colin patted her hand. "Nothing is wrong with you, my dear. You are just sad."

She trained her soulful brown eyes onto him. "Why am I sad, Colin?"

"Because—"

Graham stopped him right there. "*Chérie*, you are tired and it's making you upset. Why don't you rest before luncheon?" He kissed her on the forehead and helped her to lie back. "I'll return in a little while after you've had your sleep," he told her, stroking up and down her arm. "I want to discuss some business with Colin right now." He waited until Imogene closed her eyes and then turned to face him. The searing look he gave Colin brooked no argument.

Colin relented, and followed his brother reluctantly out of the solarium.

"What in the bloody hell are you doing?" Graham barked as soon as they were ensconced back in his study. "Why are you doing it rather? I can see what you are trying to do, Colin, and I won't allow it!"

"Graham, she must deal with what has happened to her."

Graham shook his head. "You can see clearly that she is unable to do that right now."

"Brother, please be rational about this. Surely you comprehend that in order for her to heal she will have to face the pain of it eventually. I don't think she even understands what has transpired."

"God dammit, Colin! Would you please back down? You saw how she broke when you pressed her. I cannot hurt her any more, or allow anyone else to do the same. It is my duty to protect her."

Colin threw up his hands in frustration. "This is so wrong in every way." He glared at his brother. "But you are not protecting her—you're giving her opium, aren't you? How could you? After everything, after Jasper—"

Graham would not meet his eyes.

"How, Graham?"

"It is to help her sleep…she has terrible nightmares."

"Sleep!" Colin scoffed. "Sleeping all day long, Graham? A girl who could not stand being inside on the coldest day? That's not the woman I know! Talking in riddles, glassy eyed and dazed, unable to remember things. For Christ's sake you've got her dependent upon the stuff!"

"Did Elle tell you that? What else has she said?"

"You know Elle and I correspond regularly. She loves Imogene as a sister, and she is frightened for her. And rightly so. How can you not see what you're doing to her is wrong?"

Graham shook his head slowly back and forth, his jaw set. "She is not dependent. She'll face her loss when she is ready."

"Imogene will not live a year in the state she is in. I'll go to Brancroft then, and I'll put it into his hands. He can remove her from your care if you are found unfit and putting her in harm's way. She can go to her sister and Brancroft."

The instant the threat of removing Imogene from Graham and into Brancroft's care left his lips, Colin watched as the colour drained from Graham's face. His brother began to visibly shake, and lurched toward him.

Good. Maybe that will wake your sorry arse up about the condition of your wife.

"You pretentious shit." He stabbed a finger at Colin with each word, sounding as lethal as was his intent. "You'll do no such thing, little brother. You're going to leave me now." He pointed again. "Go on. I cannot vouch I'll not kill you if you try to have her taken from me."

Colin faced the murderous stare of his brother without fear. "I know you bear great pain for the loss of your children, and the grief that traps Imogene, so I forgive your threats. I am not afraid of you." He knew his next words would burn like hot coals but he said them anyway. He had no choice. "What would our mother think of what you are doing to Imogene? Shame on you, my brother." Colin walked out of Graham's study and out into the hall.

The smashing of glass against the wall echoed in his ears as he departed.

TRISTAN visited her faithfully every day.

"Imogene, I've had a letter from Byron. I told him you've been…ill, and he is very worried about his dear *cousin*," he said the last teasingly, hoping to get some sort of reaction out of her. Imogene responded with a half-smile, clearly indulging her friend the best that she was able, which wasn't much at all. "He sent something, for you to have personally. I think you'll like it." Tristan placed a soft, bound, printed leaflet in her lap. It's a new story from the Turkish tales he's writing now called, 'The Bride of Abydos.' He's giving it to you before it's even been published. It's about a princess and her travails in love. He honors you specifically, Imogene." Tristan pointed to the page, showing her. "See here? The heroine is named Zulekia."

Zuly lifted her head from where she lay at Imogene's feet and looked up quizzically when her name was spoken.

"Zulekia?" she mumbled, trying to focus on his words. "Why would he name her after the dog?"

"He was taken with the name, remember? I believe he did it to show his admiration for you, Imogene. Byron thinks you are magnificent."

"Oh, that is so like him. Byron is a master at flattery," she said dazedly.

"One of his many talents. Would you like me to read it to you?" Tristan asked her gently.

"Yes, please. That would be most welcome." She attempted to show an interest for Tristan's sake, but he wasn't fooled. "I cannot read for myself—trouble concentrating."

"Very well, then." Tristan began to read aloud to her, his voice resonating with suppressed emotion and worry for his most dearly loved friend.

…The might — the majesty of Loveliness?
Such was Zuleika — such around her shone
The nameless charms unmark'd by her alone;
The light of love, the purity of grace,
The mind, the Music breathing from her face,
The heart whose softness harmonised the whole —
And, oh! that eye was in itself a Soul!

He read for a few moments before glancing over to find she had fallen asleep again. Sighing in resignation, he left the story for her on a side table.

As her friend, Tristan knew what needed to be done. Feeling anger at her pathetic condition, he left the solarium to seek out Graham, bracing himself for the confrontation he knew would be forthcoming.

"Your wife is overdosed with opium. How can you allow

such a thing to happen to her?"

"Not you, too. Please…she is not able to bear the pain of the loss, Tristan. Surely you can see that."

"I see nothing of the sort other than a woman completely at the mercy of the person who should be helping her. It disgusts me. You—the great watcher and onlooker. When you look in her eyes do you see anything you know? Because I do not! She is completely drowned in drug!"

"How dare you accuse me of hurting her. I am protecting her!"

"Graham, surely you can understand she will have to face her loss eventually. I doubt she even remembers the tragedy."

"She doesn't remember because her mind cannot bear the pain of remembrance, you daft idiot!"

"Fine, I'll accept that bit, but the opium has to stop, Graham. You know she cannot live like this. She would hate the state she's in if she were coherent of the fact. She would hate you for allowing it to happen to her." Tristan saw the painful wince from Graham at his words, but he wasn't finished. "Start cutting her dose and get her off that goddamn opium! Colin has spoken to me and is ready to bring in Brancroft if need be, and I support him wholeheartedly."

Graham snapped in rage. "Get out! Get the hell out of my house, you miserable fucking traitor, before I hurt you!"

Tristan walked to the door, but turned back for one last word. He spoke gently this time. "I know you love her, Graham. I love her, too. We all love her. Remember that beautiful woman who captured your heart? She is lost right now and needs your help in finding her way back. Help her, Graham. Help her to come back to the world of the living, with all of its painful realities. It will hurt her, I know, but it is the only way."

AFTER Tristan left him, Graham brooded alone in his study.

He sat there and looked out at the sweeping beauty of all he had been given and mourned. For the loss of the babies, for Imogene, for himself, for his parents, and for the paths of fate that could not be changed no matter how badly you wished for things to be other than they were. The fact remained—he knew his wife. She was strong, resilient, tireless in her determination to be independent. She would want to be well, not veiled in her delirium. *That is not my beloved* chérie.

He knew the words of Colin and Tristan were correct and true. The time had come to make a change or he *would* lose her forever.

He cut the opium dosage for Imogene that night, decreasing the amount steadily as the days passed.

There wasn't a great deal of change in her at first though, other than a general irritability, which was telling really, for Imogene was already fighting her way back to him.

And then one night he dreamt a new dream.

….A lovely country scene, the summer day, very fine. His parents were out of doors, under a tree. Mother had such a look of happiness on her face. Father looked upon her with love and admiration. She turned and spoke to him directly, 'Graham my dear, Mamma has something important to tell you. Graham, listen carefully to me. It is very important that you tell her. Tell Imogene that Father and I have them. The babies. They are here with us, and they are happy and loved. Tell her, my dear son, so that it will ease her heart. Do not forget. Tell her, Graham.

"Mother, wait! Do not leave! Help me…please!"

Graham wakened instantly, bolting upright in the bed, guessing correctly he had shouted the words out loud. The dream he had just experienced so vividly, struck him immobile.

Overwrought, his heartache and fear for Imogene so great, it all became too much to contain for even a second longer. In that moment, he felt a great rending of his heart as it tore apart and everything came pouring out. A great splitting sob came from somewhere inside him, accompanied by fear, and anguish, and loss. It couldn't be kept in, and once allowed to breech the surface, came gushing out in a flood.

He woke Imogene with his shouting, and then his tormented sobs.

"I am so sorry for everything, *chér*—"

"—I am here now, Graham. I will help you and you will help me…" Graham felt her arms come around him as she said her gentle words.

"Oh, Imogene. Have you come back to me?" he sobbed, clutching onto her like a drowning man. "It will be all right. Everything will be all right. I know it will be all right now," he repeated. "You have come back to me. Imogene, never leave me again! I cannot be without you; the pain was—it nearly killed me. You were lost and I could not reach you. I was so afraid." He struggled to pour his profound agony out to her in great gasping breaths.

She put her mouth to his ear and whispered, "I was confused at first, but then enlightened when I heard you in so much pain." Reaching for his hair, she tucked it behind his ears, as she had always liked to do. It felt like the most wonderful gift to feel her fingers trailing in his hair again. "Graham, somehow you released me from the shroud of terrible fog I've been in. I am so sorry—"

"No, Imogene." He pressed two fingers to her lips to

stop her apology. "You should not be sorry for anything. I love you so much." He kissed the top of her head and breathed in the scent of her hair, relishing the sound of her voice and knowing she was back with him in spirit as well as body.

But she wasn't finished.

"The sounds coming from you pierced through that shroud of terrible fog and shattered it like glass, Graham. And once I was free from the burden, nothing could have kept me from trying to help you, because I love *you* so much."

He didn't really have any words equal to what she's just told him.

So he switched to French and just held onto her, telling her again and again how much he loved her, and that he would love and need her always.

And in facing their great loss together, that first step toward healing was also taken together.

THE next morning, Graham made his way to his brother first, and then to his friend. He begged their pardons, and also thanked them for showing him the way back for Imogene. Humbled by their perception and caring, he told them both he would forever be indebted.

Graham made an additional request of Tristan—a favour.

Tristan agreed to carry it out.

And Graham prayed that it was the right thing to do.

Chapter 27

Let not the dark thee cumber;
What through the moon does slumber;
The stars of the night
Will lend thee their light,
Like tapers clear without number.

Robert Herrick ~ The Night-Piece to Julia, 1648

It was a first step. The clouds did not bow to the sunshine. Birds did not sing nor did rainbows appear in celebration. Things did not magically return to the way they were before. Imogene remembered now, but was by no means finished with her grief. Both were changed by their experience and would have to live with it. Their loss was a part of them now.

Graham was patient and careful. He didn't want to remind her unduly of the loss of the babies, so it was with the best of intentions that he made the decision to destroy the portrait of Imogene sleeping in the chair.

He would later recall it was almost as if she had a sixth-sense about that portrait. Because she caught him in the act, red-handed.

"What have you there?" Imogene demanded as she passed him in the hall.

"Nothing, just a painting."

"Is that my sleeping portrait? Graham? Why are you trying to hide it?" she wailed. "You keep things from me. Why do you do that?"

"No, Imogene."

"Give it to me. It is a painting of me. I demand you give it to me!"

Graham hung his head. "I don't want it to hurt you, and thought to destroy it so you wouldn't have to look at it and remember."

"No!" she gasped. "I *want* to keep it. I'll not have it destroyed. It is the only image I have of them. You see, when I look at that painting, I know they are safe inside me…alive and well." She knelt down on the floor in front of the canvas. Reaching out a trembling hand, she traced over her shawl, draped strategically to hide the swell of her belly. "My shawl covers them. I am their mother," she whispered. "Can you understand?"

"I am so sorry, *chérie.* I didn't know what to do with it…or what you wanted." He reached for her, pulling her up into his arms, breathing in the glorious scent of honeysuckle. "Forgive me?"

She nodded against him. "Ask me next time. I want it hung in the gallery," she responded determinedly. "Not for the image of me, but for them. Our children must take their place in the family history. It is what I want."

"As you wish, *chérie,*" he whispered, still holding onto her tightly.

"WHERE is my shawl? Someone has taken it and I want it back. Damn you, Hester, find it for me!" Imogene shouted at her maid.

"I have not seen it, my lady, for some time," Hester said meekly, her head bowed.

Imogene felt irrational anger boil inside her because she knew Hester wasn't telling her the whole truth.

Graham must have heard her shouting because he burst into her rooms and stepped between them. "Imogene, calm yourself." He gripped her by the arms and gave her a shake. "Hester, apologies, she doesn't mean it. You are excused." The traumatized maid fled the room in tears, and Imogene felt a pang of guilt. She would have to make her apologies to Hester later.

"I want my shawl…" she whimpered, crumpling to the floor in defeat. Not really wanting to know, but needing to hear, she asked, "What happened to it?"

Pain flickered across his face. "It is gone now. I cannot get it for you."

"Are you ever going to tell me, Graham?"

He did not speak.

"No?" She turned her back to him from where she still sat on the floor. "Get out then, for I cannot look upon you, knowing what your eyes have seen and that you will not say."

The silence of the room engulfed them both. It seemed like hours went by. Perhaps they did, before Graham spoke. "I…I will tell you, *chérie*. Even as much as I know the words will flay you, I'll do it because you wish it. Would that I could take your pain away for you."

"No one can do so for another. Give me the respect of

allowing me to own my own pain. Stop trying to shield me—I hate it!"

Graham sucked in a great pull of air at her harsh words. She knew she was being cruel but she couldn't help saying what she truly felt. Imogene had to hear it all, every excruciating word, and Graham was the only one who could tell her.

"I—I wrapped them in your shawl. Held them in my arms, swathed in the shawl of their mother, and loved them for the hour they lived. I told them all about you. Your beauty, of how much you looked forward to being their mother; how you loved them, and how sad you would be to miss that experience. I told them how we met, of how you looked the first time I saw you. That you are an expert rider and an excellent shot, competitive at games. That you laugh at little things…and love to tease. That you have the kindest heart and so much love to give."

She could tell he was having to force down his emotions in order to speak. "You see, I wanted them to have something of yours to enfold them, so they could sleep in your embrace, in a way. It is what I thought to do at the time. Was I right to do that, *chérie*?"

"Yes."

She still didn't face him. Not because she was angry, but because she couldn't stand to see the pain he bore. She did not credit his grief as she should have done. It was wrong of her—he was hurting too.

"You were right, Graham. Th—thank you." Imogene felt like she was out of her body, looking down on herself sitting on the floor, like she could just float away with only the slightest bit of effort. "Can you…can you tell me all of it?" she asked, much more gently.

"Our daughter was born first. She had dark hair like me. Our son followed in his birth about five minutes later. His hair was lighter, like yours. They were so tiny, but perfectly formed, and ali—alive." His voice broke. "I heard them cry. They breathed at first, but it seemed to get more laboured as the minutes passed. They simply went to sleep. Our daughter went to heaven first, and then our son."

"And where," she whispered, feeling strangely calm, "do they rest?"

"The Compass. They are together, wrapped in their mother's shawl, in all of her love. I buried them at the centre. They rest at the centre of…of the whole world."

"Oh." She grew still, absorbing the reality of what he'd done for her…done for their children. "Take me there? Now?" She turned herself to face him and held out her hands to her loving husband.

He took her hands.

FULL disclosure of the birth experience was comforting to Imogene. It soothed her to know her children were cherished for their short time on earth and that Graham had loved them for her in her stead. She visited their grave at The Compass and with the help of Hiram, planted bulbs that would flower every spring in a glorious carpet over them. She also chose honeysuckle vines to be placed outside of the circle so the scent would fill the space when they bloomed. Her babies would have her favourite scent all around them.

It was after one of her visits to The Compass that Graham called her to his studio. He said he had something to show her.

"Have you been painting something magnificent, my darling?" She looked toward a large canvas covered with a cloth.

"No," he whispered. "Tristan did this at my direction and from my inspiration." His hand visibly shook as he reached to remove the cloth covering, as if he were afraid to show her the painting. With a flick of his wrist, the cloth fell away.

Imogene expelled a long breath and just stood there, transfixed, in total awe of the image before her.

Long minutes stretched out.

Graham came up behind and put his hands on her shoulders. Leaning back onto him for support, she felt relief because she thought her knees might buckle.

"I had a dream the night you came back to me. It was so real. My mother spoke to me most clearly. She said—" his voice faltered as he fought for composure.

"What did she say? It's all right, you can tell me, Graham."

"Mother said I must tell you they are with them. The babies are loved and happy together watched over by their grandparents. She said it would ease your heart to know they are not alone."

Imogene stayed in Graham's arms, savouring the image before her. It was a portrait she recognized of his mother and father, painted only a five years ago. They were outdoors under a tree; his mother sitting in a chair, his father, Lord Rothvale, looking down with pride in his expression. But Tristan had added something splendid to this painting. He had added in something very precious. There was a blue blanket set on the ground. A blonde baby boy sat on the blanket and looked at his sister who appeared to be taking her first toddling step. The baby girl had darker hair and clutched in her fist the edge of Imogene's shawl, the other end of which was steadied by her grandmother's hand.

"It does ease my heart…it very much does. Thank you, Graham, for this gift."

RALPH Odeman placed the letter from his solicitor into the fire. The regimental orders received the same treatment. Best to get rid of any written evidence in the event someone came searching. Money could be traced and it was prudent to be cautious. For his plan to succeed he had to be ever watchful, and careful of what might be placed as an obstacle before him. He had new goals in his sights now. Goals much loftier than the support payments of a whore who'd birthed the by-blow of an aristocrat. Now that those monies had been stopped, he didn't have a choice but to find new sources of annuity. And they were out there for the person who had half a brain to figure out a way to gain them. Odeman counted himself just such a person.

There was more to play out with the Everleys, yes, but there was another who might serve his purposes adequately in the interim. The lovely Lady Rothvale had an unmarried cousin who'd caught his attention in the shop that day in London. Very young and quite pleasing to the eye as he remembered her. The Honourable Cariss Wilton, daughter of Sir Oliver Wilton, Baronet. But there was more—an even more attractive feature to recommend Miss Wilton as the object of his pursuits. The newly minted Viscount Wyneham was her older brother…and *that* piece of information would do very well for his plans, he decided.

Yes…indeed, she would do *very* well.

Odeman watched the wax seal on the documents boil and sizzle within the flames of the fire that licked at the paper until it was consumed to ash.

GRAHAM'S gift of *The Grandparents* portrait was the final piece in Imogene's recovery. She was able to let go of her loss and looked to a brighter future. Being young and strong, she had suffered painful losses before, so she drew on her strength to help her move forward and get on with living. There was plenty of work to do and service to give to those in need. She saw it as her duty to care for other mothers who may find themselves with such loss. She understood. She could grieve with them.

James Trenton had written to accept the position of rector to their great relief, and it was with good feeling that they prepared for his late autumn arrival. Imogene was glad to immerse herself in the readying of the church and rectory for their new occupant, both buildings having been vacant for years.

There was one aspect of their marriage that was not yet restored, though, and Imogene felt its absence keenly. She ached for Graham to love her in the way he always had because she needed his closeness, and felt ready to try for another baby.

Graham, however, was terrified of another pregnancy. The fear of losing her, either physically or emotionally, made him extra guarded. The one time they'd been together intimately had been disastrous; both of them self-doubting and insecure, their sensitive emotions smarting; neither daring enough to bring it out into the open and face their problem.

It happened the night after he showed her *The Grandparents* portrait.

Imogene reached out to him when he came to bed, and after such a long time without her, Graham was nearly frantic in his response and rushed himself. Then, he kept asking if what he was doing felt good for her, and if she was finding pleasure in it, which readily snuffed the passion of the moment. The most awkward part though, was that he pulled out of her and spilled on her stomach when he found his release. He withheld his seed from her, and Imogene was devastated by his decision to do so without talking to her about it. She felt greatly insulted but didn't tell him so. She just cried in his arms, and Graham, misunderstanding her tears, assumed he had imposed himself on her and into intimacies she was not ready to resume.

To make it easier on both of them, Graham started coming to bed late after Imogene was already asleep, and slept in a nightshirt, something he had never done before. He was still an attentive husband, loving and generous, ever watchful over her. Imogene had never appreciated his tendency to over-worry and fuss, but indulged him in allowing such behaviour because she knew he was only doing it out of love for her.

Eventually their situation had to be faced because they just couldn't keep going on as they were…

Imogene had walked to Tristan's house earlier, hoping for the companionship of her friend for an hour or so to break up the monotony of the day. Graham met her on the path as she returned, concern clearly showing in his expression.

"From where have you come?" he asked.

"I went to visit my friend, but he is not at home."

"Oh…" He looked sad and weary. "I could not find you and I was worried."

She sighed in frustration. "Do you live in constant fear for me, Graham?"

He didn't answer.

"I do not recognize this person before me. I do not know you anymore." Imogene felt her tension give way to anger. "You are not the man that healed my broken heart, Graham, you are breaking it anew. You will not touch me. I am not loved by your hands or your body anymore. I am rejected. You have broken your promise to me, as well. The promise you made when you offered yourself to me, 'with no other requirements other than to care for me and to make me happy.' Do I appear happy? Do I sound happy? Do you see happiness in my eyes when you look into them? Can you live your days and nights in this way? How can you even bear it?"

He winced at her questions as his eyes filled with pain…and what looked like shame.

"Do you love me or is it just the fantasy of me? Because if it is just the fantasy of me, then, Graham, you have nothing!"

His head snapped up, tortured eyes targeting her. "I love you! More than my own life. How can you even ask me such a thing?"

"But is it reality?" She held firm in her opinion. "Graham, if I cannot be loved by you as a wife should be, then I am already lost to you and you to me. You see me as a fairy princess—you always have. But I am not! I am an ordinary woman, who wants nothing more than the real junctures of life, with you, and if it pleases God, to be mother to our children. I want to live a *life*, not be a rack for your ornaments of beauty!"

He flinched.

"A regular…ordinary…life, Graham. You want the fantasy of me. But it is just that, a fantasy. Not. Real. And not me!" She shouted at him.

His head down, he couldn't even look at her.

"Everyone must die someday. Even *I* will die, Graham. It is already fixed for each of us, and not in your power to control. It might be fifty years from now or it might be five. But if it is five years, I would hate to think we would spend them in this way, frightened and aching for love. I can't bear that idea. I would rather wish my life over now and done with." She whispered the last part. "Face your fears, Graham. Be brave, my love. Rescue me from that future?"

HE saw that she waited for him to say something, to do something, but he was frozen, unable to step out of the prison he'd forged around his heart. *I am afraid, Imogene…so afraid of losing you.*

When no response was forthcoming, Imogene turned from him and began to walk away.

"Where do you go now?" he blurted.

Sighing heavily, she spoke slowly and with mustered patience. "I go to the house to change my clothes for I am going riding. If you would wish to join me you are welcome, if not, do not worry yourself. I will ask Ben to come along with me."

She turned again and left him standing on the path.

Graham must have stood there for a long time but he

couldn't be sure because his mind was busy. Very busy swirling with the visions of her he had created since he'd first known her—those gorgeous visions juxtaposed with the words she had just spoken to him. They spun around his head, whirling and forcing a reckoning, shifting the fear out and rattling off the chains that had bound him.

Imogene was so strong and brave.

He felt weak and stupid, ashamed of what he'd done, and of how he'd treated her.

But it's not too late…she wants me still. Imogene, I am coming for you!

Racing back to the house, he took the stairs three at a time until he reached the top and made his way to her rooms.

He burst through the door.

She was dressing into her riding clothes.

The view of her standing in her shift and stays stopped him dead. Regardless of her feelings about how he saw her, it was undeniable: Imogene was an extraordinarily beautiful woman…and she belonged to him.

Looking boldly at her, he saw the slight curl of a smile form on her luscious lips. He would have those luscious pink lips on his skin soon.

"Hester, you may leave us."

"Yes, Lord Rothvale." Hester bolted from the room.

Graham approached Imogene, locking onto her liquid brown eyes, willing her to keep them on him and not break their gaze. Without speaking any words he reached his hands around to her back and began to untie the lacing of her stays. She continued to look into his eyes for they were both familiar with this game already.

They had played together many times.

Corset removed, he reached down to grasp the hem of

her shift and pulled it up and over her head. He stroked her face and caressed her lips with loving fingers, admiring her bare exquisite flesh on display before him. He put his hands on her breasts and cupped them, his thumbs brushing back and forth over her nipples as they tightened into buds he wanted to suck and bite with his lips.

His eyes never looked away from her.

She touched him, too. By feel, she unbuttoned his shirt, pulled his arms through, lifted it over his head, and caressed his bare chest. She smoothed her hands down to his abdomen and lower. His Imogene held onto his eyes and claimed his body with her hands, showing him that he belonged to her, too.

Both of them were finding the way back to reconnecting the threads that had hung tenuously between them for too long.

Imogene was gloriously naked already. And Graham needed to join her in that state. So when she moved her hands down lower with a purpose in mind, he knew what it was and waited for it. He sucked in a breath when she unfastened his trousers and pushed them off his hips, her hands still moving until one of them took hold of his prick and stroked the length slowly up and down.

"I will never stop wanting you like this," he whispered, their lips very close but not touching.

"And I will never stop needing you like this," she whispered back in the lightest voice.

Stepping out of his clothes, Graham moved forward, forcing Imogene backward, step by determined step, until they reached the edge of the bed and could go no farther.

Their hands both grazed over the naked flesh of the other's body as their eyes stayed locked together.

He pushed her back, and went with her as they fell down onto the softness of the bed together.

Settling her beneath him he fit his hips in between her thighs and let his cock find the way to the gate of her delicate flesh. "I've loved you always, and I'll never stop loving you," he told her as he sank his cock down deep into her wet, divine warmth. It was heaven to feel her wrapped around him again, the walls of her quim tight and clutching.

He could die this way and never feel a moment's regret when he was buried inside her.

Knowing she was ready and wanton for him only fuelled his need to possess her again. And he would—thoroughly. There would be no part of her unclaimed this time.

She arched her hips into his with a gasp of pleasure as he filled her, flinging her neck backward, her throat and breasts exposed for his pleasure, and waiting for his mouth and tongue to claim them.

He did all of the things he wanted to do to her body. Things he had done before, and some he had not. All of it done in love. Nothing mattered except being inside of her.

Graham in Imogene.

Imogene in Graham.

She *was* inside of him, too. She was inside of his heart.

They became one body, one heart, and one mind together.

Love. Pleasure. Love. Strength. Love. Bravery. Loss. Graham felt each emotion. All were as important as the others he realized, while taking back his woman.

He worshipped her with his body in the only way he knew how.

THEY lay together, silently staring.

Imogene's fingers moved softly over his face, his hair, his lips. Graham stayed still for her, indulging her the joy she drew from the simple act, and of knowing he belonged to her.

"I have you back now, my darling. My heart is restored," she said on a whisper, her emotions rising up and taking over.

Graham merely nodded at her, his deep green eyes reflective of the same feelings, understanding that words were difficult to form, and more importantly, unnecessary for either of them right now.

With his cheek against her shoulder, she felt the divine rasp of his stubbly beard and relished it against her skin. His long fingers stroking over her breasts made her feel cherished. The way he breathed in the scent of her hair and stared into her eyes told her he was content.

In time he spoke, "You are so brave, and I was so weak. Imogene, your understanding and wisdom fills me with wonderment. I have come back to you, and I will never leave you again. I know I lost my way, and shame fills me for what I have done, of how I treated you. Thank you for showing me the way…to a life with you." He caressed her cheek with the back of his fingers. "My compass…guiding me, leading me. How can you ever forgive me?"

"There is nothing to forgive, Graham. If it pleases you, then know you are utterly forgiven. Accept that idea with all of my love. Take it and believe it and hold it. It is what you must do."

"I will do it then." He kissed her reverently, his lips moving over hers with gentle possession, in the way he had always done, making her feel like the most cherished woman in the world.

"Graham, I believe we'll have the fifty years. I truly do

believe in that. God owes us some charity for all we have borne."

He pulled her closer and tucked her head under his chin. "Yes, he does, but even so, fifty years would not be enough time with you. An ocean of time would not be enough. *Un océan de temps ne serait pas assez de temps avec vous, Imogene.*"

They did not ride that day.

EIGHT weeks later, when she told him she believed herself with child, she detected shuttered fear behind his kisses of congratulation. Imogene touched his face and reminded him, "Be brave, my love, for I have need of you. Fifty more years, remember?"

He brought her close and held her against him. "If I am brave it's because I draw it from you. But do not fret, *chérie*, because I go anywhere you are going. All will be well—you will be a most perfect mother to our child." He bent and put his lips to her stomach, kissing lovingly. "I *know* it, truly I do. For I have seen you…and it is my most beautiful vision of you yet."

One year later ~

IMOGENE knocked outside the door to his study.

"Come."

"Sorry to interrupt you while you are working, but we are at our wits end here." She brought the howling infant forward.

He stood and opened his arms. "That's all right, *chérie*, for I could hear you coming long before you actually arrived. I was anticipating you." He leaned over the baby to kiss his wife. "What does my little angel need to make her happy again?" he crooned down at his daughter.

"She needs her papa to take her for a stroll into the gallery I think. She loves hearing your soothing voice tell her all about the paintings. A girl after her father's heart. You know, Graham, you may not have to deal with impromptu pony rides with Byrony when she is older, rather she might demand a painting lesson instead."

Graham had to smile at the thought.

"A walk around the gallery it is then, my sweet, precious Byrony." He kissed her soft downy cheek and settled her into the crook of his arm.

The baby stopped fussing, curled her fat little fist around her father's finger and looked up at him.

"Her eyes look different to me. Do you sense a change in her eyes, *chérie*?"

"They are turning green. I told you; dark hair, long and straight, and green eyes…just like you."

He lifted the green eyes he'd been born with to his beloved wife and mouthed an 'I love you.'

"Yes, you most certainly do," Imogene whispered, her eyes glittering over at him beautifully. She would forever take his breath away even if it were something he could own in his heart…and treasure the pricelessness of the gift he'd won when he'd found her. He understood she was a real woman, living a vibrant life, and that fantasies existed only in stories. He knew this, but it still would never change how he saw his Imogene. She was beauty. The muse of beauty lived within her, and it always would for him.

"I'll bring her up to the nursery once she's fallen asleep, *chérie*."

"Thank you, my darling. You are the best of men…and fathers…and husbands." She blew them both a kiss and let herself out of his study.

Graham made his way slowly to the portrait gallery, stopping to show Byrony anything of interest along the way, or to greet a member of the staff. She took it all in, happily content to be on an adventure with him. He'd not known it was possible to feel any more love for another person than he had already with Imogene, but he'd learned his heart had a greater capacity than he'd realized the moment his daughter was placed into his arms on the day she was born.

"…Now this is the most magnificent painting I ever conceived. I did not paint it. Mr. Mallerton did this one. I merely suggested it would make a nice picture. Isn't it something? It is your mamma, Byrony. Can you see it is Mamma? She is sleeping. Asleep and all tucked up into the chair. So beautiful in her yellow dress…so perfectly beautiful…"

Epilogue

What one man can invent another can discover.

Arthur Conan Doyle ~ The Dancing Man, 1905

Present Day
Christie's Auction House, London

"Next up, lot 501. Three portraits."

"THE ARTIST: Sir Tristan Mallerton. Portraitist. Romanticist. Life 1783 to 1864. Knighted by Queen Victoria, 1850. Exhibited at the Paris Salon, 1808. A contemporary and friend to Lord Byron. The paintings of this lot were completed early in his career, spanning the years 1808 to 1812."

"COMMISSIONED: Patron and life-long friend, Graham Everley, Lord Rothvale, Baron IX, Gavandon, Warwickshire. Philanthropist and original founding member of *The National Gallery*, London. Father of the acclaimed portrait painter, Byrony Everley Russell."

"SUBJECTS: Lady Imogene Rothvale, wife of Lord

Rothvale, and other probable family members."

"PROVENANCE: Discovered recently by the Everley family at the estate Donadea, Northern Ireland. Existence unknown to the family until exposed during renovations. All have been hidden together for the past one hundred thirty years in the minimum. Excellent condition due to a superb storage situation. All have passed vigorous standards of certification as to originality, artist validity, and dating accuracy. The private journals of Lady Imogene Rothvale, made public this year, bear out these findings to be correct and true."

"SUBMITTED: Gifted by the Everley family. All proceeds to the benefit of charity administered through the *Everley Trust for the Advancement of the Arts.*"

"We begin with Number One."

"***Les Grands-Parents.*** Translation: *The Grandparents.* Date of creation, 1809. Multiple. Elder couple. Surmised to be the parents of Graham Everley, George and Isabelle Everley, Lord and Lady Rothvale VIII. Georgian dress, romanticized scenery, two babies, a boy and a girl assumed to be twins. Photographic analysis indicates the babies were added at a later date, but within ten years of origin. Items of note: intricate, fringed, topaz colour Indian shawl; indigo blue woven blanket. Size is a generous, eight by six feet. We will begin the bidding today at £100,000..."

"NUMBER Two."

"***Déshabillé.*** Translation: *Undressed.* Date of creation,

1812. Single. Lady Imogene Rothvale, lounge attire, green brocade robe, bedchamber setting. Items of note: intricate Indian shawl, appearing to be one in the same as the shawl in Number One; pearl choker necklace and matching tiara, circa1725; storybook entitled The Princess and the Toad. Artistic impression: fantasy, romanticized, staged image of a woman in bed. Unknown style for the period. In layman's terms, folks, the aristocracy did not commission fantasy portraits containing this type of subject matter in 1812. It would have been considered scandalous to sit for and most certainly was kept private. In addition, there were no known portraitists willing to paint subjects in this manner in 1812. This is unsigned but certified to be Mallerton's work. It would bear out the close friendship between the artist and the family. The style is much more indicative of 1880. It could be said that Mallerton was a good seventy years ahead of the times. He died 1865, well before the period in which subjects were commonly painted in such a manner. Size at two by three feet. Bidding begins for this item today at £850,000…"

"NUMBER Three."

"***Le Sommeil d'Imogene***. Translation: *Sleeping Imogene*. Date of creation, 1812. Single. Lady Imogene Rothvale sleeping in a chair. Yellow gown, same Indian shawl that appears in Numbers One and Two. Items of note: pet dog, Greyhound; writing journal; lap escritoire; pen and ink. Artistic impression: unique, one of a kind. Very exaggerated romantic image of a blonde, sleeping woman, arms and legs tucked up into the chair. Remarkable, flowing movement in a jonquil-yellow gown, the colour, being the height of fashion for 1812. Completely unknown style for the period. The subject and execution bears a striking resemblance to the subject of Lord Leighton's *Flaming June*, painted 1895. One must ask the question: Did Lord Leighton, at some point in his lifetime, view this painting, and was it in fact his inspiration for *Flaming June?* If true, then *Flaming June* is a ***simulacrum*** of this much earlier work. Mallerton's *Sleeping Imogene* predates Leighton's *Flaming June* by eighty-three years. In the very least this is a stunning revelation. This is it, folks, the painting setting the art world on its ear. The painting people will be talking about for years to come. *Sleeping Imogene.* Size is three by three feet square. The opening bid starting today at £10,000,000…"

"BIDDING has ended. Sold to number 317. *Sleeping Imogene* has sold for £28,000,000. Well done, California, patron of the arts. What a coup! *The Getty Museum* taking all three, for an unprecedented grand total of £44,000,000."

Finis

MARINER'S
COMPASS
NW
NE
W
E
SW
SE
S

If you enjoyed this book, please consider leaving a review.

Thank you for reading!

♥

Sign up for my Newsletter:

http://www.rainemiller.com/newsletter/

♥

If you want the discussion group on Facebook:

https://www.facebook.com/groups/TheMusebyRaineMiller/

♥

If you enjoy Contemporary Romance, you'll want to read all about Graham and Imogene's direct descendant, Ivan Everley, and the **DISCOVERY OF THE PAINTINGS CREATED IN THIS BOOK**! You can meet the present-day Lord Rothvale and his art-loving lady, Gabrielle Hargreave, in my contemporary romance series ***The Rothvale Legacy***, beginning with ***Priceless – Book I.***

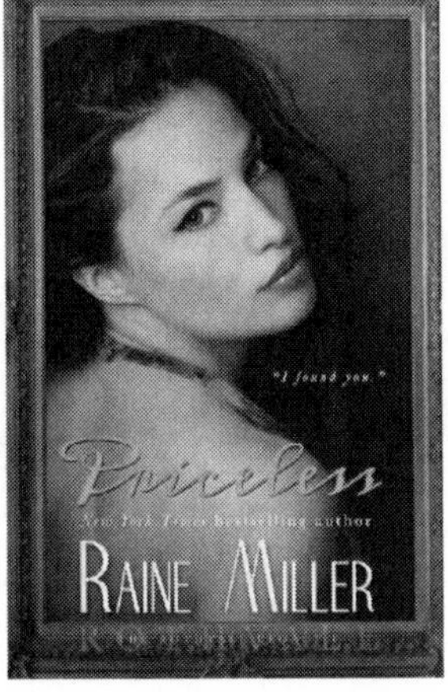

The ROGUE

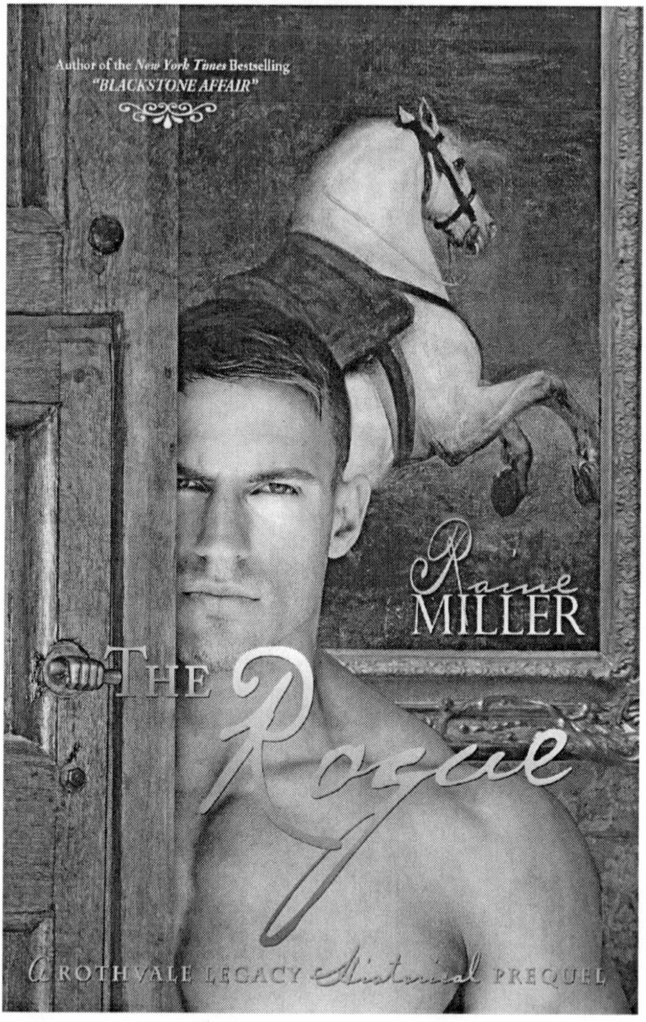

A ROTHVALE LEGACY HISTORICAL PREQUEL
Book II

Fast horses fill his days...

Fast women fill his nights. Racing horseman, **Clive Gravelle**, has never given the idea of settling down much thought at all. And why should he? His life is satisfying just as it is. Or, he would say so, even if it isn't really true. But ideas do change. New acquaintances are made. Love finds a way of pushing in, becoming something very unexpected—a forbidden dream to a man like Gravelle. He won't ever fall in love with a woman again.

Then he finds **Cariss Wilton**. Beautiful, lovely, sweet, unspoiled, Cariss Wilton.

She comes gently into his life, although the effect is anything but gentle for him because Cariss is someone he can never have. She is innocent, and far too young. A girl so far away and above the debauched world in which he's lived his life, that he couldn't possibly entertain the notion of dragging her down with him.

But Cariss is far stronger than she looks, and she definitely knows the difference between good and evil. Clive Gravelle just needs to be persuaded he is so much more than an expert predictor of winning horseflesh, and a scandalous cad with the ladies.

...Will the innocent tame the rogue?

Maybe she already has, but he just hasn't realized it yet.

*****~*Coming soon from* Raine Miller Romance~*****

ABOUT THE AUTHOR

Raine has been reading romance novels since she picked up that first Barbara Cartland paperback at the tender age of thirteen. She thinks it was *The Flame is Love* from 1975. And it's a safe bet she'll never stop reading romance novels because now she writes them too. Granted, Raine's stories are edgy enough to turn Ms. Cartland in her grave, but to her way of thinking, a tall, dark and handsome hero never goes out of fashion. Never! A former teacher turned full-time writer of sexy romance stories, is how she fills her days. Raine has a prince of a husband, and two brilliant sons to pull her back into the real world if the writing takes her too far away. Her sons know she likes to write stories, but have never asked to read any. (Thank God) She loves to hear from readers and chat about the characters in her books. You can connect with Raine on Facebook at the **Blackstone Affair Fan Page** or visit **www.RaineMiller.com** to sign up for newsletter updates and see what she's working on now.

RMR

Raine Miller Romance

BOOKS BY RAINE MILLER

The Blackstone Affair

NAKED, Book 1

ALL IN, Book 2

EYES WIDE OPEN, Book 3

RARE and PRECIOUS THINGS, Book 4

♥

CHERRY GIRL, Neil & Elaina I

The Rothvale Legacy

PRICELESS, Book I

MY LORD, Book II

Historical Prequels to The Rothvale Legacy

The MUSE, Book I

Notes

CPSIA information can be obtained at www.ICGtesting.com
Printed in the USA
LVOW11s0046211015

459127LV00003B/57/P

9 781942 095040